Subton
Switch

by

Jessica Lucci

Waltham, Massachusetts, United States
of America

Indie Woods

Watch City: Subton Switch
by Jessica Lucci

Published by Jessica Lucci and Indie Woods

Waltham, Massachusetts, USA

Copyright 2019 by Jessica Lucci and Indie Woods

e-book ISBN: 978-1-7323495-1-3

paperback ISBN: 978-1-7323495-2-0

Cover Design by Steven Novak Illustration

Dedication

For Mr. D.

"BE EXCELLENT TO EACH OTHER"

About This Book

Subaquatic city, 1886. Verdandi, a fiery teen tinkerer, is held captive by an evil totalitarian government. She is blasted into a chaos of beauty and fear, depression and addiction.

Verdandi discovers that her only chance of liberty lies not only in trusting her friends, but in challenging her mind and body to fulfill her time travel quest. What begins in compulsion becomes necessity, and Verdandi finds herself torn between two very different worlds, with the only reconciliation being time.

The "Watch City" trilogy continues in "Subton Switch," creating a testament of the power within us to change ourselves, and the world.

Prologue

Red hair bled on white sheets, flowing in sanguine dreams and unheard screams.

Part One

Chapter 1

Tess cupped the compass between her bare palms as she stared out into the night ocean. Martina left the helm and strode over to the professor.

"Besides that being the instrument that starts our engine, why do you hold that like a fragile rabbit kit?"

Tess's gaze was undisturbed. "This is all I have left from when I had it all."

"Your daughter, right?" asked Martina. Bashelle paused from twisting bait lures, and placed a strong hand on Tess's shoulder.

"Yes. My intention was to use this to find her. It has not steered me wrong on my quest to reunite with her thus far, even with the interruptions." She looked up. "Not that I see meeting you as interruptions, my dear friends, I only meant-"

"Blabbity blab," said Martina. "We know what you meant. If you hadn't been sidetracked by crashing trains, gas bombs, a military coup, and a psychotic despot, you coulda been on your quest to find your missing daughter right now."

"Yes, but, the strange, or perhaps lucky opportune circumstance is in this reprogrammed mechanism. The dials that Verdandi implanted with Dr. Kate's design are all pointing the way to Subton. So all in all, my quest is aligned."

Bashelle gestured to the window. "That beautiful orca woulda led the way to her human best friend anyhow." The three women watched admiringly as Ani gulped down a juicy cat shark. Her sleek black and white skin shimmered in the salty current.

"Who is he, anyways?" asked Martina, breaking the reverie.

"Who is whom?" asked Tess, distracted by their friendly apex predator gnashing teeth on shark scales.

"The stud. The seminal oscillator."

"The what?" Tess now swivelled in the captain's seat. Her skirts rustled in the breeze of her quick turn.

"Who is your daughter's daddy" asked Bashelle, trying to be kind, and trying not to smirk.

Tess glowered as her two friends stared in curiosity.

"I'm not telling!"

"Aw c'mon. Just tell us. You can trust us you know," said Bashelle.

"Yes, yes I know," said Tess, swatting at imaginary gnats.

"We need something to talk about while we finish this step of our journey," added Martina. "Just tell us. Come on."

Tess flipped the compass over and over in her fingers. Her breath came in haughty chuffs like a steam engine chugging up a steep hill.

Martina and Bashelle sing-songed in unison: "Pretty please? Pretty, pretty, please?"

Tess bolted up from the wide oak chair, both feet clomping on the floor together.

"You must persist, indeed, like woodpeckers on a hollow tree. Do you not accept my trust in the both of you?"

"Of course we do," said Bashelle.

"So why don't you just tell us?" added Martina.

"Because," Tess fumed, " I can't!"

"You can't?" asked Bashelle.

"Or you won't," said Martina.

Tess pulled in a huge draft of air and stood at full height, squaring her shoulders and tilting her chin up to the wooden ceiling in an exhibit of pride.

"I can't," the professor stated, "because I do not know."

The hush that followed this confession was not followed by jeers or even a snort. Martina's mouth unhinged.

"She doesn't know," Bashelle whispered to herself, her eyes wide in wonderment.

Another three seconds of unperturbed silence passed.

"Do not judge me!" charged Tess, and she stomped off to her quarters.

Martina and Bashelle pivoted their bodies to face each other.

"You look like a grouper," observed Bashelle.

"She doesn't know," breathed Martina, slowly closing her mouth. Then she grinned fiercely. "That's my girl!" She followed Tess's path and hollered, "I'm proud o' ya, lady! No need to keep names of men!"

They're good for one thing anyways, and that one did it, so what use is a name!"

Tess popped her head out from her room to face her comrades and witness the expressions on their faces. She needed to decipher their words, lest they be in jest. Upon seeing the lack of teasing around their smiles, she nodded her head.

"I will not quite agree with you on all parts of which you speak, but I do appreciate your support on the matter."

With that, she shut the door, opened her big brown bag, stepped in, and pulled the handles high over her head before twisting the bag inside out upon itself. She reopened the top, and stepped out onto plush pink carpeting. Her pale silk nightdress lay on her bed whence she had left it last. With a refreshing sigh of relief, the scent of rose perfume filled her nose, and she primed herself for luxurious sleep.

Darkness deepened within the submarine as the crew of three rested in the steady hum of steam engines. Ani maintained echelon formation, dozing as she was towed in the sub's slipstream. One eye remained open, as half her brain dreamed, preparing to take a conscious breath.

Shadows the size of mountains blocked all view from the scopes. "What in the name of the Fisher Queen is going on here," Bashelle mumbled to herself. She rubbed her eyes and peered through the scopes again. "Hey, Golden Egg, get off your nest and come ovah here." Martina lay sprawled on the hammock, her head indelicately tipped back with a layer of drool. Her long legs stretched free, dangling from the sides of her least favourite bed.

Pulsed moans followed by low-frequency pops echoed through the sound mirrors.

"What is that orca complaining about," wondered Bashelle. She diverted her attention to the vast glass window offering the helm a broad view. Two red orbs swirled just twenty metres ahead. Bashelle squinted. The glowing orbs were followed by flashes of orange. They were directly approaching the sub.

"By Triton!" Bashelle pulled the pneumatic alarm just as the first strike hit.

Chapter 2

Brilliant light blinded the small crew. A gigantic eye flashed like a stream of suns through the helm's glass.

The small submarine shuddered and pulled north, sucked in by an unknown force. Frontage windows offered a view of meaty pink. Circular suction cups pressed against the glass, and the arm behind it inflated like a soppy dirigible.

The suction cups held their force as the long arm it was attached to twisted the submarine up and around. Four metres of flesh pushed the sub through water with the force of a typhoon. A burst of heat blew from a silver cere above a triangular beak. Slimy sparkling globs splattered on the sub, covering it in goo.

Martina wound the protonic gears, building static energy. With a pound of her anvil, she hit the brass compression bar hard enough to make it ring like a bell. A wave of magnetic force flowed from the submarine's expulsion grates. The creature released its sticky grasp on the sub's propellers. Martina's head was covered in netting from her shocking tumble out of sleep. Her voice remained cooly clear and calm as she called out to Tess: "Prepare the sonar blasters."

Tess had been awakened by Bashelle's alarm. She rushed from her secret quarters and to the upper deck, too panicked to dress properly. Thus she stood with naked feet on cold oak planks, her round backside barely covered, while her small nipples pointed through her pink silk nightdress. Her brain switched to scientist mode, and she barely felt the chill in her body, or the predicament of her ladyhood.

"Incoming!" Bashelle lumbered down from the weapons cache. She pushed parallel levers as she descended, lowering torpedoes to the launchpad. All the lights in the sub shone brightly now to illuminate the crew's defensive space in the attack.

Tess pumped the sonar blaster with foot pedals. She lost balance as Ani collided with the glowing tentacled creature.

"Good girl Ani!" Bashelle cheered through short exerted breaths. The tentacles released fully now, and the crew could see clearly the shine of gold glinting beneath its phosphorus flesh.

"What in hell's bells is that thing?" Martina glanced at Bashelle and then steadied her eye for her next shot.

"Don't look at me! This is not like any creature I have plucked from the seas!" Bashelle rigged the harpoon, then joined Tess's side.

"Tis the Kraken," Tess trembled.

"Wait for Ani to get one more shove in. She looks like she is circling back for another clonk to the eerie creature. When she retreats from her attack, then you can decompress the sonar."

"Right," said Tess, jogging up and down on the pedals. "Ani will not be fond of that in the least."

Another crash sent the submarine swirling. The lights flickered. Martina rose from her puddle of puke. The contents of her stomach stuck in the fibres of the net and the feathers in her hair. "Have I mentioned how I hate the water?"

Bashelle and Tess untangled themselves from the pedal's tubes. Their eyes readjusted to the light. Tess shouted "Holy-"

"Brown Cod," Bashelle finished. Martina followed their gaze and gargled bile.

Crustacean eyes the size of cannonballs wiggled on silver stalks. A monstrous lobster with armour of bronze snapped at the submarine with giant jagged claws. Each claw had ridges of steel with rotating saws whirring upon the edges.

"I am NOT going to die this way!" Martina's adamant voice roused her crewmates from their shock.

Bashelle hobbled to the torpedo launch. "Tess, at the sonar blasters, NOW!"

Tess slid on a stream of stomach leavings but managed to maintain her gait. She hopped on the pedals, and then pressed her hands to the blaster rods, squeezing until her knuckles were white and her fists were numb.

Explosions of sound and sea shook the submarine. In sprays of fire bursting from the shelled beast, the women saw Ani plunge again at the first creature. Ani struck the part blob, part metallic aberration in the plushest part of the glowing cephalopod. The monster's glimmering beak opened to expel a screech that temporarily deafened the incredulous crew. Ani braved the chance, and risked it all. She recognized the brief opportunity that offered demise, and clamped her teeth upon the exposed beak. Her head thrashed as the monster squirmed. Finally the orca's conical teeth ripped flesh and metal from the face of death. Blood poured in a glare of red lights from hundreds of tentacles.

Around the sub, salt water boiled. Foam obliterated any view from the helm. A giant claw swiped at torn trunks of bleeding, glowing, dismembered arms. Tess unleashed another magnetic blast and the blinking limbs dispersed. The snapping claws of the second beast stopped whirring. The women watched Ani retreat to higher water.

The disabled mechanized lobster flipped backwards through the chunky water. The crew had only moments to prepare for the next attack.

"Everyone, sit!" Bashelle ordered. Tess instantly dropped to the floor, for the first time recognizing the revolting squalor she was covered in. Martina half fell, half fainted. The bounce of her head against the oak finished her stream of consciousness.

Bashelle's bald head dripped with sweat. She shifted the chute for the saline oxidizer and clamped it to the engine's steam funnel. With two hands, she gripped the pine covered knob of the double throw knife switch. Power pulsated through the tubes leading to the torpedo hatch. With a wordless shout, the propulsion beam was pressed, and the torpedo launched.

Flames enveloped the small submarine, and the kickback of the shot spun it like a child's top. Within seconds, the torpedo hit its angry mark. An explosion erupted within the chummy sea as the lobsteresque beast burst into shards of metal and shattered gems. Fire burned from within the creature's chest, searing white strips of flesh to black.

With a final tremour of green and blue sparks, the remainder of the creature disintegrated, joining the bits of tentacles in a gruesome swirl of gooey offal and crinkly skin.

Bashelle leaned over the helm and looked upon her slime covered friends. "I am never eating lobster again."

Chapter 3

"We can be as tough as we think we are, but if we try to out-tough nature, we are not thinking at all." Martina took another swig of ale.

"Agreed," said Bashelle, "yet remember: water seeks its own level. If we can even out the submarine, then we could solve part of the equation."

Below deck, an anvil clanged. "What the heck are ya doin down there?" hollered Bashelle.

Tess flitted up the trap door. In the pockets of her leather apron were all manner of glass tubes and ceramic funnels. Her eyes flashed in the triumph of curiosity. "I am progressing on an invention."

"No shite. We seen you gathering odd parts and heard you tinkering away in the wee hours when even eagles sleep." Martina poured herself another pint from the keg.

Tess did not wish to reveal her worry just yet. No sense in upsetting anyone.

"I assure you I am researching a matter of importance for the greater good." Embroidered boots tapped the hardwood as she stepped to the long work table. Her concerns regarding oxygen levels deserved discussion, but she wanted to have a solution before vocalizing the problem.

Days and nights passed within the darkened submarine. The engines were completely disabled. Inertly designed to be cozy and strong, the vessel was not a battleship. Lanterns lit the small dining table, with carefully attended measures of kerosine. Crusts of brown bread were shared along with thin soup and remnants of carrots.

The friends grew grouchy in their stagnant stasis. Tess's habit of pacing was amplified. Martina alternately pressed her face to the porthole and lay with her horsehair blanket upon bare floor. Bashelle acquired a constant headache, brought upon by her ceaseless squinting through periscopes.

Cabin fever, claustrophobia, hunger, headaches, sleeplessness; it all began to take its toll on the team.

Tess stood over the work station and pressed a nub of chalk to blackboard. The chalk crumbled like a starburst in an empty sky.

"I cannot even tell if it is night or day anymore! There are THREE of us in this torrent-swept contraption!" She raised her hands to her head and tugged at her raven locks. "Damn dumb ridiculous hellhole of a gawd awful howdy doody motor!"

She swiped her arm across the table, scattering sheaves of paper to the floor and stomped off to her quarters.

Martina and Bashelle turned stupefied towards each other.

"What the hell crawled in her panties?" asked Martina.

"Damnifino, but if it's crabs she can keep those pincers to herself. Those buggers are annoying!"

The next morning, at what they guessed to be breakfast time, Martina was gulping down her second pint of ale and trying to stomach the sardines and johnnycakes Bashelle had laid out with maple syrup. Bashelle enthusiastically crunched tiny bones between her teeth. Morning was always her favourite part of the day.

"That's a strange one," she commented to her solo audience. "What incredible stripes on that roundish flopper! These teeny shining silver slivers are barely big enough to be called fish." She chuckled in her throat while she watched the swarm dash by. "Ooh, look at that beauty!"

Martina, thoroughly disgusted by breakfast, flushed her mouth with another ale. She was irritated from lack of sleep and lack of REAL food. Bashelle's early morning rumination was annoying.

"What is the big deal? We have seen fish every day for too many days. You are a fisher by trade. We just ate fish for our first meal of the day. What in the name of unholy hell is so wonderful out that damn window?"

Bashelle's delight was undeterred. With cheeks aglow, she explained. "These fish are ones I have not beheld the likeness of, in all my years of seafaring the Atlantic coast. The glorious specimens here are decidedly tropical."

"So the water is warmer?"

"Duh, that's what tropical means."

Martina slouched in aggressive exhaustion and lowered her mug with a thump to the table.

"What is it Golden Egg?"

Martina slowly adjusted her posture and grimly met her lady's eyes. "I know what the problem is now."

Martina awkwardly lifted her arm to accept the tool box from Tess. "I can't move in this cumbersome carp trap! Human beings are not supposed to be under water. Dammit, pass me more ale afore you suffocate me with that fish bowl!"

Tess poured a pint and attempted to hand it off. Martina's face glowed red in frustration as her fingers in thick gloves refused to cooperate. Tess lifted the ale to Martina's lips and helped her sip as one would an invalid.

"Awe, it's not that bad," said Bashelle. She struggled to pull the knob that tightened the Anaclastic Jar Mechanism deep sea suit. Her bare skin pressed against the smooth glass chest plate. "A bit squashy, but it will feel much lighter once we are in the water." Her eyes darted excitedly to the porthole in the submersive chambre.

Tess placed the mug on the bolted table and stepped over to Bashelle. She averted her eyes from the brown mounds pressed against the breastplate as she lifted the heavy round helmet and placed it on her friend's head.

"I do wish you had chosen to don more appropriate attire for this mission."

Bashelle grinned behind the round glass bowl encompassing her head. "Ain't nothing you never seen before, except what you see here is likely superior to your former experiences."

Martina paused her grumbling to look appreciatively upon her Cream Puff's nakedness. "Now that's a view I don't mind seeing under water."

Tess clicked her heels together to enact the lifts. The soles of her lacy shoes expanded, affording the shorter woman more height as she bolted her friends' glass helmets securely to the joints of the shoulder clasps. The AJMs were specifically designed to be watertight, deterrent to pressure, and thermal regulated.

"I'm not sure how much longer my legs can stand this weight," Martina begrudgingly admitted.

"That's why I bolted these benches here," said Tess. She helped lower the two athletic women. "Lift your arms up," She instructed.

"But I'm still holding the tool box," Martina complained.

"Just do it. I need to roll the sound mirrors into your oxygen tubes. This way you two can communicate to each other, and to me." She pointed to a copper cover above the chute. "When you get to this spot on the outside, twist the red spigot counterclockwise and lift it up. Then press this end of the tube over the opening and twist it clockwise. Understood?"

"Aye-aye," said Bashelle, lifting one hand to her encased head in a mock salute.

Tess clicked her heels again to lower herself down to normal height. She walked to the front of the bench to face her friends. "Are you adequately prepared?"

"You tell us, professor. We are simply your henchmen."

"Please, Martina, you are just as valuable as I am in this expedition."

"Likely more valuable, as I am the one doing the daft death defying dive."

Bashelle chimed in. "This is the ocean. We are together. It's not death defying. It's fun!"

Ignoring Martina's undignified, helmet-fogging words, Tess exited the bay and closed the heavy steel door behind her, then pulled a series of levers to enact the locking system. She called through the listening tube.

"The chute will open and water will rise into it. Do not attempt to fight the flow; instead, remain seated until the seawater covers your head and reaches the cavern's ceiling. At that point you may exit through the chute." She paused, hoping that her friends took heed of her instructions accurately. "You may find it optimal to aim headfirst through the chute."

Sentiment fraught a momentary silence. "Good luck, may time serve you well."

Two voices echoed from the sound mirrors through the listening tubes. "May time circle around and serve you back."

Tess pulled her skirts between her legs and slid down the smooth pole to the engine room. She fluffed her dress out again, and reached up to the crossbeams. She bent her knees and jumped, grasping the beams in her suede gloved hands, so she was hanging like dry laundry. She lifted her legs up in front of her so that her body formed an "L" shape, and she ignored the slide of her petticoat that revealed blue flowered bloomers.

Pressing her feet against the wall, she moved her left hand to the jagged gear between the crossbeams. She inhaled for the count of three, and exhaled to the count of three. Then she joined her right hand to her left and twisted the gear, while pressing her feet so hard against the wall that the sleek muscles of her thighs became as hard as polished granite. She continued pressing and twisting and pulling. Then came an exhilarating release.

She hopped back down to the floor and rubbed her thighs briefly. "I would say tis just about tea time."

Martina's voice sounded high pitched as it travelled through tubes. "What a shame. The motor is mint but once you put a load on it, it dies, ands it's a juggernaught to start."

Bashelle and Martina were hooked together, and hooked also to the submarine. "Care to educate me on the mechanics, my dear?"

"Cold contracts; hot expands. It's the compression. So when it's warmer like these waters, from coming from our colder waters...no good." Streams of sweat rolled over her light eyebrows, dripping on her lips. Her heart raced. Was this a good time to tell Bashelle that she didn't know how to swim? What she would give for an ale right now.

Bashelle recognized the signs of a woman in full swoon. "You are like an old man worrying about everything: oh bollocks oh dang my kerchief what do I do! You forget that we have conquered much more than a little heat together."

Martina ignored the words of levity. "If the condensers are working properly they shouldn't get hot." She dug a screwdriver out of the tool box. She pushed it through a compression gasket and pulled it out. "That's black. That's carbon. That's no good."

"How can it be carbon? Those things, those attack-monsters, they were machines. Anyways isn't everything carbon?"

"Yeah but there is a difference between live carbon and dead carbon. Trust me, I know. I've blown enough glass and bled enough deer to know the difference. This muck is from a living creature, not a mechanism."

"I'll take your word for it."

"You might have to take my life for it too. Blazes! I was not born with gills, yet here I am. You have to do exactly as I say.

I am not in the mood to drown fathoms below the beautiful solid earth."

Martina took a slow deep breath, and then a strong fast one, filling every cavity in her lungs she could. Whilst holding her breath thusly, she removed her helmet, exposing her face fully to the water. With unnaturally clumsy hands, she unscrewed the steam cap. She covered the valve with her weighted boot as she awkwardly floated, and blew into the steamcap hard with her only breath.

Next, she pulled the connection inside the cap with her teeth, and pushed the cap into her mouth, licked it, and screwed it back on.

Her eyes bulged and her body cramped and seized. Bashelle reconnected her helmet and oxygen supply.

The sound mirrors connected them with a long flexible glass tube. It was attached in sections so that it could bend in joints, like an invisible snake.

Martina took a struggling breath. "It is done."

Dripping with seawater and sweat, the two AJM divers re-acclimated to gravity. Martina pulled a dry towel from the laundry cask and wiped down Bashelle's shoulders.

"Ya know, I gotta say thank you. You helped me think calmly and differently when I was feeling over-focused."

Bashelle turned and kissed Martina's hooked nose. "Golden Egg, we are the same and different. That's why even when you are an anchovy, I'd still eat you."

The couple dressed in long cotton shirts and loose stevedore pants. They stumbled into the brightly lit hull.

Tess smiled at them with her perfectly aligned teeth, her coif capped off with a long plumed hat. Her black skirt was short and flared out like a dandelion. Her legs, visible from the thighs down, were covered in white and black horizontally striped tights, and upon her feet were brass buckled clogs. Her white collared blouse was airy except where her black leather corset strapped close to her small frame. A red bandana flounced around her neck like a flag awaiting wind.

Martina and Bashelle stopped in their tracks. Martina whispered, "What the-"

"I made supper!" chirped Tess.

The two tired teammates beheld the long workbench laid out with hot food and fresh tea in China cups.

"It does smell good, and it is laid out all fancy," complimented Martina.

Martina and Bashelle stepped over their personal judgements and chose, again, to accept Tess for who she was. The three friends huddled down to chow.

"Science," Martina explained over steamy tea. "How d'ya like that, professor?"

"Well done," answered Tess. She poured fresh cups.

"The sub was damaged by the sea monster attacks. So, because of the guck in the exhaust PLUS the warmer temperature water, it overheated."

Bashelle passed a bowl of green beans and lemons to Martina. "Our problem is solved now, so eat up!"

Tess quietly announced, "I regret to inform you that we have another little issue."

Greasy onions dripped down Martina's chin. Her blonde brows furrowed.

Bashelle chewed on a lemon rind. "Well then, what is it?"

"It is not unsolvable, and we are in no immediate danger, per se."

Martina almost choked on her jerked chicken. "Spit it out!"

Tess took a breath. "We have been maneuvered off course, and our maps are not aligned. Ani has retreated, hopefully to safety. Yet we still have this to guide us." She held up the compass, and its silver shone like a small star in the submarine's dim light.

"You mean we are lost." Martina ran oily fingers through her hair.

Bashelle placed an arm over Martina's hunched shoulders. "Don't scramble your brains, my Golden Egg. You happen to be with the finest captain above and now below the sea!"

"That's nice, Cream Puff. Now could you please pass me the ale?"

Chapter 4

"If only that little redhead's orca friend was still with us." Bashelle snuggled her smooth head into the crook of Martina's bicep.

"Yes, my Creampuff." Martina reached over with her free arm and traced her fingers around Bashelle's cranium. "That gracious sea-beast, Ani, is well loved by our girl Verdandi."

"That is the beauty of such creatures. Of the sea's heart, joining the body of warm life throughout the world. I worry for her."

"Ani; forgive me, I am continually absent of her name. Verdandi's fatefully faithful friend had accompanied us thus far, leading us closer to where our beloved horologist has been kidnapped."

Bashelle's charcoal eyes melted saline water upon the hunter's naked skin. "I am grateful for Ani's help. I wonder if she will find us again."

Tess, perched upon the starboard rail, peeked up from her configurations. "I wonder if she will find Verdandi." Her chest heaved with decompressed tears.

Bashelle twisted around on the camel hair blanket to face the professor. "It is hard to track a path the ship follows in the ocean."

Tess removed her bifocals. "Yes, and science never lets one down."

Martina rolled her eyes inwardly for her own affect. Feathers of an eagle and a red tailed hawk were entwined in braids of her honey coloured hair. "Let us sleep, together, all at once, and allow nature to, if only briefly, guide us."

Dark dawn broke in blue swaths. The compass pointed the same route the troupe was headed. When they got off track, it always set the sub back to proper alignment. Tess wondered at this; it was more than scientific. Some other power seemed to have ownership here. The compass had originally been her Rose Watch, designed so she could find her long-lost daughter. Its character was enhanced with Verdandi's addition; it persisted its point to Subton.

The submarine steadily approached Subton. Beyond the portholes, fantastical creatures roamed. Sea beings, metallurgic hybrids, flora-fauna. Tess was particularly transfixed. Between blinks of reality and dreams, she conferred with her books in an attempt to identify the life-forms in her scrutiny. Her lists astounded her by what she saw that was not named in books.

Martina and Bashelle were likewise mesmerized.

Bashelle whispered between the feathers smothering Martina's ears. "In all my years above and beyond the sea, I have never encountered creatures such as these in my nets, hooks, or traps."

A moonless night broke to a sliver of sunshine sparkling in the throes of a tuna's wake.

Hoarded tea leaves steamed into regurgitated air, announcing the re-embarkment of a mission.

Tess, flagrantly revealing her perky cleavage, allowed the steam from her porcelain cup to traverse between her small mounds. She sipped slowly, allowing the hotness to meet her lips, resting briefly, before allowing it onto her curled tongue, warming it before she swallowed fully.

"We must discuss our goal to find a way to enter Subton unseen."

"Agreed," said Bashelle. "We must sneak in inconspicuously."

Martina's green eyes gleamed with mischief. "Because Ziracuny will surely have an eye out."

With Bashelle's navigational charts and Martina's star maps, the crew predicted currents and constellations.

"We must find our way into Subton during the lunar event," said Tess. "It will be the only time will have enough light to see by."

Martina shook her head. "We would risk being seen."

The trio in the sub progressed through lunar shadows. They hoped to advance upon Subton during the new moon.

"Even when we cannot see, this compass will guide us." Tess twirled the timepiece upon a chain, creating a hypnotizing whirl of silver and light. Sparkles reflected from her pink hat, creating a faery-like glow upon her face.

"Where are you getting all these fresh dainties from anyways?" Martina pulled a crisp hanky from Tess' pocket.

Tess's lips stumbled on her usually eloquent words.

"How can you still be awake? It's not human." Bashelle approached to relieve Tess of her lookout duty.

"Sleep is a decadence I thoroughly enjoy yet rarely have time for," Tess answered lightly.

Bashelle lifted an empty mug from Martina's lap and flicked her fingers upon her sleeping face. "Time to wake up, you swill pig." The two joined Tess at the table for what breakfast there was.

Tess scribbled furiously in her leather-bound notebook.

"What's got you hoppin this morning?" asked Martina.

Tess glanced up from her notes, her face manic with investigative contortions. "Just look!" The tip of her steel point pen poised like a dart towards the porthole.

Bashelle clambered over and squinted. "I only see a bunch of sea slugs and some sea cucumbers."

"Breathtaking! Flowering animals and fishy vegetables!" Tess continued her wild writing, barely pausing to adjust her bifocals.

Martina handed a chunk of cured ham to Bashelle. "Some of these fish remind me of birds. Imagine: cardinals and bluejays flying underwater."

Bashelle chewed. "I'm glad you're finally coming around to appreciating the beauty I see every day when I fish back home."

"The fish you get back home taste good, that's all I know," said Martina. Then she tapped Tess on the head. "Dear professor, if you are done gawking out the window, I could use a hand figuring out this star map."

Tess returned her attention to her crew. At times she could just barely see the sky through the telescopic periscope. She unrolled the charts on which she had been tracking moon phases. Painstakingly drawn lines connected dots across crinkly paper. Tess's heart twinged with a stab of hope.

Her quiet voice spread cooly through the echoey cavern of the submarine. "I think I've found it."

She turned to face her comrades, spreading the chart across her chest.

All three women inhaled with widened eyes as the dots and dashes combined to tell the stories of future times.

Tess's teeth shone in the dim cabin. "The way in!"

Martina broke the silence with a lift of her mug. "I'll drink to that!"

Bashelle whooped and kissed Tess straight on the mouth. Turbulent currents bounced the small sub as they all jumped for joy.

Martina's ale spattered down her brass buttoned coat, and she had no care. "Tis been a wild ride, m'ladies, with naught to offer in celebration. At this intersection of adventures, I salute you, and commend our crew as a whole."

Bashelle and Tess lifted fresh cups in spirited salutation.

Tess felt hot drops of tea spill onto her bare knuckles. Her balance was irregularly off.

The submarine tilted and shifted. The friends felt a strange buoyancy.

"Are we floating up?" asked Martina, holding her stomach.

Tess ran to the broad window. "Quite the opposite. We are descending."

Bashelle assessed the instruments and gear shifters. "Crew, We are not floating and not descending. We are sinking."

Tess's tea slid perpendicular from her body. Her feet lifted from the floor. "Grab onto the table and stay clear of the helm!"

The women clutched what bolted furniture they could reach. Martina narrowly escaped a rapid beating on the head by the spinning helm.

Air pressure within the cabin alternately increased and decreased as the submarine spun sideways. With a gentle thud, it landed.

Tess hung from the bench, her silk bloomers tangled about her swinging legs. Bashelle was clutching the handle to the engine room, her left foot braced on a corner. Martina was wrapped around the thin table in its entirely, like a sea-star on a clamshell. Her eyes were squeezed shut, and chunks of ham plopped from her mouth down to the ceiling.

Tess released her grip and landed softly upon the upturned surface. "It is okay now," she soothed with a calmness she reserved for emergencies. "We are tipped around, but we are settled."

Bashelle blinked in the flashing lights of sprawled lanterns. Martina relaxed her grasp on the table and let her feet drop to the ceiling. A rolling rhythm of spinning gears echoed from the engine room. The cabin creaked with the sound of dry timber on an icy day. Bashelle pressed her feet back into the corner and with one hand retained her grip on the handle. She desperately reached an arm out across the room, as if she could hold onto Martina with a magic touch.

"No! Don't!"

Tess felt the surface beneath her feet shift, and Martina slid in the slippery puddle her breakfast had created.

Tess screamed.

In a smooth motion that seemed to take long moments, the sub tilted onto its side and tumbled down a deep ledge into darkness.

Chapter 5

Falling, twisting, banging. Bodies pounded with a thud before a final drop at the bottom of an uncharted sinkhole. Like a mine dug by nature, the hole offered no way to the top for creatures unworthy of the sea.

"What dung-heap thought it was a good idea to put perfectly useful land-habituating mammals such as myself under water?"

"Martina, you are being a grumpy grouser. Knock it off." Bashelle's patience was wearing thin.

"Maybe if someone wasn't so stingy with the ale I'd be in a better mood" said Martina.

"We need to take it easy and ration what we have. Believe me, I'm not happy about it either."

"But I am more not happy!"

Bashelle grumbled, "We know."

"What? Am I complaining too much? Cuz I'm in a damn sardine can under the surface of the water so deep that I can't even see waves when all my life I've aimed to stay ABOVE ground level?"

Tess stepped into the lovers' quarrel. "Relax-"

Martina swiveled in the candlelight. "Relax? How can I RE something? Shouldn't I LAX first? Then I can RELAX!"

Tess tried again. "Take a breath-"

"I'd rather take a swig!"

"For cripes sake, have mine!" Bashelle pulled a draught of ale into a mug.

Martina eyed the mug. "Doesn't have much head on it."

"That's it. I'm done. If anybody is looking for me, I'll be twelve feet that way licking johnny cake crumbs offa wax paper."

The three friends joined together in darkness. They huddled together to stay warm.

"Should we evacuate this hollow barrel and brave the open ocean?" Bashelle was determined to create a plan.

"No way, nothing is getting this landlubber into open water ever again.

Mark my words. I would be more content to dehydrate like so many tinned morsels."

Martina lay her swimming head upon Bashelle's lap.

"Nothing's so tough to get through that a strong bit of willpower won't fix." Bashelle was not giving up.

"Willpower will not stop green bile from erupting."

"All you talk about are your puke habits. You spend all your time complaining," said Bashelle.

"I have all the time in the world to complain right now, and I have every right to it!"

"Blame not the currents of the sea, nor the sifting sands of timeless changes. Point no finger at one another, nor to fates or stars. The universe runs on its own clockwork and by design retains a continuous transition from present to future, dredging up the past in its wake. This force is unstoppable; no button or rewinding mechanism can slow the ebbs of the world's progress. We inhabitants of the living earth may only adapt, or not, in order to forge ahead on the waves of passing life."

"What the bollocks did she just say?" Martina turned to Bashelle.

"She's saying that we are a hopeless cause and it's not our fault, and any god you may think of, from Triton to Namaka, are to bear the full brunt of blame for our misfortune in this disaster of nature."

Tess rolled the compass over and over between her palms. Over and over again she counted: "One two three, one two three, one two three."

Martina covered her ears. "She is going to make me crazy before I die."

Tess abruptly stopped her repetition.

"Thank you," Martina grumbled.

"Look," whispered Tess. She twisted the silver compass in the darkness. Light glinted from its etched roses.

Bashelle and Martina craned their necks. Then the three women turned to the off kilter cabin door leading to the engine room. Sparks sizzled beneath the jam and bounced like fireflies across the floor.

"We need to decide NOW." Bashelle pushed Martina up and the three women stood, adrenaline awakening their exhausted bodies.

"Combustion" said Martina. "Gas must've leaked onto the manifold and caught fire."

Bashelle gripped Martina's hand.

Martina's voice crackled. "This is not the death I would have chosen."

Tess scurried into her sleeping chambre. She belted her big brown bag to the metal loops in her black and white striped corset. She returned to the captain quarters where her friends were holding tightly to each other in the sparking dark.

"Friends! All is not lost." Tess's voice held a resolved command. The couple turned their eyes towards her. She was silhouetted in the flames engulfing the inner walls of the cabin.

Tess reached with precision into her bag and pulled out three wound spools. "Quickly now. Trust me if you want to live. We do not have time for explanation, only action."

The room was aglow in flames. Bashelle and Martina released each other and stepped toward the professor. She handed them each a spool.

"This is a project I have been working on since, well, since a while into our journey. I foresaw a possibility of reduced oxygen. This tubular apparatus will allow you to breathe under water, without the AJM suits, which are currently ill-disposed." Bursting glass and cracking beams emphasized her message.

"Unroll your spools thus," Tess demonstrated. "Now lace the thin wires through the spool." The couple copied her movements.

"Next, if you trace your fingers upon the spool, you will feel an indentation. Press it in, so there is a flap on the inside, allowing an opening." The women obeyed.

"Can we hurry up here? My scalp is sweating." Bashelle was quick to learn and the heat was unbearable within the walls of fire.

Tess ignored the comment and continued her directions. "You will notice that either end of the long thin tubes end in a small, hard orb. These are ingestible and must be swallowed." She held the spool in one hand and placed both pills into her mouth. In a series of sucking saliva, they went down her throat, pulling the wires with it.

Bashelle immediately followed suit.

"This apparatus converts the oxygen in the water into oxygen which can be absorbed by humans."

"Are you out of your dagnab minds? How am I supposed to swallow this? My throat is dry and I have no liquid in me! Besides, my eyes are stinging without tears!"

"Your entire body will be stinging with fire if you do not do this!" shouted Bashelle.

Martina shoved the two pills to the back of her throat and gagged. She tried again, got one down, then spat it up. "This does not feel good."

"It will feel better than being dead. Now try again."

Three more swallows, and Martina felt the wires lower into her chest. She held the spool in her hot hands.

"Good job, Golden Egg." Bashelle was relieved.

"Watch this," continued Tess. She pressed the opening on the side of the spool to her nose. The tab pushed in further, securing the wiry tubes within, and creating a suction to her face. "Do this, and you can breathe. And talk. Even under water."

Bashelle already had her spool affixed before Tess had finished speaking.

"How will we get these out of our bodies?"

"When they have served their use, we will remove our spools and pull the tubes up. There may be some vomiting involved."

"If I am going to die puking my green guts out, at least let me die puking my green guts out onto dry land." Martina wiped sweat and bile from her face.

The three women used whipping knots to tie docklines around themselves, connected to each other. It was Martina's idea, and she insisted on leading the way up and out. With an axe, she finished off the damage already caused by the fire and chopped through the anchorage. Water swooped in, but she used the axe as a parrot uses its beak, chomping in pace by pace to climb out of the fiery water.

Once all three were eight metres away from the burning sub, Bashelle called out. "Be sure to ascend slowly!"

The jet propulsion boots they had each slipped into allowed them to accelerate their rise through the leagues.

Ten metres. Twelve metres. Fifteen. Twenty metres above the sub.

Suddenly, Martina felt the flowing ends of her mane pull back. Bashelle, behind her, blinked away bits of seaweed racing down. Tess's skirts pressed flat to her thighs.

Martina dared herself to glance down. Her worst worry was confirmed. If only she could swim! She foreignly inhaled, and shouted to her comrades: "Fireball!"

Tess realized they were being sucked closer to the incineration. "Prepare your propulsion boots!"

The pulling stopped, and the water around the women wavered, like a shaken snow-globe. "Get ready to engage your propulsion systems! Three...two... one."

Thunder rumbled at the bottom of the pit. "Now!"

The three women kicked their feet, heel to toe, and heel to toe. The boots expanded like short wings on a fat duck. From the tips of the winged forms, ionic blasters exploded, creating a centrifugal velocity of jetted power.

The women zoomed up towards the opening of the pit. Behind them a tremendous burst shook the walls of the pit. Debris loosened in chunks, tumbling down, as the pit caved in upon itself.

Martina's breath held is if a rock lodged in her throat. She could not feel her heart, only a constant pounding within her body. Her fear of the ocean churned into panic. She increased the velocity of her ascent.

"No!" Bashelle shouted, but Martina either didn't hear or didn't care. Her propulsion increased, pulling her team with her.

Bashelle pulled a cutlass from the leather sheath on her belt. With sweatless fury, she cut the rope. Martina continued shooting up while Bashelle and Tess remained tied together.

Tess screamed through the water. "What have you done?"

"We will catch up, but in order to help Martina, we have to help ourselves first."

They progressed upwards even as clomps of silt fell in their faces.

Bashelle's guilt built bricks in her stomach. She knew she had done the right thing, though. "What good are we to help if we fail to keep ourselves safe? We need to be healthy and safe for her, so we can help her. Otherwise we all die."

They reached the top of the pit just as it heaved its last blast and crumbled upon itself. Through the brown water, they followed a trail of bubbles bursting with Martina's gasping breaths.

When they found her, Martina was spinning around and around like a fish caught in a whirlpool. Bashelle swam to her and kicked her boot propellers in with as much force as she could muster in the undersea gravity. Martina stopped spinning and drooped in Bashelle's arms. Then she opened her eyes and started giggling.

"Oh, blimey!"

Tess floated closer, afraid of her friend's fate. Martina's eyes stared with pupils of different sizes, and her laugh became a crazed cackle.

"What is wrong with her?"

Bashelle lifted Martina so she was floating upon her knee like a ventriloquist's dummy. "She's high as a rat!"

The professor brought her hands to her head, "Oy vey. Nitrogen bubbles. She's poisoned."

"We must continue our way to Subton. She needs help, with real air."

Tess adjusted the chain around her neck and pulled the compass from where it rested on her chest. The trio followed the best they could toward Subton, half-dragging, half-carrying their cuckoo compadre.

"Avast! Look ahead!"

Tess squinted her eyes. Her static sleep kept her youthful, but her eyes insisted on maintaining their age. "I do not see what you are looking at. Kelp?"

"Look beyond what is directly in front of you. See!"

Tess relaxed her eyes and softened her gaze. "Something is glowing up ahead!"

"Aye! It must be Subton!"

The two women each took one of Martina's arms and kicked with renewed passion towards their fate. The glow ahead grew brighter, and formed a shape. They were so close!

A belching bromide crocodilian hippopotamidae stretched its neck. Bits of bilious chum sifted through its angular teeth. A small school of little blue and yellow striped fish nibbled on the morsels. The jaws of the scaled creature widened slowly, inviting the pretty fish in. With the hungry school within the cavern of tiny delicacies, the creature chomped down, emitting clouds of red blood through its large nostrils as it did so.

With a gulp of seawater, the women stopped dead in their course.

Chapter 6

Chunks of fish flesh hovered around the beast's head like an angel's halo. Shields of obsidian formed a spiky trail along the lizard's spine, ending with a solo curved claw at the base of its swishing tail. Tentacles sprouted from its throat like a bloody beard. Two curved horns framed its scaly face.

The beast's eyes flashed from yellow to green, and its tiny pupils dilated into black doors of evil. The massive head swayed from side to side.

"What is it doing?" Tess asked.

Martina wobbled. "Looks like it's dancing."

"Music tames the wild beast," mourned Tess.

Bashelle already had reached beneath her armpits to grasp her hooked magno-bolts. Her grip relaxed and she removed her thumbs from the triggers. She lifted an arm to Martina and joined their hands.

"May I have this dance, m'lady?"

Martina, dumfounded and discombobulated, acquiesced.

Tess heard a familiar hum in her ears. It grew louder, longer. "Oh jiminy cricket..."

Bashelle's best pub voice rose in waves.

"I'm sailing away; set an open course for the
virgin sea
I've got to be free; free to face the life that's
ahead of me
On board I'm the captain so climb aboard
We'll search for tomorrow on every shore
And I'll try oh Lord I'll try to carry on"

Tess looked upon Bashelle with absurdity. Then she realized the monster was equally perplexed, its head cocked like a confused dog.

"Keep singing," Tess squeaked.

"I look to the sea; reflections in the waves
spark my memory
Some happy some sad
I think of childhood friends and the dreams

we had
We live happily forever so the story goes
But somehow we missed out on that pot of
gold
But we'll try best that we can to carry on"

Martina grabbed Bashelle's other hand and added her voice.

"Look away, you rollin' river
Oh, Shenandoah, I long to hear you"

The creature stared. Its expression changed to confusion and then to wonderment.

Bashelle picked up the song.

"A gathering of angels appeared above my
head
They sang to me this song of hope and this
is what they said
They said come sail away come sail away
Come sail away with me"

Martina swung her arms with Bashelle in a seasick rhythm.

"Look away, you rollin' river
twas for her I'd cross the water"

Bashelle performed with unrestrained
bawdiness.

"I thought that they were angels but to my
surprise
They climbed aboard their starship and
headed for the skies
Singing, come sail away come sail away
Come sail away with me"
Martina's voice flowed cooly.

"Look away, you rollin' river
Seven more years I longed to have her"

Bashelle pulled Martina close.

"Come sail away with me
Come sail away, come sail away
Come sail away with me"

Martina leaned into Bashelle's broad body.

"Look away, we're bound away
Across the wide Missouri
Well, it's fare-thee-well, my dear
I'm bound to leave you"

The creature bobbed its head like a deranged cockatiel. One last cloudy belch erupted from its jaws, then it jumbled away.

Bashelle whooped. "That's right get the hullaballoo outta here you magnificent prick of a beast!"

Tess knelt, and Martina fell slowly and drifted above the rocky ground.

"C'mon, gals! The show must go on!" Bashelle reached her hands to her friends and forced them to stand. "Which way now, professor?"

Tess lifted the silver compass and watched the needle shiver and settle. She pointed slightly west, then lifted her finger higher.

The three woman contemplated the mountain ahead of them. Martina's skin took on the shade of her eyes. "I really, really, really, need to swim in ale right now."

Looking up at the dormant volcano, there seemed no easy way to climb the slope. Each footstep led to a deeper layer of thick quicksand. They tied each other on to Martina's bow, and she used her quiver of arrows as poles to propel the almost floating, almost sinking trio across the crater.

From the crest of the ancient mound, they gazed upon the gates of Subton. Gleaming in crystalized light, adorned with glistening mica and star sapphires, the city shone. The very fish swarming through and around the city glowed in their own brilliance.

Tess appraised the glittering Watch City in awe. "Now, how to get in?"

Martina groaned in agony.

Chapter 7

Subton was an undersea rainbow of gems. All that grew or moved sparkled with flecks of colour. In the shadows of deep grottos, glints of metal and shimmering scales swerved together. The entire colony of creatures abiding within the walls were a blend of flesh and mechanisms: squishy snails with spiraling silver shells; candy coloured parrotfish with peridots embedded in swishing bronze tails.

Approaching the crystalline valley, the women's eyes dazzled in the glint of glowing rocks. Even without their AJM gear, the terrain was difficult to pass. They lunged over crystals formed like a farm of spiky asparagus. Each step jolted up the curved soles of Tess's feet through her bruised femurs, past her cold bottom, to her aching spine. Her hot breath of impatience and pain created a brief puff of fog.

"I am not sure what we will find when we encroach upon Subton," Bashelle mused. "We had originally planned to enter in the dark, but that is now quite impossible. It seems we have no other choice than to risk peril without the protection of night." She pulled out her spyglass and investigated the view of the glimmering Watch City.

"What are you looking at?"

Bashelle handed the spyglass to Martina.

"Ahhh, yes, I see."

"Pray-tell, let me have a peek, if I may," Tess said, fumbling the telescope from Martina's thick gloves.

Bashelle pointed. "There is an air block there. A dome blocking out seawater and encapsulating enough breathable oxygen, it would appear, for a patch of grass, a few humble trees, and moving furry things."

"Those moving furry things will be my supper." Martina rubbed her belly.

"All in good time," said Tess.

"Hasten your stride and kneel here with me." Martina directed Bashelle and Tess to a fallen log on the far side of the dome. "Before we dare enter the city proper, I would firmly suggest studying the boundaries circumspectly. Keep your weapons and wits about you." She rose, and took long wobbling strides through tall grasses towards the air pod. She started cackling again.

"We need to fix her brain up, soon," said Bashelle.

"Tis nothing an ellwand of ale hasn't done to her."

Bashelle turned to Tess as they followed their harebrained hunter. "She's all bendy. If she isn't stabilized soon, her brain will pop and drizzle out her ears."

Tess cringed at the grotesque explanation, but appreciated the urgency which was required.

Tess caught up to Martina. "These moving furry things, which you say you must sup on, could be the only of their kind, the beginning or end of an unknown vertebrate, never catalogued or known to humanity. Perhaps, we could spare them, for the sake of science."

"Perhaps, we could spear them, for the sake of my stomach."

"Look over there!" Bashelle pointed to another dome. The women float-walked closer, and saw a series of glass pods, each the size of a garden shed. Within them were stacks of canoes.

"What is that about?" asked Martina.

"I do wonder," said Tess. She reached deftly into her brown bag and retrieved a pair of opera glasses.

"Where are you getting all these trinkets from anyways?" Martina asked. A rose embroidered kerchief with blue lace edging flowed from her bag.

"A lady is always prepared."

"Are you saying I'm not a lady?" Martina's eyes flashed with fire and abruptly darkened. Tess grew increasingly alarmed at her dignified friend's diminishing sense of humour.

"Certainly you are a lady, and one of such talent, style, and strength as I have never met before, and without whom this adventure would not be possible."

Martina waved her hand dismissively at this gush of flattery, but the clouds of resentment dissipated from her green eyes.

The trio continued their course, careful to crouch in open areas and sneak behind tall fronds of swaying bushes.

Martina scooped up a handful of sparkling sand and peered behind them. "We must cover our tracks," she warned the others. She pulled long leaves from the bushes and instructed the women to stick them under their belts in the back. In this way their tracks would be swept away as they went.

"I feel like a peacock," Tess said.

Martina appraised her. "You look like one too." She pulled a thorn from her palm.

Tess looked on with concern. "Are you bleeding?"

"Not yet. Give me time."

Outside the city dome, the three friends found a trap door leading to a tunnel. They followed it, and reached the dry innards of a humble building. In the tiny room was a stack of round glowing rocks and a barren marble fireplace. Sconces illuminated the space with a glimmer of warmth.

Martina immediately knelt to the tiled floor and pulled the breathing apparatus from her nose, along with the wires dangling down her throat. As they emerged from her mouth, a fresh burst of seawater poured out. "It has never felt so good to throw up."

The women started wringing out their clothes, proud of their cunning entrance into Subton. Rescuing their kidnapped friend Verdandi would be a breeze!

Tess combed her water-wrinkled fingers through her knotted curls. Bashelle adjusted her weapons cache beneath her garments. Martina lay on the floor trying to keep the world from spinning.

"Have you noticed?" she asked weakly.

"What my dear, pink elephants?"

"No. Door."

Tess rolled her eyes at Bashelle. "She's loopy."

"No door."

"I'll be duffled. Tess, look around; she is right. What ijits we are. We aren't in a cottage. We're in Davy Jones' Locker!"

A giant boulder aligned with the wall slid to the side, revealing a darkened cave.

A blast of heat burst into the chilly crevice wherein the three friends were halted.

The sconces blew out, encapsulating them in darkness.

A clang of metal on ceramic rang like a morning alarm. It stopped, and a glowing green hoop shone before the women.

A deep voice in the darkness flowed over them. "Welcome to Subton." With a flash, bright white light revealed what the women could not comprehend in the darkness.

"I am Pace."

"My stars," breathed Tess. Her thoughts fought with brain blasts of battle, synergistic escape options, and calculations of physics. Mostly, she wondered how she could quickly fix her coif.

Chapter 8

Pace bowed deeply, his mechanical arm bent at the waist, and his broad, round shoulders perfectly aligned. His bald head was half smooth dark skin, half metallic silver. He rose to full height, which was almost seven feet, at least with his robotic boots. Tess felt a flip in her stomach. Maybe it was hunger.

He stretched his left arm out, and she clasped on with two shivering hands. They rose up together, her dark blue eyes meeting his deep brown one and his pupil-less silver one, shining like scales of flashy tarpon.

"Yoki," he called over his shoulder, "kindly fetch a fresh array of blankets from the hearth-side."

A young woman; a teenager; a girl in-between a bud and a blossom, stood behind him. Her black eyes and short onyx hair lent intensity to her heart shaped face. Dark freckles accented her smooth skin. Her bodice shimmered in variant shades of blue and green, creating the illusion of motion. Her skirt was less a covering and more of a frill at her waist, iridescent in the light. Her legs were covered by rows of crystals strung together in a sort of chain mail, so that bare skin showed when the chains swayed. Tess averted her eyes.

Yoki came back with a bundle of fleeces, and the refugees were escorted to a large room with three marble fireplaces, sofas upholstered with sharkskin leather, and sparkling mosaics covering the walls. Tall shelves made of luminescent white crystal displayed rows and rows of books.

Bashelle side-eyed Tess. "Close your mouth; you're drooling."

Indeed, this was a room beyond Tess's imagination. Warm, glowing, book-laden: delicious.

Pace invited the three castaways to warm by the hearths while more young people dressed similarly to Yoki poured seagrass tea into small jade cups.

"I recognize your timepieces," Pace said. He nodded towards the glass circle threaded through Martina's hair with a ribbon, and a large face bound around Bashelle's bicep. "You are of one of our

Watch City nation." The women nodded silently, shivering in dampness beneath the toasted fleece.

"You," Pace focused his eyes on Tess, "seem familiar to me." His brown eye squinted in an effort to summon recollection.

"Yeah, everybody knows who that one is!" said Martina. Green liquid spurt from her mouth as she spoke. She wobbled on the edge of a sleek grey chaise and slid to the tiled floor as she motioned toward Tess. "She's the one and only magnificent-"

Tess rose abruptly and interrupted her sea damaged friend. "Pleased to make your acquaintance," she curtsied, balancing the fleece over her shivering shoulders. "You may call me Tess. I submit myself to you as ambassador from the Watch City of Waltham. Please allow me to introduce my fellow esteemed ambassadors from our City of Endless Time: Martina the Honourable, and Bashelle the Robust." In the back fifth of her third section of brain she again cursed with disdain regarding her limp soppy hair.

Pace stepped forward and bowed deeply again, before taking Tess's sea-wrinkled hand in his cold metal one. "We of Subton, the Great City Navigating the World, and especially, we, the Mutineers, welcome you and your company to enjoy our company. May your clocks always chime."

"May they echo in your deepest reverberations," answered Tess.

"I'll drink to that!" Martina spilled her tea upon her chest, and her eyes rolled up, showing only the eggs.

Bashelle threw off her fleece and lifted Martina's head from the floor, then pushed her onto her side, wherein she vomited ungallantly in her sleep. Tea from her belly steamed on the tile.

"My comrade is in dire need of medical attention." Tess surveyed the globs gushing from the glassmaker's mouth. Bashelle's great bosom supported her love's body. "Both of my compatriots are in need of food, warmth, and rest. Might I ask of you to allow them healing? In exchange, I will gladly offer my services to your sympathy."

Pace's silver eye dimmed as his brown one darkened. He lowered himself onto a white furred ottoman, sitting for the first time during their introduction. He slouched his shoulders forward and clasped his big hands of flesh and metal before him between his knees.

"No woman, no person, is subservient in Subton. You would lead us before I would dare try to press you under the vice of my grip."

Tess inhaled and closed her eyes. Her mouth opened as she breathed in wholly, tasting fire and salt and aged oak coals.

"Then lend us to quarters equipped appropriately for ambassadors as esteemed as ourselves." Tess rose; her legs melted, her ankles cracked, and she lay two bare, blue puffy veined hands to the mantle above the nearest fireplace. "My friend needs a medic, appropriately quickly. Now."

Her sight blurred with salt-burnt corneas and heated air. She reached out in the black of her vision, precariously balancing on the precipice of mantle and fire; standing and falling; composure and embarrassment.

She lowered herself to her knees slowly, foreseeing her imminent convalescence. Her wet body yet dripped, shivering like endless concentric ripples in a tide pool. She knew the blankness would come; not from her mind and memory, but from her body.

"I am tired, your honour, Pace of Subton, aligned with the Watch City Nation. Mutineer. Leader of youth. Powerful in your sympathy, may you find compassion for your comrades from another hydrothermic thermoclime bordering the surface of your sea's berth." She knelt in her self-made puddle, acquiescing in what may be. "Your ambassadors from your sister Watch City of Waltham are readily prepared to act and serve in the Subton Mutiny of which you represent. Forgive me. It may be quick. Please forgive me for going away."

At that, the great professor fainted.

Chapter 9

Tess, Martina, and Bashelle passed out in front of the hearths in the magnificent Mutineer library. Their clothes dried before their brains did.

Yoki exerted herself in her mission to heal the dementia binding bends of Martina the Honourable and the use of crystallized algae to deflex muscular integration of Bashelle the Robust. Pace himself oversaw the arrangements for glacial powdered nectar and gem fruits.

The three were roused and Yoki led them down a short tunnel. Three other young women accompanied them, supporting the weak travellers. Yoki stood before two doorways across from each other.

"Ambassadors of the Watch City of Waltham, please allow us to help make you comfortable in our guest rooms. We have these two prepared and you may choose as you will."

Tess's eyes darted back and forth between the two opposing rooms. There were three of them yet two rooms offered. Her head swam and her vision paled. Bashelle was conscious enough to read Tess's anxiety and tease her.

"Don't worry, fair lady. We will give you all the privacy you want. We could use some privacy too." She smacked Martina's bottom, and was answered with a jab in the bicep.

The young Subtonians lit the fireplaces in each room. They delivered armloads of clothing to the armoires.

"Please rest and partake of medicinal water and fortifying fruits arrayed for your nourishment. When you are adequately able, Pace has openly invited you to dress in fresh attire and join him in the lunarium. If you have a desire or an additional request, you may lift a conchline and voice your need. The communications sector will gladly answer and promptly respond to your comfort. For now, we shall leave you to heal and recover from whatever ordeal you pushed through on your way here. Goodnight, may time serve you well."

Yoki turned and left the hallway with the small troupe of teens following in line after her.

Tess waved weakly from the plush bed to which she had been lifted. Her voice came in a whisper. "May time circle around and serve you back." She succumbed to dreamless sleep.

"I don't like having an empty larder." Martina patted her aching stomach.

"You are as empty as I've ever seen you. Time to fill 'er up." Bashelle helped Martina rise from the bed.

"Why is the floor tilting and tipping?"

"It ain't the floor, dearest. It's you who is off balance. But don'tcha worry; the pretty lasses filled you right up with coconut water and you will find your feet soon enough."

Martina then noticed the tube stuck in her shoulder, leading to a translucent jug hung like a lantern above the bed. Within it was a rainbow of glowing gemstones soaked in a clear liquid with golden floating flecks.

A syringe inserted in the bottom of the jar streamed a slow flow into Martina's body.

"What in hells bells is this poison?" Martina tore the tube from her shoulder, and blood spurted out.

"You dinglehopper! That is the healing elixir that has kept your brain from exploding!"

"Apparently it's too late; my brain has been mash for some time."

Bashelle pulled off a soft pink pillowcase and expertly folded and tied it around Martina's bloody shoulder. "Can you do be a favour, kid, and not bleed to death before breakfast?"

"I'll try," answered Martina. She stumbled to the armoire. "Thunderation!"

Bashelle stepped behind her, and what she saw caused her jaw to open as wide as the armoire doors. "No, no, just no, nope, never, never, no way in hell."

Glittering gemstones dripped delicately from silk gowns. Pink lace trailed down pastel bustiers, and an assortment of ribboned bonnets hung from hooks.

Martina lowered herself to an embroidered settee. "I think I am going to be sick again."

Tess, Martina, and Bashelle were guided to the lunarium by cloth maps thoughtfully hung on their door knobs. Pace was sitting at a triangular table where a small feast was laid out for them. With ample water.

After proper greetings, the women sat and helped themselves to tea. Martina shoved an entire scone into her mouth and moved her jaw up and down, then brought a napkin delicately to her face and used her tongue to push the food out. Tess raised an eyebrow.

"I can't feel my teeth!'

Pace's smooth deep voice reassured her. "Madame Martina, the insensibility will pass; it is but a brief side effect of the distilled blue algae used in one of the injections we gave you. Your numbness should subside by this evening."

"I wouldn't count on that, she's always been fairly numb." Bashelle reached over and patted Martina's head. Martina did not smile at the joke.

"I'm sorry," said Bashelle. "It's always your teeth!"

Martina met her sincere expression and felt her mood soften. "At least I can still eat cream puffs!" The two chortled uproariously, much to Pace's bewilderment.

"Don't ask," warned Tess.

The three friends had agreed that morning to keep their intent secret, at least for the time being. They needed to save Verdandi, but they did not know who to trust, despite the Subtonian's kindnesses. Claiming Ambassadorship was acceptable, and not a complete untruth. So, as Bashelle and Martina emptied plate after plate, and Tess picked at her food, they described their tumultuous adventure.

"I just about lost my mind when we slid into that ledge," said Martina.

"I think you did" laughed Bashelle. "Then again, I think we all three did. Now we know to use sonar to check for depth of not just water but of sand, too."

Pace nodded. "A fall in a pit, a rise in your wit."

Tess explained how they tied themselves together and climbed the volcano.

"A mountain is just a steep path," acknowledged Pace.

Martina rolled her eyes and whispered to Bashelle. "I'll hold him; you punch."

Tess stood from the table. "Our thanks, gracious Pace, for your hospitality. My comrades and I must take to our rooms now to regroup and perhaps rest our bodies and minds after such a lovely morning."

Martina and Bashelle started grumbling in protest, but the professor's stern glare quieted their objections.

"Thank you for joining me this morning. Before you retire, please allow me, on behalf of the Mutineers, to invite you to a banquet to be held this eve in your honour."

"Will there be ale?" Martina asked.

Pace chuckled from deep in his barrel chest. "Indeed, there will be."

"I'll be there!"

Pace walked them out of the lunarium and did not avert his eyes when Tess adjusted her skirts.

Chapter 10

Tess joined Martina and Bashelle in their room. Martina sprawled across the plush canopy bed and surrounded herself in a nest of pillows. Bashelle sat on the edge of the bed and rubbed Martina's feet. Tess arranged herself on the sofa in front of the fireplace; she had not yet relieved the chill from her bones.

"Let's lay out all the cards," Bashelle began. "We need to figure out who to trust, how to find Verdandi, and for cripe's sake, where to get a decent pair of pants. I don't care how much chain mail they wrap on those things; I am not wearing a dress." She was still wearing her salt bleached britches.

Martina propped herself up. "I could creep off and scout around, find some leads to our girl."

"We need to be cautious," said Tess. "We have only seen a tiny portion of this immense Watch City. We have yet to meet anyone who has mentioned DRAKE or Ziracuny. There is no telling what kind of conspiracy we are entwined in."

"Even the more reason for me to start tracking. I am getting my senses back, and still have my bow and quiver."

Bashelle turned to her. "You are not gonna hunt a little girl."

"First of all," said Martina, "Verdandi is not a little girl. Don't be a nitwit."

Tess leaned forward. "She is a child, and while yes, I am more eager than either of you to get her back, it must be done with gentleness and grace."

Martina twisted towards her with a snake's eyes. "Who in the heck of Poseidon's tombs do you think you are? You want her back more than any of us? Feck off."

"I only meant-"

"I found her, I saved her, I raised her, I set her free. I want her back. So don't tell me you are the pinnacle of her future. You know nothing."

Bashelle scuttled closer to Martina on the bed and stroked her arm in a soothing manner. Martina shoved her hand off.

"You too. Why are you even here?"

Bashelle winced with the emotional sting. Martina saw the pain and immediately regretted her words, and tried to fix it.

"Wait, I am glad you're here. I wouldn't want to be away from you."

Bashelle softened.

"But don't pretend you would be here if you weren't following me."

Bashelle rose from the bed and leaned nose to nose with Martina. "You feckin dribble of a witch's teat. How dare you? It does not matter how deeply or how little I know that child. What matters is that I give a damn. Don't measure my love for her. Love is love."

"Whatever, I don't get it and I don't care."

"How can you not understand how I feel?" cried Bashelle.

"I gave up trying to understand people long ago. Now I let them try to understand me."

Tess stood and composed her voice to be soft and light. "It seems as if we are all tired. We have been through a lot together.

We owe it to ourselves, and to each other, to perhaps take a rest."

The other two women said nothing.

"Can we agree that we are exhausted beyond any sense of normalcy? Can we agree to let our tempers keep us warm while we sleep so we can wake to a cool new afternoon?"

Martina and Bashelle grumbled in agreement.

"If you need me, simply knock on my door."

Martina rolled over in her nest, burying her face in pillows. "If anybody needs me, I'll be in bed avoiding death."

"Move over." Bashelle crawled under the covers.

Tess closed her bedroom door behind her. She pulled her brown bag out from beneath her skirts, placed it on the floor and opened it wide. Then she grasped the handles, stepped in, and pulled the bag up over her head, encasing herself in warm darkness. She held the handles together, twisted them, and pulled them down.

She felt herself flip around and upside-down as the bag turned inside-out. She opened the bag and lowered the handles to the floor. Her feet sunk in luxurious pink carpet as she stepped out. Her room; her private world. The sight of her circle bed with precisely tucked pink silk sheets almost made her cry.

She undressed and bathed in her clawfoot tub. She scrubbed her skin with sugar and saturated her hair with honey. She had missed this so much. Besides the pampering she craved, she was determined to retain her youth for as long as possible. At least until she found her Rose.

Beneath the sheets, covered with layers of softness, she closed her eyes and counted the years. Her baby would not be a baby the next time she saw her. She would be half-grown, almost a woman herself. Would she even recognize her child? Of course she would, she admonished herself. Yet even if not, perhaps her daughter would recognize her. This was the determined hope with which she pursued eternal youth. Here in her private pocket of static time, she could escape the aging process that might deem her unremembered.

Swirls of pink spun her slumbering brain. Her lips whispered, "Rose." When you sleep, does your mouth turn down in sculpted sadness? Does the lift of your lips purse forward in sweet dreams? Perhaps a line crosses your persona cutting your dreams in half: separating colour from traces of black and white. Without words. Without music. Without feeling.

Tess startled awake and relaxed once she realized where she was. Beyond her static time, in just the other room from where her bag remained between hours, her two closest friends slept. Her eyes glazed over. If they only knew. How intense her pain was; how benignly she carried it wherever she went.

"Rose," she prayed in the darkness, "I wish I could tell you secrets. Like how much I miss you." She hugged her compass watch and returned to pastel dreams.

Chapter 11

"Dear Professor, you appear dumbfounded!" Martina's mood had greatly improved with more sleep and another jar of healing liquid dripping into her body.

"Fuzz the buzz with that professor shite," reminded Bashelle.

"Oh, yeah right. Hey, normal unbraniac nongenius lack of inventiveness typical matron of nobility: why do you have such an exceptionally stupid look on your face?"

Tess ignored the remarks, lost as she was in her befuddlement by the display of food in front of her.

"What is this?"

Bashelle stepped in to educate the scientist. "Sea cucumber."

"Is it a plant?"

"No.

"What is this?"

"That is conch pot pie"

"Oh. What is this?"

Bashelle looked at her deadeye. "Professor, that is broccoli."

"Yes, indeed it is."

Martina pinched Bashelle's thigh. "Watch it with that professor stuff."

Tess continued surveying the selections at the Ambassadors Banquet. "Feeling grossed out by the non-vegetarian bags-o-mystery?" Martina asked with a mouthful of something.

Tess stage whispered, "I swear that jam just twitched!"

"That is fish eggs, mmm, delicious on these crackers." Bashelle scooped another pink blob onto her plate.

Martina passed a brown biscuit to Tess. "One person's meat is another person's poison." She turned to Bashelle. "I would like you even if you were tofu."

"I'd like you even if you were green cheese-and you were green last night!

Martina pointed to the creamed oysters with red pepper sauce. "I might even still like you if you were this muck!"

Pace joined them at the head of the table, with Tess on his right, Martina on his left, with Bashelle next to her. "Is everything to your liking, Ambassadors?"

Martina held up a mug. "This fruity bubble water, it's delicious."

"Wow," said Bashelle.

"And this!" Martina pointed to ale.

"Oh thank gracious; I was worried for a second."

Pace took a sip of lemon water. "I am gladdened to see that despite your tribulations en route, you possess the vigour to be satisfied by Subton's offerings."

Martina answered by holding up a fresh mug.

"Everything is quite lovely," said Tess. "We are grateful for your magnificent-"

She was interrupted by the sound of Martina spitting vegetables out onto her plate. "When you cook, you need butter."

Tess politely disagreed. "I never use butter. I prefer extra virgin olive oil."

"Ain't nothing extra virgin about you." Martina high-fived Bashelle while Tess took a gulp of cold lemon water.

Bashelle chomped on white and pink meat. Grease dripped down her lips, her chin, her throat, drizzling to her two round mounds. She wiped the dribbles from her bosom and spread it across her bald head.

"That's one shiny fly dome," said Martina.

"Real meat lard makes it all good."

"Lard?" asked Tess, not disgusted or offended. Only purely curious. "Where is there lard in Subton? Surely not from fish?"

Pace looked at her intently. Science deserved an explanation. "You can find out on the morrow. I will show you."

Martina nudged Bashelle. "What's this?" She used a blue cotton napkin to wipe the grimace from her face.

"Spinach."

"No, these leaves in my salad. What is it?"

"Spinach."

"I'll have some of that. Please," Tess said eagerly. She was excruciatingly hungry but her palate could not be satisfied by the consumption of flesh.

Pace passed the fresh green salad to Tess. She dismissed manners and loaded her plate. "We have potatoes too," he offered.

"No, thank you," said the three friends in unison. Then they laughed, a giggle at first, then eye streaming cackles.

"Oy, my stomach hurts, please don't make me laugh more," begged Martina.

Tess wiped her eyes with her lace trimmed handkerchief. "Please forgive us," she said, addressing Pace. "We do not mean to be rude. Yet please understand our quandary: we have been eating potatoes for many moons." She dabbed her eyes again and hiccoughed with a new burst of laughter. "We may never eat tubers again."

"No more taters! No more taters!" chanted Martina and Bashelle, their knives pounding on the table.

Their table-mates looked upon them in puzzlement. Then Pace lifted his chopsticks together over his head and clacked them together. "No more taters! No more taters!" The table erupted in thumping laughter. Tess met Pace's eyes and felt more gratefulness than when he had swaddled her in lambskin.

Pace stood and lifted a freshly poured flute of luminescent green liquid. All down the table, each person lifted an identical flute.

"Dear Subtonian Mutineers, brave, strong, persistent, resilient; it is my pleasure to introduce these exceptional Ambassadors from our sister in society, the Watch City of Waltham." He nodded to each woman. "Bashelle the Robust. Martina the Honourable. Tess the Magnificent." The women in turn stood, holding their glowing drinks aloft.

Martina and Bashelle stood proudly, and looked to Tess, known to them to be of the noble class. She caught their subtle deference and breathed in deeply before addressing the dinner party.

"Graces of time have rung the bells of our journey, and the reverberating strength of Subton echoed through the darkness in our moments of need. The purity of your welcome has fortified us. Our combined zeal for our Watch City nation continues to support our people throughout. With shared resources and science, the Watch Cities unite our intentions for timely progress to benefit the welfare of all. We grateful Ambassadors place firm reliance on our bond with Subton, with loyalty and veneration."

"I'll drink to that," said Martina.

"So we all shall," answered Pace. At that, the entire gathering stood, and drank communally.

The feasting continued. Tess found no end to her appetite now that Pace explained what each food was. His affable attitude combined with his manners and charm made him a comfortable table mate. Tess felt confident in his demeanor. She braved a question she and her friends had wondered upon.

"If you please, could you explain away my ignorance? We ambassadors are uninformed when it comes to the terminology used to describe your culture. In particular, concerning the title of Mutineer."

Pace rose the volume of his voice just enough to be heard throughout the gathering without sounding overbearing to those seated closer to him.

"Here in Subton, we have suffered a separation of cultures. As you are familiar, DRAKE has invaded Watch Cities, and struck ours with a force we are still fighting."

"Yes, we understand," said Martina. "DRAKE: Defend, Recruit, Abet, Kill, Encode. If I was not at such a bountiful bounty with exalted comrades, I would spit at the name of our mutual enemy."

The Subtonians clacked their chopsticks in approval.

Pace continued. "DRAKE has split our community. We are all Subtonians. Yet there are DRAKE Subtonians, and we, the Mutineer Subtonians. We proudly call ourselves Mutineers, although DRAKE considers it a slur upon us."

"I like it," said Bashelle.

"Our community has been further fractioned by DRAKE's forced government. They seduce our small population of young people with promises of power. The Boundless Society of DRAKE for the

Improvement of Natural Knowledge. Or BSDINK for short.

"Feckin perfect," chortled Bashelle.

"As you know, DRAKE purposely polluted the water in Waltham so that Subton would be the only source of clean fish. As DRAKE no longer controls Waltham, largely because of you, our esteemed ambassadors," Pace paused as the table erupted in clacking chopsticks, expressing their praise of the three women who had led a revolution. "Thus, their fish industry there was a flop."

"Flop," said Bashelle. "I see what you did there!"

A chunk of braised carrots stuck in Tess's throat. Pace met her eyes and nodded. He knew who they were. She pressed her fingers around the cold glass of lemon water and sipped deeply.

"Please do continue," she said. "We respect your history and honour your people."

"Thank you, Tess the Magnificent." Pace took a swig of green ale. "We in Subton value our natural philosophers who experiment with our abundant resources. They create medicines using algae, mutating it to cure ailments to the point that many diseases known elsewhere no longer exist in Subton."

"Indeed," said Tess, "I have studied your pharmacology and scientific breakthroughs. I had a dear friend, a doctor, Kate," her voice cracked as she spoke aloud the name of her dead lover. Martina and Bashelle lifted their mugs in silent commiseration. "She had been a student of Subtonian medical science and used what she learned from your algae and crystals to design powerful healing elixirs."

"I can vouch for that," said Martina, tracing her once-crushed ribs.

Bashelle leaned over and kissed her cheek. "I am forever grateful."

Pace paused to raise his mug and sang out, "Amama." Everyone at the long table did the same with their various drink-ware and answered, "Amama."

After draining his ale, Pace went on. "Our scientists are skilled through generations of cultural teachings and modern inventions. Microscopes enable us to create variations from our vital crystals and powerful geodes, as well as build our walls of art throughout our halls and tunnels." He gestured to intricate mosaics, with flecks of fiery reflections blinking in the gaslight torches.

"Subton celebrates a love of geometry. We count the sides of crystal edges and inspect the prisms within. The powers are grown and harvested." Pace's jaw set hard and his eyes hardened briefly. "Unfortunately, DRAKE adulterates this power for evil intentions." A grim pall spread.

Pace's voice was lower, yet still projected clearly throughout the great hall. "Thats why so many were killed: DRAKE didn't like their science; they were learning too much. Becoming too independent and harder to control."

Pace poured more green ale for himself and passed the jug to Martina. "So the young generation learns only DRAKE science. Unless they live as Mutineers. If they do not join DRAKE or BSDINK they pay high taxes and are not eligible for tempting perks."

Pace lifted his robotic arm to his temple and mindlessly rubbed as he closed his eyes to painful memories. When his eyes reopened, Tess saw sadness ripple through his expression.

"After the Battle of Subton, ten years previous, most of the elder generation was wiped out. Turns out this was done purposely as a cleansing. DRAKE took in the orphans without homes and indoctrinated them into their mini militia. Weird how the older DRAKE military people did not die." He paused for breath.

"The Battle of Subton began as a massacre. Unfair. As the young ones slept after an eclipse celebration." Pace closed his eyes again, retaining tears.

"That is why," he explained in sombre tones, "we have parties in secret if at all. The young are afraid still. Joyful congregation brings back sour memories. DRAKE does not want the Mutineers to be happy."

Martina refilled her ale mug.

"They try to collect scientists and young people and thwart their ideas. They reteach bastardized science to the new generation in an effort to gain control, from the children first. That is why they effectively wiped out the generations before them in Battle of Subton."

"How awful," groaned Bashelle.

"That is the tie in to the drugs proffered to the new generation by a would-be captain of ill repute, an embarrassment to his family. To me. Now he is considered a mentor, yet he is spreading poison."

Martina felt her ribs ache. "Disgusting. Let me at im," she slurred. Bashelle poured lemon water into her mug.

The middle rows of Mutineers arose from the table and left to the galley. The bakers therein carried out a cake. Not just a cake. A geometric marvel of sugar and flour.

It took four people to carry the architectural masterpiece to the triangular marble table designated for desserts. The banquet echoed in exuberant clacking through the tiled room.

The ambassadors gazed, awestruck, at the confectionary wonderment. Four triangular walls met in a point; a perfect pyramid. Tiny cuts of red and orange fruit leather were cemented by smooth white frosting. Across the centre on all sides was a mosaic of deep blue fish eggs, forming the body of a sinuous sea dragon.

"We cannot eat this," breathed Martina.

Crystalline plates were passed up and down and across the celebrants. Phrases of mutual languages blended with sweetness.

The ambassadors listened with open ears and full mouths. Lyrical stories flowed on waves of words. They heard tales of history, mystery; truth in fiction.

Water Monsters were real. Subtonians were virulently afraid of the mythical creatures. Long whiskered grandfathers shared their fear of disrupting the apocalyptic beast. They used their chopsticks to point out the hieroglyphics on the ceiling. Pace explained the meaning behind the mosaic dragon embedded between the picture words. "A candle lights others and consumes itself."

He placed his armoured hand lightly on Tess's. "Not all dragon fire burns." She did not pull back her hand.

"What did she say?" asked Martina.

Pace translated. "Drunken life, dreamy death."

Martina raised her mug back to the Subtonian. "Ahóá"

Pace explained in a conversational tone that opened the ears of everyone at the table. "Many languages created or spoken in our city died in the Battle of Subton. A decade ago, we lost our way of life, our history, our languages. DRAKE took them and crushed them. Yet with our Blue Crystal of Knowledge we are rediscovering our languages. Nothing is lost to those who love and believe."

"Amama," agreed the Subtonians.

Pace continued, addressing Tess, Martina, and Bashelle, and the entire length of the long table within the hall. "Most people in Subton are multi-lingual, and the

Mutineers place value on it. DRAKE wants us to speak only one language, the language of DRAKE." A low disgruntled murmur rolled through the feasters.

"I am grateful to know the languages I do, but not all of us are as well versed linguistically. Could we perhaps find a mutual language for us all to understand?" asked Tess.

Pace turned to her yet still projected his voice to the attentive congregation.

"Language joins us, and should not divide us. Yet limiting ourselves to one language limits our expression. Some words do not translate; some phrases only make sense in the language they were built in."

The crowd again agreed, "Amama."

Pace continued. "Not only the spoken word is language. Written language, drawings, dances, whistles, music; these are all forms of communication. Some languages have no words; some have no dance. Yet they are each independently vital to society, and to joint Watch Cities, and indeed, civilizations everywhere. We in Subton are honoured to uphold the languages of our ancestors, and the languages of all who have come before us."

"Amama!" cheered the Subtonians.

People in the middle of the table stood and removed their plates to the kitchen. More people arrived with fresh platters of hot and cold delicacies, and seated themselves to eat. The entire gathering replenished their plates.

Tess had polished off her plate of leaves, and filled it again with another food she recognized as non-flesh: garbanzo beans with parsley. Pace added garbanzo beans to his plate with juicy fruit remnants. He handed a small bowl of pasty substance to Tess.

"I understand that you are not in desire of potatoes, yet I incur you to taste of this common food of Subton. It is the consistency of mashed garbanzo beans and pairs well with them."

Tess palmed the small bowl in her gloved hands. She had chosen the open fingered green-scaled hand coverings provided by her hosts within her dresser, to match the teal corset and black embroidered skirt she found in the armoire. She had finished off the look with her own silver hair clip affixed with peacock feathers.

"In our custom," explained Pace softly, "we scoop the poi with our fingers and eat it straight. Like this." He dipped the index and middle fingers from his brown flesh hand into the paste, swirled them in the bowl, and placed his fingertips between his lips. His tongue flicked between his fingers, cleansing the stickiness from them.

"I see," said Tess, mesmerized. She dipped her fingertips into the soft mud-like mixture and brought it to her lips. Pace looked at her intently.

"It is...interesting," said Tess. She wasn't sure if she liked it or not.

Pace smiled, his smooth lips framing a mouth of straight white bright teeth. "She says it's interesting," he chuckled.

"Is that mashed soy?" Bashelle reached over and spooned a dollop onto her already full plate. She chose a sliver of boned fish and delicately smeared poi onto it with a silver butter knife. She immersed the morsel in her mouth. "Mmm, creamy."

Conversation flowed up and down the table. Language; languages. Words over and under speech. What languages do you know? How much do you understand? Can you speak what you hear? Can you dance to your words? Can you paint an epic poem?

"I am thrilled that one language I know is Tagalog," said Bashelle. She raised her mug and met eyes with particular table-mates. "Mubuhay!" The goodwill was returned with smiles and cheers.

Across the table, Tess daintily lowered her tea cup and began to speak. Martina pointed her chopsticks at her. "Hey, you! It's my turn!" Tess felt quite awkward for speaking out of turn, but could not imagine the outdoors-woman knowing any other language.

"As a matter of trivia, I may be as linguistically inclined as certain geniuses in our midst. Besides modern English, I am well versed in American Sign Language. In fact," she looked proudly at the beautiful professor across from her, "I am one of the encoders who learned from Wampanoag residents in Martha's Vineyard. Together, we taught a language without spoken words to people who could not hear, and also those who could. Without the Wampanoag, the whole of Cape Cod could face silence and solitude."

Martina looked across at Tess. Her heart clenched. This woman who she respected, who she loved, who she trusted, was shocked by her menial knowledge? She continued speaking.

"As you can imagine, the reason I could assist in the sharing of this language was because of my fluency in Algic languages. I am eternally grateful to my Native family who cared enough about me to educate me."

She stared again into Tess's eyes. "What are you so dag-nag surprised about?"

The multi-published and well-renowned professor literally choked on her words.

Martina smouldered in her hurt and anger.

Pace cleared his throat and swerved the topic. "We Mutineers believe that language is an inborn need. It is easy for a child to learn many languages."

"Yet not so easy to understand them all," added Tess.

"Especially if you're deaf as a haddock!" Bashelle elbowed Martina.

"What?"

"Exactly!"

Tess listened intently as she ate. Her stomach felt happy. "There are language barriers. I respect the variances in nuanced meanings within languages. I do not seek to propose, at least not at this time, the idea of a universal language as you say DRAKE requires, and which I demean. Yet a system or tool to decipher...to figure out who knows what language...so we may as a nation of Watch Cities interpret for each other..." Tess trailed off.

"That is part of the dynamic of the Blue Crystal of Knowledge," Pace reiterated. "Perhaps you, all three of you ambassadors," he nodded to Martina and Bashelle, "would enjoy a tour of our pyramids."

The three friends quickly accepted the offer.

"Tomorrow then?" It was agreed.

Along the walls Martina scouted. She saw murals depicting ocean battles against a blazing dragon. Colours trembled in monstrous visions of black and red evil bleeding in a sea of turquoise.

Pace pulled blonde hair affixed with feathers back beyond the kneeling figure. "Have you had too much to drink, Martina, my ally?"

Martina's vomit splashed against the precious stones. "No." She paused to hurl. "I ate a pound of sea spinach on an empty stomach."

Pace tapped his robotic arm and let spray a cool mist upon the ambassador's face. "Next time add more parsley."

"Oy, there you are!" Bashelle pulled the red bandana from her throat and wiped Martina's face. She turned to Pace. She wasn't used to seeing a man touch her Golden Egg so intimately. "Thank you."

Pace released his gentle grasp of feathers and hair and reached into the scales of his jacket. "This will help her ere the morning." He handed her a shell from his robotic arm. "Simply pour it in her morning wash. When she rinses her face, she will feel rejuvenated. Feed her some cod cakes and beans for breakfast and she will be all set."

Bashelle was too focused on lifting Martina from the cold floor to notice Pace shifting through walls into invisibility.

Chapter 12

Bashelle knocked on Tess's door early in the morning. Tess unlocked the door as she pulled her selection of salmon scaled gloves from the armoire.

The two women took tea in the large sitting room of Tess's boudoir. Bashelle lit a pipe.

Tess pulled a deck of cards from one of the table's many drawers. A game of Old Maid passed the time before the rest of the world awoke.

Pace led the ambassadors on a on an in-depth tour of Subton, appropriate to their grande titles.

"After the Battle of Subton, we experienced an offset stabilization of climate. This shift caused our geysers to expel more frequently, essentially warming our already tropical waters. This volcano crumbled inwardly, so that our natural resource of garden fuel was diminished. Our compasses, which the Watch Cities rely on for accuracy in navigation, portrayed disturbing reversals of the poles. This created a giant suction, so that our floating islands bobbed overhead, and their natural anchors to the ocean floor had to be stabilized by ropes and chains. As you can see," he gestured through the glass tunnel to a series of coral covered trunks reaching to the unseen surface, "this method has allowed a symbiotic agreement between our need to reset the fractured islands, and the displaced wildlife."

"It is quite beautiful." Bashelle admired the parrotfish swerving in and around the infant coral groves.

"These burgeoning habitats have become the epicentre of the crystal power exchanges and transdimensional tunnels."

Pace led the ambassadors through a series of intertwined tunnels, some glowing in faint shades of purple and green. Martina felt a strange sensation in her ears and probed her auditory canals with her strong archer's fingers.

Bashelle swiped her hands away. "You're gonna bust your eardrums out, you nincompoop! Just go like this," Bashelle opened her mouth wide and closed it again in rapid succession. "Make yourself yawn." She demonstrated.

"Oh my," said Tess, covering her lips with her tight gloves of small scales.

Pace lifted his dull metallic hand to his mouth. "This is a contagious yawn!"

Tess kept her glove to her lips as she giggled. Martina groaned. "Now I'm deaf AND nauseous."

They rose in elevation, and the glass tubes became misty. Pace cautioned them. "We are approaching the surface. This is dangerous on a multitude of levels. First," he turned to Martina. She was still poking in her ears. "We have ascended slowly in order to compensate our bodies to the pressures and powers of our surrounding waters. Within our subsurface setting, we are acclimated by a system of switches that allow us to thrive without the benefits of post-surface life. It is in my opinion," he paused, looking through the humidified glass to the bubbling ripples swirling around their encasement, "that below the surface, in the sea, life rivals the existence upon dry earth, without parallel."

Bashelle felt her skin warm in appreciation.

"Second," Pace continued, "we must be aware of the dangers of the weather above us. It affects our city below, both directly and indirectly. Upon reaching the surface, we will experience a moment of breathlessness. Our bodies will feel the sensation of being pulled in a vacuum. Then we will feel a pop in our ears and a heaviness in our ribs. This is the moment we will inhale instinctually, and breathe the air of the surface. This air is not necessarily unsafe, but it is not of the same healthful conglomerate which we breathe below. It will taste different, and may make you retch."

"Oh great," moaned Martina.

"Yet this, I must most dearly caution you," said Pace, at the pinnacle of their ascent. "What we must be most wary of is our would-be comrades." The ambassadors looked at each other in confusion.

Pace continued. "Part of our agreement in the menial peace after the Battle of Subton," he paused not for effect but to subdue the hurt in his heart, "is that we Mutineers may have limited access to the surface." He paused again. Tess saw the pain in his eyes.

"I am looked upon as the leader of the Mutineers. I accept this role only because I do believe I fulfill it strongly and rightly. My mother was former Governor of Subton. We are a matriarchal society. During the Battle of Subton, she died." The giant man breathed in slowly. "As did all of my sisters."

Tess touched his flesh arm, "I am sorry for your unfathomable losses." Pace reached his metal hand over to clasp hers.

He stepped back and motioned to the dark lid shadowing them in their final ascent. "The Mutineers have limited access to the surface, including our venerated islands. Each island works independently to supply our great city with the immense power systems, health, healing, technology, language, and unique life we live. It is my dream to unify the city, so that we may connect this technology and create compass points beyond physicality, beyond time, beyond our human need for measurement. In this way we could be equal, throughout the worlds as we know them."

Tess clutched her throat. This was her dream, too: a unification of peoples around the globe to share free energy as space and time abounded.

"Because of my accepted leadership, despite the fact that my values are directly opposite of the goals of DRAKE, I and those whom I accompany are safe in our expeditions."

Martina calculated. "Why are you okay? What's so special about you? Why is it that only you of Mutineers can approach the surface without fear?" Her green eyes narrowed. "What deal have you struck?"

Pace lowered his arms from the hatch above. His jaw clenched, then relaxed. He bowed. "Martina the Honourable," he rose again to full height. "I have not struck any deal besides who I am. As I have attempted to explain: my mother, my sisters, were killed by DRAKE in the Battle of Subton. In our culture," he turned to face all three ambassadors, "women are warriors. Men may be too. Anyone who wishes. Yet it typically falls naturally upon the women to protect, grow, enhance our city with knowledge. My mother and sisters were not the only women who died. Indeed, entire generations were wiped out."

He paused in a flash of memories. Tess recognized the forced bravery of his pulled back shoulders.

"Men, women, all peoples of Subton, all manner of humanity within our community, fought valiantly. Yet a horrid dragon breathed death into life. I lost not only all of my female ancestors, and a great percentage of my body," he traced his skull and arm and legs, "but I also lost my one brother. He lives, yet he exists in the faction of DRAKE that squashed our lives. Perhaps because of some depth of shredded family allegiance, my one living sibling has agreed without reserve my rights to the surface. This is extended to my guests, but I caution you to stay close by me and not wander off, lest your presence is misinterpreted, in a moment, by a gullible BSDINK."

At this, Pace raised his strong arms, reaching easily to the last boundary between two worlds.

Three twists and a pull, a breathless surge, and then cold and warm mixed together in a stomach hurling shot. Tess tasted sand, and saw, for the first time in many moons, the sun.

Chapter 13

Pace provided a museum quality tour of the islands. "The pyramids are composed of a variety of substances such as marble, crystal sheets, beryl, corundum and diamond. The pyramids each have an electromagnetic energy, directed to its own prismatic crystal. The crystals connect in a grid throughout Subton. They create a bio-plasmatic dome protecting Subton from pollution. Its energies remain in Subton without being dispersed through the water, and echoed back through the bio-domes. In this way, energy is preserved. The city thus glows."

The women from Waltham spun around on their independent axis; one in lambskin boots, one in mucks, one in moccasins. What their eyes beheld were as individual as the women themselves. Yet, each woman saw a glory of automation, chemistry, geometry, and perhaps, some kind of magic.

Pace shared their view, always in awe of the wonders of his world. He held his arm out to Tess, and the group proceeded on the rigid dirt pathway. Parrots arced across their steps. Pace pointed out geographical sites.

"This grid betwixt pyramids allows Subton to receive and control gravitational energy waves. This power is used to run the antimagnetic caves wherein our compasses are made. It is also the source of our operational navigational systems and crystals used in all Watch Cities. The power also sends energy through Subton for various uses, like raising crops and animals, and cooking, and manufacturing."

Martina slowed her stride. She focused on individual trees, their jagged palms reaching over the walkway in a shady canopy. Her ears perked up at the sound of wings fluttering in the distance. Bashelle nudged her forward.

Tess felt Pace's hand in hers, heavy yet lifting.

"The grid also powers our time compasses that each citizen wears. DRAKE uses the compasses within the grid to control the BSDINK. A boost of crystal disentegrations, perverted from their natural and well-used pain relief and healing qualities, are inserted into these pieces. This prevents the BSDINK from using free will, and serves to diminish their personal sense of teen angst and questioning of authority."

He gestured towards the pinnacle of the closest pyramid. "The crystal atop each pyramid is a beacon, and also a barometer that measures currents and water pressure. These filter power from the gold and salt naturally present in the ocean. All the water within Subton becomes charged with crystal and algae power because of the energy diffusing naturally. The water is thus kept clean, and it allows Subton to have drinking water."

"Amazing," said Bashelle.

"The crystals use refracted moon light for use in the Inter-Dimensional Tunnel System. Direct light is refracted to crystals. This creates currents to conduct a semi-aware electromagnetic plasmic field of benevolent energy capable of retaining life-preserving frequencies."

"Holy shite," said Martina. "I only understand one-fifth of that and it is making me overwhelmed with ideas."

"I know, it is a bit much. Yet for us in Subton, this is our way of life; our heritage."

Martina reflected on her life in the wildly free Americas. "That, I understand."

Tess interjected. "Am I to surmise that crystals exist which may enable multidimensional consciousness, communication and transport?

Pace felt a swell in his broad chest. He was proud of his city, and impressed with the wonderments of the beautiful scientist at his side. "Indeed, crystals have been discovered and transformed for multidimensional transmission. Some pyramids are used as antennae to draw and amplify energies. They also create powerful direct energy for the compasses."

He pointed to a shiny rock formation up ahead. "Crystalline and electromagnetic energy help modulate weather patterns and tides."

"So why doesn't DRAKE want Mutineers up here?" asked Martina. "What are they hiding?"

"DRAKE desires to thwart the goodness of Subton's natural energy and technology. Subton's advancements in science and maths could be used towards world domination. Our crystals could be used solely for weaponry; mass destruction. DRAKE also wants to disturb the medicinal and healing powers of our crystals in an effort to change genetics, birthing human slaves like a city of clones to serve DRAKE."

He led them up a sun-sparkled mound. "Welcome to Dot Hill, one of my favourite picnic spots. At least it used to be, many years ago." He opened a compartment on his left leg and unfolded a serving tray. A flip of a switch engaged its anti-magnetic qualities so it floated above the sand. He pulled out telescoping cups and set them upon the tray and filled them with mineral water.

"Please sit," he said, rolling out a tablecloth from his backpack. Soon, the small group was lounging in the sun with an array of tea sandwiches and fruits. Tess kept herself shaded beneath her nifty parasol hat.

As they half-dozed after their meal, Pace provided more information about the Mutineers' concerns.

"Our marine biologists have been tracking migratory fish patterns for generations, and this year, a disturbing amount of schools are avoiding our waters. Particularly absent are the diadromy migrations. Our waters are a meeting place for both salt and freshwater creatures. When travel between these groups doesn't occur, it affects the ecology of creatures who make Subton their year-round home. For the past several years, our scientists have discovered fewer and fewer species migrate here each season, and dozens more seem to have vanished. They are gone."

Bashelle rolled over from her sand-bed. "What is the consensus? Climate change? Scarcity of feeder fish? Over-use of natural resources?"

"It is because of pollution. DRAKE harvests our greatest algae and crystal power resources for their own benefit. They corrupt the healing capabilities and create instead a biologic to sedate the BSDINK into submission. The byproduct is poison. This loss of our environment's enriched algae, natural crystals, and giant geodes is devastating. Those three resources in particular work to help sustain the lives of tiny ocean creatures, which in turn help sustain and attract migratory creatures."

Pace adjusted his position, the shiny parts of his body dazzling Tess's eyes. "Without the migrating predators, and without the normal predators, and with the lack of prey, the predators that do stay are larger, stranger, and hungrier. They erupt from the sea floor, unable to survive on the larvae and krill they are used to inhaling through minuscule holes in the sandy ocean floor."

"We saw steaming holes on our way here," said Bashelle. "As we approached closer to Subton, the wafts of steam grew longer and wider."

"Yeah," Martina sat up. "I wondered: could it be fire under water?"

"Of course," said Bashelle. "Geysers and volcanoes. Like the one we climbed over."

Martina looked confused.

"That's alright," Bashelle reached over and rumpled Martina's sun streaked locks. "Your brain wasn't working that great at the time."

"It isn't working that great now, either. But damn this sun feels good!" Martina lay back down on the hot sand.

"The older Subtonians warned each other, and DRAKE, of the dangers to come," said Pace. He lowered his voice. "Ziracuny insisted they were afraid of fairytales. She bragged that she was more powerful than any foe, man or beast, or little girl, that could dare to face her."

Martina mumbled. "She's such a c-"

"Could you go on?" interrupted Tess quickly.

"Yes, of course. We tried to explain but DRAKE remained deaf to our warnings. It may be our mythology, but it is our culture, and we believe it. We have faith in its factuality."

Tess brushed sand from her dress and removed her gloves. Even though the conversation had taken a more serious turn, she couldn't help but feel soothed by the orotund tones of Pace's voice.

"Eventually, as the steam grows and the holes connect in a crack, a line of fire will rise in a great hot wall surrounding Subton, and the volcano will bleed in molten streams. From the geysers will burst all manner of fiery rocks, and despicable bloodthirsty starved sea monsters will prowl."

"All-righty then." Martina stretched her arms. "C'mere and lift me up. Somebody around here needs their feet on the ground." Bashelle lumbered over and pulled her up. Martina whispered, not quietly enough, in her ear, "I think someone's swallowed too much seawater."

Pace smiled good naturedly. "It is what I believe. How about you, Tess?" He offered her his two hands and gently lifted her from the ground.

"I believe in science. Which does not mean I do not believe in you."

Pace smiled even broader and offered his elbow. "A view of the pyramids will challenge your faith."

Chapter 14

"The Blue Crystal of Knowledge stands tall. There is a rhythmic wave, like timpani, as the sides reverberate with colours of blue ranging from turquoise and aquamarine to sapphire. It is creating its memory bank and backing it up, keeping the languages of Subton alive."

Pace held out his fingers and traced the hieroglyphics etched into the gleaming blue surface of the pyramid. Above it, at the highest point, revolving in midair, was a giant glimmering blue crystal.

"Look!" Martina pointed to the flat wall ahead of them. "The surface of the pyramid is shifting as if an invisible stick was carving a path!"

"Keep watching," encouraged Pace.

"Why, it's calligraphy!" Tess exclaimed.

"Indeed," said Pace. "This is the epicentre of our languages. Within the pyramid flows the current of the Blue Crystal of Knowledge. Written words, story dances, stone pillars, all in here tells a truth of language. Geometry; the patterns in which colours are aligned in bricks; the placement of gems and crystals. Math is our art and our language, through which other languages can be communicated."

The little group continued their stroll over an extendable rope bridge. It connected the Blue Crystal Island to the Emerald Crystal Island. Tess marvelled at the engineering and mathematics required to build a sturdy bridge that could withstand the weight of grown, and in Pace's case, extra-grown, people.

"Behold the Emerald Crystal Pyramid. The rotating green crystal above shines with warmth that encourages the life of algae to grow in our waters. The pyramid itself, as you can see, is huge and hollow, preserving a cavern of growth and healing. The waters brewed within its angled vats spew fountains of regenerative liquid. It is rumoured that Ziracuny demands her tub be filled with this miraculous potion, and thus she retains a youthful glow."

"Might we go inside?" asked Tess.

Pace looked at her with a sleight of suspicion. "We could, but there are rituals we must complete first, out of respect for our ancestors' foresight, and from caution to not contaminate this powerful resource which we rely on for our legendary elixirs."

Tess blushed at her bold greed for youth.

The group swayed upon tropical winds to the Platinum Crystal Island. Tess didn't see the pyramid until they were almost touching it. Pace chuckled.

"Our Platinum Crystal Pyramid is so clear as to be almost invisible. Yet when light hits the shimmering crystal at its precipice, the stepped pyramid glows and funnels through the surface, creating a rainbow."

All three women were dazzled by colours blinking in the sunlight. A broad rainbow surrounded them within a field of platinum subatomic particles. They opened their mouths without thinking, allowing the brilliance to enter their lips, their throats, their lungs.

Pace's voice swept smoothly through the luminescence. "This is our sacred life force. It is attracted to life and flourishes life. It is brainless but self-aware. The Bio-Plasmic Field emitted by the Platinum Crystal blazes the way for the chemical reaction necessary for physical matter to become antimatter. From this, our faith is possible."

Tess's eyes gleamed with tears of discovery. "I believe."

Chapter 15

Before supper, Tess and Pace took tea in the lunarium.

"I have been book obsessed literally all my life, and I had excellent teachers, yet somehow this book was never read in my youth or avid moments of words ingrained. How did I miss this? And how I am drinking it now!"

Tess robustly turned the pages of "The Perfect Storm."

"Shall we tour the remnants of such storms?"

Tess placed the book squarely in the corner of the triangular table and raised her hand in a delicate fashion. "I would be delighted to." Pace took her hand and lifted her up accordingly from whence she sat. They walked arm-in-arm through tiled tunnels to an open-air cavern.

Tess found herself in a more rustic surrounding than she had expected, and discovered that she was overdressed. "I feel as if I am wearing a ballgown in a swamp," she mused. She used her weighted lineage slips to shift her dressage into more appropriate attire.

Pace looked at her from boot tip to hat feather. "I am impressed."

"A smart woman is always prepared."

They continued their stroll and arrived at a square deck made of driftwood. Pace invited her to sit upon a stool of swirly stone.

She pulled lace on the sides of her bustle to lift her skirts higher in the front. She balanced upon the uneven and wiggling chair. She alerted Pace to her quandary. "Is there perhaps a more steady seating arrangement?"

Pace set down the prismatic telescope he had been adjusting for the professor. His task waited while he deftly stepped over piles of rustic storage boxes to reach her quickly. Offering two hands, he lifted Tess from the chair.

Tess felt her heart beat with a force of passion from his touch. She contemplated what his robotic hand would feel like on her warmest flesh. Her face heated with the thought, so she took a breath, willing the sensuality away. The deep inhalation pulled his musky scent into her lungs. She held her breath for three seconds, absorbing the erotic impulse in her memory. She let the air out slowly between her lips, relishing his exotic aroma.

Pace felt hot breath on his neck as he lowered Tess safely to the driftwood floor. His wide hands lingered on her narrow hips as they stood in an eternal moment of time, a flicker that would light both of their memories for eons. Tess stepped back, breaking the circuit connecting them.

Pace began fixing the stool with a spinning screw that extended from the middle digit of his robotic hand. Tess watched, mesmerized by the accuracy and proficiency of this man.

"Don't worry to bother; tis fine for me. Only there could be a safety issue if someone with less balance than I were to attempt the seat."

Her brow furrowed, outlining the geometry in her mind, visible only to her possibilities.

"You would be concerned over an imaginary person's obstacle," Pace teased.

Tess was too consumed by her mathematical equations to heed the light tone in his phrase. "Yes, anyone but I, or someone with considerable adroitness, would most likely fall arse over teakettle."

Pace jolted up, amused. "Arse over teakettle?"

Tess focused her eyes on reality and smiled. "Have you heard the words of the lovely ladies I have been travelling with? I am learning a new language."

Pace acknowledged, "We adore language in Subton. Even what you may judge as coarse, professor, is a treasure of the times."

They conversed on the cultural aspects of Subton. Like how babies were exceptionally precious because there were so few of them. "We have a custom of creating hanging mobiles of fish tackle for our infants. So they have something to reach for. To get caught in the history of our people. Mining and fishing; geometry and art: these are the pillars of our society."

Pace gestured across to the rocky ledge, bubbles appearing and dispersing.

"Nitrogen in your bloodstream can damage your brain. Our deep sea divers often bring three tanks of breathable air with them to protect themselves from the possible killer effects. Our diligent scientists and mechanics have devised airlocks through which we can depart and gather fishes, lobsters, and crabs. Stacks of canoes with pods of air provide efficient means of travel below and above our beautiful waters."

"Yes," said Tess. "We saw some of those upon entering Subton."

"You must have come quite a roundabout way."

"I believe we did."

A silence of personal thoughts flowed between them. Then Tess spoke.

"As you know, we also encountered strange beasts and an anomaly of creatures the likes of which do not seem to exist naturally or unnaturally any place else on the globe. I am interested in this phenomena."

Pace's demeanor grew serious. "There are ancient ocean beasts in the water. Not just here, but wherever hydrogen combines with oxygen. They are two elements that need each other; cling to each other; exist for each other. Their mixing creates life for all of us."

He paused to hand Tess a cup of tea from his picnic backset. "Dragons live symbiotically with Subton beneath the muddy shores. Do not look so panicked, dear professor: they are of no danger to us. We have an ancient, wordless agreement. 'Let be what is.' That is a motto we live by. The dragons cleanse the sediment of illness, generate healing springs with their natural fiery sighs, and promote the growth of crystals and algae that is imperative to our way of life. Indeed, without these dragons, we would be destroyed."

"Then again," he added, "with them, we could also be destroyed."

Tess sipped her delicate blossom tea and placed the cup back onto its saucer that balanced on her knees. "What do you mean?" she asked, with alarm and curiosity.

"I mean there is one dragon whom we are all meant to fear. That one has not reared its fiery face for generations. The massacre it could bring, has brought in past ages, would engulf us all in a boiling pit of death."

"Oh my," exclaimed Tess. She thought for a moment. "What of the beast my friends and I encountered on our journey, the one who could be lulled as a child by simple song?"

Pace clapped his large hands together in laughter. "Did I neglect to assuage you of any fear regarding this silly creature? I apologize; I am not laughing at you, only at my own lapse. What you encountered was surely a ta-wa. We have compassion on these rare bumbling creatures, as scary as they look. Their unique method of circulating water through their tentacles helps clarify the sea, and their voracious appetites help control the population of pesky over-copulated fish. As long as they have the food supply they need, the likes of us have nothing to worry about."

That evening, after supper, Tess joined Pace in his den. She sat comfortably, the table beside her piled with a hoard of books she had plucked from the shelves. Misty tea warmed her lips, and the words and languages between the pages of her new treasures mesmerized her into a deep sleep.

Pace left and returned with a tray of jellies and salt bread, and opened his mouth to speak politely in greeting, then quickly closed it when he saw the lovely professor in the candlelight. He set the tray down gently by the luminaries, and deftly pulled the large volume from Tess's silk-covered lap.

He looked at the cover. "Mooolelo O na la Subton." He wondered if she could read "The Story of the Fish of Subton" as it was written, or if she was browsing only through the illustrations. In any case, he laid the heavy volume alongside her book tower. Then he opened a large trunk, removed a cashmere blanket fringed with velvet ribbons, and draped it over the sleeping lady.

Chapter 16

Pace, Tess, Martina, and Bashelle spent all the next day together as if they were on holiday. After frivolities of fish-watching, the women divulged that they wanted to help pull their weight around Subton.

Pace scrutinized them thoughtfully before clapping his hands together. "You know something ladies? There is a job we need done, and we could certainly use your help."

The women were thrilled to pay back their gracious host.

"I could assist with scientific experiments," offered Tess, hopefully.

"I am an expert with all manner glasswork, and cooking" said Martina, already imagining herself grilling edibles in the galley.

"I'm as strong as they come," added Bashelle, "and I know a thing or two or five about the sea myself!"

Pace's face emitted a flicker of mischief as he invited the trio to follow him.

He lead them to the pig farm. To their silent fuming dismay. Yet, Tess struggled to be humble. Martina teased her.

"Which silken gloves are appropriate for this particular work?"

Tess ignored her and decided to do her part. She wanted to impress Pace. At least I can wash up later in my room, she thought to herself.

Pace explained the job and looked at his navi-watch. "I have a meeting with the other Mutineers, so I will look forward to joining you at supper."

Off he went with a gleam in both eyes that Tess did not miss.

Martina surveyed the situation. "Well, I heard of pigs flying..."

Bashelle finished the thought. "But pigs swimming, this is something else."

Tess blinked. "In any case, I have never seen them with flippers!"

Martina turned to Bashelle. "Seriously, can they swim?"

"Well they sure as hell don't fly!" said Bashelle.

"Most assuredly," Tess gestured, stupefied.

Pigs jumped from an inlet, to a sandy domed shore, into a stream of natural salt.

"A salt water pond," Bashelle tasted the water in admiration.

Tess wrinkled her nose. "Their excrement is used for...fuel? Manure? Feeding underwater ecosystems? Motor lube?"

Martina nudged her forward. "This is a time for doing, not thinking, my dear Lady Professor."

"In the distance we can see a coral island," Bashelle pointed. "Just ahead of us is a dune of dung. Let's get to it."

"Okay, simply shove two hundred kilograms of live pig in a crate," said Martina. "Lather, rinse, repeat. Not a problem."

"The three of us can do it nothing flat," agreed Bashelle.

Tess pulled rain gear out of her belted brown bag. "Sissy," said Bashelle.

The three friends studied the pen. It was built from cypress, with the dimensions of a large sitting room. They were tasked with removing the pigs into a crate, one by one, and channelling them into their foamy bathing pool. Once the pigs were all squeaky clean, and the dung had been removed from their pen, the pigs would be transported back. A plan was decided.

"Time to get it done," encouraged Bashelle.

"I don't know about pets or domesticated animals." Martina's face wrinkled in disdain. "Animals should all be free, and serve a purpose in the environment."

"Okay nature girl," said Bashelle.

"No, you know what I mean, o lady of the sea!"

"Fine, I guess I agree. I can't imagine keeping a fish in a bowl as some do."

Tess asked, "You have never petted a bunny's soft fur?"

"Of course," said Martina, soothingly stroking Tess's shiny cornsilk hair. "I have a delightfully warm kit fringe on a fawn skin vest. I make one yearly in the fall. Nothing like cuddling multiple pelts from rabbit and fawn.

Tess was disgusted. "Baby deer?"

"Yes, each year. It's quite easy. October the bucks come out so I can harvest them. Their bodies are used by and eaten by many throughout town."

"Yeah," added Bashelle. "As buoys go, deer make the best. Bits of curved buck bone are great fish hooks. And of course," Bashelle patted her shoulder strap that secured an array of tools, "deer bone glides like an arrow through water. Thanks, Golden Egg." She kissed Martina on the lips.

"Anyways," continued Martina, "the does come ready to make new babies and raise them. After the young are a bit grown, BAM! Mama fills my larder."

Tess looked at her in horror.

"I have compassion; I don't wanna leave a yearling or big baby. To stay an orphan and be destitute."

"But," Tess hesitated, yet was struck by morbid curiosity. "What about the bunnies?"

"See, that's the fashion part you would understand. Rabbit kits and young deer have not yet lost their silky spots."

Bashelle shook her head and placed her arm around Tess's shoulder. "Don't egg her on. However true it may be."

Tess's mouth was agape with speechless horror.

"If you evah wanna reside in the real world you can join me and live in the seasons." Martina placed an arm around Tess's other shoulder. "Plan your life by the seasons. Follow the migrations. Learn the language of birds. Same birds of different geographical areas have their own dialects, ya know."

Tess felt her emotions switch from horror to awe and admiration. "You are an animal linguist!"

Martina removed her arm and ruffled the noblewoman's hair. "No. I am not so pompous to believe that wild creatures would lower themselves to speak with the likes of me. I am able to discern through a lifetime of listening to, and living amongst, natural creatures of the earth."

Bashelle also removed her arm from Tess's shoulder and patted Martina's bottom. "Then let's produce progress in Pig Land."

Martina got the job of lowering the pen's door mechanism. Her long limbs could easily reach the gears and levers needed for operation.

Tess was in charge of opening the gate of the crate. She stood to the side, her feet spread apart in her fancy shoes and pretty linens. Her rain gear was not ample protection for what she was about to face.

She straddled the crate just enough for stability whilst maintaining a proper stance. Her ivory prats gleamed in the bluish-white light, and her damask embroidered with pale blue and purple violets draped lavishly below her knees.

Bashelle whooped with anticipation. "I can't wait to smack some swine in the buttocks!" Her grip on the paddle was like that of a baseball slugger.

"Ready?" Martina called, her body twisted like a pretzel.

"Ready!" shouted Bashelle.

Tess felt secure in her position on the two by three foot crate. "Ready!"

Martina released the pen, Bashelle gave a pig a thunderous smack, and WHOOSH!

The pig spun and boomeranged through the professor's legs, dislodging the crate. Tess was held aloft like a reverse cowgirl upon the squealing beast's back. Her dress was trapped between her legs until she fell in a bouncing backwards roll into the sludge. Still she held on, refusing to let go. Her thighs burst with fullness of blood engorged against the plushy sides of the pink beast. Her silky ankles locked around the pig's jaw. With long limber fingers pulling on the curly tail, she straightened her desperate grasp.

Then the pig screeched. Tess was smacked on the bottom with such force that she flew three feet before landing in slop.

Bashelle held the paddle as Martina secured the crate full of pig.

"Holy shite," breathed Bashelle. "Pigs do fly."

Chapter 17

After supper, Pace and Bashelle played darts in the game room. Around them was the rainy sound of conversation and the intermittent thunder of laughter. Bashelle was relishing in the retelling of her story between turns.

"When I ever hit that thing on the arse it turned around on a dime! And BOOM!"

"You wouldn't think a pig that size would turn around like that!" Pace laughed.

"Who knew they would be able to move that fast!" She caught Pace's eye. "By Triton, you are a rogue!" They shared a laugh of fiendish fun.

"Ya know, we are similar, but you are a bit more...polished." She gazed sideways, waiting for the pun to sink in.

He playfully punched her arm. She punched back.

"Hey, don't scruff up the finish!"

After darts, Bashelle and Pace inclined themselves to play chess. Martina sat and watched for a while before returning to the bar. "Don't want my seat or ale to grow cold!"

Pace slid a piece carefully sideways. Then it was Bashelle's turn again. His piece was knocked to the floor.

Bashelle held her fist up, with her index and pinky facing out. "See this, ya know what this is? This is the bull and these are the horns. Ya play with the bull, ya get the horns!"

"I admire your methodology."

Bashelle helped tuck the hand-carved pieces into their drawers for the next players. "In all seriousness, I like your stuff. I mean Subton in general. From what I've seen, you've got quite the system here. Ample fuel, engineering of compasses that would bring any lost sailor to port, and fish harvesting techniques that even I could learn a thing or two from." She paused for a moment of self-admiration. "One thing I don't get though: why all the live-machine creations? Fish with gears and the like. It is inconceivable to me as to the purpose. Or is it for science shmience?"

Pace placed the last figurine into the box and folded it up. "The genetic engineering was used for benevolent purposes."

Bashelle raised an eyebrow in scrutiny. Pace continued. "For instance: healing wounds, injuries and illnesses. Our genetic engineers went on to investigate improved physical vehicles. This led to experiments combining qualities of life with those of machines. Thus, half live, half machine, beings were created."

Pace lifted his robotic arm, made a fist and pounded on his metallic legs. "The research from these efforts made my life possible. I would not have survived the Battle of Subton without the work of genetic hybrid engineers."

Bashelle nodded her head. "That makes sense to me."

"The genetic lab was concentrated on one of the islands as a specialized medical centre. In the chaos after the Battle of Subton, genetic engineering came under the control of DRAKE. It was corrupted for greed and power."

"How are they using it for greed and power? All I see, besides the obviously pissah way it was used for you, is a bunch of polluted fishy flesh not worthy of harvesting, and of no good to nobody."

"I do not completely disagree with your take on the creations borne of our far-sighted science. Yet, many of the BSDINK are trained scientists who believe they are learning techniques to develop progressive life improvements. They are naively unaware of the evils their research and discoveries are being used for. These young scientists are recruited specifically for genetic experiments. Every time one of our youth sides with DRAKE and joins the BSDINK, it is like we are losing the war all over again."

Bashelle reached across the table and laid a hand on his. "From my experience crabbing in Waltham, sharing the docks with Subtonian fishers, I can tell you that I have never met more diligent sea harvesters. The respect your kins-people showed for the water and the creatures they harvested was close to my heart. They shared their fishing strategies with me, and I learned more than that from them. Making a living side by side with them was one of the greatest experiences of mutual endeavour in my life."

"I appreciate that," said Pace.

"An you shoulda seen the codfish!" Bashelle lifted her hand from his and gestured grandely. "You wouldn't've believed it. Pulling up codfish with eyes poppin outta their frikkin heads! Fifty pounds easy!"

"Sounds like a good catch."

"All the damn time."

Chapter 18

"Mosaics are all over the place. What kind of shells and stones and gems are these? Floors, ceilings: mosaics everywhere."

Martina's mind narrated her trail. She had used this inner storytelling as a tracking tool for decades. Not only did it make her more aware of where she was, it helped her remember where she had been.

The walls displayed long intricate murals exhibiting Subtonian beliefs, mythology, history, and love of language and geometry.

Martina's eyes investigated the illustrations and the stories they told piece by piece.

Something tapped on the tiled floor behind her and she flattened herself to the wall.

An eye glowed red in the shadows. "The women were the tough ones."

"Pardon?"

"They were in the front lines. See?" Pace uncapped one of his fingers and shone a beam of thin light across a portion of the mosaic. Martina stepped out from the wall but remained rigid.

Pace breathed on his fingertip as one would blow on a lit candle. Instead of going out, the light increased. He pointed to the mural again, illuminating the scene.

"When the stakes were down, young girls the ages of twelve, ten, even eight, were wrenched out of their fathers' grasps to take up arms and fight. This is why there are so few women in Subton, and why Yoki is a minority."

"Yoki?"

"Yes; if you recall, I introduced her upon your arrival. If you do not remember, please do not feel badly. I am sure my niece will become better acquainted with you soon enough."

Martina reached forward to trace the lines of red gems along the wall. "So much blood."

Together the two whisperers gazed with heavy hearts upon the glyphs of babies and children pierced through with fishing spears.

"This is why I have come to you, Martina the Honourable. I did not want to startle you, and I knew that you were too good of a hunter to let that happen. I would like your help in deluding DRAKE and reclaiming Subton's youth. I wish for them to grow, learn, and perhaps even experience a remnant of childhood."

Martina kept still, staring at the tiles.

"We could combine our strengths. Together. Teamwork."

Martina turned to him in the semidarkness. "That would be wonderful, but I hate that." She walked away.

Chapter 19

"Why yes, I do intentionally coordinate my outfits to my books. Thank you for noticing."

"You are quite welcome."

Tess returned her porcelain cup to its tidy saucer. "Might I say, you serve the sweetest tea under the sea."

Pace bowed. "Shall we commence our morning walk?"

"Yes, we shall."

Pace had promised to share the science that the Mutineers saved when DRAKE tried to demolish it. He guided her to majestic door and lifted his left hand like a hammer. He saved his right arm as fleshy warmth for Tess.

The keys in his palm plucked the armoured door in the correct combination. With a bang, the door slid open. Pace turned to Tess. "Knocking on old doors. Pining for historic truth alive in the past." Together they stepped in.

"Oh my, is this a museum? A laboratory? Or a hybrid of sorts?"

Pace kissed Tess's naked hand. "Thank you for appreciating our library of art and science. We take the old and mix it with the new and then reapply it to the old. In this way the present has respect and hope. Otherwise, Subton cannot survive."

Tess's purple petticoat swished against the lavender scales and shells in her bodice. "I am beginning to understand this alignment with Subton's fashion. Listen." She twirled around in a full circle. "The sound is alike a whisk on a wooden bowl, mixing eggs, creating new life from old."

"You heighten the beauty."

Tess blushed and darted her eyes. "May I look upon the higher shelves?"

"Of course. You can see whatever you would like to." Pace pulled a rolling ladder towards her and assisted her up. Then he slowly rolled the ladder down the track so that the professor could take note of the clockwork collection.

"Thank you," she reached her hand down, "my curiosity has been thusly satiated."

Pace joined her hand to help her step down. Her free hand alighted upon him for balance.

"Your chest, it is hard like sculpted marble."

"As you can discern then, even the flesh parts of me can be hard as iron."

Tess felt both her feet securely tap the floor. "I did not mean to comment on your, difference in body." She felt horribly awkward. Pace offered his arm and they continued the tour of the massive room.

"I am not differently abled; I am exceptionally abled." He glanced down at her as they stepped leisurely together. She glimpsed the glint of masculine mischief in his deep brown eye and felt the thrum of desire beneath her breast. She reached a hand to cover her heart, as if to calm its sudden increase in tempo. The rush of blood coloured her face with shades of coral.

They paused by a window, offering a subterfuged view of heavenly wonder. Pace pulled Tess into his arms.

She had never felt so small, like a grain of sand in an hourglass, enveloped by the expanse of two globes, protecting and shielding; encasing and capturing all at the same time.

"That's it!" She pulled out of his strong embrace valiantly, like a popped balloon spurting free of its source. Pace released her but held tightly to her right hand, soft bare skin on smooth hard metal.

"I'm sorry, did I-"

"I figured it out! Pardon me, could you please lead me to your lab?"

"You need to use the lav?"

Tess shook her head vehemently and pulled her hand from his. "No, no, the lab; the laboratory." She reached into her brown belted bag and retrieved a leather-bound notebook.

"I may have discovered a connection to form a solution!" Her face shone in the brilliance of new ideas.

"I'd say you almost did." Pace's dimples deepened as confusion left his face and masked hers. "This way, dear professor." He offered his arm. Together they walked down the green marbled hallway that glistened with flecks of knowledge.

Chapter 20

The women each woke up with mint green calling cards slid beneath their doors. All people within Subton received the same card, whether Mutineer or DRAKE. It read:

The Watch City of Subton
is joining together
for a masquerade ball
in honour of the Lunar Event
we celebrate each year
and in recognition of our Watch City's dedication
to peace within and without.
Every person in Subton is invited.

Tess deliberated on fancy attire. Finally, she decided upon a gown of blue tulle with beads of gold. The corset was outlined in shimmering diamonds. To compliment her dark wavy locks, she chose a coronet of emeralds. Green silk gloves sewn with silver thread completed the look. She was "Subton Sea." She admired herself in the full length mirror of her boudoir and imagined Pace's reaction.

The conch in her room emitted a buzzing sound and the lined pattern of the shell glowed orange. It was Pace.

"How is your mask coming along?"

"My mask?"

"Yes, dear Tess. This is a masquerade ball. Part of the fun of the Lunar Event is to make the guests appear unidentifiable. It is like a game."

"I do have a costume gown," Tess explained.

"Without a mask, though, the element of mystery is lost. As a scientist, you must be intrigued by that concept."

Tess admitted she was. "What sort of mask is expected? I have never worn a mask." Besides the mask of youth I wear every day, she thought to herself. She glanced in the mirror one more time before her attempt at being incognito.

Bashelle and Tess stood in the dining room before the ball.

"It's good to be early," said Bashelle, slurping on bowls full of roe.

"I think that is for everyone," said Tess, offering a plate.

"Whatever. It's here, it's good: it's mine."

Tess looked upon the fish eggs with apprehension. "Are they not cooked?"

Bashelle wiped her maw. "Why in the name of Sam Clam would you do that? And anyways, they're pissah with whatever this green stuff is!" She slurped down another bowl.

Tess grimaced and changed the subject. "I wonder if you know why Martina has not joined us."

"She's got a case of vanity. Said she hadta do her hair and stuff for her costume, and she wouldn't tell me how she was dressing. Tryinta be all mysterious." She patted her head. "Another reason I like the simplicity of my fly dome!"

Tess appraised Bashelle's costume. On her feet were bulky black boots edged with golden thread and aligned with brass clasps. Tall red socks stretched to shabby pants hitting below the knees. The pants sported black and white vertical stripes and were tied at the waist with a long red sash. A white puffy shirt contrasted with a black vest, emblazoned with an embroidered skull. A simple black mask edged her eyes. Her head was covered by a tightly tied red bandanna edged with gold coins.

"What does your attire tonight represent?"

Bashelle's lips pressed together in disappointment. "Pirate! Isn't it obvious?"

"Oh yes, sorry dear friend. It is simply that, if you do not mind me saying so, it is not greatly differential from your daily style."

Bashelle glanced down at herself with satisfaction. "I s'pose you're right!"

People in dramatic costumes trickled in to the dining hall. Bashelle and Tess made a game of guessing what inspired their fancy dress.

A woman with a tiara of diamonds glided past. Her black flowing robes were studded with thousands of tiny white glowing crystals. "Starlight," said Bashelle. And check out this one." Bashelle let out low whistle.

A young woman wore a one piece muslin covering that fit her like a second skin. A large bustle of areophane and gauze trailed behind her, dotted with large white pompoms. Covering her face was a green mask with delicately painted white sheep. Atop her head was a spinning hat with a twirling hooked cane. "A shepherd?" guessed Tess.

"I am with you on that one."

"Oh my," declared Tess in excitement.

Bashelle looked. "A telegraph! Now that is hands-down substantially the most impressive I have seen so far."

Tess and Bashelle and the other guests continued nibbling on the expansive array of delicacies. Ices, cakes, cracker-bonbons, trifle, and tipsy cake tempted Tess with their sweetness. Substantial fare of shark tongue and roast pig made for hearty dancing fuel.

A giant Robin Hood bowed deeply before Tess. "M'lady, Our Watch City of Subton has never appeared so dreamlike."

Tess blushed. "How did you know it was I?

Pace took her offered hand and kissed the smooth white glove. "Your beauty is unmistakable."

"Okay there, Prince Charming, we get it."

Pace shook Bashelle's hand. "I am Robin Hood, not Prince Charming, you scalliwag."

"Now that you're here, could you get this herbivore of ours to please for the love of Triton eat something before she passes out?"

Tess ate bean manapua at the advice of Pace and was delighted with the fluffy filled buns.

"Where is your handsome lady?" asked Pace.

Bashelle checked her pocket-watch again. "I do not know what is taking that dame so long. Unless she found a full bottle of something too good and decided to empty it. Dagnabit, I hope not."

A conch horn blew, signalling the end of dining and the beginning of the ball. The tone echoed throughout Subton, piping through all the conches, alerting everyone that the Lunar Event Masquerade Ball was moving on to its next phase.

The doors to the dining hall opened broadly on mechanized hinges. The revelers pranced through tunnels, elaborately decorated with flowers for this occasion. The promenade was accompanied by moon lamps blinking in time with staccato flutes through the sound mirrors. The Mutineers reached an entrance of the Grande Ballroom; the DRAKE waited across the massive room behind their own door.

Above each doorway hung matching chandeliers, the epicentre of which were spectacular compass-clocks made with the powers of the pyramids. The chandeliers glowed orange, then blue. Hanging crystals refracted wavelike rainbows.
Another conch was blown, a higher tone this time. The separate crowds parted into two lanes. Between the lanes of people, antigravity bots soundlessly floated, dropping petals of water lilies along their paths.

Next came the sea turtles, swimming in the air by engine propulsion within gilded shells. Upon the back of each sat a mysterious figure hidden by deep blue silk. They were carried like sooth sayers, or royalty, or gods.

Pace patted Tess's white gloved hand resting in the crook of his arm. She pulled away, understanding his silent language. He stepped to the middle of the red carpeted pathway and paused. His eyes lifted up to the compass clocks, and a kaleidoscope of colours burst from his robotic eye. The spectators exhaled in a breath of awe.

With slow careful steps, bringing his feet together before progressing in a fashion suitable to a royal wedding, he passed the floating turtle creature with its mystical passenger, then surpassed the petal wielding bots.

On the opposite door to the ballroom, a huge red pearl was pressed into the cleavage of a long crevice etched smoothly in the doorway. The man enacting the ritual was dressed in full military regalia. There was no doubt he was of DRAKE.
From the back could be seen a long coat the colour of a boiled lobster. Worsted lace

trimmed the button-holds for white pearls in the front. The man's starched white breaches matched his white vest and shirt. Black linen gaiters rose above his patent boots. Atop his bulbous head perched a coal black hat trimmed with shining gold threads.

The compass-clocks on each side of the closed ballroom spun. Crystals hanging from the chandeliers blinked red and blue, combining into a dizzying swirl of purple.

Curvaceous fish-bots swam in streams of green gears, around and back, upon magnets tinged with teal. The doors opened.

Lead by Pace and the DRAKE captain, the flower strewing hover-bots trailed. Mechanized minnows followed up, swimming midair and dispensing purple bubbles from their gills. Another tone from the conch blowers ascended, proclaiming the promenade.

One by one and two by two, the partygoers stepped through the open doors. Tess wrote upon the numbered announcement card (she had lingered back until her number would be divisible by three) so she would be announced as

"Subton Sea." Bashelle accompanied her as "Skipper of Pirates." Together they maneuvered the steep stairs of marble, lined with purple carpet used only for lunar events.

Bashelle tripped as she looked over her shoulder but Tess held her firm. The would-be pirate couldn't handle stairs while wondering aloud, "Where in hell's bells is that woman!"

The parade of hover-bots, hybrid turtles, and bubbling hybrid minnows circled in figure eights across the ballroom. Where their paths intersected, the delegates of each side of Subton, Mutineers and DRAKE, twirled together in a circular orbit. Pace and the redcoat spun several times before releasing each other with unheard secrets.

The grande ballroom was open to Subton Sea: each side of the triangular room was made of glass. Tess realized it was indeed a pyramid of itself. The point opened up into a blank dome, awaiting the arrival of the seasonal moon to bless the Watch City with increased crystal harvesting, peace among all, and familial connection.

Once the ballroom was full, all bright lights were diminished. Through the precipice, Scorpio's stars illuminated the party, ensconced in ultraviolet fluorescence.

Bashelle and Tess clung to each other. Beauty. Undiminished.

From the centre of the ballroom floor rose a twisting spiral column. It stopped twenty feet up, and the top of the column opened like a lotus flower. Petal shaped shells opened flat and spun, slowly increasing speed. The spiral above it uncoiled so that it truly appeared as a twirling flower. Then the uncoiled wires bent in round arcs to touch the spinning shells. Sounds of gentle humming emitted from crevices in the long spiral stem.

Tess felt her heart skip a beat. "What a wonder! Tis like a glorious Victrola!"

A low thrum, reminiscent of crashing waves, filled the room. Conches trumpeted from the three corners. Men in glittering purple swim dress slid down Lally columns. They lined up single file, met in the middle, and formed a triangle around the musical lotus. The music rose in pitch, creating a chiming melody. The men danced fluidly and began to sing.

"The words she tells the stories
The numbers she keeps the dates
Together they weave the truth of history for generations
They are venerated
Separate and together
Sometimes they speak alone
Sometimes they take turns
Sometimes they speak as one
They are like the sun and the moon
And are necessary to our life"

The petals changed colour, from blue to red, blending in swirls of purple. Floating lanterns began to glow, powered by gems and magnets. Spotlights from giant golden oysters shone upon the two entrances. The music stopped, and the lotus ceased spinning.

The Subtonians began snapping their fingers. Into the room from each door, the shiny minnows air-swum leaving a bubbly purple trail. From the Mutineer entrance, Pace appeared and stood to the side of the magnificent marble stairway. From the DRAKE entrance stepped the DRAKE captain, who in turn stopped at the top of the stairs. The two men looked across at each other and saluted.

Finger snapping increased in rhythm and the Subtonians started clicking their heels against the smooth tiled floor. The accompanying hover-bots floated over, raining soft petals upon the revelers. At the far angle of the room, the orchestra plucked violin strings and timpani boomed in a heartbeat's rhythm. Bells chimed, announcing the entrance of the mysterious guests.

The turtle riders remained obscured by deep shades of silk, so that only their silhouettes darkened the light.

Tess and Bashelle watched the theatrical introduction to the ball in awe. The two turtles rested at the top of each stairway. The music stopped. The spotlight turned red upon the DRAKE stairway. The captain raised a bamboo tube to his lips and pushed the megavoice switch.

"Presenting, our Grande Marshall of DRAKE, the Dragon Queen." The red silk curtain surrounding the mystery guest parted and pulled back on revolving rods. The figure stood and took the captain's hand as she disembarked the turtle. She reached the first step and paused, allowing the red light upon her to shift to white, illuminating her beauty for all to see.

Black diamonds covered her boots to the thigh. Her sharkskin gown clung to her body more tightly than the gold claws covering her fingertips. Showcasing her figure with smooth scales, the gown was slit across the front, revealling long, powerful legs. Her red tarlatan bustle trailed behind her, and red crystals applied in rows glistened upon it. Her corset was similarly lined with red crystals, casting a sanguine shadow upon her masked face. A winged cape belted to the corset folded and unfolded. Only her blood red lips could be seen on her pale face, as a mask of red silk covered her features. Sprigs of crimson seagrass and silvery baleen splayed like darts from the mask. Her long black hair was plaited and tied with ribbons of parrotfish skin. Upon her head shone a crown of such grandeur, Tess wondered how the woman's neck could support the weight. The crown was composed of lacy hollow bone. Golden spikes jutted up and around, each one adorned with pointed gems; miniatures of the Crystal Pyramids.

The captain took her arm, and the crowd cheered as they descended the stairs. The woman did indeed appear like a dragon, Tess thought. All she was missing was the flame. Her eyes squinted, and she recoiled in recognition. Ziracuny!

The DRAKE couple sat upon thrones provided to them, and they stared across the ballroom as the Mutineer Grande Marshall was revealed.

From the blue silks appeared a woman of such beauty that the entire ballroom fell silent in breathtaking awe. She lithely leaped from the turtle's back and bowed deeply.

Pace pressed a button on his robotic chest. His amplified voice boomed with power throughout the ballroom and beyond. "Presenting our Grande Marshall of the Mutineers, the Honourable Huntress."

Blue lights strobed across the woman's face. The mask covering her eyes was beautiful in its simplicity: yellow silk, matching her soft blonde hair flowing freely in wild layers, interspersed with blue gull feathers.

Her dress was teal and silver with a sky-blue velvet train, powdered with embossed arrows. Her arms were covered to the elbows with fingerless brown suede gloves. A braided black leather bolo dangled loosely around her neck, with a precious turquoise as its centrepiece.

Black netting climbed her thighs, clipped to the garters evident below her short skirt. Her seal-leather boots were sewn with thin sinews, and added several inches to her already towering stature.

The most impressive part of her costume was her dramatic headwear. A leather cap was buckled on top of her cranium, and from the top sprung antlers the likes of which most of Subton had never seen.

The Honourable Huntress slowly turned around. Her hips rotated in a figure-eight that brought whistles from the more boisterous of Subton. With her arms raised and her back to the ballroom, she plucked a dart fringed with puffin feathers from the holster at her back. Turning to face her captive audience, she placed the dart to her lips and licked the tip. The crowd rallied in uproarious cries.

She slipped her long fingers into the garter on her left and retrieved a razor clam shell. She inserted the dart in the crevice and placed it to her lips, sliding the tip of her tongue to cover the opening. With a deep breath, her breasts pressed against the sharp neckline of her bodice. She tilted her head back and blew.

The dart arced, almost touching the open moon roof high above the ballroom. Then it curved deeply and shot down. With a burst of light and sound, it hit the centre of the lotus. The entire ballroom became warmly illuminated, and the conches blared, officially proclaiming the beginning of the ball. The orchestra picked up the excitement with a raucous number, barely heard above the jubilant cheers.

Fans and cloaks swayed in a stormy dance.

Bashelle stared dumbly as the Huntress gallantly descended the steps. Like a fairytale prince awakening from a trance, she rubbed her eyes. It couldn't be. But it was.

The Huntress approached. She stopped before the Pirate. Her exquisite body bent gracefully, accompanied by a slight motion of the right hand in front. She looked lovingly into her eyes. "Will you do me the honour to dance with me, o finest Pirate of the seven seas?"

The couple danced the night away, interrupted by a multitude of men asking to sign the Huntress's dance card. She twirled from Bashelle's arms and waltzed with the grateful gentlemen. Each time, the Pirate saluted in admiration, proud of her graceful mate.

Men and women, dressed in breezy gauze in varying shades of blue, shook their shoulders, allowing the gemstones on their scaled cloaks to shimmer in the moonlight. In this way, they danced to the whooshing music of shell tambourines and bamboo flutes.

Similarly, Tess and Pace joined hands. Pace lowered his head so that Tess could speak into his ear as they slowly swirled to the music.

"I have never experienced a gathering such as this. You've got big balls."

"Yeah I've got big balls. Nothing unusual."

"But yours are such big balls!"

"They sure are big balls," acquiesced Pace. "And many shires' got big balls, as do smaller towns."

"But you've got the biggest balls of them all."

Martina and Bashelle glided up to them.

"What the blazes are you two discussing?" asked Bashelle.

Tess readied her best teacher's voice. "In upper, upper class high society, is a zest for ballroom notoriety. They aim to fill the ballroom; the event is never small. But all the social papers would agree Subton's got the biggest balls of all."

Pace agreed. "Some balls are held for charity, and some for fancy dress. But when they're held for pleasure, they're the balls that I like best."

The orchestra paused for a brief intermission and the two couples rested with cold green tea. Pace added additional ice to everyone's crystal glasses. "I've been just itching to tell you about these balls. Oh, we have such wonderful fun!"

A gleaming hoverbot delivered trays of hors d'oeuvres. Pace rubbed his hands together in appreciation. "Seafood cocktail, crabs, crayfish... Our balls' for everyone!"

The friends admired the creatures passing by and around the ballroom's windows to the sea. Moon-lamps hung on the outside cast a shimmering glow as they crossed into view.

Martina shook her head. "Aren't the critters under the ocean weird enough without people making them ever the more grotesque? Anyways, how does one obtain ale around here? I'm frikkin thirsty surrounded by water with nothing to drink."

"What about your cold tea?" prodded Bashelle.

"Are you kidding me? I want a DRINK."

Pace demonstrated how to spin the lazy Susan implanted in the middle of the table and press the icon for beverage of choice. Martina tapped impatiently upon the ale icon. Within seconds, a mechanized octopus delivered five pints of ale.

"Now THIS is mad-scientist progress I can get behind!"

The band began a sweet introduction to a lightly lifting song. Pace pushed back from the table and bowed. "Please pardon me ladies, for I must take leave of you now. Yet we will rejoin before the autumn moon shines through the roof." Tess tried to shake her disappointment as he walked away.

Bashelle stood and stretched her hand gallantly to Tess. "Might I have the pleasure of accompanying you to the dance floor, m'lady?"

Tess's face flushed in the happy warmth of friendship, and the two walked arm in arm to join the waltz. Martina remained fist to fist with jugs of ale.

Pace approached the thrones wherein the delegates from DRAKE sat. He first acknowledged the Dragon Queen.

He bowed, never taking his gaze from her masked face. Beneath the silk, a round onyx covered a hole where an eye would be. The other eye gleamed blue as if shining from an inner power. "Yofune-nushi."

"I am not that name. She does not exist. She is a figment of your imagination. She might be dead." The woman's eye flashed with fire. Pace retained his cool demeanor.

"As you like, Madame Ziracuny. I wish to appeal to your sense regarding the power you share with Subton."

Ziracuny bared her teeth beneath her mask.

Pace continued. "Subton is blessed by our pure forms of crystal energy. They can be harvested and integrated benevolently, or malevolently. I am privy to DRAKE's plans to pursue Life-Ray technology. I must caution you, a reactionary discharge of this enormity could cause an overload of electric energy in the atmosphere, proving fatal to life-forms."

"What care have I of life if I have power over life," answered the Dragon Queen.

"The heat of your combustible machines and crystal powered lasers are causing a disturbance in Subton's power grids. Surely, you must have noticed that our islands are losing land rapidly. If you have these kinds of extreme waves superimposed on a rising sea level, then clearly one day those waves are going to have an effect that they wouldn't have if the sea level wasn't rising. The line of equilibrium is fading."

"This line doesn't exist. The only line that connects both worlds, may I say, is the material," she says.

"Madame Ziracuny, I implore you, what are you hoping to gain?"

"I want just one thing. Everything. And I want it in abundance." The majestic woman rose, and abandoned her liege and Pace.

Pace turned to the captain.

"Nero, my brother. I believe in peace. I believe in peace for all. You believe it too."

Tess retired from dancing and stared out to the sea. Her sight grew fuzzy as a devillish form behind her reflected in the massive window. She turned and faced her nemesis.

Subton Sea and the Dragon Queen appraised each other before a stream of dancers flowed between them. Then the Dragon Queen was gone.

Tess returned to the window and pressed her face against the cool glass. Her pulse raced and her stomach boiled. Her rage was like a steamy volcano, building pressure before an eruption. She closed her eyes and counted. One, two, three. One, two, three. One, two, three. She opened her eyes.

A flash of red hinted in her peripheral vision. She strained her eyes to see through the glass and lanterns and glowing sea creatures. It couldn't be a mermaid, could it? The creature flitted into sight, and Tess lost her breath. The face, the hair, the form, she would recognize that girl anywhere. Unless her heart and mind were playing tricks on her? She squeezed her eyes tight and reopened them. The girl was gone, like a snuffed candle. Only a trail of bubbles assured Tess that she wasn't completely losing her mind.

In the Coral Cove, Verdandi felt more alive than she had since her abduction. She may yet be as a fish in a bowl, but at least she could swim.

"Verdandi, come see this!"

Verdandi flipped with glee towards her friend. This one night of freedom filled her heart with hope. The glow of moon-lamps illuminated her soul.

Part Two

Chapter 21

Verdandi is focused on escape. Trying everything to the point of exhaustion. She starts out calm and organized with well drawn out plans. But she becomes desperate, banging on the walls, bloodying her hand and nub of her right arm, sending shocks of pain across her shoulder to her chest. With each hit, her heart suffers more, until she swears she can feel it bleed inside her. She collapses on the floor and can't lie down because she feels that if she does, her heart will be torn from inside her chest cavity, and the heartstrings connecting it to her body will snap like tendrils of dry summer grass. Her heart is barely attached to her body, she imagines. She clenches her teeth and tries to slow her breathing, because each passage of air through her lungs causes searing agony in her chest. The pain is so severe that rising to a stand causes her vision to turn white.

She makes it to the bed and gingerly fluffs the pillows. Every movement of her arms sparks the pain in her chest. She leans over to roll the blanket and feels like her heart is going to fall out of her mouth.

She arranges the rolled up blanket with the pillows and slowly, painfully, sits on the bed, then lifts her legs and swivels on the corner. She lowers herself to the boosted pile of pillows so she is sitting up in bed. It is less painful this way.

Drat, she left her notepad on the table. Without her bionic arm she is at a loss. She depends on the built-in contraptions she had created. They enhance her life and make common tasks a breeze, so she can write poems at a whim, or draw diagrams, or pull off and mount horology tools to tinker with new ideas.

Now, not only is she imprisoned, she is stuck in bed. Just for trying to be free. She cries angry tears. She can't even cry properly because each huff of air and moan of defeat irritates her strained chest wall. This only serves to fuel her anger even more.

It's all her fault for getting caught in the first place. She could've tried harder.

She should've tried harder. She should've been more aware.

She flashes back to the moment Nero slithered up behind her on the docks. She had been communicating with her friend Ani, the beautifully sleek orca she had helped escape from DRAKE fishing nets. Now, Ani was repaying her kindness in true friendship, fighting DRAKE militia, breaching onto the wooden planks of the floating docks and snatching soldiers one by one to the cold Charles River.

Her glistening body heaved onto the tilting docks. Her jaws opened wide, revealing a palate of ivory-white daggers. The soldier's scream came too late as Ani clamped his leg with giant force. Blood spurted in streams defeating gravity, as the leg exploded like fireworks on mid-summers eve.

The hanging skin in the whale's unforgiving grip was then pulled down, down the unstable raft of wood, so the soldier slid into the whale's face with an unpleasant bump. Flapping her fluke, Ani maneuvered off the planks, pulling her prey with her, sliding on whale bile and glops of blood. Into a sudden ringlet of water, encircled upon itself like marks on a dart board, both whale and soldier disappeared. Bubbles of blood rose to the surface and popped, smearing together like a spilled palate of water colours. The rings faded away with the increasing waves of the incoming tide. Then a burst, like a black and white shot from a cannon, erupted from the depths. Mucky radiated water splashed in a backwards waterfall upon the remaining Drake soldiers, alternately falling into the dark water or gripping, prone, onto the slimy cracking wood. As the peak of the spray returned to its source, the bulbous head of the whale could be seen, thrashing wildly. The latest conquest shook in her jaws, arms waving uselessly, mouth open in the last screech of death, eyes dripping blood across an armoured face.

Satisfied with her thrashing, Ani dove back in a spectacular feat of cetacean acrobatics, curving in a perfect arc. Her tail rose, flukes wide, and a mixture of toxic mucus, snotted algae, and fecal slime was launched into the massive DRAKE ship, covering Captain Nero and his surrounding officers in wretched filth.

Verdandi had jumped in delight, sure-footed on the wavering docks. She had played here many times with the barefoot Subton children, and had learned their skillful tricks of balance.

Her celebration was short lived. Nero descended from the ship and swam effortlessly to the dock where Verdandi whooped and clapped her hands. She smelled his sludge before she felt him wrap his cold wet arms around her. She sprung a bronze compass from her robotic right hand. The two prongs opened and she moved her powerful right arm up just enough to jab her assailant in the thigh. He released her in shock and pain. She ran two swift steps, and lifted off to leap to the next dock, when the Captain struck her bare legs with a whip. She fell forward, flat onto her stomach, sprawled akimbo on the splintering wood, as the whip entangled itself around her ankles with magnetic joints. Blood from the lash joined blood from her face as Nero dragged her across the sinking dock. He pulled her to the edge and jumped in, feet first, into the freezing water. She was breathless from her fall on the deck, and entered the water without air in her lungs. Pulled like a speared dolphin, she was at the mercy of the cold, and the whip, and the Captain.

He reached the ship without a loss for air. If anything, his vigour was emphasized with the treacherous water. He hoisted the handle of his whip up to two officers who unceremoniously pulled Verdandi, dripping, chafed, bloody, and semiconscious, up the barnacled side of the craft.

Nero stood over where Verdandi lay. The white of her belly shone like a dying fish. Her clump of recently cut hair turned redder as the abrasions in her face poured out, surrounding her head in a sanguine halo. She dared open her salty eyes, with much effort. She saw Nero's drooping jowls, and felt the slime of his clothes drip over her. She blinked slowly, as her vision dimmed. She saw a figure all in black, and heard the swift clip of heeled boots approach her as the deck shuddered beneath the force of wrath.

Was this dark figure here to help her? She cringed her eyes open again and saw a face framed by wild waves of black tresses. Was it Tess? Was she saved?

Red lips hovered in her daze, and the world went black.

She awoke, a captive, and has been scheming her escape ever since.

Chapter 22

Morning shimmered below the glass floor of Verdandi's prison. The metallic bubble that was her room branched out from the DRAKE compound. She still believed her efforts were worth it. And she was still angry.

Again she contemplated her ability to escape. Locked in a cylindrical tower. She began her morning ritual of measuring and computating.

She fastidiously wrote in the notebooks she was allowed to have. Her cell was comfortable enough, and she had everything she "needed," except her prosthetic arm. But she was getting by.

A curve in the wall flashed green, then dissipated like mist. Water dripped in a line of beads to the clear floor.

Verdandi swung her legs from the bed and dried her eyes on her ruffled collar. Droplets smashed in a tiny splash with the reconvergence of protons. The door solidified again. A lean, dark figure hovered.

The shadow stepped into the shimmering light. "Breakfast time! We've got raspberry turnovers and honey tea. Would you like to sit with me by the porthole?"

Yoki carried the silver tray, rather than placing it on the hover-bots at her side. The teen had seen enough sorrow to recognize the power of a personal touch.

Verdandi struggled within her will. Should she hold onto her miserable anger? It kept her safe from disappointment and further heartache. It kept her focused. Or should she indulge, just a tiny bit, into what little joy she had. Her freedom, her friends, her family, her home; her way of life, was gone. It was becoming increasingly difficult to remember who she was. Was this her life now, to either fight or embrace? Perhaps she should simply succumb to her circumstances. Why bother trying, only to fail and fail and fail?

Yoki was one light in this empty tunnel. Verdandi looked forward to her visits, even though she knew they were not social calls, but Yoki's duty. Yoki treated her like a normal human being. Not like a criminal or a captive. Yoki was not only her guard, but also her sole interaction. Verdandi felt tempted by friendship, but was afraid to make herself more vulnerable than she already was.

Yoki arranged the silver tray upon a bamboo tea table. She placed a blue flower into a crystal teapot and added hot water. The liquid took on a purple hue, and its steam carried a sweet inviting scent to Verdandi. She remained sitting in bed, her feet on the floor.

"You seem extra tired today. Would you prefer to linger in bed a bit? We could read together, or if you like, we could talk about what is on your mind." Yoki settled herself next to Verdandi on the soft bed and folded her hands upon her lap.

Verdandi glanced into Yoki's eyes, then looked away.

"We could talk about the adventures in our lives. I have told you some of mine."

Verdandi smiled, remembering the funny tales of would-be romances and dating snafus Yoki had shared with her.

The small smile encouraged Yoki.
"How about you have a turn today. I would
be interested to hear about your adventures."

Verdandi felt her heart decompress in
her chest. "This is my adventure now.
Dying." She fell back onto the bed.

"I see that you feel hopeless. But I
believe in your ability to make your life
better. If you let me, I would like to help
you." She paused, and her voice trembled.
"I am in a difficult situation too, and maybe
we could help each other."

Verdandi's voice was bare and
toneless. "All I'm looking for is temporary
relief of unending pain."

Yoki stood up and came back with the
crystal teapot. The blue flower was now
white with purple streaks. "Not seeing is a
flower."

"What?"

"Close your eyes and imagine."

"Imagine what?" Verdandi was too
tired to argue, and closed her eyes.

"I would like to tell you a crystal story.
You don't have to listen if you do not want

to. You can let your mind wander wherever you want. May I tell you the story though?"

"Go ahead."

Yoki took a long audible breath, inhaled the calming tea, and exhaled with a low whoosh. Her voice was soft and slow as she began her story.

"You may allow my words to form images in your mind. Blank at first, then tracings. Shadows, tails of falling stars..." She paused, allowing Verdandi time to open her mind.

"Then the shapes turn into petals. They twirl together. Now they fold in together, forming a seed." She took a slow, deep breath, and watched Verdandi's chest rise and fall in a more relaxed pace.

"Then the seed spurts up in bright hues. These are the colours seen in the fire of a Bunsen burner. Vivid blue, violet, yellow, orange, red." Verdandi could see the colours behind her closed eyes.

Yoki's voice remained smooth and slow. "The seed leaves a trail like a lightening eel. Then a series of flashes, like glowing crystals, burst from the seed. They rain upon the horizon's edge like falling stars."

Verdandi's jaw unclenched. Yoki took this as a sign to continue. She paused between phrases, allowing time for images to form and dissolve in Verdandi's mind.

"And the tracing continues, forming, curving, WORDS. Illuminating. BURST, a flower, blazing, then bursting into a thousand petals, red, then white, then purple, then a fine trace of a borderline colour; purple upon pink; pink upon purple, then a swirl, floating up, then forming a cyclone, and swirling wider and wider, erupting to red, melting down like a wax candle, to a pool of blue. And the blue continues to swirl and elongate. WORDS and blue bends back, then streaks across nothingness, and rejoins itself in a pulsating aqua ring, turning on itself and falling in, forming an orb, a blue marble spinning in felted black. VOICE, faster, ever faster..."

Verdandi could feel her heart, the strong rhythmic beat pounding through her body, the squeeze pushing hot life beneath her skin.

"...expanding, growing, solidifying..."

Verdandi tilted her head back on Yoki's lap. Yoki placed her fingers on Verdandi's temples and rubbed in slow circles. As she spoke, she dug deeper in.

"...until the expanse of every world, every vantage point, is, BLUE."

At this, Yoki abruptly removed her fingers from Verdandi's throbbing pulse-points and with each hand pushed the redhead's broad shoulders down. She could feel the strain of trained muscles give way to her upper body strength, borne from life at sea.

Verdandi opened her mouth wide like a gaping fish.

Yoki leaned her face forward so her lips felt fleshy warmth. "Breathe," she exhaled.

Verdandi breathed.

Chapter 23

Iron, bronze, and brass burst in small explosions within and without. Shimmers of gold rebounded from alchemistic scales of wayward koi. Pharyngeal teeth glowed yellow through shadowed gills. The beautiful creatures spiraled amongst each other; their own kind, their kin, and their would-be mates. Sparks flew.

Above the glass floor, Verdandi stood barefoot. She was clothed in pink ribboned bloomers from her former life, and shimmering seashells lifting the growing breasts of her new life. In dark hours illuminated by phantom lights of angler fish and phosphorescent floating algae, the young scientist bloomed.

At night she conspired within herself, challenged by her own drive. Her body betrayed her in its shifting equilibrium. Her balance was lost not by the leagues beneath the sea in which she was entrapped, but by the masses of flesh rearranging her physicality. When she at last succumbed to half-dreaming sleep upon the cold glass, or twirled in rosy silk sheets of her soft bed, her hand at times brushed against the new being which was her. It was strange, to be in the same body, yet different. She wondered if her brain became softer as her body did.

Glimmers of morning awoke Verdandi to a new day. Somewhere in her orphaned memory, she heard the words: "You are my sunrise and sunset." Typical dream. Often in quiet moments, she heard those sentiments between her ears. She knew it was nonsense. Yet in her loneliest times she felt painfully poetically placated.

She unwound from her silky cocoon. As every morning, she blinked her eyes against a lightless sun. Her empty arm struggled to untangle her head from the soft noose of her sleep. Dreams faded until she inhaled the false air and etched them into her memory. Sitting up like a rock thrown from a catapult, she remembered where she was.

She wiped the sleep from her eyes. The loss of her right arm didn't bother her anymore. It was the loss of her NEW right arm that bruised her spirit. She was a tinkerer by trade. Or by fate. Whatever it was, it served her and her community well. Her life had educated her on more than embroidery and butter. She had become skilled in horology in the Watch City of Waltham; indeed, an amateur expert. Unbeknownst to her, the juvenile experiments she engaged within her workshop had become pivotal within the government that challenged her now.

Even with one arm she was a force to be reckoned with. She knew it and reminded herself of it every day: with every dream, every nightmare. She listened. She heard the language of intelligent beasts. She knew their base thoughts. She could send her feelings back; her love was its own language.

She would gouge a hole in her breast for some of Neviah's country fried chicken right now though. Not all chickens were thoughtful. Some were simply delicious. Especially with hot sauce.

Before Yoki arrived with the view of iron-encrusted hammerhead sharks beyond the porthole, Verdandi sucked down seaweed stuffed with toasted tentacles. The consistency and taste pleased her. Lifting up the dimly reflective platter, she found the accompanying treat of raspberry turnovers that Yoki had smuggled in for her. With cold tea they were delectable. Rolling the sweet tartness in her tongue, she wondered at how Yoki knew her so well, so shortly, with so little reciprocation.

After all, Yoki was her warden, wasn't she? She delivered meals, retrieved her trays and laundry and replenished her minimal needs. Verdandi created her own cleansers from fish scales and seaweed trimmed from her meals. She missed her long hair, and the shroud it provided upon her face. Yet her strands had never grown so thick.

A slit beneath the plasma door delivered fresh parchment and charcoal on which to write. Verdandi used these greedily for her escape calculations. They inevitably were lost, or perhaps taken, during those sparkling nights whence her covered custard tasted too sweet. Yet the notebooks and pencils beneath Yoki's nasty ritual of encased morning raw oysters never disappeared.

She began to wonder if the pretty, black haired, oak-skinned, olive-eyed, warden was trying to be her friend.

Oysters flittered by the sole porthole. How funny they were! Clamped in their own shells. Hiding in the sand, she knew from Bashelle, yet she had never seen them squirt themselves into motion until she had herself been held in captivity of this artificial shell. Could it be possible to tear herself from her enclosure and swim away? Her blue eyes lingered on the bubbling shellfish and felt no communication. She wondered what would happen if their flesh tore free from their shells.

Verdandi sucked on an octopus arm. Tentacles stuck between the width of her top front teeth, her spitting teeth. Bashelle had taught her how to spit salt water in a multitude of ways, especially when her puppy teeth began to shed. Martina was the only person in town who could out-spray her in Waltham's annual contest.

Time before Waltham was blurred. Somewhat dreamlike, almost purposeful. Memory was a trail of tears and trances. Martina had told her, "You are who your future is." And she believed it. Except, sometimes, now.

How can she believe in her own future when it is endlessly estranged from all she loved and encompassed by all she hates? Or, not, hates, but distinctly dislikes, as Tess would say. The brilliant inventor had been in her life only a short time, yet at pivotal moments. Verdandi was mystified by the concept of love at first sight, yet she understood on a different spectrum, the incidence of understanding at first meeting. Was there a different word for that?

The pencil and paper were too far away from her right half-arm to sway from the night-stand, and besides, she had not ingested her morning tea to awaken her brain.

Instead, she rolled out of her fluffy bed, landing in a quite unladylike position onto the cool glass floor. The frayed ends of her copper coloured hair mirrored the scales flashing from the fish below.

She watched the school pass beneath her. Splayed upon the cold glass floor, her limbs were instantaneously alerted to life almost as an Earl Grey would do, yet without the warmth; it was invigourating.

Her view switched from fuzzy impartial rainbows to intense spectral deferences. Every movement, every colour, every differential of speed and transmission not seen by the common eye were captured in timed blinks with inward verbal notes. Alphabetized, of course. It was a trick she learned from her idol Her Noble Lady Professor Tess Alset. Or to her, simply, Tess.

Then it came to her.

New plan of escape.

Verdandi plucked out strands of her bludgeoned hair. She lined up her copper coloured specimens upon her white sheets, illuminated by the growing dawn.

With bamboo chopsticks leftover from last night's calamari, she tweezed another golden thread from her scalp. Her flesh fingers held the sticks tightly as her right limbless shoulder pushed towards her gap-toothed mouth.

She licked and secured the red follicle between her uneven molars.

Now!

Her persevered magnetic power from coils of shredded tuna scales and shards from the egg-shaped enclosure of her prison melded in her saliva.

She clenched her teeth and her eyes.

Nothing seemed to happen.

She was roused by Yoki lifting her head up from the cold glass floor.

Yoki found Verdandi half naked upon the cold bottom of her prison. Subton's unique phosphorescent algae entwined and clung to the brigades and leverages of the enclave.

Yoki held her ward in her arms and steeped tea into Verdandi's mouth. She refused to give up on her. She refused to turn her back on her solo purpose. She refused to leave her friend.

The captive choked herself awake and Yoki scuttled back to the plasma door as if just appearing. She delivered a silver tray of meat pies. She had sacrificed her own meals as a BSDINK to supplement Verdandi's diet. She wanted, more than anything possible, to conspire with this girl, who was like the little sister she had always wished for. Together they could plan for their freedom, and freedom for all.

Instead, Yoki maneuvered the levers and codes known only to her and left the prisoner to her breakfast. She returned to her post integral to Subton's safety. She was eighteen years old; she knew what was up.

She knew who she was.
She knew who to trust.
Didn't she?

The day passed. Verdandi considered herself a good prisoner. No violence or rude disdain. Tess had taught her how to be a lady, after all. She recognized that power as such.

She also remembered lessons learned. Felt, not taught. Life is its own teacher. That's what Martina told her.

The teen tried her experiment again. She hypothesized that she could flow magnetism through coils of her hair to create a circuit, thus providing energy to unlock the coded doors to her cell.

She repeated her attempts using one arm and her teeth. No sense of change was evident. Over and over, failing different ways. Nothing.

Tears of frustration threatened her focus. Then finally, she felt a vibration! Her moment of joy quickly faded into doubt. It was probably just her teeth tingling from being clenched. She flopped to her bed and dreamed of futility.

Yoki appeared for dinner, and the two girls shared plates of food. Verdandi was coaxed into describing her latest plan.

"Let's try this." Yoki pulled yards of fishing wire from her belt. Together, they attached the wire from panel to panel across the room's diameter. When they applied magnets, the room shuddered. Verdandi's eyes lit up.

"This time, let's coil the wire."

Each girl stood opposite each other across the room again. They applied magnets to the tethered ends of the coiled wire.

The room shuddered again and sparks flew.

"Shit," whispered Verdandi.

Yoki kicked the magnet on her side off the wall with her Mucks. "Shit!"

"Yeah, ugh!"

"No," said Yoki, coming over to kick the other magnet down before gripping Verdandi's shoulders. "SHIT!"

"Yeah." Verdandi raised her voice in joined intensity. "SHIT!"

"No, no, shit! I heard you say shit!"

"What?"

Yoki dropped her hands from Verdandi's shoulders. She picked up the warm coil.

"I could hear you say shit." Verdandi looked at her blankly. "I HEARD you. Through the coil!"

"Holy shit," breathed Verdandi.

"Holy shit," beamed Yoki.

The girls embraced and spun each other around. They didn't know exactly what they did, but they had done something. Together.

Chapter 24

After laughing themselves silly, Verdandi and Yoki sat upon the glass floor and cooled off with chilled lotus tea. Golden fish glimmered in blue rivulets of moon meeting ocean.

"If I could only explain how I feel when swimming in Subton Sea. Alone, yet united with the world. Glory and beauty all around me, and every choice is mine to make. Nobody telling me what to do. Complete freedom." Yoki pressed her face to the glass floor.

Verdandi lowered herself next to her, flat on her stomach, and copied her manner. The glass was cold, and refreshment spread pink across her cheek. The two girls looked at each other, their eyes meeting in mutual delight. Yoki slid her right hand across the smooth floor and placed it upon Verdandi's, and gave it a gentle squeeze.

"Freedom," said Verdandi.

"We will find a way. We can find freedom together."

The girls remained this way for thirty more minutes, closing their eyes and allowing the cold current to swirl beneath them, while between them, the warmth of friendship created a circuit of connectedness.

Chapter 25

Yoki delivered a new shipment from Waltham to Verdandi: brown paper, pencils, and chalk.

Verdandi was delighted with this treasure, but her heart plummeted when she realized from whence it came. "I'll never be free. They'll never find me."

"Who?"

"My family. I'm an orphan again." She rolled back over in bed and shut her eyes.

Yoki knelt next to the bed. "You will find a way to reach them."

"Maybe I shouldn't even try. They probably forgot about me. Or are glad I'm gone. I was always just a nuisance anyway.

"Don't give up hope. Your desire for freedom is important, and worthwhile."

"Worth what? Driving myself crazy inside this hard boiled egg? I need to accept where I am and deal with it."

Yoki's voice was soft. "You can accept where you are now, and deal with how to solve your problem. But, giving up isn't dealing. It is...giving up."

Verdandi turned over and looked at Yoki's warm eyes. "How do you always know the right words to say?"

"If I already knew everything I wouldn't be here trying to figure stuff out with you."

Verdandi scooted herself up to sit, and patted the bed next to her. Yoki accepted the offer.

"You need productive time to yourself, to create and think and build." Yoki paused, her eyes attracted to a sea turtle shadowing the porthole. "But a little adventure now and then doesn't hurt."

"I sure could use a change of scenery."

"Then let's make it happen," Yoki grinned. "In the meantime, let's do something about this." She gently ran her fingers through a short segment of Verdandi's hair.

Verdandi pulled away. "What do you mean?"

"I'm sorry, I mean it's pretty, but-"

"I suppose it is shaggy," relented Verdandi.

"It is growing, but could use a touchup."

Verdandi appraised Yoki's sleek black hair, shining with opalesque beads. "Do you think you could make my hair a bit like yours?" Her lower lip trembled in sudden shame.

Yoki lifted an arm around Verdandi's shoulders. "We can make it like mine, but specially styled for you!"

After tea and talk, Yoki lifted a silver mirror up. Verdandi's face flushed, and she reached a hand to trace the fashionable accessories in her hair.

"The black pearls are lovely!" She took the mirror from Yoki to further inspect her reflection. Yoki had smoothed out the mismatched layers and neatened up the edges into a crisp bob. Black pearls were knotted haphazardly throughout. The hair angled against Verdandi's jawline, ending in perfect points. A tiny braid wove down one side, entwined with round blue rocks, and ended with a hanging blue crystal. Verdandi realized she was not just admiring Yoki's handiwork, but also her own reflection. She set the mirror down.

"Thank you, it's beyond what I could have hoped, and...beautiful."

"YOU are beautiful," smiled Yoki.

"This crystal is a distinctive touch," said Verdandi.

Yoki nodded. "Crystals are a big part of Subton's culture. Some are used for medicine, healing, energy sources-"

"Wow! I didn't know crystals that could do all that!"

Yoki laughed and fingered the dangling charm in Verdandi's hair. "Yes, but some are just for decoration!"

The girls giggled. "I will admit though, this blue crystal has a special meaning. It symbolizes friendship from the heart, like the blue ocean can be friends to all.

Verdandi looked down and back up. "Thank you."

That night, Yoki stared at the cot above her in BSDINK quarters. Worry swirled where dreams refused to enter. No use telling Verdandi about the other ways crystals were used.

The quahog that was clamped to her right ear buzzed, interrupting her thoughts. She pushed off her covers and responded to the call. With bare feet she reached the DRAKE library and knocked. "You may enter."

Yoki closed the door quietly behind her. "How may I serve you, Captain Nero?"

Chapter 26

"Look at all these books!"

"I thought you'd like them." Yoki helped Verdandi stack volumes across the small table.

"Where did you get all these?"

"Most of them are from my collection when I was little. My mother was always reading with me." She pointed to the cameo brooch she pinned over her heart. "She and my dad died in the Battle of Subton when I was a kid. So now, I want to learn how to help my community. My main goal in life is to gain more information than I could ever use."

"I can relate to that. I'm an orphan, but about six or seven years ago, I found a home. A group of people joined together to help each other, and love each other. They are my family now."

"I am glad that you forged a new family for yourself. That is sort of like what DRAKE is doing with the orphaned BSDINK kids. Except instead of a family, it's more like a youth army. I'm lucky though; I have an uncle who took me in, and he's pretty great most of the time."

"Why then do you wear DRAKE colours, and guard me?" Verdandi eyed the red and black scales on her shoulders.

Yoki lowered her head. "It's complicated." There was a pause, and Verdandi respected the silence. Yoki composed herself and looked up. "I've told you about my goals. What about you? Well, besides to get the heck out of here?"

"I want to reunite with my family. And travel the world."

"I was hoping you would say something of that sort. I do not have the power to set you free, but I can sneak you out for a while!" She dug into the second box she had brought. "Here we go!" She laid an apparatus on top of the pile of books.

Verdandi tilted her head and squinted her eyes. Oyster shells, Bunsen burners, wooden fans, and soldering masks? "What the f-"

"Fit this over your head, strap the fans to your toes, loop the belts to the fuselage around your shoulders, and pinch the oyster shells onto your neck like this."

"Those things are alive!"

"Yes, yes, I know. Just trust me."

"You look ridiculous."

"Let me help you dress so you can look ridiculous too!"

Verdandi could barely see through the full-face visor, and every step she took down narrow hallways and shifting tunnels was a danger to her knees. How in the heck could Yoki walk with all this junk on her?

Finally, they reached a muddy, mucky, moldy room. "Ready?"

"I think so."

"Okay, here we go!"

Yoki pulled a splintered wooden beam from the wall, and a short stairway pushed itself into the small space. Verdandi tripped backwards as she avoided being struck by it. She stepped up after Yoki, and crawled behind her through a slime covered glass tunnel. All at once, she saw her leader vanish headfirst into nothingness. "Yoki!" she screamed, and grabbed her disappearing heel. Together, the two teens tumbled into murky brine.

Chapter 27

"Life is not all sea stars and coral, but I would take the squishy sea slugs and scraping barnacles with it all every day if I could just swim around and study them forever!" Verdandi was astounded by the underwater view. "It would have been kind of you, however, to not scare me into death's ghost on the way!" She kicked at Yoki, her gesture of humour made more-so by the slowness of her effort.
Yoki's laughter caused a flood of bubbles to blow through the oysters. Her yellow glowing mask was briefly shrouded.

"You look like a boiling pot of pasta!"

"You look like a fish out of water!"

The two teens took turns toppling rocks over to spy shiny sea stars. They raced over thresholds of squiggly eels and swam through swathes of undersea grass.

"What in the world is that?"

"An ocean sloth. It is a mammal that lives under water and breathes with gills. The long claws on the end of its webbed feet help dig in to decaying forestry, and enable it to creep along the ocean floor." They watched as the ocean sloth lifted one clawed foot from the dense sand. It bent its round head and slurped something into its toothless mouth. "Sea worms are its favourite meal."

"That is quite gross. Yet, sort of pretty in an ugly way, especially with the green algae glowing through its fur."

Yoki was satisfied with this astute observation. "Some ocean sloths become mobile crystal growers, as well."

The girls hovered with small twitches of their toes. In silence, they admired the live treasures surrounding them. Yoki reached out to touch Verdandi's hand.

"To me, the ocean is a living organism, a mother that nourishes and embraces. All the emotions of familial love are exhibited in her seasons and moods. I love the sea, and I feel that the sea loves me."

Verdandi joined her fingers to Yoki's. "Thank you for being my friend."

Yoki's smile was barely visible beneath her mask. "You are the best friend I've ever had."

Chapter 28

"It was so disgusting out, and in, earlier today that I was envious of your climate controlled bedroom."

Verdandi turned from her watercolour painting. "This is not exactly my bedroom. It's my prison."

Yoki pushed on with cheerfulness. "Now, finally, the sky is both pre and post storm; a heavy breeze with no rain pushing the clouds away. The city seems obsessed with some new boring meetings. Which gives US the chance for something different!"

Verdandi looked upon the shiny armour laid out upon her bed. "Are we going to be soldiers?"

"Even better. We are going to be mermaids!"

Through the airlock used for crabbing and lobster baiting, the would-be mermaids made their jovial escape. Together they wove satchels of buoyant seaweed. Verdandi quickly filled hers with ocean treasures.

"We can use these to carry things out here with us too," said Yoki.

"I am quite satisfied with collecting, thank you very much." A hermit crab snipped at her hand when she mistook it for an empty shell. She gently replaced it from whence it came. "Some treasures belong where they are." Yoki smiled in pride and agreement.

"Oh, my gracious, Yoki, look upon this!"

Yoki flipped her tail apparatus and looped back to her friend.

"Verdandi! What a find!"

"What are they? They look like mini constellations!"

"You have discovered a beautiful pair of star sapphires! See the star shimmering within each globe? Holy Triton, this is remarkable!"

"They are enchanting," said Verdandi.

"Yes, but these are twins, and each have twelve rays instead of the still gorgeous but more common six. These are prizes to Subton!"

"It looks not only like a star, but also more like a sun." Verdandi admired the opacity of the stones.

"Indeed! The twelve rays shooting from the epicentre represent the numbers on our compass clocks, and the sun they form represents our guiding light. These gems are rare and precious to our culture, and used in the very best compass mechanisms."

She pulled the two stones from their craggy shelter and held them in her hands. "Verdandi, these are extravagant. They are black, from merging with hematite crystals."

Yoki turned the gems at different angles in the ebbing moonlight. Moments of mesmerized marvel passed. Yoki broke her gaze and saw the stars reflected in Verdandi's blue eyes. She reached a hand out to hers and placed one of the sapphires in her palm. "We can be each other's guiding light."

If they were not immersed in salt water, Verdandi's tears would have been visible. Instead they became part of the ocean, much like her heart was starting to be.

The friends returned to their playground the next day, and days after that. Yoki showed Verdandi a pool of glowing algae. She explained the scientific and cultural aspects of the algae; what it meant to Subton; the religiousness encompassing it.

Verdandi traced her fingers along stone engravings as little fish hovered about her ears.

"Those things are so annoying," said Yoki, swiping her hand to brush the fish away. When she stopped, they all converged with opening and closing mouths around Verdandi's head.

She whispered along with their open and closing mouths: "Watch your step, lest you pass by, jewels thus kept, in words of time."

Yoki looked at her in astonishment. "How do you know that saying? Our native Subton tongue has been eradicated by DRAKE and only we Mutineers know it."

Verdandi answered plainly. "Nay, I do not know that language, but these elder cognizant friends of mine tell me." She turned to Yoki. "What are Mutineers?" The fish scattered.

Yoki's eyes shifted as she considered the truths which she might or mightn't share. "Most of the older generations were killed in the Battle of Subton, so now there are scores of us who were orphaned. DRAKE has enlisted most of them. The ones lucky enough to have family or friends to take them in have mostly joined the Mutiny. The Mutineers desire a combined city, with peace again. The difficulty is extrapolated by the lack of women in our society."

"What do you mean?"

"Apologies, I only now remember that you have not seen anyone besides me during your captivity, and thus would not understand the uneven population."

Verdandi felt her spirit dive at the mention of captivity but she sucked it up. "I would be interested in why there is this disparagement."

"Subton is a matriarchal culture. A great naval power, used to protect the natural environment we live in partnership with. When DRAKE attacked in the Battle of Subton, it was a civil war, because DRAKE had already formed alliances within our government. Most of our leaders erred on the side of compassion, and tried to tolerate, rather than accept, their world view. This lack of suspicion and an open-minded relent led to the city's battle, and inevitable separation. I was considered too young to fight then, but I followed my mother and aunts into the fray just the same. I saw them die. I watched my ancestors' bridges collapse."

Solemn and still, the girls steadied themselves with bamboo stalks and stood upon a spread of soft sand.

They pulled out the dyes from their pouches, and proceeded to paint pastel hued murals on the shiny curved walls of Subton.

Sneaking out became a daily thrill. It was a common part of the day, like taking tea and scribbling equations.

Verdandi and Yoki picnicked in "their" air pocket. They utilized mermaid contraptions to get there.

Verdandi motioned across the craggy shore. "Look at those busy beavers as we read our book!"

The two girls admired the mammal pulling a soft board from a burg stricken boat across the spinning stream to drier planes. Verdandi sang in rhyme.

"Busy beavers read a book
whilst wading past
their bardic brook"

Yoki closed their book and nudged her left shoulder against Verdandi's right one. "So in this scenario, we are the beavers?"

Verdandi lunged sideways and they landed next to each other on the white sandy bank. "I suppose we are!" She reached her one hand onto Yoki's left shoulder and rolled her over swiftly yet gently so as not to knock her head against the sand. Yoki laid her shiny black tresses into the gleaming granules just the same.

Verdandi grasped Yoki's right hand and pulled her to a stand with her. She stuck her already prominent front teeth over her lower lip (she still had two baby teeth that refused to escape their soft pink home) and spoke through her nose.

"I am a beavah. You ahh a beavah too. Togetha we ahh both beavahs. Lets go do beavah things together."

Yoki wrapped her arms around her bare stomach and snorted. "You've got the brains of a jellyfish. A squishy little jellyfish." She stepped closer to her friend and pinched her rosy cheeks.

Verdandi pulled her dress off and flitted away, encouraging a game of tag. Once thoroughly laughed out, the girls returned to the air pocket to read together.

"The harpoon was darted; the stricken whale flew forward; with igniting velocity the line ran through the grooves;- ran foul."

Verdandi placed her hand over the following page. "Why is our first instinct to kill? Glancing down in evening moonlight. Not blistering. Safe. Seagrass padding our bellies. A book where a pillow would be. As we lie on a bed of sand. Moving onto the next paragraph, our feet behind us in the air, still, currentless. Our legs twist and dance in the euphoria of silent sounds while our eyes dart down to shadowy words. Catching a glimpse of a creature untouched. Ruby. Emerald. Diamond. All precious things stopping for a moment in eternity. Upon your left hand, wings alight. A glorious pendant, moving upon your being without detection, without feeling. You inhale to blow the gems away while your right hand rises to, if not swat, then to slide, swoosh the winged creature away, like an uninvited angel in your darkest dreams. Where the sun shines, yet you feel no warmth."

Yoki silently followed her friend's gaze to the shimmering coral grove, the darting damselfish, the moonlike sea-jellies floating like clouds in a submersive sky. She noticed it all through not only her eyes, but through Verdandi's fresh ones. She wordlessly allowed Verdandi to continue.

"How humanity strives to tame the grasses: measuring, cutting; do not grow, do not grow. Now, nature's lives: pleasuring, tittering; let it flow, let it flow."

Yoki turned on her elbow to face her. "Geez Louise, I don't know to be gladdened or catch a case of the morbs!"

Verdandi met her warm coal eyes. "Let's choose to be happy."

"Agreed!"

They returned to their book, shadows and gold flecks shimmering around them.

Strawberry jam and lox spread evenly across split bumpy scones. Verdandi took a bite and passed whipped cream across the table. "What else should we pack?" As she chewed, she lifted her octopus point pen to thick brown paper.

"I think your list is longer than the length of our pouches combined. We can take our experiments one day at a time, you know."

"We've been doing it that way for a fortnight. Now I want to do it all, make it happen; no more messing around."

"So, no game of chess afore we hit the docks?"

Verdandi paused. "Maybe we could snip a game in our air pocket. There we go." She smeared black ink on paper. "Chess set."

"You're lucky I'm strong enough to carry all that."

"You're lucky I'm strong enough to carry YOU!"

"That was ONE time! Geez Louise, Miss Clumsybottom is more agile than I am during a geyser experiment, and all of a sudden I am a damsel in distress!"

"It's quite fine. I am also strong enough to admit that I am right and you are wrong."

"That's it, you are getting your graceful arse kicked over chess today!"

The duo swam tailless to the geyser they had been investigating and used clam shells as spades to unbury their tools.

"Do you really think this will work?"

"Absolutely. I helped create a similar agent back in Waltham. We need a timing light with a distributor; when the light comes on you're there, in static time, then can move again, from one point to another."

"Condensers of time."

"Precisely."

Verdandi held her hand out. "Could you pass me the magnetometer please?"

Yoki did, and Verdandi added it to the sedimentation bowl. Yoki stirred the geo-magnetron.

"Did you get a chance to sneak in and harvest the special algae you showed me?"

"Even better!" Yoki edged her right hip to Verdandi. "Reach into my sharkskin pack."

Verdandi pulled out a spilling handful of glowing crystallized algae. "Where did you find such perfect specimens?"

"Two words: sea monkeys."

"Those good'ol slowpokes."

"They were so cute and smiley when I combed them."

"Aww, I can imagine." Verdandi gazed into the blank space of her mind where she saw the unseen.

"I appreciate that you respect Subton's algae. Particularly the crystalline kind. We eat this regularly, and use it as seasoning in almost every meal. We boil it for tea, dry it for fertilizer, and bake it for a crunchy snack."

"It will be perfect for Photosynthetic Algine. I had a friend who discovered the formula in her medical practice. Imagine if we could recreate it!"

"We are certainly making strides in a race that Subton has been stalled in for a decade. Geomagnetic clips in desalinated water to bend light; performing alternate gravity pulleys across the reef; and now this!"

"Tinkering is a lot of fun, isn't it?"

"Mathematics is in nature and nature is in mathematics. So of course it is fun," Yoki answered.

They staked pre-coiled copper wires into rocky ground and braided them together. "If we had gold or silver the connections could be stronger," said Verdandi.

"I'm afraid not. Those metals would not survive salt water."

"They could if we coated them in zinc."

"You would know more than I would on that matter. I'm just here for the muscle and the math."

"And the food! Let's head to the air pocket and have sandwiches. I'm hungry!"

They chomped on their algae and anchovy sandwiches in silence. Their brains were as tired as their bodies. After eating they lay on top of their pouches and snoozed. Verdandi dreamed of lobsters pinching her toes. Yoki dreamed of eating metallic salad leaves. They both awoke with a start.

"Phew, it was only goldfish." Verdandi wiggled her toes.

"Zinc!" Yoki dove out of the air pocket.

Verdandi swam after her. "You've got bubbles in your brain!"

Yoki ignored her until they reached their geyser site. She scooped up a mound of algae into a geode. Verdandi watched, sensing something important was about to happen. Yoki removed the torch from her oxygen tank and pulled the trigger to scorch the outer surface of the geode. The crystalized algae glowed green, then yellow, then orange, until it turned red. Yoki stopped the heat blast, and the red algae liquefied, cooled, and turned grey.

"What the blarney is that?" Verdandi's eyes widened behind her mask.

"This, my dear, is the element you were wishing for. Zinc. Galvanization, here we come!"

"Cue the duckboats! We've got a winner!" Verdandi performed a slow motion backflip.

Chapter 29

Verdandi and Yoki stared out the porthole on a particularly grim eve, when the moon was almost at its fullest and scheduled to shine. It was the one bright thing they had been looking forward to. Yoki saw the glum look on her pal's face.

"Every moon has a turn to hide behind clouds."

"Sure." Verdandi turned from the window.

"I brought another book for us. It is about those phosphorescent fish you were asking about."

Verdandi opened the pages. "Who illustrated this? The artwork is surreal!"

"I'll never be satisfied until I'm too smart for my own good. So I drew them myself."

"Don't worry. You aren't too smart for your own good yet."

"Thank goodness! It would be boring to know everything."

The girls lay on the glass floor and watched for fish matching the illustrations in the book.

"Even though there is limited visibility at the moment, the colours in this book are so bright, the creatures look almost alive," said Verdandi.

"A book is a pocket garden."

"You sound like my Tess."

"Your Tess?" Yoki's calm heart accelerated in alarm.

"Yes, she is one of the women in my family. I've told you about her, I know I have."

Yoki pressed her face to the glass, willing her nausea to float away. "You never spoke her name."

The girls awoke a few hours later with the chiming of bells. Yoki sat up and rubbed her eyes. "Ugh, new shift. I should go."

Verdandi stood and stretched. "I will see you for breakfast then. I might just stay up and work on my diagrams some more."

Yoki peered through the porthole. Sleeping on the cold floor had invigourated her. She spun around. "Or, we could brew some puerh tea and try out your diagrams for real."

"You are officially my favourite person. I'll set the saucers out."

Chapter 30

Crystal lanterns and geode globes inundated with kerosene flickered. Excitement squelched the guilt in Yoki's stomach, and Verdandi led the way for the first time. They carried extra packs tonight, which were heavy through the tunnels and not much lighter in the open water. They were determined to engage in their shot of fun while the rest of the world slept.

"Books and diagrams are important," said Verdandi, "but living in the experiment is much more satisfying."

"I mostly agree."

"Alright then, Madame Yoki of the deep sea, connect your circuit."

"Aye-aye, Señorita Verdandi of high land. Connect!"

The two girls each pulled their switches.

A billion watts flowed through coiled current. Radio waves beamed into the twilight zone. Frequencies bounced back and forth, and against all solid mass around the geyser. The girls' masks vibrated. They felt their eyes shake within their skulls.

"Stop!"

Verdandi need not have yelled. Yoki had already pulled her lever back up. She pointed toward the airlock, and Verdandi nodded.

Once out of the water they removed their masks. "We did it! Dolphin Auroral Frequency!" They clasped each other close and took turns throwing up.

The young scientists shared taro to soothe their stomachs. Their guts churned with excitement. Yoki's dark eyes glimmered like star sapphires. "I have an idea. I have wanted to show you, at the right time, but it was always too dangerous. Tonight, I think we can handle it."

Verdandi's curiosity brought up another ball of bile from her belly. "I'm ready for whatever it is!"

"Then gather your gear. We are moving this party to the surface."

Chapter 31

One big island spread wide with a series of
smaller islands hovering nearby. Magnetism
pulled them as they rotated on opposing
poles, so the satellite islands spun around in
circles like a top. They floated a bit
through the day, sometimes bumping into
each other. This was regarded as a nuisance
rather than an emergency. Trebuchets were
hitched to each island, prepared for
inclement weather. During cyclones, the
islands were known to crash, causing
explosions of rock and metal. Even in the
dark, Yoki saw their beauty. She pulled her
friend to the shore of black sand.

"Wow," said Verdandi.

Yoki smiled. "Yes, wow."

"Can you show me more?"

"I was hoping you would say that."

Yoki hitched their packs and equipment
together. She pulled a fishing reel from her
belt and wound a hook around the straps.
Then she picked up a branch of driftwood
and looped the hook up and around it. She
wound the handle of the reel, and pulled the

knob up. Instantly, it began to spin. She handed one end of the wood to Verdandi and held the other end. The stick bore the weight and the gear propelled the packs, so the only effort upon the girls was to hold their ends lightly enough so as to not splinter their fingers.

They approached a large shape in the darkness. "Is that a ship?"

"No, that is a pyramid. All of our islands have one. They are mostly made of metals and stone. Each one is situated in relationship to the North and South magnetic poles. Each of the sides are designed to intercept as much magnetic force as possible."

"Brilliant!"

"The metal sides are embedded with crystals. These crystals conduct sub-cosmic energy to the motors within, creating vast power generators."

"Holy mackerel!"

"The stone sides are covered in a mossy algae. This algae is charged by the magnetic fields, and the stones rotate upon a shared axis keeping them together. In this way, each stone has a back and a front that can be exposed to the unique situation that allows the algae to grow on both sides."

"That is like an inside-outside greenhouse," said Verdandi.

"In a way. The generators within the pyramid transmits oscillations of high-frequency lasers, used to power the actual greenhouses and farms and time lab where the compasses are made."

"That is truly amazing."

"What I am about to show you is the MOST amazing. Just turn this corner with me, and-"

"It's like an orbitoscope made of sunlight!"

"Indeed, this is the most powerful spot in all of Subton. The star models absorb light from the half-ring of crystal pyramids you see facing it. Each of these smaller pyramids provides sources for different kinds of healing. Like illness, and injury, and mentality."

"Does no one ever get sick here?"

"Illness is rare and quickly eradicated. My grandmother was only one hundred and eleven when she died in the Battle of Subton."

"Only!"

"We tend to live long healthy lives. Partly because of our streaming fountain of algae. During the Battle of Subton, DRAKE barred the Subtonians from reaching the islands, and even now the Mutineers are prohibited from surfacing."

"Then we really are quite the rebels, aren't we?" Verdandi shivered with thrill and sudden fear.

"There is one more thing I wish to show you." Yoki placed her end of the driftwood down and Verdandi copied her. "What I am going to divulge is known only to a very few of us. DRAKE has no knowledge of it, only fish-tales. But some of us Mutineers, particularly daughters of leaders, know the secret of the pyramid ring."

"Your mother was a leader? So she knew? You know?"

"Yes." Yoki placed her arms around Verdandi's shoulders and kissed her forehead. "Now that we are sisters, I can tell you."

Verdandi's eyes shimmered in the crystal light. "I have always wanted a sister."

"As have I," said Yoki, her lower lip quivering. She gave Verdandi a quick squeeze. She cleared her throat. "Are you ready sister?"

"Indeed I am," Verdandi answered grandly, wiping away an errant tear.

"Then hook your arm to mine, and we will discover the magical truth of the crystal pyramid ring."

Chapter 32

Arm in arm, the two teens stepped into the centre of the crystal pyramids. "Kneel here," said Yoki, gently tugging her best friend's arm. They knelt together. "Spit."

"I shall do no such thing."

"Now then, you do not have to pretend to be fancy with me, you know that. Besides, I've heard you snore, in an uncontrite way." Yoki swept shiny black sand around and back in a figure eight. Then she spat into it. "Your turn. Just spit."

Verdandi acquiesced. For once, she was glad that Tess was not there to witness her indelicateness. "Why in the heck did you just ask me to do that?"

"So we can see through the bio-plasma." Yoki's answer was aggravatingly passive. Verdandi opened her mouth to complain, but instead emitted a surprised squeak.

The sand before them swirled on the traced number eight, and tiny puffs seemed to chase each other like fish in a tide-pool. The racing sand blew faster, and enlarged the path, maintaining the same shape but rounding it out. Now before them was a circle of whispering sand, twisting in an eternal destination, illuminated by the shining crystal pyramids.

"Stand up," said Yoki, taking Verdandi's hand. Together they stepped into the swishing glow.

Verdandi had to blink her eyes against the sudden glare. Her vision adjusted, and before her, she saw faint silhouettes of the crystal pyramids. Yet, they appeared almost invisible, like drops of water upon a window.

She glanced at Yoki, who nodded silent reassurance, never letting go of her hand.

Images formed like white clouds across a blue sky. The shapes shifted to create outlines of objects. There were strange creatures: a fish that seemed to fly like a bird, and a bird that looked like a fish but flew in the sea. The fish-bird and bird-fish swirled around slowly, as the black sand did in the double looping pattern.

In a flash, the mesmerizing creatures collided and became one. The cloudburst expanded, and grew colour. Palm trees shaded crystal ships along an archipelago. Children chased automatons across black sandy shores. Sun glazed women gutted marlins, pouring the red innards into bronze vats. A breeze fluttered their kerchiefs and ruffled the feathers of parading ducks. Fish rippled the water where the sea met the shore.

The image blurred and darkened. Verdandi squinted her eyes. Cannons burst from island to island. One island crumbled from multiple impacts and melted into the sea. Down, down it went, crashing onto rocky slopes and shedding its trees and boats. The water became a cesspool of sand and soil, so that the only things visible were fiery torpedoes and exploding red geodes.

Verdandi felt stuck, immobile, unable to take her eyes from the horror she was witnessing. Suddenly, she felt the wind get knocked out of her, and she fell backward.

She opened her eyes and instantly regained her breath. Yoki had pulled her back and caught her. All was still and calm. "What was that?"

"A time portal."

Verdandi sat up and Yoki poured them each a full serving of algaeic water from a canteen. "Was that...the Battle of Subton?"

Yoki nodded her head.

"I am so sorry you had to live through that."

"Thank you. I am sorry that part of my history exists. But I'm glad I lived past it."

Verdandi brightened up with the soothing drink. "We can do it again, and change it! We can go back and stop DRAKE from ever gaining power at all!"

"Sadly, we cannot. This portal only allows us to see the past as it was, not as it could be."

"Could we see the future?"

"Nay, that has not been done in my time, although I had heard elders speak of such possibilities when I was very little."

"I wonder..."

"Uh oh, here she goes wondering."

"Hmm, I simply wonder..."

"Get on with it. I know you want to tell me."

Verdandi tapped Yoki on the nose.
"Let's do an experiment."
"Here we go again."

Chapter 33

The pair looked upon their handiwork. The Dolphin Auroral Frequency was reset within the pyramid ring, only this time, the circuits looped around and through each other.

Yoki inspected the stakes. "I must say, this appears quite professional. For someone who prefers their meat burnt to a crisp."

"No meat is going to be burned," retorted Verdandi. "We are the ones going in the fire."

"That's exactly what I feared."

"I figure, this crystal pyramid ring is an epicentre of electromagnetic energy dispersed upwards from the Earth's core. The phosphorescence of the crystals reacts with the inert light of the star models, thus creating an operating system for the generators within this large pyramid to release power."

"Okay, but why did we have to take our clothes off?"

"First of all, because being naked is much more comfortable. Secondly, we needed magnetic quantum filters."

"I have a feeling this is going to give us a whole new perspective on life."

"That's what I'm hoping!"

"We aren't going to die, right?"

"Listen, sistah, nothing can kill the two of us!"

Yoki laughed. "I suppose you are right. Ready?"

"Aim!"

"Fire!

A bajillion watts pulsed into the ionosphere. Frequency waves reverberated back to Earth. Oscillating energy pulsated thousands of billions of times per second, at speeds too incomprehensible to see or even calculate. A vortex portal swirled, settled, and swallowed the girls up.

With a zap of lightening, they were gone.

Nero stepped out from the shadow of the large pyramid and fell to his knees.

"So young, Triton forgive me, please save them."

Chapter 34

Water swirled in oppositional poles. Frozen crystals melted and froze again. Curtains of sleet encompassed the invisible globe within which Verdandi and Yoki stood. Or floated. Or soared. Travelled, without movement.

Snow filled the globe, covering the girls in goosebumps and ice. Cracks of lightening burst through frozen water and shattered legions of hydrogen particles and oxygen.

Breath blew from the teenagers' mouths. The heat of their souls melted the crystals upon their lips. Hand in hand, naked, they trudged through swirling snow. Wind blew in circles. Hail twisted in leviathan forms, gushing foaming fountains into fleeing swarths of salt.

Yoki pulled Verdandi close to her body, feeling not her flesh but her desire for safety. She could not let her young friend die in the cold.

Verdandi buried her head in her Yoki's embrace. Their nakedness drew them together in their sameness. As she was protected, so would she fight. She held her grasp but raised her face to the wind.

The swirling cyclone slowed its pace. The girls felt the soles of their feet scrape sand as heat rose up from their toes to their tailbones. Before them, the sea steamed in hues of purple and red. They separated and knelt. Bile pushed from their stomachs through their noses.

Distant Victrolas spun soundless stanzas. Verdandi stood and pulled Yoki up with her. "Do you ever think to yourself, what if I really am crazy?"

Frenzied laughter shot through them. How many times had they joked about their combined lunacy. Their abnormal desires for ineffective freedom. Their individual efforts of liberty. To think in perhaps not unique, yet personal ways. Their own thoughts. Giggling together. Yoki threw her head back in a brazen howl.

Then she saw Verdandi's face. Pale and blank like a new moon. Constellations with no story fading across her rising cheeks. Sapphire blue eyes like dead stars; empty holes wherein light once shone.

The strike of love smacked Verdandi upside her head.

"Thank you."

"Anytime."

Long arms stretched from timeless waters and grabbed the teens by their ankles. Pulled into the murky brine, they succumbed to death.

Chapter 35

The two girls were pulled backward through thick water. Their open mouths took in no air as their wide eyes stared down at shadows of themselves shivering on the ocean floor. Then the pulling stopped, and they rose from their fallen deflections. "I have never held my breath that long," said Verdandi.

"We were not holding our breath. Feel." Yoki brought Verdandi's hand to her chest. "We are not breathing now."

"And we are not wet." Verdandi repinned her bangs. "Whatever light is upon us must have dried us."

"Whilst we remain underwater?"

Verdandi shrugged.

"What is that light?" Yoki shaded her eyes with her hands. "By Triton, it is the sun and moon!"

Dark swirling sand curved up and around the girls, so that the light shining through the particles appeared as bursts of brimming stars. A path cleared before them on the rocky ocean floor, and arm in arm, they felt compelled to follow it.

Higher and higher the path sloped, until it reached a moving staircase. The girls gingerly placed their feet upon it and were whisked to the roof of a long, square, tower. The change in pressure squeezed their ears from within.

Through mazes of chairs, beds, and tables they maneuvered, unknowing of their goal but sensing they would reach it if they kept going. Room to room they passed, and then people appeared, ghostlike, reclining in various fashions of rest.

One figure approached them. A man? No, not quite a man, more like an almost-man, closer to their age. His skin shone white against the black of his tuxedo, and his tall brimmed hat cast a shadow over his face. His lanky arms hung down straight, and his gloved hands flitted like doves desperate for escape.

Yoki guided Verdandi through another room to circumvent the ghostly character, but he had somehow also circled around another way so that he was still walking towards them. Yoki stepped in front of Verdandi, squishing her against an oak armoire, to shield her as the gent approached. She held one hand up ready to grab, and one fist up ready to punch. The gangly boy passed by her without having to scuttle sideways in the narrow maze. Keeping his head down, he placed a piece of paper upon her fist, and disappeared into the previous room.

Yoki held the paper and showed Verdandi. At first they thought it was a paper doll. A garish queen with a sharply pointed crown. Then the hinges of the doll's joints began to move, and the queen transformed into a gruesome beast; a dragon with gold jaws and blood flecked claws.

Yoki held the animatronic paper doll ahead of her as she and Verdandi approached another set of stairs.

Their way was blocked by a lithe young woman with golden braids. She was juggling iridescent globes.

"Beware what you bear beyond the stair." The glass balls dropped and did not shatter; instead they rolled between Verdandi's feet.

The woman took the paper monster from Yoki's fingers, and her green eyes gleamed in triumph. From behind her ear, she retrieved a beveled knife. Carefully, intricately, murderously, she chamfered the edge of the paper beast's right eye. With a hiss, the black pupil popped out, and rolled alongside the orbs at Verdandi's feet. The paper creature writhed and transformed back into the form of a queen.

Red ink dotted the blonde woman's arms. She smiled in satisfaction and jumped upon a low table, bowed gallantly, and leapt from chair back to arm rail across the room, in the same direction the strange boy had disappeared to.

Verdandi and Yoki joined hands again, lunged over the orbs, and took their first step up. The wooden plank shifted, and they fell, holding onto nothing but each other, into a wet abyss.

Chapter 36

Blue armour clanked against polished wood. Yoki opened her mouth to scream but no sound came out. Water entered her lungs and she coughed without air. She discovered that if she took quick, shallow gasps, she could breathe. Her hands grasped Verdandi's, but her friend was floating limply in the water. Where was the surface?

"You are here, and you are safe." The voice was soft and strong at the same time, like shark skin.

Yoki felt pressure lift from her body as Verdandi stood, her shoulders steadied by the woman with calming words.

Her build was slight; petite. Her shimmering armour reflected cyan sky. High noontime sunshine crowned her short black hair, and fringed the spiky edges with silver.

The woman's armour was as fabric, tightly woven to her frame. Every nuance of muscle showed, from dimpled shoulders to round biceps; curved lats and rows of abs;

buttocks like cement bowls and legs like tree trunks.

It was her eyes that struck Yoki the most. She remembered them. The dark warmth of smoky coal. "Who are you?" Yoki's lips trembled with the question and the answer she already knew.

The woman lifted her blistered hands to the young woman's face. "Yoki-sama," she said tenderly. "You know who I am. I have seen you every day, in the outer dreams of my mind. I have never forgotten you, and have always loved you."

"Mami?"

"Yes, my little fish. You have found me."

Chapter 37

Verdandi stood on thick red bricks. Her hair
was dry and warm. She reached her arm
around her body, tracing every curve and
jut, assuring herself she was unharmed. She
was barely cognizant of close yet distant
conversation: Yoki speaking at length to an
older, stronger version of herself.

Yoki held out her open palm, entranced
by the hologram the woman had placed
there. "What does this mean, Mami?"
Tears streamed down her face in
convolutions of grief, joy, and mystification.

"This is what you need to go back.
You will find me again, my sweet, strong
anemone."

"All I see is a spinning triangle." The
lightening-bright edges of the three
dimensional shape emitted heat as the figure
floated and turned.

The woman cupped her hands around
Yoki's, and the image glowed brighter in the
procured shadow. "You are witnessing the
trilogy of words, and of worlds. What we
speak, what we feel, what we dream,

happens. Who we love, who we help, who we join, becomes. As the trinity binds unendingly: solid, liquid, gas. As our blood and hearts fill with hydrogen and oxygen: ice, water, steam. We are each and all connected through the sacred triangle. Time."

Yoki's tears flowed in rivers and burnt her skin. Yet the pain was in her spirit, not her body. "Mami, I have missed you, I know you didn't want to hurt me. I think you want to be with me. But I am in a different life! How do I get to you?" She sobbed now, and her mother's hands clasped hers, encompassing the hologram in darkness.

Tears turned to mist turned to ice. The woman reached out to Verdandi and joined her hand to Yoki's. Where the sun had struck the highest point of everlasting noon hovered a smaller, darker circle; a full moon. Voices trumpeted through rising fog.

"Decade plus one has passed in your sight, yet to me the past is as yesterday. Watches click fast seconds throughout the night, yet each morning begins the same way. Without you, yet with you. That will never change."

"Don't hurt me again!"

Yoki's mother removed her hands from the tangle of fingers. She breathed an icy mist upon the cavern within, circling the pyramid hologram.

Yoki and Verdandi stood, riveted by the swirl of colours within their joint grasp. Yoki broke her reverie to meet her fading mother's eyes. "Mami! I want to be with you!"

Prisms burst from the enclosed pyramid. Winds swirled in tiny tornadoes.

"You will find me again, my ocean gem. What has been is what will be, and what has been done is what will be done, and there is nothing new under the sun."

Yoki and Verdandi stood nose to nose, forehead to forehead. Their breaths joined in crystals that fell like snow upon tumbling corners.

Time spun about them in flurries of sugary sand and snowflakes duplicated in crowns of replicated chains. The girls saw each other as snow queens: not at the edge of spring with glowing daffodils, but in the midst of winter's bowels.

Chapter 38

"You could not ask for an uglier storm."

"It's gotta be four, maybe six inches, blowing all over the place."

Bashelle grabbed Martina's hips and twirled them toward her. "Then why are we out here?"

Martina looked out into the night. "Because somewhere, somehow, I feel her calling to me."

Chapter 39

Verdandi pulled Yoki's waist as they climbed a frozen waterfall. Reaching the island's solid surface, they knelt and shivered together.

Their words were obscured by ravenous wind. Yoki pointed, and in desperation, pulled the crystals entwined in her friend's hair.

At the enclosure between the surface and the underworld, they encountered impermeable layers of ice. Verdandi thought that she might die, and willingly; the cold upon her bare skin was overwhelming her sense of life.

For the first time, Yoki panicked. The islands were iced in, trapping her and her best friend above water!

Verdandi clung to Yoki. Coldness was her deepest pain, and Yoki seemed to emanate warmth. Yoki stroked her hair. "Current is courage in water. If we stick together, we can overcome this." Verdandi shivered.

Beneath the cloudy ice sparked metal anvils of hammerheads. Yoki nudged Verdandi. "I know this talent of yours. Look and speak. Construct our refuge and salvation."

Verdandi forced her eyes open and concentrated on the ambiguous minds of the mechanized sharks. A comet flurried across the sky, and rolls of frozen salt burst open to the sea beneath.

Yoki realized too late this was not time travel, but falling under ice.

Verdandi thanked the sharks for shattering their boundary. Trapped or not, it was better to suffer by choice than to be victimized by circumstances beyond personal control.

The girls hitched a ride upon a giant seahorse and climbed into their air dock. Without taking a moment to rest, they continued on, crawling through dark tunnels.

From Verdandi's wardrobe, the girls grabbed long cotton nightgowns. They huddled together in Verdandi's bed. Yoki pulled the white sheets up over her ears.

"We made it."

Verdandi closed her eyes and smiled. "What an adventure!"

Dawn broke with rainbows of ice upon Subton.

Chapter 40

Frosty windows cleared with the current of tropical water. Nero entered the tower prison.

"What is this, a slumber party?"

The girls giggled, entwined in the twin bed. Time had slowed, but only for them. Nero could not figure out how they had returned without notice. His worry assuaged, anger took its place. Unable to prove wrongdoing without incriminating himself, Nero resorted to ordering his underling.

"Yoki, arise at once." The captain's voice was clear and commanding. Yoki did not hesitate to jump out of bed and stand at attention.

Nero eyed her up and down in dismay. "Common clothing does not suit you. Neither does your conduct. It is unbecoming of an officer. Perhaps you need to spend more time in BSDINK studies and less time on your supervisory duties."

"Yes, Captain."

"I will integrate private tutoring into your schedule. Starting today. Immediately. With me. You are dismissed to change into appropriate approved attire. Meet me in the DRAKE library nine minutes hence."

Yoki bowed, and risked a fleeting glance at Verdandi.

"Now!"

"Aye-aye." Yoki slid through the prison's seal.

"As for you, tadpole, I will see to it that your apparent loneliness is combated by more personal around the clock attention. With your would-be warden otherwise occupied, you can expect lock-bots and survey-trons to be your constant companions. Furthermore," he scanned the untidy room of scattered piles of paper and mounds of damp towels, "you could benefit from some schooling, yourself. That is one thing Yoki has been right about."

Verdandi's mask of indifference betrayed for only a moment her surprise. What had Yoki been telling Nero about her?

As Nero left, a royal blue hoverbot floated in. Its fishlike eyes beamed red lasers across the room, and Verdandi squinted as the light passed over her. "Make haste in befriending your new care provider," said Nero. The door slid shut, leaving Verdandi and the hoverbot blinking at each other.

"What in hell's bells am I gonna do now?" Verdandi muttered.

"Hell's bells," mimicked the hoverbot in high hollow tones.

"Ugh!" The prisoner buried her face in the pillow and played word games in her mind. When she peeked up, red lasers shone into her eyes.

"Piss off!"

"Piss off, piss off," the bot echoed.

"This is gonna be a long day. I wonder how long til I go crazy."

"Crazy, crazy."

Verdandi lifted the geode lamp on her nightstand and rocketed it through the air. With a satisfying crunch, it met its mark. Verdandi reveled in her small triumph and got out of bed, inspired to start a new day.

Chapter 41

Pace trailed after Yoki on her way to meet with Nero. He caught up with her and grabbed her elbow, then hurried her behind a shifting panel.

"You went up to the surface again, didn't you?"

"Sort-of, but it was different, this time-"

"How many times must we go over this? It's like you've got periwinkles in your ears. You could've been seen by one of those imbeciles, by DRAKE!"

"They're not all imbeciles."

"They're getting in your head. I do not want to see my only niece snared by the enemy's nets."

"I'm eighteen years old. I'm a grown woman. I can make my own decisions."

"You think you're an adult, but you still have so much to learn. Especially since you cannot seem to comprehend how dangerous it is to keep sneaking to the surface like that."

"But this time-"

"Enough! No more excuses, no more chances. I never, ever, want to find out you have been even thinking about the surface. You are not ready yet, and you are breaking my trust in you."

"You suck!" Yoki raced off to meet Nero's appointment, wondering with each step how Pace had found out about her latest escapade.

Still within the walls, Pace spoke. "Do you think I was too hard on her?"

Martina crept out from the shadows, both embarrassed and impressed that Pace had caught her spying. "Naw, you weren't hard on her at all. She needs to remember what respect is. If she were my ward, I'd turn her right around and show her who was the boss."

"You could be right."

"Of course I'm right. That girl wants to be all high and mighty just because of her age? Then she runs her mouth and runs off? I don't think so, no way. That dung wouldn't happen on my watch. She needs to tether that attitude of hers to an anchor."

Pace rubbed the top of his sleek head in thought. "Hmm...she needs a set of eyes on her all the time."

"Constant supervision," Martina nodded.

"And you are just the tracker for the job."

"Huh?"

Pace bowed deeply. "If it would please you, Watch City Ambassador, Martina the Honourable, to serve your comrades in this way, Subton, and most especially I, would be humbly grateful."

"Alright already. Let's go talk out the logistics over a pint."

"I'll show you a shortcut to the pub."

"You're finally making some sense."

Chapter 42

Yoki stepped out of the DRAKE library and paused as the door closed behind her. Tears threatened her countenance, so she tilted her head back and refused to cry. She slipped guide goggles over her head and repeated the code Nero had just taught her. "25, 86, 3327." Ultraviolet light diminished her view yet clearly mapped the way ahead of her with lines and angles visible only to her. In this way she maneuvered the intricate passages to the pharmacea and reported to her new job.

Sea willow branches and guarea seeds were compounded and mixed with juice of the poppy. Yoki was performing the mission of DRAKE that she most despised: making the elixir used to control the BSDINK. The sticky tincture muddled minds and rinsed brains. Each day, the BSDINK lined up to receive their cash bonuses and to accept their injections. A long, thin syringe pushed the drug into each compass clock embedded in the young soldiers' ears.

Today, Yoki had lost her privilege. Today, she had lost her freedom. She could still feel the sting of the first injection. She could feel her will slipping away.

Verdandi perched on a chair and stared out the porthole. "I am bored out of my mind."

"Bored out of my mind," repeated the newest hoverbot.

"Please, stop talking to me."

"Talking to me."

"Hmm...I just got a bright idea."

"Bright idea, bright idea."

Verdandi lifted the chair, and before the bot could swerve away, she swung, smashing it to the floor. She rummaged through the broken blinking pieces and dissected the innards. "Interesting."

A weak metallic voice whined, "Sting, sting, sting."

Three days and four bots later, Yoki slipped into Verdandi's cell. "Let's play If Today was your Last Day. Except for real!"

Verdandi leaped up from the glass floor where she had been counting fish. "One more adventure?"

"The most epic one yet." Yoki pulled a thin sliver of silver fabric from her pocket. She placed it over her eyes and tied long ribbons behind her head. "Tonight, we are gonna party like it's 1899!"

The two girls disarmed the bots and trons overseeing Verdandi.

"I can barely believe we are doing this!" Verdandi adjusted the seashell corset around her waist.

Yoki pointed. "I can't believe you have bubbies now!"

"Don't be jealous," teased Verdandi.

"Not at all. No wonder you're so clumsy: those things are knocking you off balance!"

Continuing with extra caution to elude any lingering wardens, the masked teens crept to their air pocket. Tonight was the Lunar Event, and they were determined to enjoy every seeping second of it.

In their mermaid tails to complete their costumes, they slid out into the sea. Floating lanterns, mirrored torches, and magnificent streams of light from the glass-walled ballroom created a shining spectacle the likes of which the girls had never seen before. Yoki saw the glow of joy on Verdandi's face and her own sprits lifted.

The little mermaids swam closer to the ballroom to peek at the fantastical costumes.

"It is breathtaking, all of it. Yet how is it that the Mutineers and DRAKE are celebrating together?"

Yoki explained. "During the yearly Lunar Event the two parts of Subton mingle like two jet streams meeting."

"Whoah, look!" A school of fish with clear, phosphorescent bodies converged upon a large lantern floating nearby.

"Light attracts light," said Yoki. The two girls watched as the light grew with each passing fish.

Geometric sculptures in the ballroom moved in time to matching ones in the Coral Cove. Verdandi marvelled at their complexity and synchronization.

In the Coral Cove, Verdandi felt more alive than she had since her abduction. She may yet be as a fish in a bowl, but at least she could swim.

"Verdandi, come see this!"

Verdandi flipped with glee towards her friend. This one night of freedom filled her heart with hope. The glow of moon-lamps illuminated her soul.

Yoki and Verdandi swirled around in awe. Subton's Watch City Tower lit up the sea with a blaze of red and blue gems. The giant compass upon the highest dome rotated within a numbered gyroscope. Its face emitted its own blue glow, illuminating the intricate design. On either side was a fish: one silver; one gold. With clockwork gears, they swam opposite each other; first away, then towards each other. They were indeed circling within their own orbits around the compass points, and meeting each other fin to fin at the completion of every minute's cycle.

Directly above the tower, a newer, larger, brighter light began to grow. The girls were soon joined by glimmering sea

creatures attracted to the moon.   They
created a circle, surrounding the moon
through the placid waters.

"It's astounding. Time is fleeting."

"Not for very much longer," said Yoki.
"Tonight, we get to keep control." She
motioned for Verdandi to follow her to the
gyroscope. There, she unlocked a small
metal box and pulled out the gear from their
experiments.

"How did you do that?"

"What, fit all this stuff in one box?
Haven't you ever heard of static time?"

"I mean how did you get it here?"

"I'm just a darn good planner I guess,
with a flair for hide and seek."

"Pissah!"

"I'll take your word for it. Now here,
grab this end and I will swim up and latch it
to the compass."

Verdandi fumbled with the rods and
lines. "Now to your left," she directed.
"And loop it to the right."

Yoki seamlessly configured the
magnets to the automatrons.

"Clockwise here!" Verdandi called out. "Counterclockwise there! A mirror image on both sides encased in glass. Be mindful of the numbers: each ring is etched from one to twelve."

Yoki completed the setup and rejoined her friend. "Now what?"

"You take that end and I'll take this end, and when the fish meet at the minute, we will connect our circuits to the switch on the automation."

"Why is your voice so much clearer now?"

"I think it may be from the flux pattern. It makes a magnet. It's connecting sounds and clarifying them with anticytones."

"Again, I'll take your word for it."

"Ready?"

"Set!"

"GO!" The two girls shouted together and connected their circuits through the switch. Verdandi pulled the switch her way, then Yoki pulled it back towards her. The moon spun around them, until it seemed that they were in the moon, encircled by twirling mini-moons.

Out of the automatron fish's mouths burst burning torches. Sparks of fire leaped forth through their gills.

Yoki's hair blew wildly around her. "Are we going forward or backward?"

"I don't know! Just hold on to the switch!"

The twelve tiny moons burst one by one, and the ocean divided. Yoki and Verdandi were dry within the gyroscope. Their tail attachments twitched with the changed sensation of gravity. The sea yet swirled around them in a wide cyclone. Upon them shone the undiluted full moon. Clouds beyond it spun in unreasonable speeds.

"Why is the sky so fast, but we feel like we are slowing down?" Yoki was curious, not afraid.

"It must be gravity. As you get closer to the centre of the Earth, for example, the strength of gravity increases. Time runs slower for your feet than your head."

"So we are moving slower in time and the world around us is speeding up?"

"It would seem that way. But gracious, Yoki, look!"

"What is it, an airship?"

"No," breathed Verdandi. "It is a ghost."

Double glass globes connected as an hourglass sank through the hole in the sea. Its propellers stopped whirring and it landed on top of one of the tower's domes. The figure within, guiding the gears, was unmistakable in his posture and unique grace. He unscrewed the translucent circular door and stepped out expertly, lifting his top hat gallantly.

"Who is that gentleman?" asked Yoki.

"That is Hugh. He is a friend of mine. Was. He was part of my family. He's not alive anymore." Verdandi's chest swelled, remembering the awful whoops of joy she heard from the DRAKE barracks upon her arrival to Subton, when they found out Hugh had died.

"I am sorry you lost someone you love."

"Thank you. But I do not understand this. If he is dead, how can he be navigating the shattered globes? None of this makes sense."

A wind stirred and blasted Hugh with its force. The girls were unaffected, and felt not even a breeze. A satchel on Hugh's belt was pulled so that the strap completely broke. The contents within emptied out into the wild whirl. Hugh hopped back into the cockpit. Hair brushes, notebooks, shoes, and then lacy underwear slapped the glass in front of Hugh's face. It was then that Verdandi noticed twin clocks on either side of the rudder. The second hands ticked away slowly, counting minutes as hours, even as above them clouds continued to race across the sky.

In a flash, Hugh and all evidence of him disappeared. In his wake was a cold frost that quickly met the swirling walls of water. Slowly at first, and then faster, the sea churned in tighter circles, closer and closer.

Yoki shouted over the crashing waves. "Hold on tight!"

Suddenly, the cyclone slowed, until it overcame the air filled space and smoothed out into a tropical sea again. The moon yet shown in fullness, a constant in time's drama. A thin shadow swept over it, then grew larger and darker. As it became clearer, the girls realized it was not a shadow passing by the moon, but a figure lowering towards them.

Great wings spread wide, and the figure descended in slow unyielding circles. As it got closer, it was hard to believe that this was not an angel. The creature floated before them as if in midair. She reached out one hand holding a silver chain. Light reflected off of smooth metal, and Verdandi saw the being's face.

"Martina? How did you find me?"

Martina smiled fully, showing a mouthful of chipped teeth. "A little birdy told me." Verdandi did not know how to react. Was this real?

"Here, take this." She dangled the chain in front of Verdandi's eyes. At the bottom of the chain was a large circular pendant of sorts. Martina hooked the ends of the chain together and lowered it around Verdandi's head. "Keep it here,"she said, pointing to her heart. Then she soared to the moon.

The tropical current gave way to an arctic chill. The moon appeared close enough to touch. Frozen fractals rimmed the giant compass points. All at once, the gyroscope began spinning, and a bell gonged like thunder within the tower. It repeated to the count of twelve, announcing midnight to Subton, and a new day to the world.

Ziracuny smoothed out her hair. This ball was going better than she had expected. Diplomacy: what a laugh! This was her chance to size up the unfortunate enemy. Her lips pulled back in a secretive smirk as she trained her eye on each idiot in the room. A flash of red from beyond the window wall caught her eye. She lifted one finger and motioned Nero to come closer.

He leaned over and she hissed in his ear. "Missing limbs are common enough in these youth, but that hair is from one sun." She motioned towards the figure she was sure she had seen peeking in from outside, but whatever it was, had disappeared.

"I will take care of this issue, my Queen."

"Yes, you will. Lest the dragon eat your fish flesh tonight." Nero bowed and scuttled away.

Verdandi and Yoki raced breathless and giddy back to Verdandi's cell. Yoki maneuvered the lockbots and inserted the codes to open the door. They entered, still stifling their laughter. With a dual chortled gag, their sound ceased as air stuck like rocks in their throats.

Sitting upon Verdandi's white blanketed bed was Nero, in full military regalia.

"Welcome home. I've been waiting for you." He patted the bed on either side of him, inviting the young women to sit. In shock, they obeyed.

He ran his hands over the backs of their heads, twirling their hair between his cold fingers.

In a low whisper, like a wolf's warning growl, he spoke into Yoki's ear. "You owe me." She shuddered.

He tugged Verdandi's hair. "You do too, little moon flower."

He stood up and pulled on Yoki's arm, leading her to the door. Turning his head, he met Verdandi's pallid complexion, and grinned his jagged grin. "Sweet dreams!"

He and Yoki exited, and the door sealed shut behind them.

Part Three

Chapter 43

Tess leaned over a desk in Pace's den, reading and researching again.

"Come, Tess. Why not give your professor brain a break and take tea with me." Pace set a fresh pot of lotus tea upon the console. Tess stood and stretched, arching her back in a way that Pace found tempestuous.

As their cups cooled, they exchanged pleasantries in the soft candlelight. Soon, they were arm in arm, joined on the settee. Pace pulsated with muscle and iron girth wrapped around Tess's petite, lean body. Hugging him was like wearing a suit of armour.

Tess's mind fogged with the rapture of his touch. Surprisingly, it was not cold. More like being enveloped in a steam heater, saturated to the bones in warmth. Her head was supported gently by his strong metal jointed fingers while his bulging biceps pressed against her rib cage, encasing her in safety.

Her lips parted, and the air that had been caught in anticipation within her chest gushed out in surrender. His mouth caught her breath and inhaled it in a melting kiss. Her entire body burst into burning shards, along her tongue, breasts, and shaking thighs. An empty space within her abdomen filled with fire. Her toes tingled.

He pulled her even closer and her small breasts squished against the hardness of his chest. Her erect nipples sent rivulets of pleasure throughout her flesh.
She slid a bare hand over his ear, and pulled, willing him to combine indulgences with her even deeper. His smooth head was hot beneath her palm as she caressed him, beads of sweat melting in her fingers.

His hands roved over the creamy silk on her bodice and clutched the round juicy posteriors beneath her crinoline. Her inner furnace boiled over.
Their bodies grinded together like precision gears within the most intricate clockwork.

Beyond the rushing blood in her ears, Tess became aware of a steady beat. Not a pounding heart, yet something just as rhythmic. Like a metronome keeping time, click-clacking to a promised tempo.

She opened her eyes and disengaged her mouth from Pace's. Her teeth tugged on his plump lower lip as she untangled her tongue from his.

He released his grasp on her body, allowing cool air to invade the warm space between them.

The sound came closer. Tess cocked her head and turned her chin towards the doorway. A scream stuck in her throat. Two giant floating eyes approached her, glowing red in the candlelit room. Following the eyes was the perfunctory tapping, incessantly tracking the path towards the professor's face.

In momentous smoothness, she pushed back from Pace, her finger tips pressing against his barrel chest a millisecond before they dove into her belted bag. With a flourish, her delicate fingers brandished a pair of horseshoes, which she struck together. The vibration hummed in the room with such a force that Pace clamped his hands to his ears, blocking out the whingey ring.

Tess held the curved ends and clanged the horseshoes again. She pointed the ends towards the set of gleaming eyes just before they met her face. The eyes blinked in flashes of light, then rolled back into black beads of shiny onyx. For a moment, time seemed to stand still, as the blank stare hovered and the clacking ceased to silence. In slow motion, the eyes spun over upon themselves and fell with a clatter to the rosewood floor.

Pace was sprawled backwards across the settee. He looked up at Tess in alarm. She maintained her stance; arms out straight, lunging deeply with one foot behind the other, and every tendon tensed. Her lips were firmly pressed together and tiny muscles in her jaw strained.

"Tess," he begged, "please step back. Lower the, weapons, or whatever it is you are holding. I am going to stand up now."

Tess did not move her feet, but she slowly lowered the horseshoes to her sides.

Pace stood next to her and placed his hand comfortingly upon her back, but she bristled so evidently that he promptly removed it.

Together they looked at the cracked eyeballs on the floor. Black shards spread out in a semicircle beyond a small torpedo shaped scrap of metal. Nearby, a white square lay discarded.

"What is it," trembled Tess. She brought her feet together and kept her arms down, beginning to comprehend that imminent danger had passed.

Pace let out a giant sigh of relief. He bent down and retrieved the thin paper square from the floor. "My dear Professor, you have efficiently saved us from a delivery-bot. I assume this calling card is for you."

Tess's eyes focused on the paper between his thick fingers, then at his dimples, and then down at the shattered fish-shaped bot she had demolished with her magnet blasters.

She placed the blasters hastily back into her bag and took the card from Pace's fingers. Her embarrassment prevented her from meeting his eyes. He tenderly placed two fingers beneath her chin and tilted her face up to look upon him.

"I knew you were strong. I knew you were smart. Now I know how powerful and beautiful you can be in the heat of any battle." He kissed her nose then stepped back into a bow. "I will take leave of you now, madame, and allow you the privacy of your discourse. If you need me at any time, however, you know how to find me." He tapped the watch embedded in his arm cuff and stepped out of the den, closing the door softly behind him.

Chapter 44

Bashelle brushed Tess's hair. "You should go ahead and answer the calling card. Give that stank lobster a visit. You seem to have a way with him. If you must separate his whirligigs from his root and shove them up his roundmouth, so be it."

Martina took a swig from her flask. "If only we knew what Nero was thinking."

Tess sighed and mumbled, "I think I know a way."

Martina licked the last drip of her liquid lunch. Her voice was snide. "Never underestimate the effect of a pretty face."

Tess and Nero strolled along the gardens and halls in the expanse between the divided city. A boy around the age of ten passed close by.

"Ahoy, Cap!" The boy and Nero slapped palms, and the boy continued on.

"Cap?"

Nero chuckled. "Although this is not a civilized greeting to be expected from a noble leader as myself, the younger generation responds well to our familiarity."

"I see." Tess did not see, but allowed her mind to tumble a platitude of reasonable answers. She sought to progress with the diplomatic meeting, despite her desire to bludgeon his truncheon. "Could you tell me more about this particular mural?"

Nero pulled the professor close to his side, feigning detailed interest as he pointed out intricate designs.

"If you look upon this panel, you will interpret the true value of geometric patterns. Behold: A giant dragon clamps its jaws on pillars of Subton, pulling the building down while leveraging itself up from beneath the ocean floor. Leaving its former grave, it stomps on and crushes Subtonians like stepping stones. Once excavated thusly, the dragon rips bodies open, turning the sea red with blood."

Tess felt fury fill her veins. "How can you be so bold in your demeanor? You must know that were I not a lady, I would tear your eyes from their sockets?"

Nero squeezed his hand tighter on her hip. "You have done half as much to the Queen."

"I wish I were Martina, so I could both take credit for that blinding strike of fate, as well as spit in your face with expert aim."

"Calm down, little woman. I have asked to meet you with altruistic intentions."

"Then remove your hand from my body."

"As you like."

"Shall you then share with me the inferred urgency in facing me?"

"Yes, my dear. Please allow me to continue my escort of you so as not to attract undue attention."

Tess acquiesced, yet refused to acknowledge the wisdom in his action. A dozen BSDINK boys approached.

"Hallo, Cap! Squadron C harvested the remaining citrus crystals from the minor island mine this morning!"

"Well done, lad. Extra pudding for everyone tonight!"

"Huzzah!" The boys cartwheeled the rest of their way to the mess hall.

"Impressionable youths appear to be somewhat infatuated by you." Tess glanced questioningly at the man she loathed.

Nero puffed out his chest. "Indeed, I am humbled by their affections. I am a changed man, you see, Madame Professor. Only perhaps not changed, but improved; risen in virtue. As captain and leader of this young impoverished population, it is my honour to offer support and guidance. It is part of my chosen task to provide extra portions of sustenance to the orphaned and misled among my junior ranks."

"May it be so. What is your intention with me?"

"To speak plainly, my dear, I have sought you out in humility. I would like to extend my branch to you, which is to say, a peace offering."

Tess remained silent, willing him to continue.

"May I take your arm again, madame, as we stroll?"

Tess offered her hand and he kissed it wetly before entwining his arm with hers. "Thank you, sweet lady. I knew that we of the noble class could reach a plateau of understanding, courtesy, and compassion."

Tess struggled to engage in coquettish charade. Her words poured syrupily from her tight throat. "Of course, Nero. You must understand how I felt flustered upon seeing you."

He paused their promenade and drew Tess into his chest. She gagged against the scent of raw fish and cocoa leaves.

"All is copasetic, my dear." He stroked her hair and kissed the top of her head. "We can work out the nuances together, and one day, we can go on a proper stroll through the gardens, just the two of us."

Tess pulled herself back from the captain's fleshy chest. Her words were strangled. "How delightful." He beamed, and wrapped an arm around her waist as they continued their sojourn.

"If I could divulge my allusions of our combined providence, destined as we are to align ourselves like stars in Orion's Belt, bound to be joined one day as a man and woman should be-"

"Yes, please do tell me what manner of business has brought us together today."

The flush of flourishing fantasy subsided. "I have sought you out personally. Word came that an exotic beauty of finest manner had arrived beneath our shores, and I immediately felt the pull of your tides. I henceforth have summoned you, not merely because I am admittedly enchanted by your charms. Yet also because I am besotted by your brilliant brain."

"Thank you kindly." Tess was on the edge of impatience again. "How may my brain be of benefit to you?"

Nero's fingers brushed against her ribcage and she shook in repulsion. "I know my touch thrills you," he whispered. "We can enhance on that in time. At the moment, though, I seek your expertise on matters of clockwork and navigation. Magnetic forces, to be exact. I desire to incorporate those elements for the sake of progress in the sisterhood of Watch Cities. I am close to prevailing against natural and static time, and it would be the worthiest cause of humanity if you could divulge your research to me."

"I am not sure I am the right woman for the job."

"Tut-tut. No need for modesty with me, dear Tess. I am aware of the exquisite compass clock you cherish, and wish only to share knowledge with you so we can improve the way of life for those who suffer on this day and other days."

"Go on."

"I have access to particular power sources that could fuel your timepiece, and recharge all such instruments, imbued with renewable energy. If we could turn the dials of time backward and forward, we could prevent wars and enrich lives."

"You wish to make the world a better place?"

"Yes, madame, this is my fondest dream. Aligning myself with our precious, most vulnerable children has enhanced my intrinsic selfless nature."

Tess's eyesight faded briefly to white. She took a deep slow breath for the count of three. "Nero," she lilted, "how lucky would I be to assist you in this cause?"

"Brilliant!"

"Before we begin our mission together, I have a question that has been nagging my mind during this interlude."

"Ask away," said Nero. His hand crept further up her ribcage.

"Why is there a drastic lack of females among your students?"

"Simple. Girls and women are conniving creatures. They can be mice or snakes. Either way, they act on passion rather than purpose. That's why they need men to direct their emotions."

Tess brought her hand delicately to her mouth to discourage the bile in her throat from erupting. "Of course, that makes perfect sense."

The Subton Tower chimed. "I shall call for you again, my dear. Alas, I must attend to important government matters." Nero pulled both of Tess's hands to his lips and then leaned towards her face. She offered her cheek to save her lips the indignity of kissing a frog.

Tess entered the DRAKE atrium, lost in thought. Witnessing how Nero had become beloved by the younger generation, she doubted her own instincts. Maybe he has changed, she wondered, or maybe he was not so bad after all. Could he merely be a victim of circumstance and his own idiocy? Perhaps her mistrust of men in general had allowed her vision of him to become clouded with prejudice. If so, she felt ashamed.

A red glove covered her mouth. She felt a sharp jab in her backside. "Make not a sound, and come with me." Tess was kicked in the calves, dragged to a corner, and pulled through a sliding panel, out of sight to anyone in Subton.

Chapter 45

"What's this? Why are you hard? What is this protrusion?" The DRAKE soldier's evil look turned to a grimace and he pulled his hand away.

Tess reached between her legs where his hand had just been. She fingered the hard knob and pulled.

"This is my little prick." The warm blade flashed in the dark enclosure. She pressed it where the seams of the man's pants met in the middle.

His eyes turned to fear.

"This is the only blade I need in my sheath. What say you of that?"

Fear turned to fury and he reached for her throat.

"Poor choice," she snarled. With a quick thrust she inserted her sharpness deep inside the man's body. A red burst of life sprayed across her face.

She kept her hand tight, twisting it now, as blood soaked up to her elbow. The man's pants turned purple and slick.

He pushed her shoulders and slipped in his own puddle of blood.

Tess's breath caught, and she held it for a moment that mimicked eternity. Her eyes met his, now wild with panic.

She released her grip and watched him crumble, the handle disappearing into the open hole that was once the prize of his manhood.

"Now you get the point. Get the point?" When no reply came, she rummaged through her big brown bag, and politely changed her attire into something more becoming of a lady.

Chapter 46

"Your Honour, the Subton Switch upon our Subton Tower allows the transmission of power throughout the city. This series of circuitry works on a clockwork platform. All time pieces and compasses in Subton are made from the same elements as the Subton Switch. Without our pyramids, without our gems, without our algae, we will have no Subton Switch; no Subton Tower. We will have no power."

Ziracuny traced the lace covering her right eye. "What need have you of power? You are merely a DRAKE soldier. I do not need to be schooled by a trencher."

"Next issue," said Nero, reading from the council's log. "Implementation of Mutineer Humanitarianism."

Across the long table, a medallioned officer stood. "I will speak to that. Our census has been officiated and completed. Numbers show an unlikely support of ceasing progress of our Humanitarian Huts."

"Support is unnecessary. Is the ruling being implemented?" Ziracuny leaned back in her massive leather chair.

"Indeed. My squadron is collecting Mutineers, in a very humane way, a very good way. In the end they will be happy because they want to obey the law. By the way, I care not for what they support. It does not sound nice, but not everything is nice."

"Well said. Next."

Nero checked the list again. "Fair Trade Agreement."

All were silent.

Ziracuny saw the shifted glances of the DRAKE leaders. "Is there no report?"

Nero rose. "If I may, Your Honour, I could address this pressing issue. You see, erm, it has come to my attention that, the last shipment of goods from our Watch City Alliance will be, indeed for the meantime, the last."

"You mean, the other cities are boycotting us?"

"In a manner of speaking, Your Honour, yes. When our plan of polluting the water in Waltham so that our city Subton would be safer source of clean fish was successfully carried out, our trade thrived. However, now that communication has leaked following the Rat Rebellion, both Waltham and Gustover are refusing any commerce pertaining to Subton."

"The arrogant indecency of shortsighted leaders must be dealt with accordingly."

"I agree, Your Honour, that a solution must be sought. As devoted Captain of Subton and DRAKE, I must caution you that trivial matters could be our undoing. The older officers among us will remember this saying from our childhoods: don't poke the porcupine fish." A ripple of nostalgic guffaws spread through the room. Encouraged, Nero added, "When small holes aren't fixed, then are big holes deep sixed."

Ziracuny rapped her fingertips on the tabletop. "Water flows in only to flow out." The men ceased laughing. "If you cannot fall in, you will fall out. Once you are out, you are OUT."

Nero sipped lemon water before going on. "I think we can agree that all present wish to remain present. It is understood that the older generation could not survive with their oppositional science. The remaining scientists have since seen the light, and have chosen to become part of the future legacy of DRAKE. With these positive changes of progress and correct thinking, parts of the population have become sluggishly jaded, even among the DRAKE citizens. Numbers and divisions of provisions have dwindled, and our cause is becoming less popular."

Ziracuny waved her hand dismissively. "Math, measurements, menial means... Everything ends. Hunger. Thirst. Love. But power, controlled and sustained diligently, can last forever. Eternal power. What other quest is worth living for?"

No response was uttered, so Nero quickly moved onto the next point on the agenda. "Inundation of Patriotism."

A man attired completely in red lifted his hand and addressed his colleagues. "My report concludes that all signage has been properly arrayed, not including the upgrades agreed upon at our last meeting."

"Why not," asked Ziracuny from the head of the table.

"The new flags have not been embroidered, as our workforce is focused on the drainage issue regarding the Emerald Crystal Pyramid."

Ziracuny's voice rose in volume. "There is no short supply of workers. If the Implementation of Mutineer Humanitarianism was properly carried out, this matter would not be up for discussion. Nonetheless, it must be your top priority to solve this lapse."

"Meaning, repair the Emerald Crystal Pyramid, Your Honour?"

"No, you fool! After today, you are demerited six rations."

"Yes, Your Honour."

"Do not interrupt me! Make note: follow this previous order precisely. DRAKE flags are to be displayed throughout all segments of Subton. With one small change: a big black Z where a D used to be."

A chorus of mutters flitted up and down the table. "Perhaps we could put this aforementioned ruling to a vote?"

"Why vote? I'll be absolute monarch anyway."

Nervous laughter spread around the room.

"Look at me, what's not to vote for! So let's cut to the chase. No need for a time consuming election. Here and now, boys. I am absolute monarch. Has anyone anything to say against that, you may unequivocally voice your opinion now. You have every right to stand up for what you believe."

A man with cropped grey hair stood. He cleared his throat and began. "Your Honour, I can only speak for myself, but I am certain there are others on this board who would agree with me, that although your, erm, successfulness has been, well, successful, perhaps there is another way we could promote DRAKE values without absolute monarchy."

"Well spoken. Good for you." Ziracuny nodded at him and he visibly relaxed, his fear assuaged by her words.

Then she plucked a jagged silver star from her hair and threw it. It spun through the air before lodging in the middle of his throat, splitting both jugulars wide open. Blood spurted out like water from the mouths of cherub statues.

He stood there, wide eyed, pulsating blood, before falling face first onto the long stone table. His forehead stuck with sudden force, cracking his neck back, so even when he landed with a thud to the mosaic floor, his wide eyes still looked up at the mural on the ceiling. His blood spurted up, colouring the black sea monster with red stripes.

"Anyone else have anything to say? No? Then I think we are through here." She turned to leave with Nero hobbling after her. Pausing, she turned coyly and said, "Lest I forget, after you wash this mess up, polish my star and kindly return it please. And thank you.

At that she left, in her mind, Queen of Subton.

Chapter 47

Martina adjusted the ultraviolet scopes on her goggles. From her perch above the crown moulding of the DRAKE atrium, she could see where three hallways converged. She bobbed her head as possible prey came into view.
Small groups of BSDINK consistently appeared within her field of vision, but she didn't want a boy. She wanted a man.

The Subton Tower chimed six times: DRAKE curfew. Finally, she fixed her eyes on her mark. Motionless against the pale backdrop, her trained eyes predicted the future position of her prey. Silently, she slid down the smooth thick column. She landed on the tiled floor with a clack. Damn fancy schmancy heels! She had to do it, but she hated to.

She pulled her flowing white skirts up and tucked herself into a hidden hallway. Her bare midriff was smooth with lotus lotion, and her bralette pushed her decollate to her throat. Let's get this over with, she said to herself. For Verdandi.

She stepped out from the opposing wall just as her prey pivoted around the corner. He stopped abruptly when she bent over and grabbed her ankle. "Are you in need of assistance, miss?"

The hunter rose slowly, long fingers tracing the curves of her long legs, her powerful thighs. Her shining golden curls brushed her breasts as she looked pleadingly at him with her watery green eyes. The effect on him was immediate and satisfying.

"Thank good gracious Triton you are here," she drawled. "I seem to have twisted up my ankle by wearing these spiffy new shoes. Do you like them?"

The man strode in long lengths and knelt before her. He grasped her ankle and rubbed his hands over her insoles. "I do."

Martina looked down at his muscular form, his lofty legs, his broad shoulders, his bald spot. Such a shame. It was just too easy.

With a quick jut of her leg, her knee met his jaw. He rolled to the floor.

"So don't I." She pulled her unconscious victim to the hidden pathway.

Minutes later, a gallant figure emerged. Tall, lean, athletically built. Handsomely attired in royal red with gold braided epaulets, this exquisite officer would turn any eye. Which was just Martina's intention. Fit in by standing out.

She pulled her hair back with a black ribbon and admired her reflection along the glass tunnel. She sniffed the air and followed the scent. Sweaty socks and abominable amounts of Bay Rum.

The BSDINK barracks.

She entered the lodge and all the boys stood at immediate attention.

"Parade rest!" she ordered. The boys, in various stages of undress, promptly spread their feet shoulder-width apart and clasped their hands behind their backs. She nodded approvingly. This was more fun than she had planned!

"I am Regent Master Chief of the third brigade. It has come to my attention that the extreme emotional and physical demands on a small segment of tin-brained trainees have created some disdainful situations. For example: brawling in the bunks; soapy sagas in the showers; looted linens in the laundry. You can imagine the complaints of your distraught superiors."

The boys remained silent but their red faces told all.

"Who can tell me why you, as an individual, deserve to be a BSDINK?"

A sixteen year old bare-arsed boy snapped to attention. "I am tough and highly skilled, Regent Master Chief." His eyes shifted mercifully at his comrades. "We all in your presence are equally qualified."

Martina almost melted at this exhibition of loyalty. She pulled her shoulders back more rigidly. "It has been my observation that trainees are both stubborn and stupid. Would any of you specimens care to declare otherwise?"

Newly baritone and recently cracked voices bubbled together, insisting that they were first class recruits. "We always execute our orders precisely," boomed a young gent in the back.

"Is this so?"

All the BSDINK agreed.

"I can respect that. Now you, and you," Martina pointed to the two more outspoken teens. "Come forward." They tripped over each other in their haste.

Martina snapped her fingers in the first boy's face. "I hereby order you to run headfirst into the far wall."

Looking befuddled at first, the trainee realized that he had boasted out of turn, and he had to obey the order. He pivoted and the onlookers parted like the Red Sea to clear room for him. He sprinted straight into the wall and bounced backward to the floor, dazed and confused.

Martina shook her head. The second trainee, not to be one-upped, followed suit. Naked feet slapped the floor as the entire group hustled to the front, eager to not be left out. Bouncing ballocks and swinging steeds created a kaleidoscope of young manhood. Martina could not bear it any longer. She marched out of the barracks, past the mess-hall, and into the latrine, where she rolled on the floor in gales of laughter. "Damn, stupid, ridiculous, dumb, gawd-awful, howdy-doody dinks!"

Martina gathered her composure and continued her mission. She alternately strutted and crept throughout the DRAKE compound. By the greenhouses, she spied a familiar face. She knew that girl. Yoki - Pace's niece. Why then was she wearing a BSDINK uniform, and out after curfew?

Martina discarded her own costume, and felt normalized, barefoot in her bralette and bloomers. She followed Yoki to the officers' compound. Peering behind military statues and geometric sculptures, she kept up with the lithe young lady. Yoki dialed numbered codes into boxes built in to a hallway of doors. In each box, she deposited a gleaming tube from her greenhouse harvest. Then she locked the box again.

At the final door, grandely carved with images of toothy sea beasts, she knocked. "Come in, Yoki." She spun the web of dials within each beast's jaw, and with a final twist, they simultaneously clicked. The door swung open.

"Good evening, Captain Nero. I have collected the algae-immersed juice of the poppy you requested."

"Well done, child. Now close the door and demonstrate your version of the elixir in question."

Martina did not want to believe her eyes and ears. She reached inside her bloomers and pulled a swig from her flask. Thank goodness for pockets, she thought, and she sought to clear her head with another swallow.

Martina reported back to Bashelle and Tess about her findings.

Tess paced around her friends' bedroom. "We need to clue Pace in about his niece. I think it is time to reveal our plans with him from here on. We can no longer be tight lipped."

Martina smacked Tess on the bottom. "You haven't been tightlipped in a long time."

"If loose lips sink ships, you're sunk!" Bashelle and Martina cackled together.

"Seriously!" Tess stomped her foot.

"I agree, deeply serious. There are exercises you can do for that ya know." Bashelle's hilarity caused Martina to spray ale from her mouth.

"Aw, dammit! Now the sheets are all wet."

"What else is new?"

"I have had enough for one day. I bid you both good night. We can arrange to meet with Pace on the morrow."

After quick conch conversations, the three friends met Pace in the library.

"You are right to be concerned, and I appreciate your forthcoming information. Let me alleviate you of your worry. I am aware that Yoki is spying on DRAKE and interacting with Captain Nero. This information you have shared with me about last night's transaction does puzzle me though. Please trust that I will speak to my niece about it without revealing my source."

"Thank you," said Martina.

He lowered his voice to a whisper. "As for your missing child, I will assist you in her rescue in every way I can. I recognize the strength of your teamwork, and the unique talents you each possess that bind you together in a formidable force. I must caution you: someone is always watching. With one eye," he pointed first to his own eye and then his bionic one, "or two, or none." He gestured to the gruesome face of a bookend in the shape of a sea monster.

Chapter 48

Nero crept up behind Yoki as she listened to Verdandi wailing through the sound mirror tubes. "Yoki."

Her heart jumped to her throat as she hopped to her feet.

"It will be worse for Verdandi if you do not cooperate."

"I understand, Captain."

"Good."

"Yet I would ask you to reflect: if she had my personal attention again, she would be a better prisoner. Surely your plans for her would be smoother were she not constantly blubbering."

Nero took a moment to sort his thoughts. He needed Verdandi because of her horology experience and her expertise with a compass. If he was to win the role of his queen's king, it was imperative that he solve her time travel quest. Verdandi was the missing piece in his puzzle.

His charade as a caring leader to his young troops was complicated. He absorbed their loyalty, yet took advantage of their innocence, and need for approval. Training them to recruit Mutineers with tastes of the poppy helped them rise in rank, and gave him an easy way to grow his juvenile navy. A promising young Seaman Apprentice had conceived enticing Mutineers to join BSDINK with poppy parties. The recruits sought DRAKE without DRAKE having to seek them.

From there they became a cultish gang of a family, and continued to be controlled with the drug. Compass watches were imbedded into their ears to tick and count down to when their next dose would be. It was incessantly on their minds. The watches were given as awards upon joining BSDINK and were used to increase anxiety for the drug with the continuous ticking reminding them of the drug even when they didn't physically crave it. It also made it easier for the Dosage Squadron to identify them and keep tabs on them. By offering camaraderie and friendship by way of shared poultices, the younger generation was deeper into Nero's hierarchy.

"Because I am egregiously charitable and treasure familial bonds, I shall allow you, with your wits and attrition, to retain your post as warden for our most important prisoner, erm, highly esteemed guest. But only if you have attended your chores and the tasks incurred to you have been completed, and there is no other duty rightfully dominating your time."

"Thank you Uncle Nero!" Yoki raised her arms for embrace and abruptly dropped them, sensing instantly the stalwart lack of reciprocation. "I will not disappoint this duty to our nation." She saluted and pivoted to the door, simultaneously sweating in fear and crying in hope. Nero pressed buttons on his newly designed radio remote control, and the latches to the prison opened anew, with sparks and shuddering walls. Yoki entered, saw her friend genuflecting before the porthole, and smothered her in kisses.

"I am drowning in desolation, succumbing to solitary life. Forgetting hunger for grass and sky; wind and snow, crunched leaves and crashed clouds."

Yoki sat next to Verdandi on the bed and wrapped her right arm across her back to her shoulder. She looked down at her lap, listening.

"When I get out of bed, I am stepping in recognition of a humdrum stationary life. Beneath my feet I watch the lonesome eel weave past, and I am dazed, recalling younger days' mass outcry." Yoki squeezed her shoulder and pulled herself closer so they were hip to hip, their warmth of friendship kindling the fire of Verdandi's feelings.

"Look!" Verdandi pointed at a waving manta. "Finned and slow. Followed by bunched weaves and clashed crowds of bright blue swimming gems."

"You have a beautiful way of describing things, Verdandi."

"Maybe my sadness allows me to see the beauty which I so oft took for granted."

The door slid open and Yoki hopped up from the bed. Nero smiled, his cheeks quivering like mud beneath a twisting current. He imagined his countenance to be friendly. Yoki shuddered.

"How magnificent to see you girls have become fast friends. Yet I must interrupt your moment to remind Yoki that it is time for her to attend her DRAKE training." He took Yoki's spot next to Verdandi.

Yoki reluctantly stepped to the door and turned. She hesitated, trying to catch Verdandi's eye, willing her to be safe and cognizant of the danger in her bed.

"Go ahead now," said Nero, "you don't want to miss the hot seaberry tea!"

Yoki left and the door slid back on its own.

Nero tolerated the innocent friendship between his niece and his captive. When all was said and done, it was all the same anyway. Smelling their scent through olfactory patches on the bed, watching them through spybots, hearing them through sound mirrors and hidden intricacies of dials between conch shells, he did not need to witness what was evident; they were both foolhardy females. As most of that gender were, if not all. Ziracuny, Her Highness, may she have mercy on him; even she was lesser-than. She simply was too involved with her own ego to notice. He recriminated his desire for power.

Maybe if Verdandi possessed the time travel accessibility that Ziracuny claimed she did, he could get to her first and reclaim Subton for Subton. Subtonians could be free. All happy seahorseshit.

Sometimes he caught himself caring about the ruddy brat. Then he reminded himself: she could be the key to his future.

So he forced his friendship upon the prisoner. Her horology background and experience with a compass revealed her knowledge of magnetic forces.
It was his personal and professional mission to lure the secrets from her throat. No matter what the cost.

Chapter 49

Nero chummily put his arm around a newly reformed Mutineer and introduced him in the mess hall. He was welcomed with waves of applause and cheers. Nero hollered above the hoopla: "Blancmange breakfast for everyone!" The BSDINK went wild with celebration and crowded around their new comrade. They lifted him up to surf the crowd. The boy had never smiled so broadly in his life.

"Starting my day in Shit Creek, without any decent coffee." Martina sludged through a refuse pipe and mumbled to herself. "If you wanna do shit, ya gotta go through shit, so now get this shit over with." Her newly designed sharkskin apron protected her body from the worst of the muck, and concealed her weapons. Pace had gladly supplied her with straight shears, tweezers, jacks; common tools of her glassblowing trade.

Finally, she reached the end of the line, and carefully stepped out of her galoshes.

She had tracked Yoki well enough to discern where she was, although she was in a subterranean subsea level. She shook her head and took a gulp from her flask to clear her mind.

Following clues on walls of mosaic, she found her way. The chilly chambre was decorated with dead sea creatures; a trophy room of sorts. Flanking a walrus tusk armchair was a seal's flipper holding a harpoon, and the matching appendage securing a hatchet. Floppy footsteps approached. Martina dashed across a floor of rich red rugs, and rolled beneath a long sturdy desk.

Ziracuny entered first and sat upon the large toothy chair. She sniffed the air, then Nero entered with a BSDINK prisoner.

"Ah, that's the nasty slurry I smelled." Nero was not sure if she meant him or the cuffed young man.

She turned to the bound trainee. "You are hereby accused of treason. Relaying military information to the Mutineers. Urging your fellow officers to follow you into rebellion. What have you to say for yourself?"

Nero pulled the gag from the man's mouth. "Your foresight is an impediment. You speak only of what will be, what you will accomplish, how you will prosper. What good is your glorified future if the present suffers for Subton?"

Ziracuny rose and hissed in his ear. "It is not my job to educate you. If your nursemaids died before their milk dried, that is your poverty, not mine." She trailed her silver-clawed fingertips along his jawline, then tore his throat open.

Martina heard the gurgle of death, and felt trapped within her own body. Should she avenge the murder? Or keep spying? She felt confident in her combat abilities; she had proven herself before. Yet, if she attacked, even if she was successful, it would not stop DRAKE's hold on Subton. Indeed, her immediate action could serve only to instigate a war that she was not sure could be won. Nanoseconds of flashing images ignited her fight-or-flight reactions. She used all her self-control to follow neither of them, and instead remained still. Gathering information, prepared to kill, but not ready to unleash a red army upon her friends.

Nero trembled. This horror was beyond his repertoire. "Was there nothing else that could be done?"

"Unless an idiot dies, he won't be cured." Her eyes shone in triumph. "I lust the taste of life!" Blood dripped from her teeth and landed like scarlet tears upon her bare breasts. "They are not of this world anyway; they are subhuman imposters good only for servitude."

"My Queen, are you not of Subton?"

She brutally thrashed him with the blunt end of the hatchet. "I am of no world but my own, and the world will all be mine!" She dropped the hatchet to the floor, and Nero dropped next to it. "I am destined to rule the world: past, present, and future. A queen for all ages. This is why that fiery little horologist is so vital."

Nero pulled himself to his knees and clutched his swelling head. "What is so special about Verdandi?"

"She is bait to ensnare the infidels, of course! Her pretty little head holds the key to time travel that I need in order to command all the Watch Cities."

"My Queen, you do realize the infidels are already among us, and no doubt wish to retrieve the girl."

"The matron whale can hear her calf's cries through leagues of choppy seas. And so, I will let this calf suckle, until her mama finds my milk."

Nero wobbled to his feet. "I see: why go to enemy territory when you can have home advantage."

"One who wades after two fish won't catch even one."

"Understood, and quite brilliant."

"My point, for your personal consideration, is to leave that conniving professor to me. Stop trying to seduce her."

Nero focused his dizzy eyes on Ziracuny in mock surprise.

"Do you think I do not see? With one eye I see all! This is my empire. Of course I know all that is going on. Omniscience is my gift from adapting to the idiocy of mere human half brains like you."

"I apologize for my mislaid attempt at forging paths for your empire. All words I speak are for your purpose."

Ziracuny gestured to the seal flippers. "There is naught sense in barking if you have nothing to say."

Subton Tower chimed six times. The official wake-up call for Subton. "On your way then. The BSDINK crew are not going to piss their pants by themselves."

Martina trudged back in the semidarkness of early morning and morbidity. By the time she stumbled into bed next to a waking Bashelle, she had consumed the two nips of absinthe lodged in her pockets.

"Look at what the catfish dragged in." Bashelle turned over to face the wall. She was finding it harder to trust her mate. Staggering into bed, with no grace or litheness, no soft tiptoed soundless leaps; this was not the woman she had fallen in love with.

Martina stared at the spinning ceiling. When she closed her eyes, she was haunted by her own thoughts. Could she have saved him? What if? Then what?

Chapter 50

"If she will not take it willingly, it is your job to force her to!"

"No, Uncle! Captain! Please!"

Nero and Yoki shouted at each other as Verdandi tearlessly cried beneath her sheets. Her stomach rolled in the emptiness of depression.

"You decided to risk your role as a BSDINK when you befriended your prisoner. Once removed as her guard, you persisted in treasonous actions. Despite my continual patience and lenience, you have failed to distribute appropriate dosages to young Mutineers. Thus, you have endangered our society. Now I find you delivering a strange satchel of odds and ends?"

He reached into the bag and took inventory, throwing each item one by one, so that they skipped across the floor like a thin rock on a smooth sea surface. "A sewing needle? Pliers? A cork? Scissors? A crystal bowl?" The bowl shattered into reflective fragments and Verdandi screamed.

"You fraud! What are you captain of, anyhow?"

Nero slapped Yoki soundly across her face. Verdandi screamed again. Yoki's eyes stung but she refused to cry. "You are certainly privileged, but you possess no class!"

"You foolish girl. Do you think I mean to hurt you? I am only trying to help you." He sat on the edge of the bed and pulled the blankets away from the sobbing prisoner. "If you do not inject her, I will."

He touched his flabby fingers to Verdandi's pale legs, and she shuddered in cold disgust. She pushed herself upright and wiped her wet face against a loose pillowcase. When she spoke, she felt as if her words were rocks in her throat.

"It is okay, Yoki. Do it. I'll be okay." Her lower lip trembled and she could only manage a momentary glance into her best friend's tortured eyes before tears crushed her voice. "Please, Yoki. It is okay. We will be alright. Just get it over with." She stretched out her arm.

Nero directed a floating silver tray to Yoki. She stepped to Verdandi's bedside. Her eyes filled with tears as she tightened a clamp around Verdandi's left arm above the elbow. She lifted the syringe and looked pleadingly at her friend.

Verdandi nodded.

Yoki injected the poison. Within seconds, Verdandi slumped over and landed softly upon her tangled sheets.

"Now that wasn't so bad, was it girls?"

Every three hours, for the span of six straight days, the scene repeated itself. Each dose came with less resistance. Yoki's tears fell on Verdandi's closed eyes. The redhead's voice was faint but succinct.

"It's like falling hard into a hornets' nest. The sensation of having the wind knocked out of you whilst simultaneously being stabbed by a multitude of tiny angry needles. Then later. It is not pain. You just cannot seem to catch your breath and your entire body is screaming in endless itchiness. It takes focus to remind yourself to breathe, take air in somehow, and let it slowly out. All your self control is used in the effort to not claw your skin from your flesh. That's what it feels like. All the time. I live in a continual state of self-denial. To acknowledge the pain is to feel it. I cannot effectively live with this pain. So it is sequestered to nonexistence. Only by not feeling, can I feel."

Yoki fluffed her friend's pillows and left her drooling.

Yoki waited for the empty moon, when darkness prevailed among the kelp forests. In sleek black from head to toe, she smoothly slid through silent waters. Climbing like a waving shadow, she reached the precipice of Subton Tower. Carefully, she removed the sacred crystals. She pulled a layer of the skintight fabric from her attire and pushed the jagged gems within. Their glow was barely visible through the expanded garment, but Yoki felt the weight of them immediately.

Nonetheless, she sunk purposefully to the ocean floor and in large leaps, returned to the air pocket. She reserved a minute for a deep breath, and assessed herself. She pulled the crystals from her clothing, glad to be a female human and not a male seahorse, twenty-four days in after dancing.

Through hover-bot passages, Martina kept pace, her new subatomic goggles providing her the ultimate view of the mysterious double-agent.

Chapter 51

Martina knew how to think like an animal. The need for shelter, food, safety. Predator and prey alike sought full bellies and protected pathways.

When tracking an animal, she knew the questions to ask herself. Why did the animal travel in a certain direction or take a particular route? What is the animal's mission? Animals were creatures of habit, so the ability to discern life patterns was a valuable trait for all trackers.

Hunting animals and hunting humans was no different. Martina used her touch to see. Salty fingers left grainy reminders of which doorways led to the sea. Barefoot, she could feel grains of wet sand inside recently used air portals. Wood granules swept in arcs of dust showed her where secret corridors slid behind walls. Her questions of her prey's motives were answered this way.

She found Yoki to be a meaningful target. With spectra-scopes and binocular goggles, she studied the young woman's use of codes and keys, parchments and puzzles. She followed Yoki's movements for days until she had her routine and tactics memorized.

Verdandi's whereabouts still remained a mystery. Martina sensed that Yoki would serve as an unknowing map.

Martina sloshed her way into the pub and sat next to Bashelle.

"What in the Sam Hill happened to you? Can we get a towel over here?"

A pelican shaped automaton clicked into gear and dropped a cleaning rag at Bashelle's feet. She picked it up and scuffed it through Martina's dripping tangles.

"I am so frustrated." Martina chose her ale from the button selector and a cold mug lowered from the ceiling. "I know how to find Verdandi."

"Bloomin lumen! You are astounding! So what's the problem?"

Martina looked at her miserably. "Water. Water everywhere. My eternal problem." She sipped her ale and held the chilled mug to her temples.

"How can I help?"

Martina took another gulp. "You can get me to the ocean without getting wet, without getting caught, and without puking."

Bashelle clicked her mug against hers. "We can do that!"

Pace met the couple on their way to a launch pad. Bashelle reached in her pants and whipped out a long metal lobster snare.

Pace calmly raised his arms up. "Let me assure you that I am on your side. You will certainly get caught if you continue this way because of the sound mirror tubes hidden within the murals."

"How did you find us?" Bashelle stood her ground.

"You think Martina's the only tracker around here?"

"You know?"

"Yes, of course I know. That's why you are not in chains."

Bashelle shoved her rod back down her pants and Pace lowered his arms. She looked closer and saw that the violent murals did indeed have hidden tubes. Pace pointed out where clocks and compasses had been ingrained, as motion detectors with magnetic forces. He explained.

"When the magnetic force is broken between the two magnets on either side of the narrow hallways, a mechanism goes off that propels a ball down through intricate tubing that ends at the bottom with a power surge. This sets off a ticking stopwatch so DRAKE can tell when someone has walked through. Then a clockcard tracks the time, resets the stopwatch, and a slim set of gears and pulleys maneuver the magnetic ball bearing back to the spot behind the magnet until the next time someone walks by and the magnetic link is broken."

"So in essence behind the grotesque murals lie a magnetic web of mechanized spy gear?" Bashelle was impressed.

Martina poked Pace's stomach. "Where's the key?"

"I shoved it in there."

"Don't talk dirty to me."

"How have I not noticed this before?

"This robotic air pod raft was just completed today, based on information we received from one of our operatives on the other side of Subton. He is a scientist provoked by DRAKE to invent innovative ways to build up the war industry. His creations work, but he has not implemented them. Instead he has shared his work with us Mutineers, so that we may defend ourselves or seek escape as needed." Martina's teeth clenched in guilt and grief, the sound of murder echoing in her ears.

Pace did not notice her changed countenance. "In this case, with the frequency hopping your dear Tess has been playing with, we can use the robotic craft for our stealthy mission."

"I won't get wet?"

"You will not. We however," he handed Bashelle an Anaclastic Jar Mechanism suit, "will attempt merely dampness."

"You have AJMs here?"

Pace lifted his heavy legs into his AJM suit. "We have your professor, don't we?

She thought you might be more comfortable with technology you have experience with."

"She knew about this? Our plan? She knew you'd find us?"

Pace screwed the glass bowl, and his grin was magnified. "Tess and I have been quite busy together as of late."
Martina stretched her legs in the robotic pod. "I bet you have been getting busy, no doubt." Bashelle cackled.

The trio communicated through magnetic transmitters. Pace used radio wave remote control to maneuver the robot, and Bashelle swatted curious pilot fish away from the craft's shifting gears.

Pace swept a large arm in a wide arc and pointed seventy-eight degrees North. "You were on the right track, Martina. Verdandi could not be found because her tower cell is made of photosynthetic blocks. Green enamel shades the dome so sunlight cannot pass through."

"What does that mean for us," asked Bashelle.

"The prison tower supplies the oxygen she needs, but if we attempt rescue now, she will drown."

Martina pressed her face against the dashboard of switches she did not know how to use. Pace continued.

"Further hindrance to us is the properties of the enamel. It not only blocks sunlight, but it also blocks the magnowavegraph that Tess designed to seek her."

Circumventing the tower, they returned to port, no more successful than when they had ventured out.

But now Martina knew how to stay dry.

Martina preferred hunting alone.

She "borrowed" the robotic capsule and figured out how to navigate the radio waves with radio control from within. She crunched in, her long legs squished. "I'm packed like a sardine and am beginning to smell like one. Blast it, couldn't the damn Subtonians build a vessel for humans of non-shrimp stature?"

She tilted her neck up and her breath fogged the glass. She remembered Bashelle spitting on goggles. Flung saliva dripped into her eyes.

"Dammit to Neptune!"

She peered upwards at the glass floor of Verdandi's prison. She knew she was taking a risk, but if she succeeded, it would be a risk worth taking.

First she saw shadows. Feet. An IV, the red head falling to the floor and trembling. Then stopping. Eyes open yet unseeing. Saliva drooling onto the glass. "We are each being self-digested," mused Martina. "I will help you, dearest warrior."

She pushed the mechanized levers of the swimming robot's long arms. Squeezing the grips allowed appendages to open and close like lobster claws. She rotated a dotted dial to ignite an extending heat torch to write words on the outside of the metal cell. From Verdandi's viewpoint the letters would be backwards. Martina trusted the girl's reading ability over her own. The letters, however, faded quickly because of the nature of the metal, leaving no trace.

Although she did not ignore the seriousness of her task, Martina was enjoying her new toy. The torch was a tool previously unknown to her, even as a professional glass worker. It was not simply a torch, but a plasma cutter. It was powerful and precise enough to separate the plasmatic metal by breaking magnetic attraction within the tiny pieces melded together. So as it cooled, the metal re-attracted to itself.

"What a pissah tool!" Upon returning the robotic craft, she made sure to klepto her new favourite tool in her inner vest pocket.

Tess, Martina, Bashelle and Pace devised a plan to rescue Verdandi together. Pace spoke in deep, husky whispers. "Suspicion around Verdandi's tower, where very few people are allowed, would most certainly alert the DRAKE magnetos. Artillery bots will surely be prepared."

He lead them to a better, safer way to Verdandi. Martina swiveled dials as Yoki had, and Pace shot her a questioning glance.

"What? I'm wicked smart!"

At last they had circumvented the alarms and militia. Pace stood guard while the women passed the sliding door to Verdandi's cell. Their heated rush froze when they saw their girl.

Draped sideways over a soiled bed, with greasy hair and a face covered in acne, the skinny figure lay motionless. A tube dripped liquid into her left ankle.

Tess unfroze first. She dove into the bed and pulled Verdandi's cold body to her. "Wake up! Wake up!"

Bashelle clutched at her heart. "Is she...dead?"

"No," moaned Martina, "not all the way." She pulled a dropper-bottle of acidic modafinil plasma and squirted 5ccs into the girl's nostrils.

With flailing arms, Verdandi bolted upright, pushing Tess to the floor. Her eyes were wild and crusty. From her throat came an animalistic growl.

Tess popped back up and reached out to touch her arm. "It's all right, dear one; you are safe now, we are here. We can help you. But we must make haste."

Verdandi swatted Tess away.

"Come on girl," said Bashelle sternly. "Wake up and get up. We haven't got time for sleepyheads."

Verdandi rolled herself in her sheets like a caterpillar that changed its mind.

"She can't." Martina's voice was soft and thick. "Do you not understand? She is sick. Drugged. She cannot relate to us in her lost mind."

Tess barely listened. "Come, child; tis us, your family. We are here for you darling." She approached the bed again and gingerly sat down.

Verdandi's bloodshot eyes glared at each of them. "Traitors!"

"That's it. No more games. You're coming with us." Bashelle tried to muscle her away but Verdandi flopped in her grasp like a struggling tiger shark.

"If you try to take me I will set off all the alarms, I know how, I'm not stupid, I've figured out a thing or two while being stuck in this jar with no one and no thing."

Bashelle grunted and scooped her up nonetheless, pulling the spasmodic young woman close to her chest.

Within her roll of sheets, Verdandi enacted the magnets worn as a necklace around her throat. The force pulled bolts from alarm systems.

They ran from the room still clutching Verdandi. She worked her arms free and punched whatever was within reach, mostly Bashelle's face. Pace hustled them down a short stairwell.

"You may have forgotten yourself, but we will NEVER desert you!" Tess shouted encouragement to the lost girl.

The group turned a corner and Verdandi grabbed a copper pipe. Bashelle lost balance and tripped down the remaining flight of stairs, pulling the sheet, but not Verdandi, with her. Scaling the pipe like a monkey up a tree, the pale, bony young woman beat her would-be saviours up to the top floor, crawled like a reptile to the prison door, and locked herself back in. She attached the tube of life taking liquid to her throat, sighed, and slunk to the hard glass floor.

DRAKE militia raced towards the source of the alarm. Pace blocked their way while Martina guided the remaining rescue crew through secret tunnels forgotten by the DRAKE.

They huddled together in Tess's room. "What has happened to our girl?" Tess wailed.

Martina clutched her knees in a corner and rocked back and forth. "She is not our girl any more."

Chapter 52

Yoki climbed in bed and lifted Verdandi
from the pillow. She straddled her, sitting
behind her. Verdandi laid back against her.

A tear escaped Yoki's eye and trailed
down Verdandi's red river of hair.
Verdandi took a short, halting breath, then a
longer one, letting the air out slowly, feeling
real air entering her lungs for the first time
all morning.

Yoki rubbed her hands up and down
Verdandi's upper arms. The right arm
ended above the elbow, and Verdandi had
still not been given the privilege of working
in the metal shoppe. Yoki had delighted in
hearing her friend's plans for a new arm; the
magnifying glass, telescope, and microscope
she had drafted to incorporate into it so she
could study the ocean life beneath her glass
floor. Now her friend had little ambition.
The injections had seeped it out of her. Her
soul was drained out little by little each day,
and no human spirit was infused to
counteract the emptiness it left.

Yoki could feel Verdandi's body tremble. Her lips parted to allow a small phrase to escape.

"Did I take, my elixir today?"

Yoki held her tighter, wordlessly, struck to silence by her guilt.

Days passed, and Verdandi became less coherent the more the needles pricked. Yoki missed her friend.

Verdandi moaned in half-sleep.

"What are you trying to tell me?" Yoki's voice lilted sweetly, offering soothing encouragement. "The other half of my shell, I am listening."

Verdandi used all her energy to lift her eyelids beyond halfway. She rolled her eyes up, valiantly attempting to focus her pupils upon her friend's face. Her eyes dulled with the effort.

"Go on," encouraged Yoki.

Verdandi shuddered.

Then she coughed, and Yoki heard a gurgle in her throat. She pulled her up and laid a hand on her back, pressing in as she rubbed.

"You've got this, you can do it," coaxed Yoki, furtively scanning the bed and nightstand for the petulant bowl. Finding none, she cupped her left hand and held it in front of Verdandi's mouth. Verdandi heaved, her breath hot and empty.

"Keep going, you've almost got it."

A blast of mucus shot from the young horologist's dry mouth. It sprayed Yoki in the face.

Yoki closed her eyes and felt fat globs drip down her cheeks. Her left hand still cupped, she pounded her friend's back between bony shoulder blades with the fist of her right hand. "Let it out!" Worried sweat from her forehead joined the yellow muck on her face.

Verdandi's lungs rattled once more before spouting a massive glob of green mucus and bright yellow bile tinged with bronchiole blood into Yoki's awaiting hand.

Yoki rubbed her eyes on the rough plates of her shoulder pads. The scales scraped her eyelids, and pulled just enough body fluids with them to tempt her into opening her eyes. Phlegm diluted with

perspiration and melted into her vision. She
blinked rapidly. Her back grew cold from
hot sweat beneath her armour.

"You're almost there, don't stop,
you're doing great!" Yoki stopped pounding
her friend's back, and instead used her fist to
twist into the fleshiest parts below her
armpits.

One more thin pull of air shook the
remnants of poison in her tubes, and
Verdandi spouted out streams of green
strings.

Yoki shifted her blurred eyes back and
forth in controlled panic before deciding to
dump her dripping handful of human blob
onto Verdandi's pillow. She wiped her hand
in a swift swipe upon the white sheet,
leaving behind a trail of black and green.

Verdandi's eyes were closed but she
maintained her body in an upright position
in her defecated bed. She tried to inhale but
was stopped by a warning in her throat.

"It's okay," Yoki instructed,
understanding the dilemma. Threads of
solid green hung from Verdandi's bloody
lips. "Just relax," she cooed. She ran her

fingers through her hair to erase the slime from her fingers and encourage gription.

In a light sing song voice, she spoke to Verdandi.

"Now my dear, it is going to be all right, it's almost there."

She rearranged herself on the bed so that she was straddling Verdandi's legs over the white sheet, her knees bent, her back straight. This was her position when harpooning salmon. Now though, instead of vaulting a spear, her goal was to withdraw something more deadly.

Verdandi did not speak. Her pale face bobbled upon her neck. Between the forefinger and thumb of each hand, Yoki pinched the two threads of slippery green that hung from Verdandi's mouth. She pulled. The threads gave way, and Yoki leaned back as far as she could before the armour dug into her hips.

Verdandi's head pulled forward then dropped back like a buoy in a storm. Yoki's fingers lost their grip on the sleek green poison.

Yoki ran her fingers through her hair again but it was too thick with globs of human excrement to dry her skin. She rubbed her fingers on the front of Verdandi's soft nightdress, feeling the moisture leaving the creases of her engraved DNA.

"Remember the moon that night?"

She reached up and pulled the green strands again, wrapping them around her fingers like a bobbin with embroidery thread. Short bursts of hot air escaped from Verdandi's throat.

"The moon was so full and lovely that night. The fish were so happy splashing in the brilliant pools." She continued narrating as she pulled back, harder this time, her heart pounding.

Verdandi faintly moaned. "Good," said Yoki.

The tips of Yoki's index fingers were bright purple. She spun her thoughts of pain away and pulled again. Her story became more frantically paced and the pitch of her voice rose, yet she maintained the even keel of wordy distraction.

"The moon glowed upon the inner lake and cast rainbows of streams upon the currents. Remember that?" She yanked, and urine escaped her bladder in drops. "The fish below were like tusks of narwhals. We called them moonstone fish, remember? They were white as cockle shells beached in dry sun."

She could feel the threads grow taught. The thickness had increased. She knew this was the end. She didn't know how she knew, but she knew.

"It was beautiful, Verdandi. It was so indescribably beautiful."

She fell backward on the bed as the ends of the green threads launched from Verdandi's throat.

White stones engulfed in blood were wound at the bottom of the threads. They hit Yoki in each eye. Her vision erupted in sparks of yellow and red.

Verdandi breathed in deeply and her eyes widened so round that when Yoki glanced up at the whooshing sound, she feared her friend's blue orbs would bound out upon her lap.

Verdandi's massive inhalation reached its sucking peak. There was nothing, a moment of silence. Verdandi's eyes focused and met Yoki's in tribulation. They both understood, but too late.

From Verdandi's quaint mouth burst a volcanic spew of viscous fluids in every colour, covering the bed and both girls in hot and cold and a rainbow of wrathful expectorant.

"Uh, ugh, oh," gasped Verdandi, "I'm so sorry, yuck." She gagged chunks of stomach lining and spat lazily so that yellow drool dripped down her chin. She fell back onto the pillow that was covered in squishy globs from her own body, and closed her eyes.

Yoki pulled herself to her knees, inhaled the spattering of her friend's convulsions, and exhaled a sour breath of relief. Then she fell forward, her forehead a direct hit to a particularly jelly-like blob of human juices. She pulled her right arm out from under her, and placed it over her friend's heaving stomach.

This is how Ziracuny found them.

Chapter 53

A hook and pulley attached to the ceiling drew the naked captain up by his hands until his webbed toes barely touched the floor.

Ziracuny brandished a switch of sea nettles and struck his softest flesh until it bled. "What have you to say for yourself?"

"Whatever you desire of me, I also desire, my Queen." The sea nettles struck again.

"I desire vengeance on you for poisoning my prize." The spiny heel of one golden boot pressed the lever to engage the pulley. Nero was now fully suspended, and all the flab of his body succumbed to gravity.

"Your Highness, it was easier to control her that way. She is headstrong and willful."

Framed by a mask of golden beryl, Ziracuny's eye blazed with fury. "That is the spirit I hoped to brandish and burnish, not diminish! You obtuse moron!"

This time she reached for a rope of wound seagrass, and thrashed him thoroughly. When he stopped crying out, she slowly lowered the hook until his knees touched the ground.

Her voice softened as she ruffled her short petticoats about his sweat-drenched face. The swivel of her hips provided the faintest fan of relief to Nero's misery.

"I will acquiesce the point that Verdandi is like a tiger shark that needs to be tamed." She pulled the leather belt from her thigh-breaching skirt. "Like some dogfish I know." She snapped the belt between her hands. Nero bowed his head before her. She tenderly placed her glittering shoe upon his face and reminded him who was in charge.

Chapter 54

Verdandi used remote control to steer herself across the table from Ziracuny. The motorized chair enabled her to move independently throughout DRAKE quarters, and even to tea with the leader of them all.

"Thank you for joining me. I would have understood if you declined my invitation."

"I didn't know I had a choice."

Ziracuny feigned surprise. "Of course you have a choice; you are my guest. You must believe me, I had no idea of your situation."

Verdandi lifted her head and glared, too weak to challenge the lie.

"That is, I had an inkling of your visit here in Subton, but I understood that you were free to roam the glorious halls as you wished. Ah, so many treasures to behold. From this moment forward, that is how it shall be." She looked to Nero as he placed a tray of caviar on the table. "Understood, Captain?"

"Yes, Your Honour." As he walked back to the kitchen, he patted Verdandi's head.

"Keep your hands off of her!"

Nero winced and kept walking.

Verdandi wondered why Ziracuny would care to protect her.

"Please, drink your tea. This particular pot was brewed specifically for us to share. You will find the fragrance to be lightly floral, and the steam to be soothing. Sip slowly, close your eyes, and savour the goodness of health." Ziracuny demonstrated, and for a moment, Verdandi saw her as exquisitely refined, elegant, and resplendently charming. She brought her teacup to her lips to distract herself.

She closed her eyes to her challenging thoughts and inhaled the delicate aroma before sipping. She opened her eyes in glorious surprise. The tea seemed to enter her body immediately, invigourating and calming at the same time. "Splendid!"

Ziracuny smiled at her from across the table. "Only the best for you."

When Verdandi returned to her prison, she found it had been upgraded with the finest linens, a huge canopy bed, and crystal chandeliers. She didn't mind being back in her cell; rather, she felt grateful for the improvements. Reality was a blur. She changed into a nightdress of the softest, lightest, fabric she had ever felt, and lay in plushness, willing her insides to stop itching.

"Where you run from, you will not find what you crawl toward." She awoke speaking the words of her dream. She hastened to write it on the lovely new notebook placed at her nightstand. It had been so long since she had experienced one of her visions, or premonitions, or whatever they were. Maybe that meant she was getting better?

A fresh pot of her special brew floated in on a tea tray, and she drank thirstily. She poured cup after cup, sensing strength and healing flow through her body. Whatever it was that Ziracuny had come up with, it was working! Verdandi whistled a tune and chose a violet dress from her sumptuous wardrobe.

After breakfast, Ziracuny surprised her with a workshop all her own. Long tables. Bunsen burners. Jars and jugs; plants and rocks. Tools galore.

"Thank you."

"My pleasure. You are a grown woman and deserve to have the things you desire. Is there anything else I could provide you with?"

Verdandi lifted her armless shoulder up.

"We can have you fitted immediately, with the finest artists Subton can boast of."

"To be contritely honest, I would prefer to design and create my own."

"Of course, how thoughtless of me. You will find drawing boards, chalk, and all manner of paper for your musings."

Verdandi's brain was becoming less addled now that she was no longer a slave to the endless drip. "It would be helpful if I had an assistant. My facilities are not what they were, and an extra set of hands and a sharp mind would allow me to succeed in my endeavour."

Ziracuny's lips strained in the pretense of patience. "Did you have someone in mind?"

"Yes, I think Yoki, since she and I communicate well and understand each other's methods, would be the optimal choice."

"I agree. I will activate her conch straight away."

The day wore on and Verdandi felt the sluggish call of desperation overcome her mind. The opportunities before her sucked her energy. Her thoughts turned dark and lonely. What use was any of it. She was of no use.

Ziracuny held out on summonsing the disgraced BSDINK, but finally made the call when she saw Verdandi failing to thrive. She needed the girl to be alert and upbeat. How else would she do her bidding?

When Yoki entered the workshop, Verdandi started crying. "I'm sorry, I don't know what's wrong with me. I'm just so happy to see you."

"No need to be sorry! I've missed you as well! Shall we sit and chat?" A sofa rolled out from a blank wall. A tea tray with petit-fours settled upon a low table that rose from the floor. "Whoah, this place is quite something!"

"I did not even know those things were here!" The surprise technology sparked a lighter mood in Verdandi.

Yoki was sensitive to the fact that her friend was ill, confused, and recovering. So she attempted to entice her in light conversation. Verdandi was not interested in talking about her new dress or shoes though. She pointed at the compass embedded by Yoki's ear.

"I will be as honest as I can be. Always. I do not doubt we are being listened to and otherwise spied upon, yet I will always speak the truth to you. You are deserving of that."

Verdandi placed her cake back on the tray. "Go on."

"I have been coerced into administering the poison throughout Subton. Mixing it, delivering it, injecting it." Her voice strained in shame. "I do not want to do it."

She paused again and Verdandi did not seek to interrupt her. "This compass I wear, all the BSDINK now wear. They are tracking devices, time pieces, telephonic communicators, and energy gauges. They are also how I, every morning, inject every BSDINK with poison. Right through the plasma dial."

"Do you also inject yourself?"

Yoki leaned forward to whisper in Verdandi's ear, and hesitated. "I will not lie to you. So I will not answer."

Verdandi nodded. Confusion, broken trust, and frustration took turns pounding at her heart. She reclined on the sofa and closed her eyes. Yoki moved so that she could rest her legs on her lap.

"Breathe. You do not have to talk, or think, or even listen to my words. If you want to, you can just focus on the sensation of air entering your lungs, slowly, filling your body with freshness, and then if you want to, you can focus on the relaxing sensation of the air slowly leaving, passing past your lips. Then you can breathe again, at whichever pace you desire, and can choose to focus or not to focus. You can just let your mind be free, and see the colours behind your closed eyes. Reds, oranges, yellows...and maybe...blue."

Verdandi found her voice. "I'm worried about getting my hopes up. Whenever I try, I seem to fail. When life is smooth, it crashes. It makes it hard to believe in lasting peace. I don't think I believe in the possibility of a happy life any more."

"I'm listening," whispered Yoki.

"Sometimes I hate myself. Even when I am doing good things. I wonder at my motives. It's like I don't know who I am because I play so many parts. So which is the theatre and which is reality? Am I a blur of both, neither here nor there; a no one; a ghost? Existent, but only as a dream?"

Yoki gently brushed the palms of her hands up and down Verdandi's stockinged shins.

"I don't want to die now. I just don't want to live this life. Tears and blood dripping to tile. If I could live for something I would. I wish... Naw forget it. I don't wish anything."

"What is it? What do you wish for?"

Verdandi swung her legs to the floor and sat up. "Why do you even like me?"

"When you're friends, you don't have to ask why. You just are."

Verdandi contemplated that and took a sip of the lukewarm tea. "Well now, I sure had a case of the morbs for a minute there!"

"You sure did! And that's okay. You're allowed to; we all are. But, right now, do you feel like doing something fun instead?"

"Yes! Wait until you see all our nifty new gadgets!"

Yoki was permitted, or ordered, to visit Verdandi at length each day. Ziracuny kept close tabs, and disallowed Nero from interrupting them at any time.

Yoki held up a drawing as a sample of embellishment when Verdandi's arm was near completion. "When we put a little of ourselves into our tasks, it makes the job personal, more real, and somehow beautiful."

Verdandi traced her fingers along the paper. "Now I want to make it perfect! Your art tells a story. Now that the tale is in my head I can look at the facts instead."

"You're a poet and you didn't know it."

"Pardon me?"

"But your feet show it."

Verdandi inspected her buttoned boots.

"Because they're Long-fellows!"

Verdandi dropped her chalk and tackled her friend. "You would make a stuffed bird laugh!" They tumbled to the floor alternately hugging and pinching each other.

Verdandi's health improved daily. Yoki told her, "You don't look like a sun-bleached mollusk anymore!"

"Whatever that witch put in my tea, it worked!"

Verdandi's new arm was a work in progress. Ziracuny watched appreciatively and even entered the workshop from time to time to offer sweet treats and compliments.

Now that the horologist's brain was functioning again, she would be prepared for her real job.

"Could you turn the wrench please?" Yoki followed Verdandi's directions.

"It would be," she paused and turned, "a whole lot faster," deep inhale, "with a ratchet." She pulled and tightened all the way up. "But this will do."

"It sucks working with wet wood. But Bashelle always told me, wet wood still floats. Now for avulsion...backing plate...ignition wrenches...because this piece is wood and that part is metal."

"I don't understand what you're doing, but it makes sense to me when you tell me."

"Dagnabit, why won't this stick together?"

Yoki approached the bench. "It seems to me, here you have a square inch you are working with, and you cannot use this same quarter inch washer, so..." She secured a welding helmet to her head and carried a roll of metal to the vice. Verdandi watched.

Yoki lifted the mask. New washers made cheerful pinging sounds as she dropped them to the table.

"You are a genius."

"No, you are."

"No, madame, you are."

"No, oh perfect one, you are."

"Yeah, I suppose I am!"

Ziracuny sashayed in and the girls regained a more adult composure.

"I am utterly delighted to hear joy and laughter. There have been too many dark days, and I am indubitably pleased that you women have graced me with bright ones."

Yoki tapped her imbedded compass, and the inner chimes related the time. "Much obliged, Your Honour. I must take leave now for garden duty." She turned to Verdandi. "See you on the morrow!"

As Yoki streamlined out the door, Verdandi stepped closer to Ziracuny. "Thank you for letting Yoki come be with me."

"Of course! She is a lovely woman, and I am delighted that you and she enjoy each other. I enjoy it too."

Before Ziracuny could stop her, Verdandi lunged towards her and wrapped her arm around her neck. Then she said something about getting ready for supper and left.

Ziracuny was alike a polished statue. Pure astonishment froze her body.

She could not recall a time whence she had been hugged!

That evening, Ziracuny and Verdandi shared an exceptionally lavish meal together.

"My appetite is back in full force!"

"I am thrilled that you are so ravenous." Ziracuny winced as Verdandi chose forks at random and fingers more usually.

"Mmm-mm."

Ziracuny sipped her flute of bubbled ginger. "Your appendage project appears to be coming along quite nicely."

"Yes, it sure is." Verdandi scooped a mouthful of shredded roast pork.

"I wonder if you would be interested in something new, once your arm is complete."

Verdandi nodded her head but her mouth was too full to talk.

"I have noticed you and Yoki have been playing with, or rather experimenting with, magnets."

Verdandi stopped chewing, fearing a lecture.

"Which I think is quite wonderful," Ziracuny added. Verdandi resumed chewing.

"As I am sure a woman of your obvious intelligence is aware, magnetism and tides are sisters in Subton culture. Common mechanisms are based on that relationship. Our next full moon will play a part in our newest compass design. So the Watch City of Subton will experience a rare and powerful phenomena, whereby all compass points will lead directly into each other."

"Hmm." Verdandi was only half-listening, as she was decidedly more interested in the next course of buns with sweet cream butter.

"Indeed." Ziracuny could not have hoped for a smoother progression towards her goal. "In the morn, and at your leisure, you will find a rather dull collection of ordinary materials and minerals abundant in Subton, such as iron and sulphur. I have confidence that you will thrill at exploring their properties."

"Sounds fun!"

"Wonderful. Perhaps you could investigate Subton's natural resources, and research their qualities for thermodynamics, petrology, and geochemistry."

"Wow, that would be an incredible opportunity. Thank you."

"I must admit, I am not offering this solely for your entertainment or benefit."

"Oh?"

"Once you feel you have mastered general nuances of these sciences, I would be exceptionally proud to ask if you would design our newest timepiece, the Gold Moon Compass."

Verdandi's knife scratched across her plate. "You would like me to design new technology?"

"Yes, Subtonians, such as dear Yoki, would be honoured."

"I am so tired and full, I could almost believe I am dreaming. I heartily accept. Thank you!"

Ziracuny hadn't realized until then that she had been holding her breath. "I hope you have some room beneath that corset. Savoy cake and whip sauce are our final course."

Verdandi wiped her mouth on her sleeve. "I can handle that!"

Chapter 55

Amphibious birds flew beneath the dome. Their hollow golden plumes quivered in the invisible breeze. Travelling transmitters, aware of their hunger for fish and ignorant of their use in telephony, the winged creatures intermittently circled and dove, piercing still waters with hooked beaks. Plunging to shallow depths, they sought supper. Rising back through the thin line separating liquid from gas, they tore into fish flesh, leaving scrappy scales behind for their cannibalistic prey. Yoki paused to skip rocks across the subaquatic pond.

She stopped with a gasp and looked at the greenhouse.

The poppies were swaying.

"They can't be," she thought. "I am the only one with a key."

She wouldn't investigate. She knew who it was.

The poppies kept on swaying, the red blooms swishing hypnotically, mesmerizing her eyes, her brain.

She mustn't investigate. She wouldn't.

The poppies kept swaying.

"No," she said.

Swaying, swaying, swaying.

She stood motionless, completely focused. A bird screeched behind her.

She jumped straight up and spun midair one hundred and eighty degrees. She launched the rock in her hand like a discus and struck her mark with a crack.

With a thud, Martina landed on the pebbled shore. She reached a hand to her already lumpy forehead. "What the f-"

"Following me much?" Yoki stood over her, another rock at the ready.

Martina rose and brushed the sand from her chaps. "Was that really necessary?"

"I know you have been stalking me. I do not know the extent of your spying, but I have at times, upon noticing, allowed myself to drop clues. I'm not so ignorant. I'm grown. I'm an adult. I'm not a kid, so it is not that easy to outsmart me."

"Except, you have been outsmarted."

Yoki hung her head. "Outsmarted, yes. Wait, no!" She lifted her chin. "Outwitted.

I have the smarts, I need more wits. Instead of spying on me, why don't you talk to me?"

"I suppose it is easier to watch from afar and guess. Yet now that we are in the throes of oblivion, we can speak on the same level."

"Agreed. No bending angles; our communication can be a straight line."

They sat and Yoki pulled lotus tea from her small satchel.

Martina pulled her flask.

They spoke among swishing anemones and darting clownfish.

"I know you have been scouting for Verdandi. I kept this from her, not because of malice, but because of friendship. If I told her, she would have flipped her lid, either from desperation or fear. At first, I admit, I was selfish and sought only praise from my leaders and respite in friendship. I did not want to be out of the picture."

Martina's silence unnerved Yoki and built upon her guilt.

"Secondary, Verdandi would be in trouble with DRAKE if she found out you were looking for her. I would be outed as the double agent that I unwittingly have become. At night in my bunk with over a hundred other BSDINK, I struggle through dreams of broken allegiance. I am split between so many people, so many sides. In it all, I have done my best by Verdandi. She is my friend, the sister of my heart. My intentions were always for the greater good."

Martina grew pale. Yoki's conundrum was uncomfortably familiar.

"I obviously picked the lock to the precious poppies and enacted a motorized propeller to swirl the air and distract you. Now would you care to explain, as we are speaking as allies, why only you of all the lunatic kids in Captain's Camp Cuckoo are unaffected by the pretty little jewelry you wear by your ear?"

"Firstly, I must explain, that the DRAKE mission here is to overhaul and sell mineral goods from our unique oceanic city. These goods are important to trade within Watch Cities, and are used in all manner of technology."

"Tell me something I don't know."

"DRAKE is not interested in trade. The goal is domination; a monopoly of resources. In this way, to control the ebb and flow of technology as they see fit, or rather, as Ziracuny sees fit. She seeks wealth and power beyond any government; she seeks an empire."

"Again, I ask you, tell me something I don't know. As in the answer to my question." Martina reached over and tapped the compass on Yoki's ear. "I can only assume by your general non-zeal for DRAKE and by the fact that you are speaking so openly with me about your apparent disdain for your commanding officers, that you have switched the calibration of your timepiece and do not fear the repercussions of being overheard."

"I will explain, and you will understand. I have managed to avoid becoming victimized by the poison because I have discovered an antidote. It is my job to create the poison and provide it as needed, and as wanted, to all BSDINK, and to Mutineers who may be lured to the red navy. I was forced to hook Verdandi on the controlling liquid, even as I felt myself slowly succumbing to the low doses required of me to take. I realized that the only way to save Verdandi was to save myself, before the potion clouded my judgement so thoroughly that I no longer had a mind of my own, before I could become a buzzing unthinking drone like my peers. Through experiments that Verdandi and I had conducted together, and because of the lessons I received in my childhood, and ironically, by DRAKE training, I managed to remain unaffected. Look." She turned her head and pulled her beaded braids back so Martina could inspect her other ear.

Martina peered in, and adjusted her goggles for monocular telescopic vision.

"Just as I suspected. You've got rocks in your head."

"In a manner of speaking, yes, I do. I have discovered a formula using genome strands, algae, and our holy crystals from the pyramids. When these crystals are cut and shaped precisely into thin triangular layers, and seeped with the formula, they act as an antidote to the DRAKE poison. As long as I keep it deep in my ear canal, it is effective, even as Nero insists I inject the poison into my compass chambre every day."

"Are you willing to create this antidote in larger quantities, to clear the clouded brains of your peers, and most importantly, MY friend Verdandi?"

Yoki took a final sip of her tea. "Why do you think I stole the Subton Tower crystals?"

The next day, Yoki and Pace were working on a remake of Metzmarine Steam 86, a common hobby they enjoyed sharing. Pace passed a boiler gasket to Yoki. "We missed you at Wednesday spaghetti day. Did something fun, I hope?"

Yoki remained tightlipped. "Yeah, something like that. Can you hand me the brackets?"

Chapter 56

Ziracuny's obsession with power was reaching a boiling point. Verdandi needed to hurry along with her work, but it was a delicate balance; Ziracuny still needed to endear herself to the little brat. If the young horologist knew the true purpose of her pet project, she would certainly refuse.

She had it all planned out. Place Subton in time constraints, in an endless looping day. Thus preventing the gullible groups from escaping her course of action, stunting any attempt to follow her or change their fate.

This bright morning, Ziracuny was teaching Verdandi how to play the water organ. "It is all math and measuring you see, my dear. Music is nothing short of numbers talking."

That afternoon, Ziracuny invited Verdandi to take tea with her in the DRAKE board room. Nero ran his finger down the dotted list of Ziracuny's demands. Polite conversation entwined with matters of business.

A DRAKE officer sat across Verdandi. "What have you been doing all day, young lady?"

"I have been practicing the water organ."

"Well, that is certainly useful to our cause." A few other officers snorted snidely.

Ziracuny slammed her teacup to the table, and shards of porcelain flew into the tarts. Her calm, cold voice belied her actions.

"The water organ and this woman's increasing skill with it is indeed useful, important, and valued." She poured honey into the new cup served by a floating tray. Her voice warmed with the tea.

"After all, what better accompaniment to my coronation could there be but a rousing anthem of Subton's finest musical instrument, by the most brilliant woman to grace its amphitheater?"

Verdandi began to think she had misjudged Ziracuny all along.

Coronation Day. The entire city was involved, from human to cyborg to seafolk. Creatures, salt, sand, water; all were called upon to greet their first queen.

"Huzzah for the Queen! Huzzah for Ziracuny!"

Within the new throne room (that had once been a giant infant nursery school) Nero whisked a bloody BSDINK servant out.

"Kids heal, clothes don't." Ziracuny removed her white gloves and stood gallantly for her servants to redress her.

"Absolutely, Your Highness. Yet perhaps the punishment for dripping a spot of sea-maple upon your corset was a bit harsh?"

"Your voice is taking my time away, and my time is too valuable for the wind of your breath."

"If you keep killing your supporters, you won't have any left."

"You are dreadfully mistaken. I will have more supporters, for how darest they not?"

Nero left the inner chambre and saw Verdandi practicing her music. He passed by with a whisper. "Don't trust the devil with your fins."

Ziracuny's hair shone black upon red above the cheering crowd beyond the balcony. Verdandi played the water organ in the background with an enchanting effect.

Ziracuny's voice projected strong and clear, like a song.

"Your patience with my exotic nature, as the expressions of my desires fall upon you; how I yearn to serve you despite my past. Naysayers will slander the woman before you who once was one of you. No matter how I appear, destiny led me here. From the drought to the flood; from the cliff to the cave. Freedom. Flying, diving, running. Industry; innovation. Still I sought the unseekable.

Cry out for me, Subton! My truth is your truth. Throughout the infancy of my womanhood, growing with you, grasping my fate, and the secret promise I kept for you. For those whisperers who wonder at my beauty and grace: those were bequeathed to me unassisted by any natural power. My only will was to serve you. My presence here today is a tribute to you. Long live Subton!"

The crowds cheered.

Ziracuny stepped back to swallow a flute of ginger bubbles. Nero patted her brow with silver infused cotton. "Do you think you may be overexerting yourself, Your Highness, or expecting too much of the serfs beyond your recognition?"

"Boundaries, dear Captain, are tokens of safety, breathing in the smoke of sin." Steam billowed in a crown around her head, as the towers rose in shimmering crystal behind her.

"I do not have to bring the show; I am the show!"

Nero clutched at her iridescent robes. "Wait, allow me to accompany you in your endeavours; I may yet prove myself to you!"

"Nothing makes me leave faster than asking me to stay."

She glided back to the balcony amidst ecstatic screams of worship.

Horns blew throughout Subton and delivered the message to all whom were not blessed enough to attend the euphoric spectacle. Landscapers, chefs, doctors. All listened through incessantly opened sound tubes, unclickable conch shells, pounding telegraphs, and radio wave telephony.

Verdandi was escorted to a giant nautilus carriage. A dashing young groomer with mahogany skin guided her hips up to the tiller's bench. Hands reached over to adjust her crinoline and she swatted them away.

"Hey, just trying to help!"

"Yoki!"

"Did you think I was going to let you endure this disgusting dram without me?" Blue chiffon and pink silk swathed together as the girls embraced.

"Don't let my mascara drain from my face!" Verdandi laughed as Yoki pulled a dainty kerchief from her bralette and dabbed her best friend's eyes.

"Who cares?"

The teamsters cracked the reigns of geometrically appendaged seahorses. The royal carriage paused aside the princesses' escort. Curved glass dissipated and the girls were the first to see the new queen in exquisite glory.

Ziracuny looked upon the young women. Her proud heart faltered with reminiscent memories of roses and baby's breath. Then she remembered pain and toil and darkness within unending caverns. Her eyes relit with focus on her future. Elaborately gilded dolphins pulled the queen's carriage, guarded by DRAKE officers.

The route to Subton Common was extended to allow for more spectators, commencing a circular route. Sunlight burst through shining underwater waves, caressing the domes with warmth and golden joy. Seating galleries had been erected. Orchestras, bands, and operatic singers overcame the precession with swirls of emotion, causing many a dry eye to tear, and normally silent voices to cheer.

Ziracuny's majestic entrance was the most mesmerizing scene of all. Bouquets of sea flowers, strands of beads, and glowing shells were waved enthusiastically.

Pace and Nero stood side by side. Pace's ultra-eye revolved in schisms of introverted sight. Without speaking, he communicated within the realm of steam-powered creatures. Half alive and half dead; bionic and unbionic; all formed from the same elements. They listened, and within their own geo-compressed eyes, saw.

Tess could not believe her eyes. Beyond the spectacle of sickening grandeur, past the apocalypse of the Watch City sisterhood, she saw red strands of sought after love, and heard the stanzas played by her fingers.

Verdandi's flesh fingers rolled the organ in a spinning aquatic rainbow. Her new arm lifted a baleen bow upon the shimmering surface. Propelled by bellows of coal and oxygen, an epiphany of sound christened the coronation.

DRAKE officers held a red cloth above Ziracuny's head. Glowing algae and crystal were poured an amethyst geode. Nero anointed her head and hands. Then the DRAKE, all in a line, passed the specially designed Royal Cape over Subton's revered Trident, then the Crystal Triangle. One by one, each officer genuflected and kissed the holy artifacts. Nero was the last in line, and presented Ziracuny with each object.

The crowds silenced. Ziracuny did not kneel before the historic relics of leaders before her.

Two soldiers opened a treasure chest, revealling rectangular gold plaques made of manatee hides. From afar, Martina adjusted her goggles and interpreted them as chest shields.

The display was impressive, and compelled some to realize that they were taking part in a religious ritual – not merely in a pageant.

Ziracuny stepped forward, not as an emperor, but as a god.

She reached out to the purple pillow that hovered between her and the pair of brothers before her. Neither Pace not Nero lifted an arm to swat her hands away, although the Mutineer's natural cornea glowered in disdain, and his flesh fingers trembled with restrained impulse.

The Queen crowned herself without reverence. Without beguilement or humility. Without question.

"Ziracuny! Ziracuny! Ziracuny!"

She threw silver coronation coins to the crowd, causing an undignified scramble among the poor and the greedy.

The carriages of the Queen and Princess floated by each other again; two ships in the night.

"Now that I am Queen, dear child, I can give you everything." Rumbles of thunder and smashing currents burst. Sparks of lava and torches illuminated dark corners of the future.

Chapter 57

Caramel skin, caramel voice, caramel touch. Swirling in sweet dreams with simmering ends.

"I am here looking for you. Always. I will never leave." Lightening flashed upon a lone tombstone high on a vacant hill.

Black and red flooded her mouth, as sharp white tridents bloodied her lips.

"Professor Alset, I apologize, you must wake up. Forgive me; I do not know the proper address to speak to you. So I must speak to you earnestly." Yoki shook the worldwide renown inventor.

"Wake up! Verdandi needs you!"

"Yoki? What are you doing here?"

Yoki looked at the man deep within Tess's bed. "Uncle Pace! What are YOU doing here?" She shook her head. "No matter, please, help Verdandi! She is losing touch with her own brain, and I don't want to lose her!"

Tess tapped Morse Code on Martina and Bashelle's door, and the four women and one man dashed into darkness together.

Through wet slimy pipes, the noblewoman clutched her skirts. Her bodice slipped beyond her hips as she slithered through. Without cover, her bare breasts slid through syrupy liquid, smelling faintly of bleach. Her cold-erected nipples paved paths below her body, like a snail in shallow sand.

The tight copper tunnel curved. Tess's bodice burst. She plied herself through, flattening her palms against the converse walls. Her corset stuck and then released with an exhilarating reprieve. Pulling her crinoline and skirts with it, her bloomers yet remained, caught on the taught muscles of her hard glutes. Beneath her, a trickle of thick liquid passed between her thighs.

With a vacuumed pop, Tess fell to a redwood floor. "Wipe up lest you make tracks." Tess caught the heavy towel in one hand.

Yoki guided her through the secret tunnels, stairways, and platforms to the regal enclave.

Tess whispered at last. "This is yet the same prison!"

"Aye, and the prisoner is no less caught."

Yoki pulled Tess close. "Pardon me, Professor, but this must be done." In a seismic flush, the pair rolled down vines of wound kelp through a minuscule opening in the plasmatic moon ceiling.

"Be patient and kind and knowledgeable," murmured Yoki into Tess's breasts. "Your girl's brain is washed with salt, and her words are fueled by noxious gas."

Yoki dropped the noblewoman unceremoniously to the glass floor and pulled her own way up like a monkey in jungle swings. She raced off to her DRAKE duties as the rest of the rescue team caught up and lowered themselves down.

Tess rushed to Verdandi. "Please, come with me. I love you so much, and I know we can get through this together. But we must leave now!"

Verdandi shot up from her desk. "You don't know what you're talking about. I'm fine. You have no idea what it's like to be me. You just crashed into my life and expected to form some kind of twisted lifelong bond with me? What are you, some kind of sicko? I don't even know who you are! Oh yeah, the damn special almighty Professor Alset. So damn frikkin special and elegant and noble. With your fancy dresses and oh so proper etiquette."

Tess took a step towards her, hands open, pleading.

"Feck off! Don't think I'm stupid. You pretend to be classy. Yeah, you're a real classy broad. You don't think I know what the hum of a rumble seat sounds like? Don't look so aghast, dear lady. Do you think you were the only one admiring the moon up at Mount Feake during sweet summer nights? I'm not an idiot. You, and a lorry driver! Are you insane? Some precious lady you are. Some noble."

Martina landed lightly from the ceiling. "This is not about Tess, or Hugh, or me, or the moon. This is about YOU. And how we all love you. We love you, Verdandi. You can be mad all you want, call us names, be a pissy little brat, but the fact remains. You are loved. By us."

She gestured around the room. "You may claim not to know Tess, who if you remember correctly, you recognized before any one of us did, because she was your idol, your mentor through books. Sure, you had never met her before she, as you say, crashed into your life. She crashed into all our lives, and although I empathize as her almighty nobility and prissy politeness grinds my gears, she has sacrificed herself, her life, for you. If that's not enough to know her for, then that's your loss."

Martina reached out her arms and cupped the teen's shoulders in her palms. "But I, Verdandi, me, you know me." Their eyes met, and Verdandi faltered. Her lower lip quivered as tears fought the anger in her eyes.

Martina continued. "I know you deeply and dearly. Your secrets, I would never divulge. My dreams which I have shared with you, are ones I trusted solely to you. We have been a team. We have been friends. We have been family before any of these other gnobgashers came into the picture."

Bashelle grunted.

"I still trust you. If you are having trouble believing, and are confused of what is truth or lies..."

Verdandi's eyes widened in surprise at being understood.

"...then please, remember, and trust who you once were. Trust the girl who trusted me. Trust the girl who believed in herself. You are still that person."

Martina laid a hand upon Verdandi's left arm. For moments, long seconds, blending together without the tick of a watch, the glassmaker's long fingers warmed the cold skin of the lost child.

The warmth dispersed the sentimental spell. Verdandi shook Martina's hand off.

"You are wrong. I am not that person. I'm not a girl. I'm not a dumb little thing. I'm grown. I'm a woman! I know what's best for me."

Her voice rose in pitch and volume. "How dare you come in and try to tell me what to do! I don't have to answer to you!

You're not my mother! I don't even have a mother! I am fine on my own, and always have been. You are just a control freak." She scanned the small gathering. "You all are."

Bashelle sobbed mutely, her round shoulders hopping up and down.

"Verdandi," Tess spoke softly, her own heart pulsating with broken seams, "we can help you. You do not have to go this alone. We love you." She stepped forward again and lifted her hands in front of her, tentatively, wishing to hold the girl as she once had, to hug the tears out. But she didn't dare. She was at a loss of what to say or do. Logic didn't exist in this longing emotion. She took a breath in Verdandi's silent stare. "I love you."

Verdandi crumbled. "No, you don't! You don't! You just want to possess me. I don't need you to be my saviour. I can do what I want. By myself. I don't need you!"

She leaned forward and spat out a green and white glob, and winced in secret pain. "Leave me alone!" She used the back of her scaly sleeve in an attempt to wipe the tears and saliva from her face. It only streaked the snotty mess further across her lost composure. "Go away!"

With that final shriek, the women felt their hearts crumble to their feet.

Bashelle tumbled.

The floor crackled.

"Whoah!" shouted Martina. "Grab on! Climb!"

"Onto what?" asked Tess, tripping over her own feet.

"Damn plasma nets! Those wild donkeys!"

It was too late. The invisible net shimmered in red strobe lights. Nero entered the room, and smiled. His jagged teeth gleamed red and black in the flashing darkness.

Chapter 58

Tess, Martina, Bashelle, and Pace were carried below all decks to the bowels of Subton, where they were caged like rats before a snake's meal.

Tess knelt in a corner and held her hands to her eyes. "It's all my fault. If I had just managed to grasp her from the ship that day. If only I swam after her. I could have rescued her, and none of us would be in this mess, and she'd be safe."

Bashelle's voice cooed in calm reason. "You did more than any human could be expected to do. You were superhuman in your attempt to save her. I didn't even know you could swim!"

Tess cradled her head in her hands. She lowered one hand and looked at Bashelle. "This leads me to another aspect of that day which I mean to discuss with you." She lowered her other hand flat on the floor and sat up with straight proper posture. "Where were you when she was being strung up like a prize fish. Like a scaly, revolting, tuna!" She choked the last word out like a cat coughing up a bone.

"Where was I? I could not be more flabbergasted by that question. I was right there, I was at the water before you were!"

"Indeed. So why didn't you do something about it then? Why was it left up to me to dive, stripped and ragged, into that nasty ice water, to save that girl?"

"Hey now," growled Martina. "Get your gears back on track. I was with Bashelle, side by side, fighting in that bloody chaos. All we could see was the DRAKE navy, and blood, much of which was our own."

Tess pushed her dainty hands against the wall and stood. "Why then, oh hunter, could you not leave the mighty Bashelle unattended and get that girl back yourself?"

Martina took two swift strides across the cell and landed within the professor's breath. She bent at the waist to stare with ferocious eyes into Tess's face. Their lips briefly touched as Martina spoke, in low tones, clear and cold.

"Shut your trap, now. This is not a warning. Close that sweet little squirrel mouth before I squeeze your soft tummy and choke out your nuts."

Tess shivered in the unwavering steel of the mark-smith's gaze.

Pace lifted his hands up and slowly walked towards the two women. His velvet voice spread softly past his gently parted lips. "Ladies, we all have valid points, and justified frustration. If we can all take a collective breath and step back just for a moment, I believe we will see we are all in the same boat."

"Careful there," Bashelle half-whispered to Pace.

Tess and Martina simultaneously broke their stare of predation and turned to the Mutineer.

"What boat would this be?" Martina hissed. "I see only three women who have traversed colliding seas and escaped a serpent's wrath, only to be confined in unholy bubbles beneath the surface of natural earth. There is no boat for us. If there were, I would be on it, by myself, using any and all fuel to blast out of this forsaken hovel of what you call a Watch City, irregardless of what manner of creature I demolish in the action."

Bashelle, stung by these words, felt her heart drop. "You would leave me?"

"Is coal black?"

"Never mind all that. I have heard enough from the pair of you." Tess shook her head in frustration. She stepped around Martina and approached Pace, who still had his hands raised in supplication.

"What makes you think you are in any boat in which I, or these two imbeciles, would be in?"

Pace lowered his hands, "Tess, I only meant-"

"Only meant what? That you-"

Tess's retort was cut short by a fist to her face. She spun as stars swiveled around her eyes. "How's that for an imbecile?" Martina's eyes shone with the victory of a killer, and her grin spread like a snake's before the last strike.

"Look at her!" Martina turned triumphantly to Bashelle. "I knocked the words clear outta her mouth!"

Bashelle did not return the smile of success. She did however, return the punch, removing the shine from Martina's smile.

"Look at THAT!" Bashelle picked a tiny object up from the floor as Martina clutched at her bleeding gums. "I knocked the gold right outta your words!" She threw the false tooth at Martina and stomped to the far end of the cell.

Martina retrieved the precious tooth from the rocky floor. "Why, Why, mutht it alwayth be my teeth?"

A shadow darkened the dungeon door. Nero.

"Your quest seems quite impossible of late, ladies, dear brother." He bowed with magnificent farce to each of them. "I must interrupt your little tea party. It would not be fitting for a would-be ruler to be entwined in such riffraff." Behind him, a line of DRAKE soldiers marched.

Nero stepped safely back from the iron bars and called his order. "Engage power, and, blast!"

The soldiers drew round canisters from their shoulders and twisted them clockwise. Then they snapped a shining lever, and glowing rings shot forward through the bars. The rings targeted the prisoners' hands, and pushed them all towards the bars. The connectivity of the rings embraced each wrist and bar with dynamic magnets.

Yoki lowered her magnet barrel. She couldn't let herself show emotion. She hid her fear and guilt behind a stoic mask.

Pace saw her and called out from his magnetic chains, heartbreak in his deep voice. "Why, Yoki? You are my family. You chose to work with us. You were chosen to lead." His voice cracked in sorrow. "You have betrayed yourself, worst of all."

Nero unlocked the cage, and Pace was dragged away.

Yoki arrived late for supper at the BSDINK mess hall. As she walked in, the tables erupted in applause. All her peers were whooping and hollering for her. They surrounded her and patted her on the back for a job well done: leading DRAKE to the infidels.

She gained new DRAKE followers, admirers, and friends who were drawn to her power. Keys clanked against her armour: she had been rewarded with a new commanding office and a snazzy new sub-glider. "The life of a rat," she thought late at night, in her elegant dark cave.

The Queen insisted on visiting the prisoners. She had to witness the incarceration of her dreams. Upon seeing dried mud clumped within the professor's curls, she threw her head back and laughed. "When I was a vixen of your current age, I experienced moments equalling the stupidity you exhibit." She appraised the scroungy aristocrat from top to toe. "Nay, I was never nearly quite as dense as you are now."

"Why did you even take our girl anyways!" said Bashelle.

Ziracuny kept her eye on Tess. "A minnow can bait a hungry shark."

"You bloody quim," growled Martina.

Ziracuny focused her masked eye upon each of them. "The absurdity of your ignorance is offensive!"

"You have what you want now," said Tess. "You have everything. Why not let Verdandi go?"

"Where you see light, I see shadows. I have lived in those cold depths, unseen and unknown. Now is my time to claim the light for myself!"

With a flash of lightening and burnt plasma, Ziracuny disappeared.

Pace was led in magnochains to Yoki's desk before his hearing.

"Please, Yoki. I am not worried about my own freedom, but of yours! The truth will set you free, and you will have your whole life ahead to rebuild yourself."

"How dare you ask me to speak the truth?"

"Ever since you were in my sister's arms, at her breast, in her heart, you have always reflected her light. And shone with your own. You were born with the faculties of a leader: empathetic, kind, fair, just, trustworthy."

Yoki cringed at the last word. "When I snuck you the fuel to send to other Watch Cities in need, you never asked me where I got it from. So you are complicit in my thievery! I played both sides, maybe cuz I had to! How dare you judge me when you took the fruits of my forced labour. I did what I thought was best for me, for you, for all of us!"

Pace was pulled away with invisible power of the magnetobot guarding him.

Chapter 59

In the dank prison, the three women had been relieved of their wrist cuffs. Their freedom was yet no closer, and the minutes droned on slowly.

Tess paced a trail within the dirty cell. "I simply desired to reach Gustover. I never wanted to step a foot in Waltham in the first place. Now look where I've wound up."

Martina picked her teeth with a spike of dry seagrass and mumbled. "You're not the only one who's lost a daughter."

"What?"

"Just shut up!"

Tess hung back quietly feeling sorry for herself. Then the pity built itself up into anger.

"You can't talk to me like that!"

"Oh really?" said Martina. "Cuz you're so damned important? Ohh-la-la it's fancy pants Professor Pussycat!" She skipped and curtsied, and raised her voice to falsetto. "At your service. Oh my, I am too precious and special for the lot of you, you must deliver my tea and open my door and brush my long luscious locks. Everyone everywhere just can't get enough of me!"

"That's enough," warned Bashelle lowly. But Martina carried on.

"Oh dear, my sweet little noble hips require silken attention. I accept all hands on deck; I do not discriminate. As long as my fascinator is properly aligned with your belt, I have no qualms about our meeting of the minds!"

"I said that's enough!" Bashelle lumbered over next to Tess.

"Oh sure, be on her side. Little damsel in distress needs help from big bad Bashelle."

Bashelle stepped forward into Martina's face. "She gave as much as you did. Maybe more. Hey, maybe less. It's not a competition. We are in this together. Do you hear me? And you slug, how dare you say I'm not on your side! I am ALWAYS on your side! Sometimes I'm on somebody else's side too."

The three women retreated to different corners and slept, out of weariness and boredom rather than tiredness. Martina awoke to a sound like chickens scratching for seeds. She looked groggily toward Tess, and saw the rows of calculations she had etched on the ground. "Don't you ever sleep? What's wrong with you?"

Tess ignored her.

Bashelle sat up. "I feel like I'm rolling on a carpet of anemones."

"Whatever that means," grunted Martina.

"Ahoy, a water moccasin is slithering in!"

Nero approached the bars. Martina spat in his direction. "Get outta here, ya glasscock."

"Yeah, you eel piss!"

"Madame Bashelle," the Captain said, "allow me to appeal to you as a fellow creature of the sea."

Bashelle felt her demeanor soften for a microsecond. She was intrigued, wondering just what he wanted from her. Once the sea was mentioned, it was like someone invoking the name of her god. She pushed mercy aside and settled on curiosity.

"What could you possibly want to say to me that won't make me bash your skull in?"

"I confess that yes, I am from Subton. I recognize you a person of the the sea, even though you were not born here." He dared to step closer to the bars. "I have seen how you keep our customs. A bit brashly," he added, and Bashelle's eyes darkened with the implication that she was not well-mannered, then brightened when she found the compliment in that.

Nero continued. "I do not necessarily want to join my countrymen in certain efforts. I wish to be part of a new world, a new order, a new government. I will not be the worm. I will be the hook."

A cold sourceless wind blew into the musty cavern. Nero hurriedly whispered: "In the darkest days you are not alone. The devil is right beside you."

Ziracuny appeared in a flash of light and snow. "I gazed upon my watch and realized it was time to torment the captives."

Tess leaped to the bars and pressed her face against them, her teeth bared like a rabid wolf. "Empty the blight of your presence from this chambre. Prison would be heavenly were I not to see your one mad peeping eye ever again!"

Ziracuny applied fresh stain to her lips where snow had melted the colour away. "Just because you're an enemy of the state doesn't mean we cannot be civil."

Bashelle joined Tess at the bars. "Seems like you've been civil with your share of men...and women perhaps?" She darted a look at Martina who shifted her eyes. "And even, various other fishy substrates?"

"How can you dare to talk to me this way?"

"Because Ma'am. We are in a place where ladies piss and shat. It doesn't get more equal than this."

Ziracuny turned her attention back to Tess. "If you got your nose out of the crevice of freshly inked pages now and again, you would learn how to live a better life, not some subaquatic fantasy. You and your Verdandi. It is about time you decided to grow up."

"I have read tens of thousands of books. I have lived a hundred million lives. I have witnessed a million heartaches. I do not need my own. So when you open an invitation thusly, and my voice is singularly heard, I gain your approval. But I don't need it. That's on you. I know who I am. I suppose that doesn't make it hurt any less, but it makes it easier for me to exist."

"A pity with all your expertise you never learned how to be a proper lady. Quite a shame; all the schooling you were granted; such a waste. You would be better suited shuffling cards somewhere in the western frontier of your adopted nation. Your land of emigration. Your un-noble science."

Tess pulled her face away from the bars but still squeezed them tightly so that her thumbs went numb. "Using science as a tool is an ethical responsibility. Not a game! Your perversion of technology hurts instead of helps. The reverberations of your evil intentions will shake the earth for generations! Stop now, before you ruin the magic that science is, before you devastate progress, before you inadvertently destroy the future for us all!"

Ziracuny flung her otter furs around her shoulders. "I need not be lectured to by a tyrant of the people. Stir up your pot, and be boiled in it."

The Subton Tower echoed. Ziracuny swiveled on heels of sharpened narwhal tusks. Her breath and haste left a wind of deadly sweetness. Nero saluted as she exited.

Growling in a tone meant only for the captain, she said, "The bell tolls for you."

Chapter 60

Verdandi pressed her naked body to the window floor. She was too weak to dress. Too cold to move. Too tired to try. Too broken to care.

She watched the empty black depths below her. No moon shone upon the coral, invisible in the night. No ostracod flashed with starlike bioluminescence.

No wayward blackdragon slithered through the sea within her sight.

No friend tapped in hello. No one lay a blanket upon her, or brushed her hair.

Nobody listened to her tinny cries.

Not a care. Not a word. Not a sign.

What if instead of escaping...she just left.

She didn't want to be here anymore.

She didn't want to be.

She lay there all night, bare and barren hearted, willing herself to die of cold.

Bells chimed. Again and again. Or perhaps once, endlessly. Rivulets of echoes across streams of cognizance and time.

Does time in sleep without dreams count the same seconds as the hours that flash in a minute's nightmare?

Verdandi was awoken from her daze with the sensation that someone was calling her name. On and on repetitively. Finally she sat up in bed. She looked around and still heard her name inside her head. "I must be losing my mind." She noted that Nero had snuck in again. There was a needle in her arm, poked in while she slept. She pulled it out.

She continued hearing her name, and was drawn to the sensation of the voice inside her head. She rose from the bed with her white shaky legs and gazed down. Could this be real?

Was she truly mad as a hatter?

She dropped to her knees in prayer and hope. She pressed her face against the cold glass floor.

It was true!

Ani, her friend, had found her!

The black and white whale bumped against the glass. "I see you!" rejoiced Verdandi.

For the first time in a while, since last she spent time with Yoki, she felt happy. Her heart panged with the memory, so she brushed it aside and revelled in the joy of seeing her whale friend.

Verdandi talked through the floor, blubbering thanks to the orca who had sought her out. Something switched in her brain. She was reminded of familial love, and the mutual faithfulness she once felt.

She and Ani conversed in their telepathic language. As Verdandi moaned and cried, her eyes became clearer. She saw now, she understood now, she realized now, that all that Ani was telling her was true. She was trapped. Her family had been trying to help her, and now they were suffering because of her mistakes.

She continued silently, exchanging ideas, and nodded her head in agreement. The whale nodded back and flicked her tail, waving goodbye.

"As an animal can mantain loyalty, so may I," thought Verdandi.
She gulped down an entire pitcher of water. Then she wrapped a shred of blanket around

her left wrist and ran the IV tube under it. She reclined back in bed, exhausted from the little movement. Her eyes closed while the IV drained into the empty pitcher that she had placed on the floor beside the bed. She fell asleep, her arm hanging down, the poison filling the carafe instead of the skeletal form of her body.

Chapter 61

Bots hovered to and fro sliding crevices within the sanctum of her prison. Adept at following, inept at deciphering. The teen barely ate breakfast before attacking her new idea.

She had been watching the sea floor long enough, from high in her tower, fascinated by the trickles and traces of fishy pathways. Mesmerized so often by the liquid dripping into her blood and by the phantasm of wonders below the glass floor, she had, in her dazes and dozes, retained blips of thoughts. If she could just clear her head, she might connect the dotted plan in her mind and make it real.

She experimented. First with her tea, then with her scone. She lifted her conch communicator and asked to meet Ziracuny in the music room, but alas, the Queen was currently involved in pressing government issues. Instead, BSDINK acquiesced and rolled in the water organ that she had asked for. "Even better," she thought to herself.

"Now I don't have to pretend I'm not up to something."

She turned to the trio of spy bots chasing each other across the room. "You really are quite stupid, you know."

"Quite stupid, quite stupid, quite stupid," they alternately echoed. Verdandi felt a laugh rise in her belly.

She pressed in the chalk button on the end of her right pinky finger and began scribbling on the walls. Numbers, letters, dots, and dashes. Magnetic volumes and gravitational measurements. Anomalies on the sea floor.

She popped open a case from her polished bicep and withdrew a set of intricate goggles. She knew stealing things was wrong, but so was kidnapping people! She placed the goggles over her eyes and maneuvered the bejeweled maps within. She took them off and soaked them in her bubbling algae potion.

When they were saturated and stained green, she let them cool before placing them on again. Now she could see! The graphs of Subton, wherein the inner routes lay between and beneath floors and walls. Moreover, she could see the pinpricks, like ghosts of red ants, floating across and through the maps. Her heat sensor worked!

Encouraged by this triumph, she embarked on her next mission.

She sat at the water organ and slowly played. She added sand to the bottles and watched the tiny granules float above the surface as the pitch grew higher. She clamped her magnetron project to each glass cup and felt the hair on her arms rise. Her right arm grew heavier, resisting the magnetic force. She played higher, faster, a wild tune that soon she could not hear. Yet still she played, her fingers flashing around the brims, sand hopping into the air, magnetic pulses pulling her body. Her goggles clouded in faint green fog. She saw a flash of blue, and the glass exploded.

The spy bots crackled in harmony, merged in a twisted mashup of metals.

Chapter 62

Verdandi's goggles froze to her face. Ice crystals bound her layered hair to the nape of her neck. Engulfed in cold mist, she could not see.

But she could feel.

Within the goggles, the maps flashed and shifted. She had transported through layers of rock, metal, wood. Under ground, under water. Just where she intended to be.

Her icy fingertips traced the demons etched in the wall. Images of fire glistened with her touch. The fog followed her.

A red spot emerged from the corners of the illuminated map within her goggles. It floated closer; was she approaching it, or was it approaching her? With nowhere to hide she stood still as a statue, wishing for invisibility.

Her wish was not granted.

Hot hands grabbed her arms and leather straps wrapped around her body like a team of boa constrictors. Soft hair brushed her cheek as a hoarse voice whispered in her ear. "Did you think the spy bots saw with only their own eyes?"

Ice melted over Verdandi's goggles and streamed down to her throat like a river of tears. Through rivulets of water trailing past her eyes, she saw her captor.

A dark form cut a stunning silhouette in the lifting fog. Cascading chains rattled from black leather straps. Light filtered through the cage dress rotating around the wearer's bare hips. Long, shining, patent leather boots squeezed fleshy thighs. A clenched fist rose and dropped sharply down, cracking a whip with the sound of struck lightening.

The snap of leather broke Verdandi's mesmerized focus. She struggled futilely against her entrapment. "Let me go!"

Gold moons reflected off mahogany hued eyes. The dark figure leaned in and kissed Verdandi's cheeks, softly, one at a time. She shivered.

"Why would I leave you now, when we have finally met?" The woman's voice was alluring, yet dangerous at the same time. Verdandi rolled her mechanical fingers together and sparked a flame, scorching through a band of leather.

The woman unhooked a gun from an O-ring at her throat. She pulled the trigger, and clear liquid shot forth, immediately extinguishing Verdandi's fire.

"Did you think a woman such as I would be unencumbered by a water pistol?"

Verdandi's curiosity was stronger than her fear and fury. She could see that her captor was not much older than she was. "Who are you?"

"Why, I am Ricci, and after these many months, I have destined this as our time to bond. For you see, dear Verdandi, it was through my eyes that the bots could see." She pressed her face nose to nose with the teen. Verdandi saw that the glowing crescents in Ricci's eyes were not reflections, but rotating lenses. "I have been keeping careful watch on you."

"Are you a DRAKE officer come to snatch me back to oblivion?" Verdandi struggled again against the restraints.

"I am simply Ricci, no need for a formal title or rank. I am the boss. I am in charge of myself. If I choose to help DRAKE, I do, and if I choose to hinder, I may do that also. As long as I am always choosing to help myself."

"Then why don't you choose to untether me so that I can help MYSELF?"

Ricci kissed the tip of Verdandi's freckled nose. "I would like to help myself to you first."

"Just let me go."

"What are you willing to do to secure your freedom?"

Verdandi contemplated the question as the dominatrix contemplated her. "What would you want me to do?"

Ricci's red mouth opened with a tinkling laugh, exposing brilliantly white fangs. "Now you are catching on." She ran her fingers through Verdandi's tousled hair. "I would be willing to loosen your bonds if you would permit me to feel your hair."

"Sure," said Verdandi. The weird person was already touching her hair, after all.

"Hold this for me, would you, cutie?" She placed the grip of the whip in

Verdandi's mouth. Verdandi sucked on the end so she could pull it into her mouth further and secure it with a solid bite.

Ricci held Verdandi close to her, and began untangling the long leash. Every movement was accompanied by her sugary breath in Verdandi's face.

Finally, the teen was completely disengaged. She rubbed where tightness had numbed her arm. Ricci removed her black lace gloves and crouched before Verdandi's legs, massaging her way up: her calves, her thighs, her tender glutes; thoroughly digging nimble fingers between Verdandi's ribs, edging along her spine. Finally she stood before her and rubbed the smooth cusps behind her ears. Verdandi felt pressures release from deep inside her. She sighed in pleasured relief. Ricci pulled the girl's ears, guiding her head. Red strands from a tangled coiffure brushed against soft breasts. Ricci closed her eyes.

"This is the hair I have longed to feel."

Verdandi allowed her face to remain pressed against Ricci's decollate. Ricci kissed the top of her head and tenderly pushed her away. "I have wanted to do that since I first saw you with the dragon," she murmured.

"The dragon?"

"Yes, you know who I mean. Her Royal Pain in the Neck."

Verdandi shushed her. "Beware what you say; spies are everywhere."

"Do you forget that I am a spy?"

"Yes, well no, of course." Verdandi fumbled with her corset and rearranged her striped skirt.

Ricci watched as the pink silk ribbons on Verdandi's collar were retied. Her face clouded. "I used to be her pet too, you know. Before you came along."

"You think I am Ziracuny's pet?" The freckles on Verdandi's cheeks became comets.

"I do not see what she finds attractive in you, but if she sees it, it must be so. She used to trade fresh dainties with me, and dress me in pearls." The glow of her oscillating irises flashed. "I have no need of her now. It matters not that she clutched you so daringly. I take what I want, and she has no enticement to me now." She rolled up her whip and snapped it onto a dangling ring at her waist.

"I need to leave now. I appreciate that you untied me, after tying me." Verdandi curtsied. "Good luck, may time serve you well."

"May time circle around and serve you back," answered Ricci politely. "Yet my time would be well if you served me."

Verdandi steadied herself. "I need to save my family."

"Your family? What need do you have of them? What can they do for you that you cannot do for yourself? Tis better to save yourself and align with me. I could give you what you deserve, and you could be my pet, a much pampered pooch."

"No," Verdandi insisted, backing away from the impetuous sadomasochist. "I must free my family! You say you have spied; have you not understood my need to be with them?" She continued her backwards trail.

Ricci's deep eyes shone bright in scorn. "You want to be with them so much, you ungrateful brat? Join them!" She twisted the handle of her whip, and a piercing shriek blasted through the sound mirrors. Throughout the halls, tunnels, and staircases, gaslights flashed at the checkpoints of each guard as the sound travelled past. Verdandi, still weak from imprisonment and poison, reacted too slowly to prevent the DRAKE enforcers from cuffing and shackling her.

She glared at Ricci as she was carried away. Ricci lifted her hand in a delicate wave. "Toddle-loo! May you serve time well!"

Chapter 63

It was a teary reunion deep in the depths below humanity's reign. Where DRAKE served and Ziracuny lead, prisoners found freedom in tin-tapped togetherness.

Ziracuny harassed them every day, demanding the Watch that would give her power over all the Watch Cities. She terrorized them. And smiled whilst doing so.

The dungeon cells joined with open doorways, so the prisoners could walk throughout the rows.

Ziracuny purred. "We removed the inner doors long ago during the Battle of Subton. Tis more efficient to squish in more Subtonian radicals in that way."

Bashelle squared off. "See my fingers, see my thumb, see my fist, you better run!"

Tess hugged Verdandi close to her side. "Failure is the mother of success."

The coppertop melted briefly into the sideways embrace. "Mmm-hmm."

"Remember when you what you said? You had all that time to figure things out-"

Verdandi rubbed her sad groggy eyes. "Yes, I'm sorry, I never should've said those things, I never should've-"

"Child, my love, listen. You are smart! You figured out how to set off the alarms. Do you think you could do that now?"

Verdandi blinked the fog from her eyes and a glint of memory glimmered in her petulant stare. "Yes, I could so do that! I see what you are thinking. Let's do it!"

Bashelle wiped her brow of oozing platelets pulsating from her DRAKE inflicted lesion. "Would either of you like to clue us in to just what in the blazes you are talking about?"

Night fell without accompanying darkness. All was grey, slatted by slits between bars and light through layers of carbonite. With sleep, without sleep, within sleep; Verdandi fell into depression again.

Martina secretly approached Verdandi. At first Verdandi ignored her and walked away.

Martina paused her step with a solid open hand upon her shoulder. "I get it, I'm with you." She held out a palmful of geodes.

Verdandi twitched, turning, seeing. Her breath stuck in the bones of her throat. She stared at Martina's hand. Then her body quivered. She cast a furtive glance at the other women, each asleep.

"Nobody knows?"

"Nobody," answered Martina.

Verdandi leaned into the crook of Martina's arm.

Martina kissed the crisscrossed trails in red hair. "What you love will tear you or clear you; cut you down, or mend you up. What do you love? Make whatever you love worth the effort of giving yourself: your body with scars, even those that do not fade; and your heart with its broken-ness which may never be whole, but filled with cement of friendship in its crevices."

Then she slipped a rock into Verdandi's hand.

"You might think you need this now. But you do not need this always. Always awaits you."

She kissed her beloved girl, and rolled onto the floor into sleep.

Chapter 64

Pressed lungs dimpled and deflated. Blazing fire choked to char. Strums ebbed to thrums ebbed to empty sums. Circuits lost voltage, and suns turned to pinpoints of galaxies lost in fallen stars.

A young woman who had defeated all odds fell.

Blue lips, black veins, red hair.

All colours faded to nothing.

Chapter 65

Ambulatory medic bots answered the cries for help echoing through the alarm systems of the dungeon. While the women were magno-blasted with invisible chains, spindly metal arms lifted the limp body to a floating cot.

Dark terror faded from horrified screams to deadly silence. The lack of sound became tangible; the nothingness of grief filled the cell.

The magnetism of the chains released, so the three women could move again. Yet they stood, as if their bodies had forgotten how to function.

The pressure of inertia pressed upon the prisoners, and inevitably, their emotions exploded like burst balloons.

Bashelle shouted across the cell to Martina. "You of all people should have known better! Giving her certain death? An empty soul! Don't you remember at all what it was like to be a shell? Did you forget the feeling of false air in your lungs?" She paused. "Triton's testicles! You have been crushing crystals too! You've been crushing with her!"

Martina tried to explain and held out her hand. Bashelle pulled away.
"Don't touch me! Don't ever touch me again!" She planted her right foot back and raised her left arm, her giant fist clenched in ribbons of purple veins. She stood, poised for a knockout punch. Then she lowered her arm.

"I love you. How could you do this? I am so angry, that I want to hurt you! How can that be possible?" A stream of hot tears erupted from her flushed face.

Martina reached two hands out, in silent pleading.

Salty water dripped in lone dots to the dusty metal floor. "Don't. Just don't. You sicken me. You have broken my heart."
She pointed to the far corner. "Now leave! I never want to see you again! How dare you! How dare you make me feel this way!"

Martina twitched in grief. She glanced at Tess, whose face was sculpture-like: pale, unmoving, lifeless.

"Please," whispered Martina, "please let me explain. I'm so sorry-"

"Go!" Bashelle's finger remained pointed at like an arrow strung for discharge.

Martina raised her arms in supplication and was met with icy stares. She lowered her head. Her golden hair hovered over her sun etched face, and her green eyes darkened in the shadow of shame.

Bashelle sought sleep that would not come. Her thoughts chased dreamy images away. Had she been too hard on Martina. She grumbled into her hands. "Feck that."

Tess snuck a cotton robe from her bag and rolled it up into a thin pillow. Between meditative outlooks, her feelings clashed with her thoughts. At the time they needed to be coming together most, they are separated the most. Can the mission survive? What is the mission anymore? Is it hopeless; is all life hopeless?

Tess attempted to solace herself with pride. She was indeed gratified by her lifetime of ingenuity, and mentally counted off some of her major accomplishments in science. Even little things have improved little parts of life. But now what is the use? Is she fated to forever lose at any cost? Maybe she never should have trusted Bashelle and Martina to begin with. Like they said, what is she to them? She is a coincidence. Coincidence is not science.

So maybe their friendship never existed.

Chapter 66

"All I'm looking for is temporary relief of unending pain."

In the hospital unit, Yoki frantically switched dials and pressed fresh algae into pulps, then melted them into liquid form to drip into her best friend's eyes, ears, nose, mouth. Then, with a needle three inches long, she shot the clarifying elixir into brittle blue veins.

Verdandi opened her glassy eyes. "Martina says I can't promise to stop. But I can promise to try to do better."

"You are not alone. You have people who love you and want to help you. Like me." Yoki removed her latex gloves and smoothed back Verdandi's hair.

"I'll never be free. They'll never find me. I'm an orphan again."

Yoki watched and worried while Verdandi became increasingly depressed.

"It's good having nothing. Nobody can take anything away from you."

Yoki filled a long syringe. "One day is one life. Each day we get a new life to witness."

Yoki continued to replace the brain poison with her clarifying elixir each day. The BSDINK students slowly became hungrier and curiouser. Unblurred by the potion, their thoughts became clear yet confusing.

Nero studied the medical unit and decided it would be best to place Verdandi into solitary confinement. Something was unusual in the expected treatments, and he did not know what it was. The safest choice was to shut down Subton's most special patient before she could figure out how to climb her way up.

This dismal change gave Yoki an opportunity she had wished for. Out of sight of the other patients and staff, Yoki attended to Verdandi often until she could continue progress on her own.

Verdandi built her strength slowly. She spent a week violently ill, and kept the auto fill bubbler in constant use. She drank and drank and drank until her veins were visible again. She started to eat from the selection of freeze dried food offered to her. She watched the splotches on her arms fade away, leaving only her constellations of freckles. She could see clearly again.

She made her escape plan.

Verdandi used the materials in her medical unit to create a magnetic force. It could instantaneously clamp open and shut, allowing her to escape just as the door opened slightly and closed immediately.

She lost a few strands off the back of her head in the narrow opening as the door snapped shut, and she covered her mouth to suppress an exclamation of glee. She still felt weak, but she was determined. She was going to save her family.

Chapter 67

Tess and Martina were screaming at each other in the dank darkness.

The professor stomped her foot. "She is like a daughter to me!"

"She was my child before she was yours!"

"What in heaven's bells are you saying?"

"I'm the one who found her. I'm the one who carried her emaciated bloody body from the train tracks that night 6 years ago. I'm the one who shared my home with her, my HOME, where I barely allow ANYONE to enter; it took Bashelle two summers to get through the door. I kept that child, I cleaned her and healed her and fed her. What care I couldn't give, where my abilities had reached their limitations, I reached out. I asked for help! I humbled myself. Do you know what that means? I brought Kate, yes your precious Kate!"

Tess blanched at the name and her face turned to stone even as her eyes watered.

Her lips didn't move as her breath pushed the name between them: "Kate."

"That's right, Doctor Kate, how I loved her." Martina's voice softened. "She was beloved, and rightly so. She was an angel on earth."

A quiet pause blotted out words of ruin. The silence of individual grief swirled together in invisible currents of emotion, combining as one double strand of mourning.

"She was," whispered Tess.

"Anyways, I rose above myself, I made connections, I invited people into my life. Because of Verdandi. I would do anything for that kid. Anything. When Kate took over the healing, it was a symmetric alignment of cures. The child healed fast and strong. But that wasn't really cuz of me or the good doctor. It was cuz of her. Verdandi WANTED to get better. She WANTED to heal. She WANTED to live."

Tears tugged the professor's eyes and she dabbed at them daintily with a double edged kerchief.

Martina's voice rose. "Verdandi is tough as nails and stronger than any force, natural or otherwise. She is bricky! She forged her path and I was proud of her for it."

"Yes, she is strong, I saw that right away."

"She was probably born strong. When she was weak, she willed herself to become stronger. I am the one who set her on her path, cared for her, taught her, admired her, LOVED her. And then YOU show up!"

"I can't listen to your malarkey anymore." Bashelle glared at Martina. "Typical. You are either a hero or a zero."

"You cannot judge me until you have suffered my same pain."

"Yeah I can!"

"The human body is an enigma. With a full belly, you do not imagine famine. In a coal car in June you remember not December snows. When your body craves that which harms it, the craving is incessant, until the poison thirst is quenched. In that satisfaction, the pain it brings is forgotten."

"If you're so frikkin smart, why did you even-I just can't have this conversation right now. Again. It's too frustrating."

"Damn, it must be hard work being bitter."

Bashelle turned away. "You can't unfry a fish."

"I don't even understand what that means. But it doesn't matter! Just please stop being mad at me! You don't know what it's like, to be torn within yourself, trying to do the best thing. And the pain-it's like having a tooth ache without the tooth!"

"Shut up. Shut up, shut up. Stop talking. I don't want to hear you. Just stop." Bashelle lumbered away and sat against a wall. Tess fluffed her skirts and sat next to her.

In low voices they commiserated, their friendship solidified by their mutual distaste.

Bashelle and Martina spoke in Tagalog, a language they were both confidently correct that Martina could not understand.

"I wish I was wrong so I could apologize and be sorry forever," said Bashelle.

"I share that sentiment. Alas, as I reflect on wrongdoings or ill-will from my past, I bear similar guilts. Were it not for me, Hugh might still be alive today. And Kate. How many lovers must I lose? If I had reacted differently or made different choices, maybe Verdandi would not have been kidnapped. My own child has been missing these one and a half decades past, and I am no closer to finding her than I was the day I lost her. I shame myself each time I make a poor decision. Nothing can make up for it; nothing can change the past or provoke the future to bend towards our needs. With futility I have researched, experimented, built, and burned ideas and configurations for plausible time travel. I could save us all, or just myself, if I was not so daft and utterly hopeless."

Bashelle scooted closer so that the eyelet trim on Tess's dress ruffled over her own bare knees. "We have each, and all, spoken words we cannot retrieve with nets. Our decisions and whims are hiccoughs only heard if a different ploy is interrupted. We are our worst enemies."

Tess lowered her head onto Bashelle's broad chest. Bashelle stared into nothingness as her heart tore itself over and over again.

Martina glanced hopefully, daring to look upon Bashelle's beautiful face. Tears soaked silently into her burlap blanket. This is what she was down to, she thought. Exiled within her own community.

Her friends have abandoned her.

Chapter 68

"May we sit here?"

"Sure," said Martina. She edged over on her burlap sack. She was afraid of what Bashelle would say to her next, but she still longed to hear. Tess sat down on Bashelle's other side.

Bashelle spoke smoothly and plainly, with lack of her usual jovial tone. "I would like to try to talk to you, about your mood, and how it is affecting us. I am not trying to attack you. Is that okay for me to talk to you about right now?"

"Yes."

"Okay then." Bashelle breathed in long and deep. "Lately, you have not been a real teammate. It has been decidedly unlike you, and for a prolonged time, so that I do not know if you have changed in such a way that you are interested in working towards our mission here, and if you are at all interested in keeping a relationship of any kind with me."

Bashelle turned her head to look at Martina's face. "Are you? Interested? At all?"

"Yes," said Martina. Her words stuck in her throat and she had to cough them out. "I want all of that, I want to help, and I want to be with you."

"I want that too, but it seems impossible the way things are now. Remember when we first set out on the submarine from Waltham?"

"Yes, it seems so long ago now."

"Indeed it does. A lot has happened, a lot has changed. Has our mission changed? Have we changed so much that we are no longer able to continue together?"

"No," pleaded Martina. "It is not too late."

Tess spoke softly. "When we left, you were devoted to saving the girl you had helped raise. You took a bullet for her at the Battle at Mount Feake. What has happened to change that passion?"

Martina's hands shook. "I am sorry. I do not know what is wrong with me."

Bashelle's deep voice became more gentle. "Maybe because you are imbibing not in your usual way, that you are used to, and that is affecting your body and brain."

Martina paused to contemplate that and shook her head. "No, it's just that I don't like being stuck in cramped spaces, you know that I have never been a fan of open water, despite your valiant efforts to introduce me to your great joy of seafaring. I'm just not cut out for this."

"None of us are cut out for this," said Bashelle. "But we have to recut ourselves into a form that can adapt to what we cannot control, to not just survive but thrive in new worlds that we never knew existed. We need to undergo the pain of change to understand the power within ourselves to become stronger than we ever imagined."

"When did you become the great philosopher?"

Bashelle reached over and stroked Martina's limp blonde hair. "When I became a sardine with the love of my life." She leaned in and the two women shared a soft kiss. Afterwards, Martina exhaled in refreshed breath.

A trio of hugs turned into one massive squeeze. "Alright already," sniffed Martina. "I love you guys too but that's enough squishing for one day."

"Quite fine. We could take this time to share calculations and form a plan," said Tess.

"Yup, back to work." Bashelle stood, stretched a strong hand to Martina, and pulled her up.

"Okay, just one more hug," said Martina. She and Bashelle embraced until Tess interrupted.

"Calculations, anyone?"

Martina smacked Tess's bottom. "I was almost starting to like you again."

Chapter 69

"I'm pretty pissed you kept the bag a secret so long," said Martina.

"Yeah, that was sucky," added Bashelle. "But now we've got a good secret that nobody else knows about neither, right?"

"Correct. Once we each step into my bag, we will be safe in static time."

"But how will we reach through the iron bars to move the bag and step out on the other side?" asked Bashelle.

Martina's eyes squinted. "I have an idea for that. And I think the idea already knows it."

Bashelle and Tess looked perplexed.

"Go ahead, idea. I know you're there. Come into the light."

Silent feet pushed against clay walls. Like a gecko defying gravity, a sleek form crawled towards them in the shadows. With a soundless landing, the figure leapt and appeared before them.

"I do not want to be a traitor to my people anymore."

"You agree to partner with us?"

"Yes," said Yoki. "It's a deal."

Chapter 70

Yoki followed the plan perfectly. She knew how to be a good soldier, knew how to implement tools, and was skilled at interpreting information. She did not intend to stray from the course of action.

She would perform the final duties of her shift. Then she would disable the spy-bots and alarm systems in the dungeon. Promptly at the strike of three upon the Subton Clock Tower, the women would climb into the bag. With the guard equipment disabled, it would be simple for Yoki to carry the bag through hidden tunnels and neglected stairways to the infirmary. At that point, she would create a diversion by faking an accident in the chemistry sector of the medicinal lab. This would provide the opportunity for the women to step out of static time. They would use the codes Yoki had supplied them with to enter Verdandi's private medical unit. Together, they could fight their way out and board a robotic steam-pod. Thus they could zoom away from Subton Sea. The plan was prepared.

When her shift was over, Yoki crept towards the inter-Subton radial dial switchboard. She pulled the lever to disable spy-bot systems WCS397412A. Then she twisted a metal key to close the circuits of the alarm transponders. She was scurrying past the BSDINK washroom, when she heard a terrible sound.

A mighty blast, louder than an oceanic avalanche, shook the walls and bent the drainpipes. Yoki looked up and calculated the distance and direction. The blast had come from the medical centre. Verdandi! She had to make sure she was safe!

She rushed past bots and guards, DRAKE militia and BSDINK trainees. She needed to get there first; she needed to be able to see her friend. She needed to save her, no matter what else happened.

She was so close. Just one more corner, and one more hallway, and WHAM! Yoki was tackled by a force of speed and substance that knocked her off her feet. The collision sent her tumbling in a somersault of red and bronze and silver. Whatever had struck her was tumbling too.

She pulled an ionizer dart from her lace trimmed brassiere.

"Hold off! It's me!"

The tumbling stopped and Yoki was flattened indelicately beneath her oppressor. "Yoki! Get up!"

"I...can't...you...dungheap!"

"Oh, quite sorry about that." The assailant rose and helped her to her feet.

Yoki's eyes glittered. "What the heck happened? Are you all right?"

Verdandi hugged her best friend tight. "Some crazy bitch has been treating me with something, and whatever it is, it worked!"

"I am so glad to be a crazy bitch right now," said Yoki.

"Me too! Now let's move! I've got enough magnetism for the both of us."

"You sure do! Now come this way. It's time to kick some arse!"

They dodged soldiers and disengaged robots together on their race to the dungeon. The Subton Clock Tower chimed three times. They burst into the dungeon and stopped so fast they almost skidded into each other.

They watched as Nero stood in the open cell. Tess's big brown bag was in his hands. His long brows furrowed in confusion and curiosity.

"Get him!" yelled Yoki. She and Verdandi ran at the shocked captain and knocked him flat on his back. The bag went flying, bounced off the bars, and hit the rough ground with a series of thumps.

"Come out! Get out of the bag!" Yoki howled loud enough for not only the women in static time to hear but also the BSDINK squad patrolling the region.
A dozen black and red uniformed teens entered the dungeon. They saw their captain surrounded by three foreigners, a pretty redhead, and their leader, Yoki.

"Captain Nero," called out one strong voice. "What is your order?"

Chapter 71

Bashelle grabbed Nero from behind and used her sea-strong muscles to clamp his arms to his sides. Martina pressed herself against him and grabbed the nape of his neck closer to her. With her other hand shoved a fist in his mouth so he couldn't speak.

"Oh my good god," Martina flinched.

"What?" asked Bashelle.

Nero locked eyes with the hunter. Her stomach churned as she glanced down. "You sick duck. You are actually enjoying this!"

Yoki turned to face the BSDINK crew. "Comrades, you may lower your weapons. Or you may not. You may sound the alarms. Or you may not. For the first time in, well since we all played at diabolo together, you have a choice. We do not have to answer to Captain Nero, or DRAKE, or even Ziracuny. You do not have to answer to me. Yet we each must answer for ourselves."

Martina interrupted with a whoop and a yell. "You rantallion! Slimy blimey fish eater!" She shook her saliva covered hand. "Captain Finger Munch here just bit me!"

"Yoki!" Drool dripped from the captain's flabby chin. "You dishonour yourself, and all of DRAKE. Shut your silly little mouth and let the real BSDINK do their job."

"You're not allowed to talk to me like that. Nobody is. I think you have me confused with somebody I used to be."

The BSDINK soldiers stood, uncertain. Yoki addressed them again.

"You have been bamboozled, separated from your kin, and utterly brainwashed. Drugs have been forced upon you." A murmur of disbelief washed over the group. "It is not your fault; you have trained with dedication and bravery. Your trainer, however, has been your tormentor. Only recently have I been able to liberally inject a healing serum into your ear pieces, instead of the continual doses of mind-numbing poison that Nero subjected all of us to. I am troubled and grieved to admit my role in that. I only hope to redeem myself by continuing the healing process for all of you, all of us, all of Subton."

"This is an outrage!" Nero struggled against Bashelle's grasp. "Traitor! You would be the undoing of us all! I had nothing to do with any of the abhorrent practices you just described. I have done nothing!"

Yoki did not bother turning her head to answer him. She kept her eyes on her peers. "Nero, you went from being a mentor to being a menace. You are no longer my captain."

"You bucket of chum! How dare you entrap me, hold me in disdain, and portray me as that which I am not!"

"Uncle, you are not a liar. You are just a stranger to the truth."

Gas exploded through flues stretching from the sand to the surface. Nero grinned. "It is already too late for you! Surely the Queen has discovered your treachery. Best to surrender here, now, before me."

"Never," said Yoki.

"Go ahead, boys! Grab her!"

The young men looked at each other uncertainly.

Yoki's voice remained calm. "You do not have to rush to a decision. I simply ask you, please take a moment to think. For yourselves."

"Yoki, WE need to make a decision. Fast." Martina pointed to the ceiling. "Even now the walls are crumbling with stampedes of DRAKE soldiers, and this dungeon will surely be blown to bits by the time the gas flues enact one small chain reaction." She looked around at her reunited family. Her eyes settled on Verdandi. "I could just spit nickels, I am so happy to see your face."

Another blast shook the room. Verdandi touched Yoki's hand. "I know what to do. I believe in us. I believe in the power of the Watch City people to bind together and create new connections. We got this." Yoki nodded at her.

"Martina, Bashelle, Tess," Verdandi's voice cracked. "I am not going to hide my emotion. I want to cry and hold each of you and just BE. But," she wiped tears from her eyes, "we are going to have to take a rain check on that. Schedule it in for a week from Thursday. Right now, we need to get OUT."

"That's my girl!" Martina whooped.

Another explosion scattered bits of tile from the ceiling. "Go!" directed Yoki. "I will be all right here. I, too, believe in the power of our people."

"You need to follow me. I know where to go," said Verdandi to her family.

"What about this scale-less fish?" asked Bashelle.

"Leave him. We need to focus on safety right now. Justice will come in its own time."

Bashelle pushed Nero into a corner of the cell. She, Martina, and Tess followed their girl out. The BSDINK soldiers lowered their weapons and fists as they walked by.

Captain Nero shouted. "What are you doing? Have your brains evapoured? Seize them!" The squadron did not move. Another rumbling approached, of feet, not explosives.

Young Mutineers poured into the dungeon. They were prepared for a fight, but when they saw the BSDINK with lowered arms, they stopped charging.

"How pathetic," roared Nero. "When no one loves you, you have to pretend that everyone loves you."

Yoki's next words hit the captain in the heart. "You would know best." She shifted sideways so she could see him while purveying the growing crowd in front of her.

"Mutineers, BSDINK, we are together. Our mission is the same. We have been pitted against each other by the older generation, the ones who refused to release control, the ones who used us as pawns in their sick games. We are people, not property. If you will be allegiant to a cause, be allegiant to your own, and to the true spirit of Subton." She took a breath in tense moments of bickering between two sides.

"We have all been victimized by DRAKE. DRAKE made us orphans when our parents were killed in the Battle of Subton. DRAKE divided us into separate nations. DRAKE seduced us with power and poisoned us with deadly promises. DRAKE tried to overcome us, pushing us into either servitude or death. Now is our time, our choice, our lives. Right now, we have a chance, a real chance, to free ourselves. If we can come to a truce together, then together we can break the bonds of control. We do not need to be subservient. We can be victorious! The clock is ticking, the tower is chiming, and our city is bursting. Our home. Our future."

Nero took a feeble step toward her. She lifted her hands to an imaginary sky. "Scales meet each other in common waters. The things that took us apart are the things that can bring us together. We are invincible now, we are unstoppable! But only if we unite!"

Four score feet stomped in enthusiastic agreement. The Mutineers and BSDINK closed the gaps between them and became one loud multi-coloured congregation.

Nero stared at the scene unfolding before him. His knees buckled beneath the weight of his fear.

Yoki's voice called bold and clear. "We are not fighting for DRAKE. We are not even fighting for Subton. We are fighting for ourselves!"

The young people cheered.

"Our futures do not depend on one rule or another, only on our willingness to volunteer our powers, our strengths, our passions, to the futures we desire, together!"

A low murmur became a blasting chant. It swarmed the gathering with a charge of freshness and strength.

"DUMP DRAKE! DUMP DRAKE! DUMP DRAKE!"

They converged upon Nero, who scuttled backwards like a soft-shelled crab in warm sand. "Yoki," he pleaded. "Stop them!"

She looked down at her uncle, whom she had loved. "I do not have that power. Nor would I use it if I did."

Yoki made her way through the chanting crowd. She paused at the entrance to the cavern and turned around. She lifted a voice excelsiator to her lips, and her words boomed. "When what is done is done, please follow me to reclaim our lives. Woe to the one who tries to stop the flow of our combined efforts. DUMP DRAKE!"

Chapter 72

Heels splattered blood in hard steps along the metal floor. Nero, blind, his eyes bloody pulps, lay in his own blood. He was repetitively mumbling and groaning. "Tell her I love her."

Ziracuny glared down. "Tell her yourself."

She lifted her left leg and extended her foot out beyond her knee. A blood-splotched black stiletto shoe shone in refracted light.

Without blinking her eye, the queen stomped her dagger heel through the captain's jugular.

A fountain of blood spurted like hot lava from a lively volcano, painting Ziracuny in all shades of red.

She pried her heel loose. She regarded her clothes. "Time for a bath."

As she pranced toward a water portal, she couldn't quell her sense of disappointment. "I wish there was more of him to kill."

Chapter 73

Verdandi and her family escaped into the ocean, but DRAKE militia disrupted their plan with torrents of torpedoes.

Pace saw Tess across the steamy sea. He launched himself toward her. "Be safe, please, let me protect you!"

Bashelle bounded between them. "You will soon discover that she is as good at procreating peace as she is at sacrificing her own blood for war. She's a big girl." She zoomed forward with her jet-pack harness, pulling Martina's robotic pod behind her.

A hybrid shark opened its giant mouth. Bashelle destroyed it with one blast of her plasma rocket. "This thing is sweet!"

"I thought you would like it," beamed Martina. She readied her bow and pushed the clear dome of her capsule away. She still didn't like the sea, but she could never turn down a fight.

Pace's multiscopic eye pinpointed his niece amid the battling youth. His self-propulsion closed the space between them within seconds. She saw him coming and placed a hand on his head.

"I am sorry uncle. Now I understand."

He nodded and handed her a geode compass. "Take this, and fight well. I believe in your success."

"Thank you," said Yoki, but he had already zoomed off into battle.

And not a moment too soon.

A gigantic beast with a twisting metal tail emerged from an algae covered cave, and upon it a rider. Slimy seaweed floated from the gears, appearing as a billowing cape in the swirling current. The rider held a sword of hewn iron, and it was brandished in smooth strokes, cutting through the vortex.

Behind this monstrosity followed a pride, for what else could they be called, of sea lions. Their breath was governed by lungs of coal bellows, emitting steam through cavernous nostrils. From their toothy mouths shot bursts of fire that cut through the water with amazing velocity. The wide hind feet of these cephalopods were not of flesh, but of metal blades, forged deep in the hollows of Dot Hill. Swooping up and down, they prevented close-range attacks from behind.

Moray eels with jeweled fangs led the procession, coiling as they swerved up and down across the sea floor.

DRAKE soldiers bore breastplates of black and red. They aimed torpedoes of molten lava. On and among terrible contraptions of flesh and metal they rode, floating on a wave of black smoke.

Yoki, in her mermaid gear, raided the greenhouse. Armed with a sickle, she swooped down to the softest silt and swung. This glorious nutrient rich earth became a dust cloud, aimed perfectly at the oncoming DRAKE militia on their hybrid beasts. Swirling up to the seahorses' bridles, live eyes became clouded and stung by the unavoidable dirt. Riders kicked in dismay at their bucking broncos. The shooting pain of copper heels on iron ribs sprung in rivulets throughout their bones. A cry of anguish and anger, unmuffled by elaborately plumed helmets, echoed in the chaos.

Behind Yoki followed a legion of BSDINK. They discarded their black and red symbols of despotism, and replaced them with the traditional scaled armour of previous Subtonian generations. The young tribe joined the fight against Ziracuny's would-be empire. Shimmering in flecks of aqua and teal, they gripped the tools of their ancestors. With justified anger, they were strong.

Yoki swam forward, slashing the flesh from a hybrid tiger shark. As the beast burst into a splash of blood, a harpoon sailed through the black cloud. Ziracuny's diamond studded eye patch glittered in the darkness as she met her mark. The harpoon found her prey's heart easily, but was deflected. Yoki looked down at her sapphire encrusted bosom and pulled the offensive harpoon out. Not a gem had been shattered. She smiled, feeling the freezing water floss her teeth and fill her cheeks.

Sharks picked apart armour from DRAKE militia. The red emblazoned breastplates cracked, and bodies squished between giant jagged teeth. Blood squirted in the water, creating a feeding frenzy. Malicious mayhem was quelled row by row; by rows of teeth and rows of battalions too unaware to halt their courses. Crunch, crunch, crunch: the sound of DRAKE defeat.

Pillars holding up the floating islands crumbled. They sank, covering parts of Subton. Other islands that were tethered to columns floated away. An earthquake cut through the city.

Martina shot her crystal galvanized arrows, taking down scores of red and black watercraft. "I always thought I'd die peacefully. Perhaps in the jaws of a bear. But yet, it appears that wistful dream is not to be. Alas, I will accept my fate against the torrid nature of the evil ocean. Fire and water, take me on! I've seen worse. Perhaps I won't see worse again."

Bashelle reloaded her hook launcher. "As long as we are together, I can fight. Even if I lose. I will fight for you."

"And I for you."

A cannonball soared through the tumultuous sea. Martina ducked. "My fate is to be bear bait! You can't drown me!"

A school of manta rays flew overhead, blocking the humans beneath from the humans above. "Go get 'em you glorious devils!" cheered Bashelle.

Chapter 74

The Blood Moon shone through ionospheres. Subton Sea glowed red with shrimp and krill and blood. Verdandi parted the sea using sonic waves to bring the young Subton population to safety. An aquamarine glow illuminated the fresh battle site.

Hybrid sea beasts galloped and brayed. Their red scaly flesh was branded with the name of the oppressor: DRAKE.

Crossing a cold current, a giant white seahorse was bridled and saddled. Its rider bore a bow of the most exquisite mangrove vines with a crown of crystalline arrows for easy reach. Martina's wild eyes sought her targets with fervour.

Alongside the seahorse crawled a red and white crab of gigantic proportions. Its tongue was a hook, and its iron fists opened and closed with levers directed by the operator. Bashelle smoothed her hand over the rough shell she sat upon.

Pace floated among Mutineers clothed in shining luminescent armour. They jolted towards the fuel cells of the Coral Cove.

A battalion of DRAKE beasts roared with such volume that the sounds carried through water like the tumult of locomotives. The DRAKE drivers maneuvered them towards air pockets within the cave and unleashed noxious gas, trapping several Mutineers beneath the craggy hills.

The young scientists who had been corrupted by DRAKE heard the freedom cries of their peers. Encouraged, they joined the battle to preserve the goodness of their studies and experiments. They enacted stabilizers to protect their creatures, old and new. The ancient beasts they had been studying remained intact. Their Frankensteinish creations, and hybrids, and mutant offspring of these, were secured.

Geysers blasted inescapable heat and debris. Inert volcanoes awoke, coughing up black crystals. Fireballs shot through the salt water, igniting sea trees.

Skeletons of people lost after the Battle of Subton became dislodged. Dead mutilated bodies and bones danced in the bloody currents, swirling around the chaotic battle.

The ocean floor grumbled. Two giant sea worms living beneath the sand shifted their slime-filled bodies and sifted sand between their rows of gills. They were harnessed up on ropes and spurred on by long tridents, like circus lions provoked by their tamer. They were trained to attack, but were soon found to attack indiscriminately, as they were dumb beasts. Pace easily destroyed them with his arm canon. Their writhing parts curled upon themselves, twiddling their legs in broken segments throughout the sea floor.

A dark shadow grazed the highest layers of sanguine sea. Golden jaws chomped through the smog. They opened, and from within the hybrid dragon's bellowing chest, there burst a massive roar that reverberated through the battle. Thus Ziracuny appeared upon the gruesome scene, standing on top of the magnificent beast. Her lips dripped Mutineer blood.

She blazed red from head to heel. Calcite plated armour stuck to her body like an exoskeleton. On her head was a crown of scrimshaw with embedded onyx. A patch of scarlet silk covered her empty eye socket. Her feet were strapped to mother-of pearl flippers, and she used her long toes, flexing and pointing, to enact the gears for speed.

"I am Queen of the Sea! The oceans are mine! The waves bow to me while my buried comrades rise up to greet me!"

Dirt swirled in the spiral from her spinning trident. Long-dormant creatures emerged from the ocean floor.

Bashelle and Martina edged forward.

"I'll be the son of a sea monkey!"

"If ya gotta die, might as well have some company."

Chapter 75

Ziracuny appeared on the battle's horizon. "Follow me or else all fury will be released upon you!" She pointed a finger, and a fireball burst forth, incinerating a   hill of coral.

"Thus with my power shall your old city of Subton crumble, disintegrating into nonexistence. Your worn out libraries, pathetic sculptures, gaudy architecture, and disdainful farming methods will be obliterated. Your songs will be muted; your buoyant glow will be snuffed out, and your senseless sorcery of shapes will be forgotten as worms on hooks."

She lifted her hands above her head and faced their palms together. Between them swirled a zapping globe of plasma. "Behold! I possess the life-ray and can use it at will! My gift of damnation will submerge Subton and kill the naysayers and enemies of my truth! A new era, of MY rule, MY life, will glorify this new empire. The Life-Ray will do this for you, Subton."

Bashelle shouted. "Can someone please kill her so I don't have to hear this anymore?"

"I'm on it, Creampuff!" Martina hopped on a runaway seahorse. Though it bucked, she managed to maneuver it with her into her battle, her quiver full.

Ziracuny deposited the evil globe into a proton blaster to complete the life-ray. "Supplicate yourselves as Nero did, as DRAKE has done, and exist with me in progressive dominion."

Glowing arrows swept past her. Martina climbed rocks, scaling a tower of gems and fossils.

Bashelle spun the knob on her hook launcher, then pulled the lever in a series of rapid clicks. The three pronged hook struck the precipice upon which Ziracuny stood. Perfect shot! As the long rope rewound with antipolar force, the rocks beneath the queen's feet dislodged and crumbled.

Ziracuny leaped onto a low overhang of shale, just managing to balance the life-ray without tumbling. She turned the weapon towards Martina, the closer target.

Ziracuny aimed the life-ray directly at her. Martina pulled the modified harpoon on her bow.

Bashelle knelt to the ground and covered her eyes when she saw the fatal error.

Martina's weapon hit the cavern below the overhang on which Ziracuny stood. Ziracuny shrieked in triumph. "You missed!"

Martina clutched the side of the rocky mound. "No, I didn't."

The stones below Ziracuny's feet crumbled and she stumbled. A lanyard on her tool belt suspended her between life and death. She swung into the cave. Just behind her, Tess swam in, and the cave collapsed, blocking entrance to all others.

Chapter 76

In the watery rubble, a single eye shone in the darkness. "Following your god; good girl."

Tess ran her fingers and toes through the devastated cavern and crept towards Ziracuny. "Writers are gods. Scientists are gods. You are not a god; you are a monster.

The killer queen led Tess to an air pocket and pushed a boulder aside. The ocean flooded in. When the pocket filled, Tess would drown.

Tess gulped pints of seawater. Her globe helmet cracked, as did her awkward glass swimming suit. She pried the jagged covering off, and quickly became sodden. Her clothes dragged her down. She pulled them off and resorted to swimming in her undergarments. Her body numbed to the coldness but luckily, she had retained a set of her breathing apparatus, tucked in the shallow cleavage of her corset.

Dodging rocks and oxygen bombs, Tess managed to catch up with her nemesis.

Bubbles of laughter ensconced Ziracuny's face. With a weaponless hand, she pointed hysterically at Tess.

Tess looked down at herself and cringed. Underwater, day-clothes removed, Tess floated in her undergarments. The thin white cotton clung tight to her skin, revealling all which a proper woman should keep secret.

Tess grappled with her brown bag still belted between her breasts and around her crotch. "Screw it! I'm still a lady!"

A net of black lace fell upon the professor. Tess saw Ziracuny's teeth shine in triumph and heard her cackling cry of victory. It was then that she discovered her foe's advantage. Ziracuny had gills!

"I will not be caught in a fish's net!"

Amidst noxious gasses, fumes, and oxygen bombs, Tess dared not use a torch to free herself. Instead, she used her handy-dandy sewing scissors in pocket 88, row 16, of her bag. She cut her way through the netting, and as she untangled herself, inadvertently pulled on it. Entwined in stalactites, stalagmites, and shattered walls, it caused the cavern to further crumble.

She grabbed a rock and wrapped it in a length of torn netting. Then she pulled a loop and threw it towards Ziracuny. Braying with glee, the queen dodged the rock. Too late, she realized she was not the target. The lasso caught the trunk of minerals standing strong in the whirlwind of the cave. Ziracuny's dive placed her at the mercy of the storm.

A subterfuge pulled with sucking gravity, displacing Ziracuny. She was spun like a wild top, around and over upon itself. Sucked backwards, she collided with Tess.

Ziracuny lunged face first and bit into Tess's scalp. The gravitational pull forced her away. A chunk of hair ripped out with a hideous grin.

Tess remembered the glow in the dark algae fuel that Verdandi added to her silver compass watch. She wound the bi-directional rotating bezel and pulled the helium escape valve. A streaming beam of green light shot forth, illuminating her blind maze.

Subterranean oceanic creatures with phosphoric tendencies were attracted to the light. Her view thusly enhanced, she could navigate and dart away from Ziracuny, who tumbled half-sightless in the slippery dark behind her.

Ziracuny called out in a menacing sing song. "That's right precious professor. You think you are getting away. But I am on your tail. Wait until you find yourself in open water. That is MY element." Her creepy cackle echoed in the cavern.

Chapter 77

Ziracuny chased Tess through dark grottos and caverns. Steam spurted uncontrollably. In places, the grottos were flooded with deep basins of rushing water from cracks above.

"You will boil in your own broth, little frog, with your luscious grin spreading like the ocean around you." Ziracuny aimed an arm cannon at the ceiling as they both struggled through the twisty caverns. A section of limestone crumbled through the rock matrix. Fresh springs from the surface poured upon Tess with such force that she fell backwards and slid on slippery algae.

"Are you trying to drown us?" she screamed.

"I am not quite sure that is possible," answered Ziracuny. The gills in her throat widened and pulsated.

Tess clung to a strong-rooted kelp. She knew she couldn't hold on much longer. Heavy masses of water beat down upon her. Displacing it was out of the question, and she couldn't achieve the buoyancy required to swim. The kelp started loosening from its home. Her body spun uncontrollably in the tumult.

She flashed back to the terror that had brought her to Waltham.

The train.

The steam.

The spinning, spinning, spinning, before the final crash.

Bodies flung with metal debris. Wood and flesh, steel and bone; all cracked.

A shock of heat brought her back to the moment. Ziracuny was using jet propulsion to swim!

No, re-thought Tess. She is flying.

The professor yet wound her fingers around the struggling kelp as she watched the queen accelerate towards her. She closed her eyes and counted to three.

Then she and the kelp let go at the same time.

Chapter 78

Tess fell and rose again, then fell. She bent her knees and her feet landed on Ziracuny's head. Straightening her arms, she sprung from Ziracuny's face.

The opposing stream of rushing water caused cavitation. Tess was suddenly glad that she was down to her skivvies; less drag on her momentum. Curving her shoulders before the surface's imminent impact, she prepared for landing.

With a crash like the sound of smashing glass, Tess and Ziracuny broke through the surface. Tess rolled onto wet sand and bounced like a ripe coconut.

The sky bled red into the churning sea. The glare cast fiery shadows upon the island, so that everywhere Tess's eyes darted, she imagined she saw Ziracuny creeping upon her.

Lightening flashed across the moon.

Tess fingered her silver compass watch mindlessly as she assessed her next move. She pulled magnetic-block bands from her bag and slipped them up her biceps.

Thunder boomed and hail splattered, sizzling upon hot sand. Tess turned slowly in a full circle. She needed to get her bearings. She unhinged the clasp of the compass watch. The needle searched for North.

Where was Ziracuny? How would she defend herself? Anxiety flooded Tess's neurons.

Lightening flashed again in rapid succession. The horizon became illuminated by the spinning crystals above each pyramid, creating cataclysmic rainbows. It was then that Tess realized she was standing in the epicentre of the pyramids' power grid. She threw herself prone to the shiny sand, but not soon enough.

Ziracuny pounced and the two women tumbled together; hands and claws, teeth and fangs; lace and leather.

Electricity crackled between and throughout. With matching cries of pain, the professor and queen were zapped into oblivion.

Chapter 79

Tess and Ziracuny heard their screams within their heads, and felt their bodies simultaneously freeze and burn together. Green fog escaped their combined breaths.

Pain and intense temperatures subsided, yet the two women were inexplicably paralyzed. They could only clutch each other's throats and blink their eyes as they witnessed the future.

Horizontal rows of expressionless soldiers marched with perfect synchronicity. The emblem of a red dragon glowed from black breastplates. Behind each wide row, machines of human form scraped along the dusty parade path. Their round eyes were sightless; their mouths nonexistent. Large ears rose from their heads like dueling trumpets.

Mechanized taxidermied creatures maneuvered grotesquely along the crowds eagerly watching the procession. People pressed flowers into the dead orifices, and were rewarded with chewy candies from the non-being's bowels. Following close by in scattered masses were naked children, making sport of collecting the most sweets.

Bugles announced the royal carriage.

Ziracuny's lips curved up, and Tess's stomach turned upside down. This sight was too much, too real, too wonderfully horrible.

For on top of an automaton dragon of gold, there was latched an onyx throne. Upon the throne, amassed in furs, was the unequivocal Queen Ziracuny.

In her hand she pulled chained reigns. They were not directing her vehicle, however. They were pulling and dragging the political power of her pride.

Tess's throat emitted an involuntary scream of lamentation.

Connected to the chains by rings around their necks, three human forms alternately dragged and dredged in the dirt. Tess recognized herself first; her black hair matted with dried blood. Then she saw Bashelle, with half her skull missing. Afraid to discover the further horror, she yet could not divert herself from identifying the next human. Verdandi. Her face pale and expressionless like a statuesque drone.

Skeletal, yet beautiful despite the deathly shadows within her eyes.

"I won," bleated Ziracuny. The words echoed in Tess's ears.

The golden dragon opened wide its jaws and roared with thunder. It belched a flame of green gas. The chemicals drifted over the time-lost enemies, and they felt their bodies regain control, even as the world around them began to spin.

Chapter 80

Hail the size of hockey pucks pelted the two women as they disengaged from each other's grasps. Ziracuny rose first, aiming her plasma blaster at Tess's crotch.

"You think that hasn't been done before?" asked Tess. She snapped her fingers and pulled a loose thread from the lacy cuffs of her bloomers. A blue light travelled from her fingertips to the thread, then spread over the entirety of her being, so that a thin sheath of blue veiled her. "No conductors for your electric weapons here, ma'am."

Ziracuny pulled the trigger nonetheless. Sparks flurried around Tess's countenance. Fire arced, connecting the women in an alternate current. Lightening shattered the sky, and hail evapourated with jolts of green haze.

Ziracuny and Tess instinctively blocked their heads from the impending flurry of falling stones. Tiny white pebbles of crystalized ice descended upon them in fast fury. Within seconds, they were covered to their necks in teensy rubble.

The hailstorm stopped, yet the thunder continued. A bell gonged, drawing the women's attention.

Before them was a large, crumbling, chipped brick building. Generations of ivy clung, dead and alive, trailing over and around bare branches and nubile leaves, in an endless quest to climb, rising ever upward, tracing the crevices between each brick.

On top of the building hung a large bell. Below the bell, partially shrouded in the overgrowth, a sign: BOT.

"The BOT building," breathed Tess, barely believing her eyes. "I haven't seen this place in, fifteen years? Eighteen?"

"Try twenty," said Ziracuny, taking strange delight in her stuck situation.

"Yes," said Tess, remembering. "It has been twenty. How did you know?"

Tess was distracted from the answer by movement nearby. A gilded pony shuffled up the cobbled walkway to the landing and whinnied. The door opened. A governess stepped out, balancing a babe in one arm and a broom in the other. The pony whinnied again.

"Oh my," said the old woman. "I haven't enough hands at any time." She turned back toward the door. "Mistress Alset," she called, "please come at once to retrieve your parcel."

Tess gazed in wonder at the young girl who slouched through the door. Dirty feet bore no witness to the hot rocky stairs. The pony opened its mouth and regurgitated a small blue box.

"I know what this is," said Tess out loud.

"Of course you do, you fool; you are witnessing your past."

Tess, enchanted by the memory, ignored Ziracuny. "My silver timepiece. My most treasured possession. This is when it first touched my fingers."

A westerly wind blew, and the scene floated away with it. In its place was a new scene, same setting, different time. Over and over, young Tess was called out to retrieve exorbitant packages addressed to her at the Boston Orphan Trainlot.

Chromexel boots from Alden's; hobble-skirts from Jordan Marsh; Abalone hair pins from Grover Cronin's; flirty undergarments from Filene's. In each scene, Tess grew taller, stood higher, and stepped stronger. The old woman got older, but she always had a babe in arms.

The scene switched again, and this time, young Tess walked out alone, her brown leather bag shiny with beeswax. Her elegant skirt featured horizontal draping with hidden strings and hooks. Tess remembered designing the accruements to this gift, her favourite princess line dress.

A hansom carriage clopped towards the orphanage.

"How strange," said Tess, "to see oneself as young, to know the journey ahead, and yet not knowing how the journey started. I never found out who my benefactor was."

"You truly are a dunce," said Ziracuny. Just then lightening flashed again, the wind swirled, and the imprisoning crystals disintegrated in thunder's sonic boom.

Ziracuny was on Tess before she could think a thought. "Now I have you, and we go where I want!" The women were caught in the swirling vortex. "Immortality!"

Chapter 81

"With time travel, I can be immortal! Never die! Always rule!"

Ziracuny's words travelled in currents through air and space. The Earth spun, Ziracuny spun, Tess spun. Suns and moons do-si-doed across murky skies. The world faded to black, then blue, then green. A flash of light like an exploding star blinded the time travellers until they felt the solidity of their bodies and the world around them again.

Before them was a palisade dripping with red roses. Their scent permeated the women's lungs.

All around them, life flitted and flew, sprang and sang, swayed and played. God's Eden could not have been more lush.

A red serpent slid up creamy birch logs and flittered its spiked black tongue.

Tess and Ziracuny followed closely behind, effortlessly. It felt as if they were moving only in their minds.

The serpent continued its path intently. A fledgling pterosaur swooped low and crashed with fright into the briar when it heard the cobra's malevolent hiss.

"I know this place," hummed Tess.

"I do too," said Ziracuny, her eye never leaving the hood of the snake.

Smooth zephyrs swished sheer curtains. The snake slid beneath the silk.

"No," trembled Tess. "No, no, stop! No!" Within her body she flailed, but she could not move, trapped as she was within her own mind.

A white bassinet rocked on its own accord. The child within hiccoughed in her sleep.

"Rose," cried Tess. "Someone! Save her!"

The serpent turned towards Tess as if hearing her plea. It curled its long body into coils of diamonds. Then it struck.

Tess screamed.

The serpent lunged at the baby. It wrapped its long body around chubby limbs. Its forked tongue flicked into the child's mouth, and went on to lick the entire sleeping face.

The snake continued to coil. Soon the baby's face and body were obscured by black with sharp bands of red.

"Rose! My Rose!" Tess blubbered hysterically.

She continued screaming for help.
None came.

The air shifted. Zephyrs were displaced by a southeastern gale. Winds whipped the nursery curtains and beat the basinet with blustery blows.

Birdsong died. In its place was a wild whomping sound, like giant wings spanking the air.

Green mist oozed with the gusting ozone. The serpent was gone. But as the song of birds was replaced by a foreboding clap, so was the snake replaced by something much more treacherous.

There stood Ziracuny, cradling the sleeping child in her arms. Her blue eyes chanced a glance into Tess's.

Tess gasped.

"How can this be? How can this be real?" Next to her, Ziracuny howled like a coyote after a kill. "What have you done?" Ziracuny continued to howl.

"You demon, hellhound, savage monster! Bug buggerer! What did you do to her? Where is she? I'll mangle you to bits!"

Ziracuny's howl turned to laughter.

Tess broke the seal of her subconscious and her body awoke. In seconds she had knocked Ziracuny to the thorny ground and hog tied her with a length of hanging vine.

"So help me, I seek to do no harm, but I will kill you little by little, bit by bit, as you have killed me each day since you stole my daughter. You do not have enough blood to bleed for the life I have lost. Where is she? I demand to know! I will count to three, and if I do not have my answer, then pray to all gods and devils you might, for no heaven or hell will restrain my wrath."

She pulled Ziracuny by the scalp so she could look directly into her eye as she counted. "One...two...THREE!"

The ground beneath them rumbled, cracked open like a hungry dirt-filled mouth, and swallowed them up in one gulp.

Chapter 82

Unified forces enacted upon the buried women. Electromagnetism and gravity intersected and bent in jagged waves.

Beneath the entombed women boiled an ancient hot spring.

The ground gurgled like a hungry belly. Then it vomited chunks of long-forgotten ore and columns of steam.

Spewing towers of water dislodged Tess and Ziracuny from their graves. Their bodies fell upon a rocky ledge. A deluge of crusty shells fell upon them as they grappled, inches from the high shore.

They worked independently but with the same goal: staying alive.

The island shook. Chunks of larva floated and cooled in mucky patterns.

Tess and Ziracuny sprinted to the closest pyramid and scaled its leaning facade. At the top, they stood, staring at each other. Through the glow of living emerald, they each saw death.

Tess shouted an unintelligible syllable and dove at Ziracuny. Her fingers found the hidden gill slits of her foe and pulled them open. Cold flesh bled in Tess's fiery hands. Ziracuny responded with claws to Tess's breasts. Tess yelled, not in agony, but in the hopeful death of dying with her enemy.

The emerald glowed brighter and brighter. Green; everything was green. In a flash, the spinning emerald shattered, piercing the women with a thousand points of light. The pyramid shifted, and disintegrated into sandy wind.

Down, down, down dropped the deadly pair. Down into darkness.

Chapter 83

Geothermal energy from deep inside hot springs simmered in Subton Sea. Seismic waves carved through rocks, creating tunnels circulating with steam. Dormant volcanoes awoke with shifting fractures, and the sea floor quaked.

Tremours shook the ground, the sea, the air. Islands trembled. Floating awry, they struck each other. Smashed masses of land drifted down to the oceanic cityscape.

Down also, fell Tess and Ziracuny, through an abandoned magma tunnel.

Verdandi watched the human rubble fall. She knew what to do, how to help, if only she could swim quickly enough.

She flipped her metal mermaid fins and jetted towards the airlock wherein she and Yoki had spent so many carefree hours, hidden from stresses of the world.

There it was! The contraption they had built together. Its purpose was to provide a sanctuary in the tunnels, without being seen or heard.Now it would be used not to keep evil out, but to trap evil in.

Verdandi prepared the tunnel block. First she used a pressurized hose to soak the sea weed balloon within the tunnel. It expanded, filling the inner entrance. Then she deployed the plasma wall they had created, inspired by the one surrounding Subton. Their version incorporated an invisible airlock in the tunnel. So when they swam in, they could apply the plasma screen while water was suctioned out.

Verdandi employed the tunnel block just as Tess jumped out. Ziracuny was right behind her, and became shut in the tunnel. Mere seconds passed until she could blast her way through, but Tess gained a head start. A defensive stance was better than a fleeing one.

Ziracuny's armour sparkled in the reflections of battle. A legion of DRAKE soldiers cheered when they saw her.

Her voice reverberated loud and clear. "All my descamisados expect me to outshine the enemy. I will not disappoint them!"

Tess gulped and swallowed seawater in astonishment at the sight of a little mermaid.

The sultry siren swam closer through the sandstorm swirling in briny turmoil. Rounded hips, buoyant bosoms, floating strands of red hair crowning her head naturally.

Water went up Tess's nose. Her ears, throat, and brain tingled. Then she finally figured it out. "Verdandi!" she shouted, more in surprise than in attempted communication.

Verdandi did not hear the professor, so focused was she on Ziracuny. "In your palace almighty queen? Do you know what I know? Do you?" She pulled her robotic arm back. Young people from BSDINK and the Mutineers came up behind her to help, but they were too far away to encircle and entrap Ziracuny.

Ziracuny calculated the opposition and decided to attack Tess. To the shock of all, she sprouted winged appendages and flew through water.

Tess raised her hands and used her arm bands to emit electromagnetic pulses. Ziracuny swerved, and snatched at Tess's brown bag. Her talon-like fingers grabbed the belt tightly, and whisked Tess to deeper water.

Tess and Ziracuny fought for the bag and its contents. Ziracuny's wild eye found the gleam of her prize. Tess unbelted the bag from her body, but too late. Ziracuny palmed the treasure she had been seeking.

"All this time. Every battle I waged. For this trinket. This trifle!" She laughed maniacally. "How trivial it is now! It was all I had wanted, and now I no longer need it! I have what I want. And nobody else can have it."

Tess watched in horror as Ziracuny twirled her precious silver timepiece between her fingers. Releasing the Tiffany chain, it sunk slowly down to the depths of Subton Sea.

Tess did not hesitate. She would rather lose her life than lose this, the only instrument she trusted to lead her to lost happiness, her one hope of finding her daughter. She darted towards it, intent on its retrieval.

"Not so fast little fishy." Ziracuny unholstered her proton blaster and casually aimed.

Electrostatic particles fired in a fine stream of radially polarized neutrons. They attracted instantly to the silver timepiece. Tess was a metre away when the circle flashed in a millisecond of prismatic light, then disintegrated into nothingness.

Tess felt her heart stop ticking.

She continued her descent to the depths, incapable of processing this newest pain.

"You continually make life too easy for me," said Ziracuny. She aimed her proton blaster again.

A bronze bolt struck the blaster and removed it completely from her grasp. "What insolence is this?"

Verdandi sprung her crossbow on her mechanized arm and loaded another bolt.

In the deepening darkness, Tess saw a flash of light. When she saw Verdandi's silhouette, hope reentered her heart, and she dashed up.

Ziracuny removed a subatomic tangent missile from her tool belt. Tess recognized it at once; she was the one who had invented it. Quickly, she retrieved her sinking bag and scavenged through pockets. She pulled out her diffusion rod and fired it before Ziracuny could pull the plug.

Tess, Verdandi, and Ziracuny were discombobulated by the high pitched squeal. Ziracuny regained orientation first. "It did not have to come to this. But who can resist two fish with one hook?" She snapped her fingers and pressed them to the onyx gems upon her head. Then she cupped her hands and pulled a glowing electric globe from her palms. "The Life-Ray is yet mine, but I will share it with you, just this once."

Silently stalking, the sleek predator approached. Perfectly camouflaged, it was almost impossible for even a fully sighted person to discern from the shimmers of waves and patches of shadow.

The alpha mammal was not alone. She was guiding a partner; a peer.

Gecko glue covered Martina's right hand. With it, she could hold on to Ani's smooth skin without pinching.

In Martina's left hand was a blow dart.

She whispered to Ani. "I see my bullet twice. Once when it leaves my scope. Then just before it hits the target. When have you known me to miss?"

She lifted the blow dart to her lips and lined up the beads. She pressed her tongue over the chamber and inhaled as deeply as she could. Then she closed her lips tight around the tube, withdrew her tongue, and blew with all her might.

Tess and Verdandi had scarcely regained clear thought when the prey was mortally wounded. Blood exploded from every orifice of Ziracuny's body.

Bells rang out from the Subton Tower. Martina sang along. "Ding dong the witch is dead!"

Chapter 84

Ziracuny detached a syringe of bubbling green liquid from her arm garter and pierced Tess's breast with it.

The needle did not inject; instead it drew. Fresh clean red live blood.

She shook the vial, mixing the liquids into a blinding yellow. She grasped the syringe tightly before her, and plunged it into her own chest.

"What the heck?" said Martina. "I already killed her! She doesn't hafta die twice!"

Ziracuny's body stopped pouring blood. Her mutilation regenerated, healing beneath torn armour.

She lifted her eyepatch. A white ball rolled round and round within the socket, before strapping itself in with strips of flesh. A blue iris formed and the pupil dilated.

Tess floated backwards in astonishment, realizing the incredible truth of what she had just witnessed.

Bubbles escaped the queen's mouth as water pulsated in and out of her gills.

"Tess," said Ziracuny with a wicked gleam, "I am your mother."

Chapter 85

Just then, Yoki whizzed by on her blue skidoo, followed by her mongrel navy. She zoomed in and snagged Ziracuny by the hair. Her crew dashed from their vehicles and tied the sea witch securely with lengths of seaweed.

"What do we do with her?" they asked.

"Kill her," said Martina.

"Enslave her," said Verdandi.

"Torture her," said Tess.

Yoki considered her options. With a deflated breath she decided for all of them.

"Pity her."

The skidoo crew unceremoniously pulled their captive back to the city and deposited her in the dungeon.

A series of canon blasts drew attention back to the battle.

Yoki held her hands out. Her cupped palms faced the surface. She moved them in a clockwise circle three times. Her crew, even those unaccustomed to this ancient Subtonian ritual, copied her.

She revved her engine, lifted her fist to the sky, and shouted, "Steam on!"

Chapter 86

Verdandi, as a mermaid, with her self-styled weaponry and mechanisms, was an even more dangerous hybrid fighter than the monsters of DRAKE.

Anglerfish with glowing grenades incinerated themselves upon encountering her coconut smokers.

Electric catfish lost their currents when sprayed with tubes of hagfish slime.

Hybrid squid squirted hot whale oil at the Mutineers. Verdandi launched an antimatter shield to protect them.

Bashelle whooped. "Now THAT is some anti-dis-establishment-tary-ism!"

Young scientists who had been corrupted by DRAKE were inspired by the rehabilitation of their BSDINK peers. They tore off their lab coats and joined the calamity. This was their best dream and worst nightmare combined!

They enacted their stabilizers to save their creatures, old and new. The ancient creatures they had been dissecting. The

Frankenstein creatures they had created. The genetically hybrid beings they had borne. All were reanimated, recharged, reassembled, and reprogrammed. With jet packs and megaphones, they unleashed the beasts.

E to the X – DY -DX
E to the X – DX
cosine, secant, tangent, sine,
3 – point – 1 – 4 – 1 – 5 – 9
square root, cube root, log of pi,
DISINTEGRATE THEM, die, DRAKE, die!

Dormant volcanoes awoke. Their restrain lost, they burst with bullets of rock, fiery lava, and sooty ash. The sea darkened. Chunks of floating islands sank, destroying the buildings below them. Geysers continued their thrombotic pulse.

Pace marched heavily across the sea floor, aiming his arm cannon and enacting multi-sonic force fields. He called out to his compeers. "The closer we come to annihilation, the closer we come to freedom!"

Waves bubbled with boiling hot breath, creating quick currents, and melting sandy island shores away. The coral covered metal beams lending support to the islands collapsed.

"Frikkin electronolisis!" raged Bashelle. "It kills ANY steel under water." She sought cover where there was none. The battleground was a blind abyss.

Long defunct organisms buried beneath solid inches of hazardous runoff stirred. Rerouted in a whirlwind, tiny microbes floated and joined together. Jubilant spurts of fresh red streams exerted new life into the battle, unlike the whisping wafts of blood.

A steam powered race ensued, as both sides sought safety. In the chaos, bridges were crashed and docks were demolished. Superheated molten machines scathed their drivers' hands and blistered skin so that metal vehicles had to be abandoned.

All of Subton was being demolished in furious anarchy. The Subton Tower chimed and clanged in agonizing complaint.

Yoki checked her compass. Everywhere was North; nowhere was North.

She retrieved her satchel from the grotto, using her memory rather than her senses for navigation. She made it to Subton Tower and traced her hands upon the base. She could feel sand granules hopping up from beneath it. Sonarized quicksand!

She was prepared for catastrophe, no matter what form it took. Up she floated, using her hands as guides upon the vibrating structure. She knew what she must do, before the tower, and perhaps all of Subton, was swallowed whole.

At the top of the tower, the noise was so loud that Yoki could feel the nerves in her teeth shake. Her eyes were burning in the ashy, torrid, haze.

Straddling a vibrating chime, she reached two hands into her satchel. The holy gems felt heavier going back than they did coming out. She replaced the gems with exactness. Then she leaned over, grabbed the switch, and pulled.

Chaos ensued upon chaos.

Yoki clung to the spire. She closed her eyes, protecting them from debris. Strange, she thought. She could feel the world spinning around her, but her body sensed no momentum. Her hanging legs weren't swinging. Her satchel wasn't pulling at her chest. She opened her eyes.

The world was spinning around her. Or rather, around the Subton Tower. The red and blue gems blazed. The giant compass upon the dome spiraled and spun in the dizzy gyroscope. Its blue glow grew stronger, deeper, brighter. The clockwork fish swam around and around and around, intersecting endlessly.

Around the tower, water swirled in an incessant twirling dance.

The bell stopped ringing. The chimes stopped chiming. All at once, everything was silent. The world paused, as if frozen. Except for Yoki. She saw what happened next. She heard the glass break. She felt the gold burn.

An explosive shock wave broke the peace. The compass, all compasses; all timepieces in Subton, melted. Their faces dripped, their numbers smeared, their colours blended. The Subton Tower turned bronze.

The melting continued throughout Subton Sea. Just as the metal merged with the tower, so did the individual timepieces and compasses melt. They absorbed into water. They absorbed into skin.

They blended into bodies and spread throughout with a golden glow.

People screamed in panic. "What's happening," they demanded of each other. They could see through themselves as if they were living, breathing X-rays. Arms and legs and bloody ribs; cheeks revealing the teeth within.

Martina remained sitting on the ocean floor. She cradled Bashelle's bloody body in her arms.

"Please, don't leave me, please!"

Bashelle smiled wanly. "You can always forget me; I'll never remember."

"No, no, stay, please! I'll do anything! I'll even learn how to - GADZOOKS!"

Bashelle opened her eyes and squeezed Martina's hand. "Gadzooks? You're tapped."

Martina grabbed Bashelle's face and kissed her hard.

"What in crab nuggets and curly fries has gotten into you?" Bashelle pushed on Martina's shoulders for leverage and stood.

Martina jumped up and clung onto her. "Thank you, thank you, thank you!" She cried so hard that she cracked a rib. It healed instantly.

All over Subton the scenario replicated itself. The wounded were healed; the dying were refreshed to life. They were whole and well again.

The X-ray apparition faded, but the rejuvenation remained.

The battle was over. DRAKE no longer existed.

Chapter 87

Tess poured hot tea and Verdandi passed around scones and lox. A fortnight had passed since the Second Battle of Subton, and a new sense of normalcy was being forged.

This morning, the women were discussing the artifact that had been discovered the previous day.

"What good fortune," said Tess, "to be reunited with some of the original pieces crafted by Verdandi."

"I could've simply recreated it," said Verdandi.

Bashelle bit into a muffin. "The new engine just needs a little tune up, then we can begin our journey."

Martina groaned. "Please no, anything but being in that old tin can again!"

"No worries," soothed Bashelle. "It is a new and improved tin can!"

After breakfast, Bashelle, Tess, and Pace met in the machine shop to work on the engine.

"This thermo syphon system you use here for your watch maintenance and vehicle propulsion is just the thing I needed to get this baby going right," said Bashelle. "Now the pumps are perfect. Top of the radiator cools, and it immediately lowers. This woulda come in handy the first time around."

Pace looked up from his task of winching the engine. "Glad to help!"

Tess handed an L drive to Bashelle. "The zinc is a marvelous idea."

"No big deal. Zinc for electrolysis; it is a sacrificial mineral. There is friction with watercraft, and it causes electrolysis which wears away the good stuff. Zinc bonds to it first, preventing rapid onset of rust. You can apply zinc to the L drive because it's in the water, and the zinc attacks it before rust can."

"You are one smart sailor," said Pace.

"I'm not that smart. But it works."

Pace finished winching and stood back from his work. Tess handed him a cold glass of lemon water.

"You're gonna laugh when I tell you the parts we need," said Bashelle. "It's like a two piece set. They don't even exist anymore. It is a set of points, I figured there would be a problem there. It needs nine times horsepower if that is even possible, with the magnanimity to force through high lunar tides and cataclysmic reactions."

"Cataclysmic?" asked Tess.

Bashelle brushed her aside. "Hush up, the grown ups are talking here."

Tess crossed her arms but managed not to stomp her foot.

"Oh you mean these?" Pace pressed a pocket on his abdomen and a drawer slid open. He reached in and twisted a lever, then rotated a tiny knob with his thick fingers.

"Whoah." Bashelle was enraptured by the mechanism. Then she felt her face grin. "Not easy to find the nub with big cold fingers now is it?"

Pace lifted his gaze questioningly.

Bashelle held up her fingers, closed them together, and rubbed an imaginary spot in the air.

"Oh!" Pace self-consciously chuckled. "You surely understand being a cyborg does not preclude me from having a human touch." He winked at Tess, who was increasingly reddening.

"I shall leave the two of you to continue your fine work," said Tess, and she pranced out.

Moments passed and Pace said, "I wish we could have shared more time together, Bashelle. I have a feeling I could learn a lot from you."

"Yeah, you probably could."

He finished retrieving the needed pieces and handed them to her. "Now, these parts are more common than you have assumed. Here in Subton, these switches are our specialty; it is what makes us a vital Watch City. We use them in all our compasses. I'll gift these to you without reserve, in honour of our friendship. But next time, you're buying me a draught of ale."

"Consider it done. Why don't we have a downpayment on it now?"

"Always thinking and planning! Lets go."

They lumbered off to the former Mutineer building for a pint.

Pace stopped. "Hold on a minute."

"What now?"

Pace pointed to the abandoned DRAKE officers' quarters. "I bet they have got quite the setup in there!"

"Now you're talking. Always planning!"

"That's what we do!" agreed Pace.

Martina and Verdandi were completing their own contribution to the new vessel.

"We have the technology," said Verdandi. "And if not, we'll make it. It's not gonna be a total failure."

"You got that for sure. Cuz if you wanna do it right, it takes time!" said Martina. "Aw, dammit! Lookit this!"

Verdandi walked around the workbench to see what had Martina so upset.

"The condenser is a problem cuz it cannot have cracks in it. That is definitely a problem." She fired up her new plasma torch and used crystals to repair the glass.

She met Verdandi's eyes. Her commanding voice softened. "Only scars are permanent. And even they can fade with time."

Chapter 88

The moon waned and waxed. Yoki was voted the rightful governor of Subton. The dead were mourned in Subton fashion. The injured were being healed and the addicted were being treated. Ziracuny awaited trial.

All of Subton assembled to bid their Waltham visitors farewell. Verdandi and Yoki embraced as the moon rose.

"I really wish you would come with us. It would be a grande adventure."

"One day, I will join you on many quests, no doubt. Right now, though, my crusade is here."

"This is just the reason you were voted in so quickly!"

Yoki laughed. "Are you sure it wasn't because of my hairstyling talent?" She ruffled Verdandi's red locks.

"Yeah, I'm sure. One hundred percent."

Timpani announced the start of the celebration. Yoki pulled Verdandi's hand.

"We'd better get going to the ballroom! Bashelle is providing musical entertainment tonight."

"I am not sure that is something we need to hurry for."

"You might be more entertained than you imagine!"

Governor Yoki took centre stage and began the ceremony.

"The Watch Cities have been a steady unified force in our ever-changing modern world. Fair labour conditions, environmental health, social and economic development; these are just a few examples of the great feats our cities succeed at and strive for.

Subton and Waltham are specially bonded now through all of time, and thus, we would like to bequeath to you, Watch City of Waltham Ambassadors, this Freedom of the City Award. For each of you, this award comes with Subton's friendship, partnership, and citizenship. Tess the Magnificent, Martina the Honourable, Bashelle the Robust, and

Verdandi the Valiant: may your clocks always chime."

The Ambassadors bowed, answering the courteous reply: "May they ring in your harmony."

Pace stepped across the stage and bowed before each woman individually before stopping before Tess. "Subton hereby acknowledges and awards Waltham with Freedom of the City, to come and go as is pleasurable and necessary, at any time, for any occasion. Our hearts go with you where you go. Please accept this symbol of our mutual admiration and respect. You will discover it will propel you through turbulence, and steer you through rough waters. I present to you, the Subton Switch."

Tess accepted the heavy gift and stepped forward. Her voice projected clearly through the many amplification horns.

"If there is nothing to stop the flow of water it will flow forever. So with time. If you are on a boat floating in an endless river with no barricades you will forever propel.

Gravity itself is a barricade. If you defy gravity, you can defy time. We travel in time each day, moving forward at its leisure, regardless of our watch hands. We can wind our watches ahead, so that the hands pass hours within minutes, but it does not change time. When we make static time we can stop the time within us but not outside of us. When we leave our static time, we have effectively stepped into the future. Each step we take is into the future, and there is no way to get ahead. There have been experiments with time mirrors to look past, but never have we been able to look ahead besides those people gifted with visions. Just seeing the future is not experiencing the future. What if you had the power to swim the river of time? You could swim ahead upstream or backstroke against the current. It is possible if there was no force stopping it. Time is unstoppable; now we need an unstoppable force to guide us through it. Together, we are unstoppable."

The Subtonians cheered. "Good luck, may time serve you well!"

The Walthamites responded. "May time circle around and serve you back!"

Pace addressed the energized populous. "It is now my privilege to offer the stage to Bashelle the Robust. Please feel welcome to dance and sing and eat and drink the night away!"

Equipment strange to Tess's eyes were pulled onto the stage. "What manner of tools are these items?"

Verdandi took her hand and jumped with excitement. "Musical instruments!"

"Bashelle? And music? Oy vey."

A prismatic ball of light was lowered over the stage, reflecting the colours of Subton with millions of rainbows.

"Hello, Subton!" Bashelle's voice was unusually loud. The crowd went wild.

Tess delicately placed sound blockers in her ears. "What in all of humanity is that object she is speaking into?"

Verdandi blushed. "It's nothing much."

"Excuse me?" Tess removed a sound blocker.

"It's just a thing I made. A transducer that converts sound into an electrical signal."

"You invented that?"

"Well, no, maybe, yeah, but Yoki did too. We did it together!" Verdandi's humility faded as the joy of inventing with her friend filled her heart. "It uses a coil of wire suspended into a magnetic field. Yoki calls it a dynamic microphone."

Tess removed the other sound blocker. "You truly give me hope for the future Verdandi!"

Bashelle's voice bounced across the ballroom.

"Are you ready Yoki?"

"Uh-huh."

"Ricci?"

"Yeah."

"Martina?"

"Okay."

"Alright gals, let's go!"

"I swam with the smelts and the snappers
Floated with the pikes and the jacks
Dove with the chubs and the croakers

I'd still like to get my stickleback

Oh, I see a man at the back as a matter of
fact
His eyes are as red as the sun
And the girl in the corner let no one ignore
her
Cause she thinks she's the passionate one

Oh yeah! It was like lightning
Everybody was fighting
And the music was soothing
And they all started grooving
Yeah, yeah, yeah-yeah-yeah

And the man in the back said everyone
attack
And it turned into a Subton Switch
And the girl in the corner said boy I want to
warn you
It'll turn into a Subton Switch
Subton Switch, Subton Switch, Subton
Switch, Subton Switch"

Pace and Tess danced until Polaris
stopped winking.

Part Four

Chapter 89

Verdandi operated the sonar station. "We are going too fast for me to get accurate readings. Tess, can we please slow down?"

"I am trying to reduce acceleration, but the controls are not responding. Bashelle! What is the situation down there?"

"The steam has stopped," Bashelle hollered from the boiler room.

"What do you mean?" asked Tess.

"Can't be," said Martina.

"Crawl down and see for yourself!"

All four women gathered in the sweltering room.

"What is the issue?" asked Tess.

Bashelle pointed to the manifold. "I can't see it!" She reached towards the tubes. "I'm thinking if we open it up, we can dislodge a blockage."

"Stop!" screamed Verdandi.

Bashelle froze, her palms just centimetres from the tubes.

"Everyone: don't touch it!" Verdandi held her breath.

Tess's eyes widened. She realized what was happening. "Verdandi, you just saved us all!"

Verdandi breathed again.

"What, what is it?" asked Bashelle, hiding her hands in her apron pockets.

Tess turned to Verdandi. "Would you care to explain?"

"The steam is so hot and under so much pressure it is invisible. That's why we are going so fast!"

Tess climbed back up to the control room. "Look at these levels!"

"Whoah," said Verdandi, following close behind. "That's a lot of electrostatic discharge."

Martina sat in the captain's chair and strapped herself in. "I know what that means."

The control boards crackled.

"Yup. Here it comes," said Martina. "Been there, don't care." She closed her eyes and clutched the arms of the chair as lightening struck.

Chapter 90

The submarine spun like a zeppelin in a
hurricane. Tess held fast the steering wheel
and clacked the change valves. She didn't
need to check the compass rose to know that
she was directionless. They were
directionless.

"The rudder is stuck!" shouted
Verdandi.

"Dammit," added Bashelle, "the bell-
crank shaft on the control cylinder is
unresponsive, immobile!"

Tess rotated the periscope, unbelieving
her eyes. She referenced the compass at the
helm. The needle shivered. Magnetic
North, true North, then it flipped to South,
and the needle spun backwards. The poles
switched, and switched again.
She lunged for the microphone that Bashelle
had insisted they bring with them.

"Crew, we have a problem."

"Get on with it," moaned Martina.

"It would appear that we are nearing a
black hole of sorts."

"A what?" Bashelle shouted over the humming sound of blood rushing through her ears.

All at once, the submarine stopped. The conserved momentum sent the crew flying, except for Martina who stayed strapped to the chair. Chicken brisket flew from her stomach.

"What is that humming sound?" asked Verdandi.

"Oh, heavens, you hear it too? I thought was losing my hearing with my lunch," said Martina.

"It's getting louder," said Bashelle. "The hum is increasing. Look - the control panels brightened. Yet the engines remain nonfunctional."

"How are we not sinking," wondered Verdandi.

"Because," said Tess, "it is a black hole! And we are in its pull." Shock took the emotion from her voice.

The submarine jerked forward, and slowly increased speed. Beyond the windows, the sea drifted on ultraviolet waves.

Faster and faster, the sub was pulled. The distance between the black hole and the crew shortened leagues by the minute.

Verdandi clasped Tess's hands. She slipped something hard and smooth between her palms.

"Where did you get this?" Tess asked.

Verdandi turned to Martina. "You gave it to me."

"Strange," said Tess, "it feels heavier now."

"We don't have time to talk now, just use it!" said Verdandi. She led Tess to the new lever above the steering wheel. The Subton Switch.

Tess lifted her precious silver rose compact to the switch. Magnets slid apart, revealing a circular well. Tess placed the timepiece in, and it was a perfect fit. "Together we can steer through rough waters," she whispered.

"Do it," encouraged Verdandi.

Tess pulled the lever. The submarine dipped and jolted forward ever faster through the oceanic black hole.

In a looping funnel, colours of stained glass filtered through the blackness. The submarine propelled with invisible power towards questionable time.

A shadow followed, writhing in monstrous tendrils of extinguished flames. The black hole closed. Thus entered the dragon.

Chapter 91

"That's a nondairy whipped product you know," said Bashelle.

"Shut. Up." Martina unbuckled and took her puke-covered shirt off.

"Is everyone all right?" asked Tess. She covered her nose and mouth with a handkerchief. "Besides the obvious gastrointestinal mishap?"

"We have definitely landed. But look!" Verdandi pressed her face to a porthole. "Tess, I've a feeling we're not in Subton anymore."

Tess nudged her out of the way and peered through the frosty glass. "Mertensia!"

"Who?" asked Verdandi.

"Not who; what. Oyster flowers. I haven't seen so many since," Tess's eyes glazed over, "since suffice it to say it has been a long time."

"My dear professor," said Bashelle, "methinks ye hath swallowed too much seawater. Oysters are mollusks, not plants."

"Right you are, but these flowers have a reputation for tasting like oysters, thus the name. They are quite lovely."

"Hold on," stumbled Martina. "Do you mean real actual flowers, growing from real actual dirt, on real actual land?"

"Why, yes," said Tess. "It appears to be a mountainous-"

"I'm outta here." Martina opened the hatch with belching fury.

Chapter 92

By the time her friends caught up with her, Martina was waist-high in blue heather and naked.

"You long-eared galoot! Your brain has gone fizzy!" Bashelle tackled her, which only made her laugh. She pulled Bashelle close and rolled over on top of her.

"Huzzah! Huzzah to buzzing bees and mossy trees! To honeyed breeze and dirty knees! Kill me afore I'd rejoin the seas!"

Verdandi and Tess looked at each other.

"Those two are knackered."

"Indeed." Tess sighed. "Go on ahead then."

"Really?"

Tess's disapproving gaze melted into a smile. "Of course. There are many ways to be a lady. I do not doubt that one of them is running through insect-infested fields with your friends."

"Yahoo!" Verdandi tripped while attempting to run and kick off her boots at the same time. Then she joined the madness that was friendship.

"Beware of hidden dangers!" warned Tess. "I am going to take a walkabout."

"Silly priss," said Bashelle, "doesn't want to take a piss in front of us."

"You beware!" yelled Martina. "I am ready for a bear to eat me! But you, sweet little morsel, best look out for a big bad wolf!" She cupped her hands to her mouth and howled. Bashelle and Verdandi joined in.

"Absolutely nipped," said Tess, walking away. "Complete whooperups." She paused to admire the roots of a sycamore.

"What are you doing here?"

Tess jumped up and shook her skirts vigourously as if shaking off dust. "I am simply taking in some nature," she explained in agitation. She looked up to address the speaker in a more conservative fashion.

Then she saw.

Her eyes focused. And refocused.

Barren whiteness blanked her brain.

She was deafened by oxygen-rich blood struggling to keep her conscious.

It couldn't be.

"What? You?"

"What am I doing here?" The man twisted his neck to look over his shoulder. "How'd you get here so fast?"

Tess could hear again. Her heart. Her pounding, pounding heart.

"What in the world are you wearing?"

Tess didn't answer. She stepped forward, tentatively, as one walking in the dark. Then she lifted her hands to the man's chest, and felt the life within him. She slid her shaking hands up to his shoulders, and leaned in to smell his throat, his scent. Leather and oil, and something unattainable that she desperately desired.

Her fingertips touched his bristly face. "Kiss me, Hugh."

She did not care if this was real or a dream or a post-mortem spasm. It felt real.

His tongue met hers.

Oh yes, this was incredibly real.

With raucous voices not far off, obscured by trees, the lovers felt somehow alone.

Flurried. Wild. Like a dream.

Green leaves, cool wind, rain!

Clutching wet clothes, Tess felt bark against her back, then a rock between her legs.

Rotating, the couple cleverly balanced over a cold mossy boulder: a remnant of volcanism bursting forth onto a glacier.

Tess and Hugh lay in the puddle they had created. Being drenched had never felt so satisfying. In the distance, voices frantically called.

"Oh, my," said Tess, blinking back raindrops. She tugged at her sopping skirts. "Make haste! They will not believe the miracle of you!" She kissed Hugh firmly on the lips and took off through muddy trails.

Hugh stumbled and fell, entwined in his suspenders. "Wait!" A crash of thunder erased his call.

"There she is!" yelled Martina. "Grab her!"

Bashelle half pulled, half carried Tess down the hill to the sub. "Verdandi says we are in for it!"

"Pause, please! We need to stay! You need to see-"

Martina interrupted. "Listen, missy, nobody wants to stay on dry land more than I do. But that coppertop has consulted her brainiac weather maps and insists we take cover in the sub." She took Tess's hand and lifted her to the hatch.

"We need to go get Hugh, he will need to be safe too!"

Martina and Bashelle exchanged a significant look. Bashelle spun an imaginary gear by her ear.

"Yup," Martina nodded.

Verdandi's voice was high and strained. "Hurry!"

No sooner had Bashelle tightened up the hatch, then the first bolt of lightening struck. Hail the size of limes barraged the sub.

Verdandi occupied the helm. "Push the switch! Push the switch!"

Bashelle pushed, and they jolted forward, through the mysterious black hole.

Martina stripped Tess's wet clothes off and wrapped her in one of the quilts that Subton had donated. Then she joined the others at the helm.

Tess tried to compose herself with soothing thoughts. "Tell yourself over and over. Remember. The trees, the air, the sun, the moon. The wind, the leaves, the stars, the earth..." She passed out.

Chapter 93

Sound waves smashed and combined, bouncing frequencies throughout the hull. Powerful blasts shook the dials of the steering system's main manifold. Randomly intensifying, it was uncontrollable.

The whooshing sound dissipated, became a hum, and ceased.

"That felt like we were locked inside a conch shell!" said Verdandi.

"A strange sensation, surely," agreed Tess.

"I don't sense any movement, and the hydraulic system is unperturbed," said Bashelle. "How are you doing?"

Martina coughed and cleared her throat. "No launch to report, Captain."

"Perhaps you are seaworthy after all!"

"I'd rather not be."

"Geez Louise," gasped Verdandi. "We are home!"

The women disembarked.

From the dock, they could see the columns of the music hall; the steeple of

Saint Mary's; the curving pathways at the peak of Mount Feake.

Yet something was off. Strange.

Then they realized the landmarks of Waltham were there, but they were different somehow.

Things were there that weren't there before: trees were taller than buildings, other buildings stood taller than trees that had never existed.

Tess pulled binocular telescopic goggles over her eyes. "El Museo Telefonico," she read on an awning. "I am fluent in nine languages, and have no idea what that means."

A clickety clackety rhythmic roll approached them.

"Neviah?" Verdandi could not believe her eyes.

"Neviah!" cheered the other women. Joy, shock, gratitude; all combined in streams of tears.

The beloved innkeeper approached them. Then she stopped, without a puff of steam.

She daintily flicked a small switch. Tiny gears hummed. Her wheelchair converted.

Neviah stood, and propelled by a platform on wheels, greeted her friends with her brightest smile.

"I have been waiting for you."

After repeated embraces, Neviah placed her hands out in supplication. "Now, now, my dears. I have a bit of a trinket for you." She reached into her green silk pocket and held the treasure out for inspection.

"It's a tiny pyramid," said Verdandi, "like the ones in Subton. How intricate!"

Neviah's laugh was like a tinkling of bells. She turned the pyramid over in her palms. "Look again. What do you see?"

The women peered over each other's shoulders to see the shiny shape.

"It's shifting!" said Martina. "Or growing? Is it alive?"

Tess calculated in her brain and counted with her breath. "One, two, three. Three, six, nine. Three. Four. Twelve. What sort of mad science is this?"

"It's gotta be an optical illusion," said Bashelle. "We are undoubtedly crazed."

"Keep looking," urged Neviah.

"It is a pyramid," mused Verdandi, "with multiplying sides." Her head shot up in surprise at her contemplation. "Am I right?"

Neviah placed the gleaming object into Verdandi's hands. "Yes, child."

She continued explaining, to everyone's awe. "It shrinks, and grows. A trilogy of words and worlds. A trinity: ice, water, and steam. Then also, plasma! All created from the same element. Different forms of identical components. This is the key to the time equation you are so valiantly seeking to solve."

"Shrinking, of course," said Tess.

"Although this brings me some bittersweet flutters, I must encourage you to return to your vessel." She escorted them back to the submarine, with much heartfelt goodbyes.

"I will see you in time, my dearest friends," said Neviah, waving her silk scarves.

Verdandi was the last one to crawl inside. She peeked up from the hatch. "Why have you been waiting for us? When did you discover the pyramid? How did you know we would be here?"

Neviah sang out through the increasing wind. "You told me."

The hatch twisted and locked. The travellers spun again.

Chapter 94

Through the porthole, the women glimpsed shadows and shapes of variant lucidity. Patterns of time, pasts and futures, assailed their senses.

"I really want to get home. Home, home," said Martina.

"I understand," said Bashelle. "I think we all do." She gauged the relief valve. Verdandi poked Tess in the arm. "Are you sleeping?"

"No, I am meditating. I am trying to remember." She opened her eyes. "The Subton Switch. We pulled, we pushed? In what order? We are missing something here. I am attempting to retrieve my memory."

"Push, pull, push, push, pull?" guessed Martina.

"Naw; push, push, pull. Right?" asked Bashelle.

"Just one pull and one push, wasn't there?" Verdandi squinted her eyes into her imagination.

"I cannot grasp it," sighed Tess, "yet it seems to me, to configure our travel more precisely, we need to go backwards in order to go forwards."

"As in the proverbial two steps forward, one step back?" Martina asked.

"Precisely!" Tess clapped her hands together. "This is what I dare recommend. We pull back, then push forward. What say you?"

The women all looked to Bashelle. "Well, I guess I'm the captain then! A'right, so be it. Engage the plan." She nodded to Martina who quickly strapped herself into the wooden chair. She reached up, and pulled the switch.

With a flash of light like a bursting sun, the submarine whirred and hissed. Darkness shielded the scorch of days, and radiance warmed the bite of night. When the women emerged into their new world, they were brought to tears by its innate beauty.

Deep pine forests rose upon an ice-capped mountain ledge. Cool air ascended and descended with scents of salty sea and fruity seeds.

"Where are we?" asked Martina, gazing longingly at a purple meadow.

"Wrong question," said Bashelle, her nose to the East. "When are we?"

"Whichever the answer, tis not our intended destination," said Tess.

Martina shuffled away, her eyes fixated now.

"What is it," asked Verdandi, following closely.

"Look," she whispered, "do you see them?"

Verdandi followed the hunter's sharp gaze upon a stiff glacial peak. In the highest crevices were immense nests. Flickering reflections blinked back at the sun.

Bashelle whistled. "There's gold in them thar hills!"

"Better than gold," said Martina.

A long, broad, shadow flew over them. A screech alike a braking locomotive caused all four women to clutch at their ears. Tess screamed.

An eagle shining like platinum dove at them. Tess reached for her blasters and Bashelle tackled Verdandi.

Martina stood, unwavering, unafraid.

The colossal creature pulled out of its nosedive and circled the women. It stretched out its lethal talons.

Another sound filled the air; not a screech this time, but a squeal, and a gurgle.

All four sets of eyes stared and their muscles relaxed, relenting to the glorious death before them.

Black blood oozed from the eagle's slimy prey. Its pale serpentine body twisted in the bird's piercing clutch. Two red horn-like filaments waggled from its head.

The eagle winked its eyes at the stunned audience, and with one large flourish of wings, sailed off to the shore, where it dangled its writhing prey. Then it shook the slimy, bloody creature, and dropped it, down, down to the sea.

Just before the monstrous wiggling thing hit the water, a whale breached. In an instant, its black mouth opened, revealing teeth larger than any sharks' of Subton.

Snap! The jaws closed. Spurts of oily blood darkened the water. Then, with a flap of its flukes, the whale disappeared.

The women looked at each other. All was silent. No bird; no serpent; no whale. Just a far roll of thunder beyond the mountains.

"I want to stay here forever," murmured Martina.

"Nope!" Bashelle pulled her away. "Captain says all aboard!"

"Aye, aye!" agreed Verdandi and Tess in unison.

Chapter 95

"Push harder!" screamed Martina.

"No," warned Tess. "Careful lest we break it."

"Oh bejeezus I don't want to be stuck here forever!"

"It will be okay, and just fine," said Verdandi soothingly. She took the silver timepiece out from its spot, blew on it, and pressed it back in.

The engines recharged and the throttle responded.

Bashelle wiped sweat from her bald head. "What kind of science was that?"

"Just luck," said Verdandi. "I think we've got it this time!"

In slow motion, the women floated within the buoyancy of time and space. Then, a hollow crash reverberated through the submarine, through their bodies, through their lives.

They broke through ice.

When they disembarked, it was without curiosity, or hope, or thrill. It was with weakness and tepid lethargy.

They tasted sea and sand in their throats. Dizzy and discombobulated, all four fell to their knees.

Green fog surrounded them. They could see nothing but themselves. Slowly, the coloured cloud changed to turquoise, then pale blue, then smoky white.

A floating orb approached them.

A man in black stood inside the clear globe. As the women watched, a rectangle of glass unhinged from the top and opened up, forming a ramp. A woman in a steam chair emerged. She wheeled over to them where they now stood in astonishment upon a glorious dock.

"We have been waiting for your return," said Neviah.

Verdandi ran into her arms. Bashelle pulled Martina forward into the hugging fray.

Tess remained, dumfounded. Tears poured down her face as the man in black stepped down the ramp.

"Aren't you a sight for sore eyes!"

"It can't be, it...can't be," she stuttered.

The man held out a hand.

"Hugh? Is it really you?"

"Yes, I will always be here waiting for you."

"I thought you were dead, we thought you were-"

"Aw that whole being dead thing didn't work out that well for me. Nice headstone though, I really appreciate it! I visited it once I dug myself out of the sand pit beneath the would-be-deadly cliff at Mount Feake."

"I have so many questions, like..." She gazed into his melting brown eyes, and felt his warm bronze skin heating her body with just his hands.

"Oh, blazes!" She wrapped her arms around him and they clutched each other, crying and laughing in delirious relief.

They pushed apart, admiring each other, amazed with each other, in wonder.

"Hugh," Tess whispered, reaching up with one shaking hand to touch his scruffy beard. She stepped closer so that her breasts pressed against his silk shirt. She closed her eyes and inhaled deeply the scent of oil and leather that was uniquely him. "Hugh," she repeated. "Kiss me."

He placed his rough hands on her smooth shoulders, and traced her arms before landing his fingers on her hips. She reached up and grabbed the back of his head so suddenly that his top hat fell off. They pulled each other close, and their lips met in a burst of desire.

"Here we go again," Bashelle grumbled.

Verdandi hollered. "Get a room!

Neviah placed an arm around Verdandi's waist. "I know where there is a room, for everyone! Shall we?"

Arm in arm, the troupe promenaded to Days Inn.

Martina retched. "I am never going near water again."

Chapter 96

After a large meal and a larger nap, the motley family visited the newly christened Waltham Hospital. Each of them, Bashelle, Martina, Neviah, Hugh, Verdandi, and Tess, solemnly bowed heads beneath a shining plaque. The dedication upon it denoted the accomplishments of the brilliant doctor honoured in this part of the hospital, "Kate's Wing."

Then they visited the Subtonian Memorial, and the Watch City Memorial etched with the names of all who died in the battle of Waltham Watch.

They travelled by horseback to Mount Feake Cemetery.

"I suppose you will have to erase your name," said Tess.

"Nay, I kinda like being a ghost," said Hugh.

"You are ever so cunning," teased Tess. Her heart pounded with thoughts of the mysteries yet to unfold between them that night.

Verdandi and Martina unsaddled their horses and walked along a hunting trail. The air was quiet and calm. Martina felt like she could breathe again. She sat on a broken branch and rested her eyes, while Verdandi talked to herself in the way that Martina found precious.

"I stand. Slipping my toes into nature. Wriggling my heels amid long green blades of grass, of which I know the taste, the particular flavour. Adjusting my hat, I pivot, glimpsing shadow against rows of evergreen bushes. Pulled tight in corsets during frigid winter, now cut loose to expand in springtime's warmth.

My shadow. Long and lithe.

I remove my hat. Evening sun plays tricks on what is seen and unseen. Gone are my counted ribs. Smooth flesh and muscled arches have replaced them.

Gone is my flowing hair, drifting in lingering winds.

Here I stand. At six of the clock. In the shadow of myself. I see the girl, hidden in blotted pain.

And I wish her well."

An eagle silently circled down. Closer and closer. Martina remained perched on the charred birch. Talons extended. Martina took one long glorious breath, and smiled.

The eagle landed lightly upon her leathered shoulder. Something knocked against her head.

"Alright already. I have missed you too, my friend. No need to whack me in the cranium." She opened her eyes and met the eagle's brilliant glare. Then she saw what the eagle was holding in one clawed foot.

Verdandi heard the eagle's silent voice. "Hello, I am eager to share some time with you, golden one." She looked at the object the eagle carried. "What is that?"

"It appears to be a message in a bottle."

"Ooh, how fanciful!"

Martina pulled the cork from the blue frosted glass and retrieved the parchment within.

"What's it say? Who's it from?"

Martina didn't speak for a minute. She was deeply affected by the message, and declined explaining. The eagle lifted off, and she stood.

"Verdandi," she gently encompassed the girl in her arms. "I love you always, even when you don't know it."

The next day, afternoon, and early eve, they all remained in bed and accepted trays of hot cross buns and marmalade. Upon rising, they rode orbers (which is what they discovered the spherical glass vehicles were called), and sought refreshment at The Tea Leaf truck.

Tess and Hugh sat knee to knee. Hugh motioned towards Verdandi, standing before a hovering tea tray. "Look at that," he whispered.

"At what shall I look?"

"She has hips now."

Tess's whisper spat through her teeth in outraged astonishment. "Shut your mouth! How dare you! Thoroughly disgusting! She's FIFTEEN!"

"I was not being lascivious. I was simply pointing out. She is changing. She is growing up. She is a woman now, not a child."

"A child she is!" Tess craned her neck to assess the ruddy sprite. She noticed the curved hips, the round posterior, the stretched legs, and the bulbous breasts of the girl. She turned her attention back to Hugh. "Why are you looking, you dirty hog?"

"Please do not disgust me with your insinuation. Lest you forget, I have watched this brave creature grow from a straggly waif to a tender child to a strong-willed young woman. A real person. Not an imp. Now, she is grown."

"I say not."

"Nay, she is grown. Not all the way," he conceded. "But mostly. She is smarter, you know this Tess, she is smarter than all of us."

Tess winced and stared again at girl's curvy body.

Hugh continued. "She is. She is your student or apprentice or whatever in hell's bells you wish to call her."

Tess looked at him defiantly.

"If you look at her, REALLY look at her. All of her. Not just her genius stuff or whatever it is that you focus on-"

"I know! She is strong and independent, and has been through too much in too little time."

"She doesn't need your pity, she needs your-"

Tess interrupted again. "She spent her babyhood in an orphanage. I bear no ill will to the Sisters who cared for her. I hope they hugged her, and believed she was precious, as all children are." Her eyes glimmered. She boiled in an emotional flood. Her vision blanked to white.

Hugh recognized her dissociation. With alarm in his heart and control in his body, he pulled an iced tea from the cart and placed it in her hands. The chill seemed to wake her up.

"Thank you."

He pulled an iced tea for himself. "Cheers."

"There you are, my sweet Creampuff!
Where'd you wander off to? Ah, never
mind; sit and drink with me!"

Bashelle joined Martina under the Tea
Leaf's expandable awning. "What in the
blazes are you drinking?"

"This, my dear, is called iced tea.
Look! It has ice in it! It's cold!" She took
another swig. "I didn't even know it
existed!"

"Nor did I." Bashelle took a swallow
from Martina's glass. "It's delicious!"

"Toldja."

"Anyways, I went to take a fresh look
at the docks, and Ani is flapping up a storm.
The fishers are quite pissed off. So I came
back to fetch that girl of ours. Where is that
little mermaid? Somebody oughta nail her
fins to the ground."

"I'm right here!" laughed Verdandi.
She pushed aside the awning.

"What is this mess?"

Verdandi's robotic arm was a mish-
mash of tools. She and Neviah were
surrounded by an archipelago of floating tea

trays, each covered in bits and pieces of indiscernible source.

"We are redesigning the mechanisms of Neviah's robots. What if, at the inn, we could talk through the clocks and watches...as long as they are in the city using magnetic waves or sonic waves...wait til you see! We can build new communication devices! Allow me to demonstrate."

She pressed the button on her arm-watch and whistled into it. "Now look: here I added a rounded gear. You turn your gear in a series of numbers. Each timepiece has its own code, got it?"

"I'm listening."

"Then you pull the gear out, and...the timepiece matching the code you just entered vibrates with radio waves!

The timepiece that Neviah wore as a brooch gave off a buzzing noise.

"Jiminy cricket!"said Bashelle.

"Then what?" Martina asked.

"Then, when that person's watch vibrates with the radio waves, they can pull their gear out. This allows the time pieces to open a channel of communication! And then!" She pressed a button in the centre of the gear. "C'mere Neviah! I need you!" She released the button.

Her voice emanated from Neviah's brooch.

"What the dickens?" said Bashelle.

Neviah pressed the button upon her time piece's new gear. "I am right here," she chuckled.

"Holy smokes," exclaimed Martina, "even her laugh came out!"

Tess witnessed the demonstration with great astonishment. She joined the growing crowd.

"That was a project I had investigated, and backlogged, and never got around to making time for. Verdandi, you beat me to it!"

"Your advice would be greatly welcome."

"I guess you're catching up to me!" said Tess proudly.

Verdandi teased her with a squinty grin. "Maybe someday YOU will catch up with ME!"

Tess joined her voice to the roaming laughter. Then she walked away to ponder. "Maybe it is true," she thought. Verdandi could surpass her. "I am unsure how to feel about that." The idea of not being the best, the greatest, the most brilliant, scientist in the world itched her flesh.

"Yet," she thought, "how privileged would I be, if I could mentor the next world-renowned inventor. Imagine the progress that bright girl could bring, the light she could shed on science." Tess perked up. She could be part of that. She could assist Verdandi instead of the other way around.

Or, better yet, they could work together!

She circled around and returned to the scientific display.

"This looks like fun," said Bashelle.

"Yeah!" agreed Martina. "I could be in my glassworks and holler down to you at the docks to bring me some supper!"

"Dangitall, the docks!" Bashelle turned to Verdandi. "Ani is going to make a lot of enemies if she keeps up that fuss. You'd best check on her, and ask her to calm herself down."

After supper, messenger bots delivered calling cards to the fisher, the hunter, the inn-keeper, the mechanic, and the professor.

Please take tea with me in the parlour at half-past nine.
Much love, Verdandi

"I do hope I can stay awake that long," yawned Martina.

"Worry not; I'll find a way to keep you up." Bashelle pulled her in for a long, mutually exhilarating, kiss.

"Thank you everyone for being prompt," began Verdandi. "I have some disconcerting news to share, and wanted to think it out before I expressed it."

Neviah nodded encouragingly.

"I was delighted to meet with my friend Ani at the docks, and utterly relieved to find her healing quickly from her wounds and tribulations." She paused, and when she spoke again, her voice trembled. "Even though nothing should've happened in the first place. It's my fault she got hurt." She blinked back tears.

Hugh lifted a carafe and poured a glass of iced lemon water. He walked across the room and brought it to her.

"You are doing fine," he said quietly. "After this, let's make plans to talk and listen about whatever you like."

Verdandi sipped the cold beverage and nodded gratefully. Hugh slid back to his seat.

Verdandi took a cleansing breath and continued with renewed vigour. "Ani told me distressing, cataclysmic, information. Ziracuny has escaped Subton."

A collective gasp resounded in the small room.

"Go on," coaxed Neviah gently.

"The guards chased her, but lost her trail beyond the crumbled islands. It seemed as if she had controlled, or commanded, or communicated, with all sorts of devilish sea creatures to aide in her getaway. The Subtonians simply could not find her."

In the silence that followed, Tess's voice rang low and clear. "I think I know how to find her."

Questions chorused throughout the gathering. "Truly? How? She could have gone anywhere!"

Martina added, "We know she desires control of the Watch Cities. So we can find the cities she is drawn to."

"True," agree Tess solemnly. "But perhaps... She pulled out her silver rose compass watch. She held it aloft so everyone could see. The needle spun. The friends hovered closer in a circle.

"What in the heck is it doing?" asked Bashelle.

"One moment," said Tess. She pulled out a syringe from a pocket in her big brown bag. Inside it stuck crusty dry brown crud.

"What in the royal jelly?" Hugh was startled.

"Pardon me," Tess said primly.

She opened the syringe and spat into it.

Martina was aghast and fascinated. "I think I may never have been more intrigued by you."

Tess remained focused, her eyes deep in concentration, her lips pursed tightly together with no breath entering or leaving.

She lifted the dial of the compass and unscrewed a tiny silver plug. Then she shook the syringe so the crud mixed with the saliva, turning it faintly red.

She fit the needle of the syringe into the tiny hole the plug left, and pushed a drop of solution within.

"What the blazes are you doing? You're going to ruin it!" said Bashelle. Tess didn't answer. Her attention was unilateral. She replaced the plug and rewound the watch.

The time ticked. Then stuck for three seconds. During those three seconds, the needle on the other side of the watch, where the compass was, spun around crazily. Then it stopped, shuddered, and remained still. The watch regained its ticking of time.

"What does that mean?" asked Martina.

"It is a secret I have recently discovered. It only makes sense. I cannot explain it. Not completely because I care not to, but because I know not how."

"In time, you may," said Neviah.

"Yes, I do not doubt that. The best I can do right now is to call attention to our departed Kate's genome experiments that were melded with Verdandi's brilliant horology. I have a theory that Kate added an elixir to this timepiece that caused the compass to specifically point in Verdandi's direction." She held up her hands as questions were again murmured. "I will figure it out, and I will inform you all, in full. What I have attempted right here, right now, is to inject the compass with Ziracuny's blood. It could serve as an extra resource, however unreliable it may be."

"Always good to have a back-up plan," said Martina.

Bashelle took the compass and consulted the many globes and maps available for weary travellers in the parlour. "I would say that Martina's assessment of the situation is correct. Ziracuny is likely headed to a Watch City. This compass is pointing towards Gustover. So if we choose to follow our instincts, and choose to believe the information from the compass is correct, we can conclude that Ziracuny is in Gustover."

"I for one would love to hunt that evil witch down!" said Martina.

"As would I," said Tess, "but how do we get to Gustover?"

Martina knocked her knuckles on Tess' head. "You are a tough nut to crack, oh genius professor. The glass orbs I made!"

"Will they suffice? Are they destroyed? What manner of fuel shall we use? What provisions do we need?" Tess held her hands up in frustration. "What will I wear?"

"We will figure out all this, and more," suggested Neviah.

"Funny thing," Tess said, "Gustover was my original destination. Then I met all of you, when I was put offtrack to Waltham."

"In some ways," said Neviah, "it is good that your plans were derailed. Think of all the positive things that came from an otherwise horrendous incident."

"We would not have run DRAKE out of Waltham," said Martina.

"Or adventured successfully to Subton, and added our skills that led to the abolishment of totalitarianism in their government," added Bashelle.

"And we would have never met," said Hugh. Tess blushed.

"Now, the best thing of all," said Verdandi, "is that we have become a family."

"For all time," said Tess.

"For all time."

Acknowledgements

To the Steampunks before me:
Mary Shelley, Jules Verne, H.G. Wells,
Terry Pratchett, Studio Ghibli... Sharing
worlds in multiple formats shows me that
we each have our own steampunk homes.
To the Steampunks amidst me:
Watch City, Silk City, Jewelry City... Your
enthusiasm, friendship, support, and
encouragement has cemented my love for
the steampunk community. I could not have
survived this year of book touring without
you at my back.
To the Steampunks beyond me: We are
connected in a circle of unending time and
community. Art surpasses the boundaries of
time.

KK: I will have to write another book just
about my thankfulness to you. And how I
want your baby.

My big little brother: you encouraged me
with you friendship, cynicism, honesty,
acceptance, jokes, and love. I never knew

my baby brother with the curliest hair in the world would become my best friend. I was the meanest teacher in our pretend basement school. But I loved reading your fave book to you: "The Monster at the End of this Book." Your giggles and astonishment at that book made my heart soar, and I always loved your ability to be honest with your expressive face emotions. I really owe it to you. I wouldn't be who I am without you. And don't even say something snarky like it's not your fault!

My sunrise and sunset children: my love for you exists forever in endless days.

To Vincent Valentine and The Telephone Museum. Your friendship, knowledge, and mind-blowing tours changed the ending of this book in the most time-blasting ways! Your passion for children's education and your welcoming atmosphere for all abilities and talents has created a culture that I treasure. Thank you for including me in The Telephone Museum family.

The Waltham Museum has been an upbeat resource of facts and friendship. Every time I visit, I learn a new tidbit that helps me honour history in my writing.

The Charles River Museum of Industry and Innovation continues to educate me with historical lectures and presentations.

The New Bedford Whaling Museum and the Nantucket Whaling Museum provided me with visual and tangible examples of the era in which "Subton Switch" takes place.

Ricci: you did it again!

The soundtrack of my mind plays Pink's "It's All Your Fault" to an imagined anime video of "Subton Switch." Listening to this song while envisioning key moments helped me clarify emotions in the storyline.

My Blog Buddies With Benefits! Thank you for your readership! Free stories and books continue, all for you!

Inspiration

Literature:

"Lodore" by Mary Shelley

"The Toilers of the Sea" by Victor Hugo

"Twenty Thousand Leagues Under the Sea" by Jules Verne

"The Perfect Storm" by Sebastian Junger

"Moolelo Hawai'i" by Zepherin "Kepelino" Kahōʻāliʻi Keauokalan

"The American Claimant" by Mark Twain

"Moby Dick" by Herman Melville

"Experiments With Alternate Currents of High Potential and High Frequency" by Nikola Tesla

"Amid the Pyramids" by Ernest L. Norman

"Hedy's Folly: The Life and Breakthrough Inventions of Hedy Lamarr, The Most Beautiful Woman in the World" by Richard Rhodes

Film:

"Ponyo" by Studio Ghibli

"Atlantis: the Lost Empire" by Disney Animation

"Elvis and Me" adapted from the memoir by Priscilla Beaulieu Presley
"Total Eclipse of the Heart" music video by Bonnie Tyler

Song:
"Come Sail Away" by Styx
"Oh Shenandoah" an American folksong
"Big Balls" by AC/DC
"Rainbow High" by Andrew Lloyd Webber
"E to the X DY DX" football cheer by Rensselaer Polytechnic Institute
"The Ballroom Blitz" by Sweet

Art and Artifacts:
1849 Fresnel Lens used in Sankaty Head Lighthouse, on display at Nantucket Whaling Museum
"Shinagawa Oki no Kujira Takanawa yori Mita Zu [Seeing the whale in Shinagawa Bay at Takanawa]" Woodblock print triptych on paper, c. 1798 by Shuntei Katsukawa, on display at The New Bedford Whaling Museum

Also by Jessica Lucci

Watch City: Waltham Watch
Behind Time - The Facts in the Fiction of
Watch City: Waltham Watch
Poetry in the Prose of Watch City: Waltham
Watch

Coming Soon from Jessica Lucci

Sneak Peek
"Watch City: Gustover Glitch" by Jessica Lucci

Pinning the last silver braid behind her ear, she realized she would have to be someone else for the rest of the day; someone who she used to be, and would have to speak in that voice to faces she decidedly did not want to see.

From behind the closed door, sounds of happiness were too much to bear. Without unclipping her intricate silver braids, she lay her head below the open window and sought the peace of thunder.

Sleep refused safe harbour. Electricity through shallow clouds blinked hopefully, whilst beyond the stairs below her, tepid joy befouled the air.

One bird, one book, one sacred nook. No one ever thought to look for her here. She had borne the pain of invisibility, and now it was her reprieve.

When all had gone, night slid in. Gaining strength from solace, she stretched her arms and felt her fullness. She could be a ghost again, hiding in plain sight.

Resources

Telephony: https://telephone-museum.org
Oceanology and Marine Biology: https://www.ocean-science.net
Gemology: https://www.gia.edu
Fossils: https://brettonrocks.com
LGBTQ Human Rights: https://www.hrc.org
Missing and Exploited Children: http://www.missingkids.com/home
Alcoholics Anonymous: https://www.aa.org
Al-Anon: https://al-anon.org
Substance Abuse: https://www.samhsa.gov/find-help/national-helpline
Opioids and Teens: https://www.hhs.gov/ash/oah/adolescent-development/substance-use/drugs/opioids/index.html

About the Author

Jessica Lucci writes about modern issues while maintaining historic integrity. She makes her home in Massachusetts, USA, where she is currently writing a steampunk trilogy with strong heroines based on events in New England history.

A book review is the easiest way to support an author.

Amazon Author Page: https://www.amazon.com/Jessica-Lucci/e/B075JMNK1S

Goodreads: https://www.goodreads.com/user/show/69847566-jessica-lucc

Visit Jessica Lucci online.

Website: https://www.jessicalucci.org

Facebook: https://www.facebook.com/Jessica-Lucci-1574551225939780/

Twitter: @Jessica__Lucci

Instagram: https://www.instagram.com/jessica__lucci/

Tumblr: jessica-luccijessica-lucci.tumblr.com

Pinterest:
https://www.pinterest.com/indiewoods/pins/

Your Page
This page is for you, dear reader, to write as you wish.